HYPERSPACE WAR

TEARS OF THE SUN

CALVERT

aethonbooks.com

TEARS OF THE SUN

Aethon Books
www.aethonbooks.com

Print and eBook formatting by Josh Hayes.

Published by Aethon Books LLC.

ALSO IN SERIES

Behemoth

Leviathan

Gates of Hell

Tears of the Sun

CHAPTER 1
PASCAL

Orbital ring of DeGaulle, Archimedes system, 2334

SPARK LED the small group of civilians, still far too many for Pascal's liking. It wasn't that he wished there were fewer of them, because that would have meant even more deaths. No, it was simply an exhausting and terrifying task to save nearly forty souls. Part of him longed for the days when he sat alone in his office, poring over witness reports, surveillance data, and psychological profiles of suspects, looking for patterns. His only responsibility then had been not to knock over the coffee mug on the edge of his desk while he scanned the data in his mind. Of course, it had also been his responsibility to find the culprits and offer some form of restitution to the victims. But those had been abstract thoughts and tasks.

Now he ran after the frightened crowd of people who had been left behind, having voluntarily given up their places in the Evac capsules to allow the women and children to go first. He could literally see their anxiety and fear in front of him, as well as his responsibility. Their very survival was at stake, and the looks they gave him were as hopeful as they were pleading.

They expected nothing less from him than their survival and reunion with their families who were already out there, rushing through the vacuum toward DeGaulle.

Don't let the pressure get to you, he thought tersely, casting a tense glance over his shoulder for the hundredth time.

"You cover our backs," Spark had instructed him. How that was supposed to work, other than looking behind him every now and then, Pascal didn't know. So he resorted to keeping a tight grip on his HV pistol while constantly expecting Alpha's trigger-happy puppets to come barreling around the corner. Then his back would undoubtedly be as riddled with holes as the orbital ring was, as he couldn't constantly walk backward while keeping an eye on everything. But as there was nothing else for him to do, he simply did his best not to get too nervous.

They moved like a silent procession through the corridors of the ring, which meanwhile trembled at ever shorter intervals. From time to time, one or the other violent jolt traveled through the floor and walls. Some tremors were so violent that they knocked them off their feet.

"According to the technician, we should be there soon," Spark radioed from the front. Pascal couldn't make him out because the front half of the line had disappeared behind the corner of another security gate. On the one hand, it was good to hear the sergeant major's voice, because it proved that he was still alive and everything was going relatively well. On the other hand, it made Pascal nervous, because at least when there was silence, he felt like he could possibly hear pursuers right away. With Sparks' voice in his ear, instinctively he was overcome with fear that he might miss something dangerous. Not for the first time, he wished for his NeuroSmart and its filtering and amplification routines.

If I don't get my act together soon, I'm going to turn into a wimp, he thought bitterly, and radioed back to Spark: "What do you mean 'soon'? I don't think this place is going to last much longer."

As if to emphasize the point, they were rocked by another tremor. Structural groans and rattles reached Pascal's ears and proved to him once again that the space station was doomed. Surprisingly, their battered and bedraggled-looking charges remained perfectly calm. Here and there, some were knocked off their feet, but they quietly picked themselves up and helped each other, then rejoined in orderly rows of two. Just as Spark had instructed them to do.

The lack of raw emotion and physical reaction shocked Pascal more than if they had screamed and shouted. It almost seemed as if they were driven solely by some kind of emergency program rather than any belief in their survival. Hope was a luxury they must have lost somewhere between the massacre, the hostage-taking, and their families leaving.

"How soon will we be there?" he radioed back after picking himself up and checking his pistol again.

"We have to make two more turns and then we will go through a maintenance node into an airlock. Behind it is the next rescue bay."

"Does he have any data on whether the capsules are still working? Or access to the cameras?" asked Pascal hopefully.

"No. All system resources beyond the control mechanisms of the Evac capsules are being used by Alpha's and the Neuromorph's warring codes," the soldier replied in the negative, and his radio message was nearly swallowed up by another tremor in the walls, which continued as crashes and creaks across the acoustical spectrum.

"Oh great," Pascal grumbled as he helped an elderly man in work clothes who had fallen to his knees. "That means we're going in completely blind. There might not even be any atmosphere left in the bay."

"But at the latest, we will detect that in the airlock. There are warning lights for it."

"Oh, I see," Pascal answered meekly, annoyed with himself. He just didn't know enough about space, spaceships and orbital rings to be of any real help. All his life he had been painstakingly careful to avoid assignments that led him into the clutches of the cold vacuum. If an investigation required it, he had either sent subordinates or kept his stay as short as possible. However, what weighed heavier on his mind was that he perceived himself as becoming more anxious and fragile. Ever since WizKid had sacrificed herself for the group, and by extension him, some of the synapses in his gray matter were apparently no longer firing the way they had in the past. He still didn't know whether it was a good or bad sign.

What was definitely a bad sign, however, was that he seemed to be developing a tendency to brood more and more. When he was at the academy, every high-ranking investigator had to attend a series of lectures from time to time, he had always drummed into his students that brooding was the most inefficient form of thinking the human brain was capable of. Brooding meant mentally circling a problem over and over again while being sucked into it like a whirlpool. There was nothing constructive or even helpful about it. Thoughts had to revolve around a problem until they produced solutions and new approaches, while brooding always spat out the same results and caused ones thinking to become rigid. Just like his inner victim monologues.

I'm useless without my implants, he mimicked himself in his mind. *I used to be much tougher and more efficient.*

It sucked, but now it was over. He straightened his shoulders, casting a glance over his left shoulder to make sure they weren't being followed, then helped the man in front of him climb over the pressurized bulkhead threshold.

When they reached the maintenance bay, a large room with a central work area designed for half a dozen technicians, Spark's giant figure and that of the much smaller technician wedged themselves against the control panel of the security airlock at the far end.

"Take a moment, keh?" the soldier suggested, turning briefly to Pascal. With a gesture he signaled that they should sit down and rest.

"All right." Pascal turned to the civilians while manually locking the bulkhead. "We'll take a short break until the security gate is unlocked."

Without a murmur the crowd started moving again. It took a moment for them to sit crisscrossed on the floor, tightly packed together and silent. He counted the disheveled heads and nodded with satisfaction when he got to 39.

As his gaze roamed over the crowd, something struck him as odd. At first he couldn't put his finger on what it was, but then it struck him: the small crowd formed an almost perfect circle around a spot where an old lady with white hair was sitting. He would have chalked it up to a coincidence if their eyes hadn't met at that exact moment. Her eyes were deep blue and piercing, but that wasn't what grabbed him. Instead, it was the character in her eyes. They shone as if someone had switched a lamp on in her eyeballs. Her gaze had a clear alertness that seemed both attentive and deeply serene at the same time.

As if drawn by a magnet, he walked up to her.

"Hello," he said somewhat lamely, unable to think of anything better to say.

"Hello, Inspector." Her voice was firm and clear, which surprised him considering her age was probably well over ninety.

"You know who I am?"

"Of course," she replied, smiling candidly. "You introduced yourself before leading us to the last escape bay."

"Oh right," he replied and would have liked to slap his forehead at his own stupidity.

"Who are you?"

"Who am I, or what is my name?" she asked, her smile taking on a mischievous, almost childlike expression.

"It's nice to see that you appear to have kept your sense of humor. When you have a chance, you will have to tell me how you do it," Pascal said with honest admiration. Something about this woman put him at ease and at the moment that was exactly what he needed. The other civilians seemed to feel the same way, sitting surprisingly close to her. "But first, let's start with your name."

"My name is Kathleen Mitchell."

"Pascal Takahashi." As he held out his hand to her, he half expected her to say, "Of course, you've already introduced yourself," but she simply shook his hand and smiled as she pointed to the floor in front of her.

"Thank you," Pascal said and sat down as if she had just invited him into her living room. Still, it didn't feel strange and he couldn't resist accepting her invitation. As he looked at her while she returned his gaze in a relaxed manner, he noticed she was sitting very straight.

"Are you a nun?" he asked.

"Oh no." She chuckled happily—a sound that was at odds with her surroundings and the general atmosphere and yet did not seem out of place.

"What are you?"

"By that question, I'm sure you want to know what I'm doing here, is that right?"

"Yes, something like that," he admitted.

"I was conducting a workshop here for three days."

"A workshop?"

"Yes. Meditation."

"Ah," he quipped as the answers started to roll in. "I see."

"What do you see?" she asked, the amused look in her eyes making it clear that there was more to the question than the words suggested.

"Why you're so quiet."

"You think it's because of the meditation?"

"Yes."

"Why? Do you have experience with meditation?"

"Yes," he confirmed, nodding slightly. "After I broke up with my ex-partner, following the advice of my Nanonikerin, I meditated for a while to get my blood pressure under control without the help of medication from my NeuroSmart."

He couldn't remember the last time he had spoken so openly about it with anyone. Probably never.

"And? Did it help?" she asked, eyeing him with interest.

"Yes. At least the high blood pressure disappeared after a while."

"Did you feel better too?"

"Yes, I was maybe 10 percent happier."

"Ten percent, that's good," she chortled, looking youthful, almost childlike, despite her relatively advanced age. The wrinkles on her cheeks started to move, as if they had taken on a life of their own.

"I thought so too. So you held some kind of seminar?"

"Yes, exactly."

"Did you do it for a non-profit organization?" enquired Pascal, not knowing exactly what he was getting at. He just wanted to talk to her because it felt good.

"Oh no!" she shook her head decisively. "I've been paid very well for it."

Seeing his furrowed brow, she laughed uproariously.

"What do you think of me now?" she asked with interest, her smile still a picture of alert attention and clarity.

"I briefly had the image of an esoteric rip-off in my mind," he admitted honestly.

"I love people's thoughts," she explained, gesturing happily around her. "They're so exciting, don't you think?"

"Oh yes, I think so too. That's why I became a policeman."

"See. You think you shouldn't make money out of spirituality and meditation, it's a rip-off, and I think it's great. I like living in the countryside because I love nature and silence plus it's a bit more expensive. I also like to use some of the proceeds to enable penniless prospective students to attend my seminars, as well as offer my books for free."

"Oh, I didn't know that," he replied somewhat contritely.

"Of course you didn't." She laughed. "Tell me, Inspector, why do you look so worried?"

Initially, Pascal wanted to say something angry like, "Can't you see that this crappy station is about to fall apart at any moment? Can't you see that these people are distressed? But something stopped him. He didn't feel like arguing.

"I'm worried about you and the others as well as my friends," he finally admitted.

"What are worries?" the old lady asked lightheartedly.

"Fears." He knew this line of questioning from the academy. Most worries, even the most negative emotions, could ultimately be traced back to fear. All one had to do was investigate it long enough.

"Yes, naturally," she said, much to his surprise.

"All emotions are the body's reaction to thoughts, and I love thoughts."

"Now?" he asked, surprised. "Normally people would prefer to turn off their thoughts."

"Yes, because they are afraid of their thoughts," she

explained, and from her mouth it sounded like the statement of an exceedingly amusing thing.

"What do you mean?"

"Let's say they're afraid of the station breaking apart, yes?"

"Yes!"

"Good, you've been on this station for how long now? A few hours?"

"About."

"How long have you been worrying about the fact that this space station might break apart?"

"At least half that time," he replied.

"Good. How long would it take for you to die if one of these walls," she made a gesture to the left, "ruptured now and we were hurled into the vacuum?"

"A few minutes, I think."

"That's interesting. You're plagued by worrying thoughts of possible death in the vacuum, not even knowing if it will happen, and even if it did, at most you'd feel miserable for a few minutes before it was over. The thoughts of a possible future you fear strike me as much more momentous and unpleasant than the dreaded end result."

"Hmm, now that you mention it... But there are advantages to being afraid of death," he insisted. "After all, I wouldn't have been able to get you and the others out otherwise."

"That's because you weren't just worried about your own death, but about the deaths of all these fine people," Kathleen Mitchell continued. "But why are you afraid of death?"

Pascal considered for a moment while his gaze flitted briefly to Spark and the technician, whom he could clearly see over the heads of the seated people. They still seemed engrossed in gaining control over the door.

"I don't know," he admitted. "That's what everyone's afraid of, whether they admit it or not."

"I think it's quite amazing."

"Why?"

"Do you like sleeping?" she challenged him with a surprising counter-question.

"Of course I do. A good night's sleep wouldn't be bad right now."

"Everyone looks forward to sleep. But where are you when you sleep?"

"What do you mean?" he asked, puzzled.

"Where are you, Pascal Takahashi, Inspector of the Abducted Citizens Directive, when you sleep?" she repeated with a smile.

"I don't know, I'm just sleeping."

"You're not there. While you are sleeping, you are not there. Only in the morning, once you open your eyes again and your thoughts return, are you back, existing again."

"Hmm," he mused. "I hadn't thought of it that way."

"People love sleep because at best it restores them and allows them to believe the thought that they will wake up in the morning. But that is just a thought. Yet it is quite similar to death. When you die, for all you know, you are no longer here, just like when you are asleep. What frightens you about it is only the thought: *I won't wake up again, that's it.*"

"Hmm," he went again.

"Sleep or death, the only difference is how you think about it. No one really knows anything about sleep or death, only that we experience both," she continued, chuckling her sincere chuckle again. "Don't look so concerned, Inspector. We may not be able to control what we think, but we do have control over whether or not we believe the thoughts that pop into our heads. I think that's a very good message."

"It sounds reasonable but not particularly simple. After all, we are not all meditation teachers," said Pascal.

"I'm just a woman from Trafalgar who doesn't believe in thoughts. I am a teacher, if others think that I am."

"I see." He nodded and couldn't help but return her smile. He envied her lightheartedness.

"You know, Inspector—"

"Please call me Pascal," he said.

"All right, Pascal. What do you need right now?"

"Um, pretty much everything."

"Like what?" she probed.

"For example, I'd like to be safe, and I'd like more support right here." He thought of Lieutenant Goretzka and the soldiers from Bismarck, who were currently holed up somewhere north of their position, buying them enough time to rescue civilians only to die doing so.

"You do have a lot of support," the lady said, pointing first up, then to the ground.

"The solidity of the ground supports you, the air provides you with oxygen, your fellow humans' warmth keeps you from freezing, and your companion and the technician are taking care of the door. That's wonderful."

"But this section could break apart at any time, even now, at this very moment," he returned, and as if to underscore his fears, the orbital ring sent another jolt through the floor and walls, shaking them up properly.

Once they had righted themselves, Kathleen Mitchell still looked absolutely relaxed.

"This is a thought for the future. As we don't know what the future will look like, I don't believe in such thoughts. They have no relevance to me. What I do know is that right now I have everything I need to live, in this moment."

"Of course. What you mean is that I should be more in the present. Living in the here and now and all that." He had read a few guidebooks in his life with a similar message, and while he had found them interesting and the arguments quite compelling, he didn't find it easy to put into practice. Or how was it even supposed to work.

"It's not that easy, hmm?"

"No."

"It's just a thought too. Really intriguing."

When he didn't say anything for a moment, her smile grew a little wider. "You know, the Indian sage Jiddu Krishnamurti said, 'The day you teach the child the name of the bird, the child will never see that bird again.'"

"The thought bird is not the bird."

"Exactly. Just because we give something a label, doesn't mean we understand it. However, because of the label, it loses its ability to inspire. What an incredible creature, defying the pull of gravity with delicate wings, don't you think?"

"Yes," he admitted thoughtfully, as something started to stir in his mind.

"Cop?" Spark's radio call made Pascal flinch as if he'd been struck by lightning.

"Yeah?" he asked, his pulse pounding.

"We're all set. Ready to go."

"Got it, thanks."

Turning to the older woman, he continued, "We're good to go. Thanks."

"For what?"

"For the conversation."

"Oh," she said, laughing, "you were talking to yourself."

He was about to ask what she meant, but a tremendous tremor knocked him off his feet, and this time something did break. Across the room, the cold composite floor burst, crunching and creaking so loudly that it rang in his ears.

"Holy crap," he cursed. They didn't have much time left. If they had any time at all.

CHAPTER 2
JEREMY

In orbit above DeGaulle, Archimedes system, 2334

THE BATTLE WAS FAR from won, it had merely shifted. However, with the appearance of the fortress habitats in orbit above DeGaulle, the cards had been reshuffled. Jeremy's tactical overview map clearly showed that the Locusts' gigantic lasers were tearing deep holes into the ranks of Alpha's Earth Protectorate. Where its energy, generated by dancing photons, was not stopped by enough absorbing mass, it shot off into cold dead space where someday it would eventually vaporize something.

Or eventually burn out, Jeremy thought, trying to ignore the onset of fatigue in his limbs.

On the holoscreen, he watched as two smaller Locust starships emerged from the *WizKid*'s hangar and slipped through hyperspace windows at lightning speed. Growling, he glanced over his shoulder and regarded the members of the Conclave with brows drawn together in disapproval. He hated that they controlled all the systems and could overrule him. On his own ship!

We have dispatched two couriers to inform the trailing fleets of our new location, sent one of the Locusts, giving him a piercing look. He had better shield his thoughts.

"Macella," Jeremy turned to his first officer. "Your assessment, please."

"The enemy ships are regrouping into an open formation. Soon the lasers' penetrating power will decrease significantly and they will only be able to hit individual ships and not formations," she said, tapping something on her arm display before standing up and tracing some trajectories on the holoscreen with her finger. "I would recommend that we move into low orbit and shield the planet as best we can. They could try to target DeGaulle and split our forces that way."

"That's what we'll do," Jeremy agreed, nodding with approval.

He allowed himself to study her for a moment. He traced her elfin features with his eyes, which seemed so at odds with her straightforward military demeanor, before getting lost in her deep blue eyes. After the battle on Exo, when they had become intimate, he had wondered if it was just a hormonal surge after the adrenaline had worn off, but now he was sure: he loved her, with every fiber of his being.

"THOSE FUCKING SWINES!" roared Walter suddenly, startling Jeremy out of his brief daydream as if a bucket of ice water had been poured over his head.

"What's up?" he asked in alarm, digging his fingers into the armrests of his command chair.

"That's what's up!" the engineer growled, pointing at the holoscreen. His voice had changed enough to concern Jeremy. Walter no longer sounded angry but... captivated.

The image on the screen flickered briefly due to interference, and then the tactical analysis display with its many colorful curves, diagrams, and columns of numbers switched to the *WizKid*'s telescopes, which hadn't yet been obliterated: they showed a glowing planetoid covered with black spots that looked like boils. Red veins of lava stretched along the edges, spreading out in all directions. Superstorms of hot plasma raged in the atmosphere, looking small on the camera feed but destroying entire continents on the surface.

"What is that?" asked Jeremy anxiously, and a sinking feeling in his gut told him that he wasn't going to like the answer.

"It's Bismarck," Walter whispered, every single word stabbing Jeremy like a knife. Something inside him wanted to break loose and make its way out, screaming, but it didn't happen. It didn't happen because a memory surfaced that he had suppressed a long time ago. During the time he had suffered most at the hands of his parents, before he had become a teenager and started fighting back, he had hated everything that had happened to him. His father's callous attempts to raise him to be an obedient boy. The traumatic experiences of having to slaughter game and poultry at their country home in Heusinger Plain. However, he had even worse memories of his mother, who had spanked him for running and crying to her for protection. "A soldier doesn't cry," was the only thing she had said about it.

Back then, Jeremy had often fantasized about the end of his world. He had imagined a heavenly body colliding with Bismarck and destroying everything he hated. He had imagined firestorms that incinerated everything, as well as huge waves and little green men that killed everything and everyone, starting with his parents.

The images that flashed across the holoscreen were so similar to the fantasies of the little boy he had been that he was speechless. Part of him felt guilty, as if his past thoughts alone had brought about the death of his home. Another part was shocked that everything he had grown up with was coming to an end. Then the consequences of the destruction came crashing down on him: all the people they had had to leave behind: the elderly, children, the sick, those who could not take part in the fighting in space—dead. And Newt. Exterminated by Alpha's revenge after their escape, by their plan. By Jeremy's plan.

Bismarck had been the second moon, after Europa, to orbit the gas giant Zeus I, and be explored and colonized by the European colonists. It was there that they had discovered that the observations of the Archimedes system were correct: there were five moons with atmospheres in the habitable zone of the solar system. No measuring errors, no nasty surprises at the end of a one-hundred-year journey with no return ticket. Nobody could have guessed that the nasty surprise would come many decades later, in the form of an AI. An AI that Moreau had created.

I would have loved to kill you twice, you damn dog, he cursed inwardly, allowing his anger to surface. It was definitely better than the toxic mixture of guilt and grief that threatened to well up inside him.

A hand touching his left arm almost made him jump out of his skin. It was Macella, who had leaned over to him and was looking at him with reddened eyes. Shock and compassion filled the deep blue. Relaxing his hands, which were clenched into fists, Jeremy looked down at his burning palms and discovered fresh blood on them where his nails had bored into the flesh. He looked at them for a moment as if they didn't really belong to him—at least he felt nothing. No pain, not even a burning.

"Jeremy," Macella said in a soft voice. One look at her face was enough to know that she wanted to say something but didn't know what.

"Hold your course," he ordered hoarsely, feeling a wave of apprehension wash over him that was alien. It didn't belong to him. He didn't need to turn around to know that the Locusts of the Diplomatic Conclave were reacting to his strong emotional reactions that had spilled over into the Gaia field. This was confirmed by the subsequent wave of compassion and warmth that poured over him from their spirits like a therapeutic drink from the Fountain of Youth. Although their compassion also felt somehow distant, like a note that was just a little off, but still it did him an incredible amount of good. The effect was the same one he had experienced on Bismarck when humans and Locusts had met for the first time in the colony-spanning Gaia field. No, not met, touched. The aliens' feelings were different. Alien and always a little out of reach of one's own experiences. Nevertheless, the intention behind it was clear to see, as it was now.

Jeremy did not presume to understand the aliens, but he believed that he understood at least a few things about them. For example, he was convinced that they reacted with greater empathy and immediacy to the emotions of others. The compassion that the six Locusts of the Conclave just showered him with was as sincere as it was natural. Where they felt suffering, they automatically shared in it, whether it was their own or not. The Gaia field did not distinguish between two participants. Feelings were simply shared and therefore lost some of their severity and intensity. They did not disappear as a result, but their burden was noticeably reduced by the social warmth that spread through the field. As much as Jeremy had enjoyed SenseNet—he would never give up the Gaianest in his head. At least not willingly. All the alien technology, based on evolution, seemed organic and real. Somehow more direct and intimate, as if it fit into the natural course of things, while the undeniable wonders of human ingenuity felt more like unnatural interventions in the grand scheme of the universe. In short, human technology was cold while that of the Locusts was warm. At least, that was the most appropriate comparison he could think of.

"Thank you," he finally said, addressing no one in particular, as his gratitude included both Macella and the Locusts.

No one said anything. Macella squeezed his arm once more and seemed to have a thought, as her eyelids twitched briefly. But she said nothing. Instead, she sighed softly and sat back down in her chair. Walter remained silent, though Jeremy could clearly feel his anguish in the Gaia field, while Felicity stared uncertainly at her console.

"Hold course for DeGaulle," Jeremy finally ordered hoarsely, switching back to the tactical overview. There was something reassuring about the unexciting symbols of triangles, dots, squares, arrows, and lines. What had happened to Bismarck had happened, and nothing they did now would change that fact.

With DeGaulle, however, it was different. They could still make a difference there and ensure that Alpha didn't repeat its act of mass murder. Fantasies about how he would punish the AI for its crimes welled in him, despite knowing how stupid it was. An algorithm didn't have base motives, it didn't do anything with the intention of causing suffering or to punish humanity. Instead, whenever it did anything, it was out of pure calculation.

"It wants to provoke an emotional response from us," Jeremy said aloud.

"What?" asked Felicity from the front, turning to him with a furrowed brow.

"It wants to provoke an emotional response from us," he repeated after clearing his throat. "Alpha considers emotions to be a weakness we humans have because they fall outside the logical pattern of the cause-and-effect principle. Being an artificial intelligence, it tries to analyze and predict everything that happens in the universe by using data sets and calculations.

However, as you once told me, emotions are the body's reaction to thoughts."

He looked at Felicity, who nodded slowly.

"That seems logical to me, yes," she agreed.

"Nothing tangible could be gained by Alpha burning Bismarck to ashes. Virtually all resources had already been depleted, all able-bodied personnel had been withdrawn, and there was no military equipment there either. Therefore, it was trying to provoke an emotional reaction out of us so that we might break formation, giving it the opportunity to destroy the fortress habitats. Perhaps also throw Pascal's fleet off their target, a target it doesn't even know they have."

Jeremy, of course, failed to mention that he had actually briefly toyed with the idea of flying to Bismarck. For the first time, he was almost glad that the Locusts were ultimately in control of his ship.

Over the holoscreen, he saw Macella advising all the remaining intact units in the system not to head for Bismarck but to protect the remaining colonies. There were so few of them that Jeremy's eyes moistened.

"How long until we arrive in orbit?" he asked.

"Fifteen minutes," Macella returned.

"All right." He turned to Walter. "Put all the Earth Protectorate's movements on screen for me."

The engineer didn't answer, but the green dots representing friendly ships and their trajectories disappeared and a 3D schematic view of the inner system appeared. Red triangles popped up, a few at first, then more, appearing faster and faster one after the other. The onboard consciousness calculated the trajectories which appeared as red arcs, following the movement of the celestial bodies. Alpha had spread its fleet among the remaining colony moons, DeGaulle, Verdi, and Trafalgar. That was to be expected.

When he added the allied units consisting of humans and Locusts, it didn't take long for him to realize that they couldn't do it. At least not without more alien friends showing up soon. What they needed now was the Neuromorph.

Where the hell are you? Jeremy kneaded his hands as he instructed the onboard consciousness to keep searching for Behemoth. He mentally replayed how the outline of the space monster would appear on screen, but it was a tiny bit different than he remembered. Because he wanted it to be. He thought hard about these outlines so as to provide them to the onboard consciousness as a template for its scans.

"By the way, where is Commander-generator?" he asked Macella, as an idea came to him, which he carefully hid between his emotional pain over the demise of Bismarck and his thoughts about the outline of Behemoth.

"In the engine room," Walter answered in her place. "He's working with some of the Locust technicians to further integrate some of their systems."

"What about the damage we sustained from the two direct hits we took when we arrived?"

"We still have no atmosphere in about 16 percent of the ship. Multiple hull breaches on the starboard side and destroyed superconductors. I could go on with this list forever," Walter grumbled.

"I see," Jeremy replied, getting up from his chair to step next to his engineer, who gave him a puzzled look from his workstation.

"Can any of this be fixed in the engine room?" he asked, squinting his eyes slightly as Walter started to shake his head. Fortunately, they'd been flying together long enough for the Bismarcker to understand.

"Yes, absolutely," Walter finally answered, actually sounding convincing. However, nothing concrete could be gleaned from his thoughts in the Gaia field, since they were overshadowed by his turbulent emotions. Trying to see a clear thought in it was like holding a blade of grass in front of the sun and trying to make out its contours while your eyes burned. "The solenoids need to be rearranged and the heat exchangers replaced," he said.

"I'll take care of that. Meanwhile, you supervise the current repairs," Jeremy said tersely, returning to his chair. "Macella, you have the bridge!"

Macella wanted to protest and her confusion was clearly evident in the Gaia field, but after he shook his head briefly, she snapped her mouth shut again and nodded. "Aye, Captain."

He gave the six Locusts of the Conclave a quick sideways glance, expecting an objection, but apparently they had no objections. His attempts to camouflage his thoughts by amplifying his emotional distress had apparently worked. It probably helped that not only were their thoughts alien and not always transparent to him, but that it was similar the other way around. Or before long, he would be done for.

To avoid thinking about the possibility, he logged out of the virtual bridge.

When he opened his eyes—his real eyes—the lid of his acceleration tank was already open and his head was above the gel. The onboard consciousness had taken control until the viscous green slime had emptied out of his lungs and stomach, so as not to traumatize him, which could possibly prevent him from wanting to get into the tank again. Carefully, he climbed over the edge and down the ladder, showered in one of the tiny washrooms, and then slipped into his exosuit. A glance at the chronometer in his helmet told him that it had taken him about eight minutes to do everything. That meant he still had a few minutes before they reached orbit.

The *WizKid* was no longer accelerating, because otherwise

they would have had to turn and brake too hard since the distance to DeGaulle was so close—an advantage, as he would be able to make much better progress in zero gravity than under a few g's of acceleration. If the time until their arrival above DeGaulle was correct, he had about five minutes left before the turning and braking maneuver would kick in and send him crashing into the nearest wall. So if he didn't want to end up like an insect on the windshield of a MagCapsule, he had to hurry to reach one of the emergency acceleration seats in the engine room.

With practiced movements, he shimmied along the handholds of the corridors and shafts to the next elevator where he said, "Engine room."

Silently, he glided through the central axis of the battleship. It only took a few seconds for the elevator to accelerate to around a g, momentarily giving him the feeling that he was standing in a normal elevator. As the car turned, as always, he felt nauseous for a moment as gravity reversed its direction and matched the direction of the brakes.

A beep preceded the opening of the doors and he pushed himself out into the short corridor that led to the engine room. He slid through the zero gravity like a stiff fish, stopping just short of the bulkhead labeled Engine Room C1 to give the door controls time to respond to his command and open.

Seated inside was Commander-generator, whom he recognized by his battered biosuit, which he still hadn't replaced, and two other Locusts on acceleration seats that had extended out of the wall. If they had noticed his arrival, they didn't let on. Instead, they were typing away on touchpads and alien devices that were somewhat reminiscent of the paraphernalia in the habitat recovery room.

Without hesitating, Jeremy floated to a wall panel and hit the red emergency button. The panel silently slid back to reveal an acceleration seat hinged to the front of a gimbal. He sat down in it and the nanomembrane straps flowed around his torso like black mercury before gently tightening.

Jeremy, sent Commander-generator. *I am surprised to see you here. Shouldn't you be flying the ship?*

The ship can handle it, Jeremy replied nonchalantly.

I meant an unspoken question: what are you doing here?

We can talk about it once we've slowed down...

He didn't get to finish his thought, because he lost his bearings for a moment as the massive battleship turned around. In his mind, he saw the *WizKid* ahead of him, its huge propulsion flare, glowing dimly as most of the nacelles were destroyed, going out. At that moment, the massive hull spun once on its axis and then the nacelles ignited again, heading a little more forcefully this time toward the planetoid DeGaulle.

The deceleration was brutal. He was pressed into his acceleration seat by at least four or five g's and felt like a tomato that someone had smashed against a windshield at full force. All the cartilage and joints in his body screamed and burned like fire. The medical monitoring systems in the seat responded by jamming thick needles into the side of his neck. They injected a cocktail of drugs, including amphetamines, analgesics, and blood thinners, designed to keep his veins open and his blood flowing. Still, he gritted his teeth in a snarl and prayed that the ordeal would soon be over.

Ultimately, it took a full three minutes, during which time the opposing momentum continued to decrease until at last it had subsided and given way to a comfortable microgravity of 0.3g.

Groaning, he removed the straps and checked his muscles and joints. They felt like jello but cracked like dry wood.

That was extremely unpleasant, he thought.

Yes, Commander-generator agreed with him, releasing his

seatbelt as well. The other Locusts didn't even look up but continued working on their insect-like alien devices.

Can we talk?

You mean speak? Commander-generator inquired.

Yes.

Wait a moment, please. The Locust went to a small flap on the wall and pulled out a toolbox. After rummaging around in it, he pulled out his arm display, which was now looking pretty beat up, and strapped it on. The two aliens briefly looked up and tilted their heads—no doubt a gesture of disapproval.

"I'm ready," said the translation program. "But confused."

"I need to talk to you confidentially," Jeremy explained.

"That's what I thought. The reason is what has me confused."

"Can they understand us?" he asked, nodding toward the two Locust technicians who were once again poring over their equipment.

"No. Without aids, they can't use any equipment to convert acoustic signals into Gaia, and even if they could, they'd need practice, and they wouldn't get it because they fear the *Cold Death*.

"What about your thoughts when you speak? Before translating, don't your thoughts go into the Gaia field?" questioned Jeremy.

"I can shield my thoughts. As you know, I'm a part of my faction's secret service. How secret would we be if we couldn't shield our thoughts?"

"Good point."

"So, my friend, tell me what this is all about," Commander-generator asked, pointing at the toolbox.

"Are you really? My friend?"

"I hope so. If you're alluding to my apparent betrayal on the approach to the Fortress World, I hope you believe me when I say that I saved all our lives by doing so."

"Yeah," Jeremy grudgingly admitted. "Still, it felt terrible."

Instead of answering, the alien tilted his big V-shaped head.

"All right. So we're supposed to destroy the Neuromorph because your species dictated it as a condition for an alliance and thus our survival," Jeremy explained, "but you know as well as I do that the Neuromorph isn't the problem, but a way to save us all."

"He's not malicious and he's been good to us," Commander-generator agreed with him. "However, the Conclave is afraid of him, and I can understand it from their point of view. While the purity of thoughts and emotions can be understood through memories, they aren't easy to comprehend."

"Yes. So they believe us that we believe the Neuromorph is good. Nothing more."

"Yes." Commander-generator nodded, almost humanlike.

"We have to save him," Jeremy urged the alien.

"That would be treason. We swore to do otherwise."

"I think I know a way we can keep our promise while still keeping the Neuromorph alive."

"You have my attention," the rich baritone boomed from the translation computer.

"We'll need Pascal's help to do it—I hope he's still alive. Plus, we need to find Behemoth, and fast."

CHAPTER 3

PASCAL

Orbital ring of DeGaulle, Archimedes system, 2334

THE SURVIVAL INSTINCT that had driven him through the fires of hell during the Battle of New Rome stirred in Pascal. A huge furrow 1.6 foot wide cut through the floor like a ripped scar. The deck below came into view, as debris, dust, and two hapless civilians tumbled down onto it. They screamed and flailed their arms wildly, then there were two brief, ugly sounds in quick succession and they fell silent. Smoke poured into the room from somewhere, which had suddenly become far too small, and settled beneath the ceiling like a black poison.

Coughing, Pascal ducked his head, straddled the torn chasm, and followed Spark's wild gestures. At one point he collided with someone and was thrown to the side. His armor broke most of the fall, but a sharp pain erupted in his shoulder.

As Pascal picked himself up, he remembered that he needed to seal his helmet, which he had opened while talking to Kathleen Mitchell. He did so, and the supply of internal oxygen kicked in. There were three more steps to Spark and the airlock he had just opened. They seemed a million miles away to him.

A bang caused the audio filters in his helmet to activate as two elderly men in front of him pressed their hands to their ears and fell to the ground screaming. The ground was shaking as if in an earthquake. Glancing briefly to his left, he saw the wall blistering through the thickening smoke.

"Cop, hurry up! This place is about to blow up in our faces, keh?" radioed Spark, sounding genuinely anxious for the first time.

"I'm trying," Pascal groaned, frozen to the spot. He wheeled around and searched, but couldn't find her. Kathleen Mitchell. The wise woman who had smiled like a calming force in the midst of chaos. "Where is she?"

"What?" radioed back Spark.

"She's not here! I don't see her!" cursed Pascal and was about to jump back into the cloud of smoke when he was grabbed from behind and yanked back.

"Bad time to lose your mind!" It was Spark who was roughly dragging him through the airlock that had just been opened. Behind them, the bulkhead crashed down like a guillotine. Pascal jumped up and pressed his visor against the small porthole.

Then he saw her: most of her gray hair was burnt, but her friendly face had not lost its smile. Kathleen Mitchell was standing just in front of the bulkhead that Spark had closed in front of her.

"Open up!" yelled Pascal, pounding on the door handle, but nothing happened.

"It's too late," Spark radioed from behind. "The emergency lock activated when the first plumes of smoke came in."

Pascal pressed a hand to the window, unable to think of anything that would better express his helplessness. The old woman smiled and her eyes were free of sorrow or pain as once again the ground trembled and he was yanked off his feet again. He banged his helmet against the bulkhead and went down.

"My God," he heard from somewhere. It was possibly Spark, but it was hard to tell over the ringing in Pascal's ears.

When he got up again and peered through the porthole, Kathleen Mitchell had disappeared along with the entire room on the other side. Where a moment ago there had been a half-destroyed room blanketed in toxic smoke, now the blackness of space yawned. To the left of his field of vision shone the black silhouette of DeGaulle's dark side with its brightly lit cities, while straight ahead the other half of the orbital ring was busy drifting away. The gigantic structure had been torn open as if a giant had taken a bite out of a donut. Fires flared up on several hundred decks before quickly dying out in the vacuum, just as the many fountains of escaping atmosphere were disappearing. A little farther away, just short of the planetoid's terminator line, the ring ruptured at another point, and the severed piece appeared to be spinning. It would soon crash into DeGaulle, and he prayed to God that the forces acting on it would tear it apart before then, so that it would burn up in the atmosphere. It was strange to wish for such a thing, and the mere thought of the many souls that may have gone to their deaths on the falling part almost turned his stomach.

So much death, he thought, seeing WizKid in his mind's eye. Followed by Lieutenant Goretzka and the faces of the nameless Bismarck soldiers who were dying or had already died on that piece to help them survive.

"Hey, cop! That sucks, for sure. But we've got some people here who still need help," Spark radioed, and Pascal tore his gaze away from the apocalyptic scene in front of the porthole. He tried not to think about the fact that only a single bulkhead now separated them from the cold of the vacuum.

"Yes," he answered hoarsely and turned around. Two steps

and he had passed through the airlock. He was accompanied by a heaviness in his stomach.

If he didn't know that they had only been going in one direction, he might have thought that they had arrived back at the original escape bay. The only difference between this and the previous one was that all the Evac capsules were still here waiting for them. The light on the ceiling flickered a few times before returning to a constant glow. For how long remained to be seen.

Only five older men and one woman had made it besides him, the technician, and the Sergeant Major.

So few.

"Jerome, get an escape capsule ready. I don't know how much juice we have left," Spark ordered, looking up at the ceiling lights, which were once again flickering ominously. Obviously, Jerome was the technician, who nodded briefly and then hurried to the control panel with his analyzer.

The gravity changed slightly, decreased significantly now that the ring had redirected. Not to the point that one of the walls would become the floor, but just enough for Pascal to feel like he was about to fall. It couldn't mean anything good. Either the fragment they were on was also hurtling toward DeGaulle and would soon crash, or they were moving away in the opposite direction into space.

"Which capsule?" Pascal asked the technician when he reached his side. Spark was busy sealing the inner airlock door with his plasma torch.

Instead of answering, Jerome curtly gestured to the hatch directly behind him and again, with narrowed eyes, immersed himself in the inner workings of the open control panel.

"Okay, everyone," Pascal said significantly louder than necessary, beckoning the six survivors over. One of the few useful things he had learned at the academy was to always speak extremely loudly in dangerous situations. It signaled confidence and a sense of urgency, two things that frightened people needed to hear. It was working now too. They followed his gestures and lined up in front of the Evac capsule with blank, tired faces just as he indicated. The fact that they couldn't even muster the strength to cry anymore struck him like a hammer blow.

"When that door opens, you go in, find a seat, and buckle up quickly, understand?" he continued. They probably already knew what to do, but he needed to do something now, or for the first time in a long time, he was going to lose it. As if the dying space station was trying to push him to do just that, the ground shook again. Sinister squeaks and cracks echoed off the unadorned steel and ceramic walls. No one screamed, which meant the sounds grew more menacing as they echoed back and forth.

"The door is sealed," Spark reported, trotting over.

"Are you all right?" he asked as he came to a stop in front of Pascal, looking down on him like a fatherly giant. His eyes, illuminated by the passive light of his helmet, looked tired but focused.

"Yes," Pascal murmured, nodding slowly. "In there..." He paused, and the soldier looked back toward the sealed airlock. Turning back around, he said nothing, giving him time to continue.

"There was a woman there, she was special somehow," Pascal finally added. The lady's face had burned into his retinas like a tattoo of memories.

"We lost a lot of good people today, and we're going to miss them," Spark replied, putting a hand on his shoulder. "But now is not the time for that. There are still people we need to save."

Pascal snorted and Spark raised an eyebrow.

"What?" he asked.

"Oh, nothing. A few months ago, it would have been me saying what you just told me."

"Hmm," the soldier went.

"All this," Pascal said, making a vague hand gesture, "has changed me. I'm not sure I like it, but it's changed me. I used to be clearer, more focused, but I also think more protected, in exchange for being tougher and more callous. Right now, I'm wishing for that armor back."

"Let your armor be your armor and your thoughts be your thoughts," Spark replied and Pascal looked up at him in surprise. He expected a lot from the giant, but not philosophical wisdom.

"Our job now is to get these people out of here," Spark added, and Pascal nodded.

Jerome took a few more seconds, during which time the entire escape bay shook and the gravity continued to shift, making it harder and harder to stay on his feet. The change in direction was making him feel nauseous, so he could barely contain himself when the round hatch finally opened, revealing the inside of the Evac capsule.

"Go, go, go!" he shouted, herding the six survivors and Jerome inside. He and Spark closed the door and manually locked the hatch with a red lever on the cabin wall. Then he jumped into one of the acceleration seats, which was facing aft rather than forward. The Evac capsules were ejected from their tubes toward the surface and had a rocket engine on the nose that fired to act as a brake as soon as they had completed their ballistic flight. Consequently, they would suffer the worst g-forces facing in the direction of the braking force, while the ejection would feel more like a wild roller coaster ride. At least, that's what he hoped.

A hiss announced the hatch locking and then it was silent for a moment before a jolt ran through the cabin and they were catapulted out like a projectile. Everything shook and rattled, somewhere a cover from the ceiling came loose, which Pascal experienced as a disturbing movement at the edge of his field of vision. At first the acceleration jerkily, then unyieldingly, pressed him into the simple three-point harnesses. His arms and legs were stretched out as if by a puppet master. The whole thing lasted a full minute before weightlessness set in and with it the feeling of nausea in Pascal's stomach.

"You all right, cop?" radioed Spark.

Instead of answering, Pascal turned his head toward his seatmate and in slow motion raised a hand with his thumb up. "Right now, I'm trying to force my vomit back into my stomach by sheer force of will," he said.

"The suit has a suction valve." The soldier tried to reassure him. It didn't work.

"Good to kn—"

A metallic screech tore through his sentence like paper, and suddenly everything began to tumble. Up and down alternated every second and his harnesses snapped harshly against his armor. He hoped that the civilians, who were not blessed with military equipment, did not suffer serious injuries.

Loss of balance and sense of direction protested in the form of a nauseating vertigo moments before it happened: his stomach flipped over, sending a surge of vomit up his esophagus and gushing into his helmet. It slapped against the visor and individual chunks splashed back onto his face. It stank putridly and for a brief moment he fought down panic as he thought he was going to choke. Once the last chunks of half-digested food left his mouth, he calmed down a bit. There was a hiss and a roar in his helmet and the vomit was sucked out. A residue remained and the display in his helmet warned him that a wash was imminent and to hold his breath. He did, and shortly thereafter the suit pumped recycled water from autonomous fluid reservoirs into his helmet before jerkily sucking it back out again, leaving the display reasonably clean. Vents on his shoulders automatically expelled the contaminated mix, spraying small bubbles out in all directions.

"Really gross," Spark remarked. His voice sounded strained, as if he were grinding his teeth.

"I'm sorry," Pascal returned, and was just glad that there was nothing left in his stomach to vomit out. The nausea remained, of course, but the gagging stopped and for that he was extremely grateful.

"What... what was that?" Pascal pressed out against the ever-changing gravitational pull.

"I guess we got hit by a piece of debris and catapulted out of our ballistic trajectory. We're now tumbling uncontrollably toward the surface. As the gravity direction keeps changing, I'm guessing we're already being pulled relatively fast by DeGaulle," Spark explained, his voice strained like a high-tension tightrope.

"But... doesn't that mean..."

"Yes. If we don't enter the upper atmospheric layers facing forward and in a controlled manner, we'll burn up while being torn apart," the soldier confirmed his worst fears.

"I hate space," Pascal grumbled. *And I hate not being able to do anything while sitting in a damn sardine can with nothing but a vacuum around me,* he added in his mind.

"You're not the only one, keh."

"Jeremy to Pascal, do you read me?" The voice, punctuated by static, sounded in his ears, catching Pascal by such surprise that he had to clear his throat before he could answer.

"Jeremy? Is that you? My God! I hope you brought backup."

"Yes, it's me. How nice to hear your voice. I'm seeing a completely destroyed orbital ring plummeting uncontrollably toward DeGaulle here. I was afraid—"

"Perhaps your fears are still justified," Pascal interrupted him, having to force each syllable out with great effort. He felt like a ball of plasticine being pulled in all possible directions by a group of extremely rough giants. At least that was the best inner image he could come up with. Or the worst.

"What's wrong?" asked Jeremy, but before Pascal could answer, he added, "Shit, don't tell me you're sitting in that out-of-control escape capsule!"

"Sorry," Pascal sighed, smiling fatalistically to himself. "Unfortunately, it was getting very uncomfortable on the orbital ring."

"We'll get you out of there!"

"And how are you going to do that?"

"I've got Walter on board here, remember?" Jeremy replied, and Pascal could almost hear his cocky captain's smile in his voice, which on the one hand was part of his youthful charm and on the other one of the biggest clichés of space travel.

"Accomplishing the impossible in an impossible situation? Sounds easy for the old grouch."

"Give him a moment and don't you dare explode before we figure something out," Jeremy returned. "Because I need your help."

"With what?" asked Pascal. "I'm a little... tied up at the moment."

"When you land on the surface, I need you to do something for me, or rather for the Neuromorph, or rather for all of us." The static in the background increased momentarily, making it very difficult for him to understand the young captain.

"The Neuromorph? Behemoth?"

"Yes. We found him. Only problem is... we did bring reinforcements, but at the price of the Locusts wanting the head of our ally and friend," Jeremy said, his voice sounding like crackling paper.

What is going on with this damn connection?

"Why would they want to kill the one who made this alliance possible in the first place? The one who ended the war?" he asked, racking his brains. However, he couldn't think of anything that would make sense.

"They clearly hate AIs as well as technology a lot more than we would have thought from the Locusts on Bismarck," Jeremy explained. "They clearly don't trust any AI, no matter how friendly it turns out to be. When something nearly wipes out your entire civilization, it's certainly an understandable reaction. How do you think our descendants will feel about artificial intelligences one day?"

"If we survive this crap, you mean?" Pascal wasn't at all sure at the moment that that would be the case. After all, his brain was literally still spinning in circles.

"Yes."

"You're right, not particularly great," Pascal finally relented. "Nevertheless, all evidence points to the fact that the Neuromorph is not up to something evil. He's put his own head in the noose too many times for that."

"They are a truly emotional people, who place at least as much importance on the emotional world as they do on the intellectual."

Of course. How was he supposed to recognize a pattern if it wasn't made up of puzzle pieces he could understand?

You're slipping, Pascal Takahashi, he scolded himself inwardly, grunting as a particularly relentless attack of vertigo struck him.

"Hey, I have an answer from Walter," Jeremy suddenly radioed, snapping him out of his self-critical thoughts.

"So, can he make the impossible happen?"

"Of course. It's Walter we're talking about here," Jeremy gloated, "though I seem to have a part to play in it."

"How..." Pascal continued, but the young captain refused to be interrupted.

"Well. We'll try to get you out of there right away, but when the time comes and we do get to set you down on the surface unharmed, I need you to do me a favor."

"What's that?"

"I need you to rescue the Neuromorph while we destroy Behemoth," Jeremy returned.

While other people might have reacted with lack of understanding or inquired about the apparent paradox in that statement, Pascal however didn't. He understood these pieces of the puzzle all too well and they came together in his mind to form a coherent pattern faster than he would have thought.

Apparently I'm good for something after all, he thought and smiled to himself. Albeit a small pleasure, it helped him get past his groaning muscles and sinews for a moment.

"Send the details to my suit. You should be able to use the military precedence codes," he finally said.

"Good luck, my friend. Jeremy out."

CHAPTER 4
JEREMY

In orbit above DeGaulle, Archimedes system, 2334

When Jeremy returned to the bridge, he no longer felt nervous about the audacious plan he had set in motion. It might turn out to be completely idiotic, but for the time being it was the best plan he could have come up with in such a short time. He only wished he could have worked it out with Macella, Walter, and Felicity, but with the Conclave on board, he didn't want to run the risk of their new allies getting wind of it.

"It's good to have you back, Captain," Macella greeted him with a smile. There was a noncommittal politeness in the smile that hid something. A sign of understanding, perhaps?

"Our guests have instructed me to question you regarding what happened in the engine room, your conversation with Commander-generator, and the radio signals that left our ship," she said, tilting her head toward the six aliens.

Jeremy looked toward them and tried for an innocent grin. "So they want to monitor my thoughts based on the conversation between us and probe for possible untruths? Fine by me."

"Good. What did you really do in the engine room?" asked

Macella without any real interest, like a computer emotionlessly and monotonously rattling off questions.

"I rearranged the solenoids and changed the heat exchangers. Commander-generator helped me do that," Jeremy answered truthfully, following the helpful tips from his Locust friend who had told him to always go directly to the memory of what he had experienced when being questioned. So during his answer, he focused on the specific visual memories of how he opened a wall panel, pulled out tools, and wedged himself behind a small console.

"The Conclave was unable to monitor Gaia emissions from Commander-generator. Why?" continued Macella.

"I asked him to keep our conversation confidential."

"Why?" It was obvious to him that his girlfriend would rather not have been having this conversation.

Instead of answering, Jeremy turned to the Conclave's Locusts, who were eyeing him with tilted heads as if he was a lab rat.

"If you want to know something from me, just ask me. My crew is not just one of your tools, okay?"

Yes, she is, Captain Brandt, the female in the middle contradicted him. Commander-generator had called her Matriarch. *Once this battle is fought and both sides have gotten what they are fighting for, then we can think about an equal alliance. Until then, you need our help, without which you will be annihilated.*

"You'd fight Alpha the same way, after all, it's a goddamn AI," Jeremy said aloud.

Yes. Normally, however, we would destroy its creators as well. Just to be sure, she answered directly into his mind, and the accompanying images of mass destruction were almost unbearable. He wasn't sure if she had just made some kind of Locust joke, but either way he didn't like it, joke or not.

"I'm sorry, Captain," Macella said formally, and her eyes

showed how reluctant she was to continue. "Let me repeat the question: why did you want to talk to Commander-generator without the Conclave being able to hear your conversation? This process is very unusual for Locusts."

"Like I said," Jeremy replied angrily, not even having to struggle to feel real anger. It came naturally. "I wanted to talk to him without being interrupted."

"Why?" inquired Macella, but in her eyes Jeremy could see a conspiratorial glint. He would have liked to smile at her to let her know that he was indeed following a plan, but he had to remain believable, so he continued to focus on his anger.

"Because you commandeered my damn ship! I can't even vent my frustration at you for taking control of it away from us!" It burst out of him, and he turned directly to the aliens again, stabbing an index finger at them as if he wanted to skewer them. Every word that crossed his lips made him angrier, because every single one was true.

"This ship is named after our friend and you have dishonored it with your dictatorial behavior! She gave her life so that Locusts and humans could live together. She saved not only us but your people on Bismarck as well, and you know it! How dare you come aboard and act like big shots, you slimy waterheads?" he rumbled angrily, hoping he hadn't gone too far. "That's what I told Commander-generator!"

There was no reaction from the Locusts, except for their overwhelming auras of authority and composure. Even now they didn't crumble. The fact that he had shared his plan for the Neuromorph with Commander-generator and asked him if Locusts could receive and interpret radio signals, he carefully hid under his all-consuming rage.

Macella looked questioningly at the six figures on their perches, then nodded and turned back to Jeremy. "What were those radio transmissions you sent?"

"When I learned from Walter that escape capsules had been launched from the dying orbital ring, I was hoping that Pascal was in one of them. They don't have directional receivers, as you know, so for that reason, and because we were close enough, I asked Walter to set up a secure radio link," Jeremy explained truthfully.

"The signal was scrambled," Macella opined.

"Of course! Radio signals are easy to intercept, even by Alpha."

"What was the radio message about?"

"You probably noticed from my communication with Walter here that it was about the rescue of our friend. What else would it be about?"

"They don't mean that radio message, Captain, they mean the other one," Macella replied. It was becoming increasingly obvious that she was tired of playing the human translator for the Conclave.

"I see. The other radio message was sent to the Neuromorph," he replied tersely, shrugging his shoulders as if it was nothing of importance he was talking about.

The Locusts on the podium started moving, exchanging uneasy glances.

Explain yourself, human, came directly from the Matriarch, whose ganglia at the back of her head snapped for a moment.

"Well, you want the damned Neuromorph in return for your help. I haven't seen him yet, have you?" he asked, letting his genuine anger and despair over this seep into the Gaia field. "I haven't seen him yet, and if we don't see him, we can't destroy him. I've sent out a system-wide radio message to him to lure him to Trafalgar and then to us at DeGaulle. With any luck, he can defend the colony there until your units arrive and then jump here."

Why would the Cold Death *respond to your message*?

"Because he's a good guy, that's why!" hissed Jeremy, "and you want to kill him. I'm only doing this because it would be worse to throw away the lives of my entire species. Don't have any illusions about how I feel about this!"

The Matriarch remained silent, as did the other Locusts of the Conclave.

"I'm sorry," Macella said, raising her palms apologetically.

"It's all right," he returned, trying to calm his rapid breathing. His heart was hammering in his chest and even he couldn't tell if it was because of the excitement or his anger. At least that gave him hope that they couldn't see through him either. If they couldn't do it, then the aliens wouldn't be able to do so for a long time.

Or?

At any rate, the Conclave remained silent, and he took it as a good sign for the time being.

"Give me an update," Jeremy finally ordered, addressing Macella and finally settling into his command chair.

"Aye, Captain. We are in orbit over DeGaulle, as is the rest of the surviving fleet of Locusts and Navy units. The fortress habitats continue to fire on Alpha's ships and where they hit, they vaporize everything. However, the AI has reacted quickly and the number of hits has dropped significantly. Currently, their ships are split between us, Verdi, and Trafalgar. For now, Europa seems to be left out of the equation."

"Do we still have units over Verdi?" he asked with concern.

"No. But according to our sensors, most of the orbital defense platforms are still intact, as is the orbital ring," she returned, pointing to the updated schematic on the holoscreen.

"Did Pascal say anything about whether his mission was successful?" interjected Walter from the front.

"It was," Jeremy confirmed curtly.

"Good."

Now that the mission is complete, every colonist should have turned off their NeuroSmart by now to protect themselves from Alpha. All autonomous and semi-autonomous systems, such as defense systems and drones, would also have received the Neuromorph's basic program code along with the signal to fight Alpha's algorithms. Jeremy only hoped that the battle would end well and that their ally's confidence would prove to be justified. The prospect that all computer systems in the Archimedes system that were connected to the colony-wide SenseNet contained semi-autonomous copies of the friendly AI reassured him. However, there was also no alternative; after all, he had sent his radio message for the Neuromorph to all the system's radio stations, for lack of a better idea, in the hope that it would be relayed.

"The war spheres will be entering weapons range in a few moments," Felicity reported from her console, her voice a prime example of professionalism.

"Fire at your discretion. Just keep an eye on the drones," Jeremy ordered. "Walter, I want us to hold back 20 percent of our drones, just in case. I don't want to end up being naked when Alpha springs its surprise."

"What surprise?" asked Macella.

"I don't know. What I do know is that it's definitely got some sort of plan cooked up."

"Hmm."

"It's not just going to fly up to our position and shoot it out with us, believe me," he replied, shaking his head decisively. "No, it knows we're bringing in reinforcements, and it knows that it has to surprise us. Believe me, it will, and soon."

"Any idea how it's going to do that?" asked Macella.

"I've been trying to figure it out for some time. If anyone has any ideas, feel free to share them."

"Maybe it'll go back to flinging asteroids from the belt at the colonies to split our firepower," interjected Walter, who looked like he hadn't slept in a month since seeing the images of Bismarck.

"Unlikely," Felicity objected, giving her friend and companion a sympathetic look. Her eyes said, *A mess like that wouldn't normally get to you.*

"True," Walter agreed with her, nodding weakly. There was no sign of the bad mood he normally wore around him like some kind of medal, and that worried Jeremy more than anything else. "In order for them to arrive here in time, Alpha would have to have sped up the asteroids even faster than is possible, even for it. But even if it were possible, the ice and rock that they're made up of would just shatter."

"Then what?" asked Macella. "Maybe it has more ships in hyperspace just waiting to jump into our midst?"

"I don't think so. Behemoth has deployed hyperspace barriers of its own—at least if its mission was successful. Alpha is likely to know about them." Jeremy shook his head and sighed.

"It's always possible that it has some new technology up its sleeve," Walter mused.

"But we can't count on that," Macella agreed.

"Nah. But we should keep our eyes open."

"Speaking of eyes," Felicity interjected, pointing to the holo-screen. "Here we go."

Jeremy saw it: on the screen, for the first time, the weapons ranges of Alpha's advancing armada and their defense forces, shown as red shaded circles, overlapped. Tens of thousands of flashing icons came to life: battle drones and their spherical counterparts from the Locusts' cruisers. They kept a seemingly leisurely pace as they headed toward the approaching Earth ships, but appearances were deceiving. Because of the vast distances, which looked tiny on the screen, even a predator drone that accelerated at over 40g looked like a snail. The swarms of missiles that had followed shot past them at double their acceleration, with hyperspace missiles simply disappearing before reappearing moments later amidst the ranks of Alpha's war spheres. But only a few managed to outwit all the AI's mobile barriers with their ECCM measures. Most were lost. However, where they did find their target, there was little hope. The hyperspace windows the smart missiles opened were so close to the hulls of the enemy ships that their short-range defenses barely had time to react. Hyperspace exit and impact occurred so quickly that a human brain was unable to detect them.

"Walter, how long before the two mammoth drones get to Pascal's escape capsule?" While he was still in the engine room, talking to Commander-generator, he had asked Walter to implement his plan immediately. In the meantime, several minutes had passed, and even the rather ponderous Atals work drones had made good progress.

"Forty seconds," the engineer replied without looking up from his console.

"Should I take over?" asked Jeremy.

While mammoth drones basically operated autonomously, such as when they repaired starships, hauled loads back and forth between starships, or carried out predetermined blueprints for space stations or ships. But everything else was subject to strict limitations imposed by the AI laws. In short, the drone piloting software was fast and accurate as long as it was following fixed instructions, but stupid and useless as soon as it had to tackle more complicated things. It was rather ironic that after all the laws and measures in place against the dangers of AI, an AI, of all things, had plunged the colonies into chaos. To say that the Progressives had been right would be a mistake, of course, since ultimately they were to blame for the whole mess in the form of Moreau. Nevertheless, he couldn't help but acknowledge that simply looking the other way and saying "no" had hardly been a good solution. If the problem had been dealt with earlier, it might have been possible to develop a Neuromorph to protect the people sooner.

"It's probably better," Walter recommended, and Jeremy shook his head to clear his thoughts.

"All right, patch me in."

The transition was smooth. Once he agreed to a request from the ship's consciousness to enter a new virtual space, the bridge simply disappeared like it had never existed and he found himself standing in space. High above DeGaulle, but not as high as he would have liked, he gazed across the blackness at Pascal's escape capsule. It was tumbling right beside him through the top layers of the atmosphere like an out-of-control boomerang.

"Zoom in," he commanded, and the capsule, its movements projected into the virtual space in real time, became huge. Had it been real, he could have touched it just by extending his hand. He examined the thick steel plates with their smooth welds and covered bolted joints and walked quickly, but carefully, along the hull. There were two protrusions that might pose a problem for the mammoths.

"What's behind these protrusions?"

"Extendable wings for atmospheric flight," the onboard consciousness replied in an androgynous computer voice.

"Simulation: can two mammoth drones provide the capsule with enough counter-thrust to allow it to land like a rocket without aerodynamic properties?"

"Simulation in progress."

A few seconds passed, during which time Jeremy looked at the black-ringed propulsion pod, which had long since gone out.

"Yes," the onboard consciousness announced the end of the simulation.

"Good. Will their pilot software be sufficient to adjust thrust and position quickly and efficiently enough to allow the capsule to fly and land stably?"

"Yes."

"Excellent. Next simulation: my concern is that those two protrusions for the wings stick out too far for the drones to get close enough to the fuselage with their magnetic grappling arms. Or at least not without jeopardizing their own stability. Is that correct?"

"Simulation in progress."

Then: "Simulation complete: structural integrity of C2-type mammoth drones 78 percent compromised. I advise against it."

The real mammoth drones arrived, maintaining a distance of less than three hundred and twenty-eight feet from the plummeting escape capsule. Their massive forms were somewhat reminiscent of oversized cockroaches. During flight, their grappling arms hung backward like the tentacles of an octopus, but now slid forward in anticipation of work.

"How long before the capsule enters the atmosphere and burns up?"

"Four minutes," reported the onboard consciousness.

"Simulation: if the drones cut off both bulges and used the covers to weld the holes shut, how long would that take?"

"Simulation in progress," the monotone voice announced again.

"Three minutes twenty-six seconds."

"Holy cow, that's cutting it fine," Jeremy cursed.

"You'd better make up your mind fast," the onboard consciousness recommended unnecessarily, eliciting a frustrated snort from him.

Per military priority code, he took control of both drones and ordered them to strip and seal the bulges before clinging to the outer hull and stabilizing the escape capsule.

There was no delay. The two space roaches shot forward so fast that he feared they would collide with the capsule before they attached themselves to it like spiders with magnetic legs and their countless fission cutters sprang to life.

"Calculate a trajectory to the Élysée Tower. Have the capsule land on the roof. It should be sturdy enough to allow such a landing. Plus, nobody lives there. Feed the flight data into the drone's pilot software. Also, calculate a thrust pattern for their atmospheric flight that will keep them stable. I don't want to have to stress about their stupidity or protocol limitations," Jeremy ordered, watching as the mammoth drones did their work with precision and accuracy.

"Roger that," the onboard consciousness obediently replied. "Calculations in progress. Transmitting."

A green hologram appeared before Jeremy's eyes, showing four minutes that rapidly counted down to exactly two seconds.

"Sufficient time," the androgynous voice announced emotionlessly, the best news he could have asked for just then.

"Fabulous! Transmission to Pascal: we're bringing you down safely," Jeremy exulted, waving his fist in satisfaction just as a third voice joined them, seemingly out of nowhere: "This is Walter. You'd best come back, we have a problem."

"Of course," Jeremy sighed and switched to the virtual bridge environment.

"What's wrong?" he asked, shaking his head briefly to get used to the abrupt change of environment.

It was Macella who answered him. "Drones from Alpha's ships have broken through our defenses and are heading for Pascal's escape capsule." She pointed to the holoscreen, which showed actual telescopic images: a swarm of shiny objects were racing toward a red dot silhouetted against DeGaulle's huge black outline. The lightning-fast war machines looked like a swarm of meteors targeting the colonies, which were orbiting peacefully. But it was his friend they were targeting, and at that moment, that was far worse.

"Do we still have Predators in reserve?" he asked tensely.

"Not an active reserve. Just the 20 percent we were told to hold back for an emergency," Macella replied.

"This is a freaking emergency! If we deploy a swarm now, will they make it in time?"

"Just a moment," Macella requested, tapping away on a datapad so believably rendered by the virtual environment that an uninformed observer might actually have thought they were in the past.

"No," she finally said, as all color drained from her face.

"What do you mean 'no'? Those things are fast as hell," Jeremy shouted, watching in horror as Alpha's battle drones moved across the holoscreen like ravenous sharks. There were sixteen of them and they would reach his friend in exactly two minutes and thirteen seconds. At least their weapons systems would.

"Yeah," Marcella muttered. "But they've already reached full speed, so from our launch angle, the Predators just aren't fast enough."

"Railguns?"

"They aren't following an exact linear trajectory, making them impossible to hit," she objected, sounding almost apologetic, as if it was all her fault.

He couldn't believe Pascal's life expectancy was ticking down on his holoscreen and would run out in two minutes and there wasn't a damn thing he could do about it. Surely there was *something* he could do!

"Son of a bitch!" he yelled, pounding his chair in exasperation until his knuckles hurt. He wished for a moment that the pain wasn't just a figment of his imagination.

The bridge became deathly quiet, except for the overwhelming emotions of grief, anger, and frustration that surged toward him from all sides except from the Locusts. These emotions mingled with his own feelings of powerlessness, and he could barely stand them.

Although he knew it wouldn't help his soaring adrenaline levels, he paced his command platform like a tiger, accompanied by the concerned silence of his friends.

There must be something I can do, he repeated inwardly like a mantra, racking his brain for a solution.

"What about a hyperspace jump?"

"We're still too badly damaged," Walter replied, shaking his head.

"Can't we get slingshot again?" asked Jeremy, chewing so hard on his lower lip that it hurt.

"Just attaching the necessary cables and calculating the jump would take longer than the one minute and sixteen seconds Pascal has left," the engineer grunted sadly.

Jeremy's eyes darted to the time display, which was diminishing far too quickly.

Dammit!

"Hyperspace rockets," he shouted, as if he had just had an aha moment. But he knew better.

"The targets are too small for the targeting computers to get an accurate bearing," Macella pointed out as the remaining time dropped below one minute.

"You've got to be kidding me," Jeremy wailed, slumping into his command chair, completely exhausted. He felt as if someone had pulled a plug, sucking all the life force out of him. There was nothing he could do for the inspector now. A tiny number of red pixels that were not even real told him the exact time of his friend's death.

When it reached twenty seconds, his heart began to race. He wanted to turn away from the live feed of the speeding drones, didn't want to watch the capsule explode, and yet he couldn't take his eyes off the screen. Jeremy felt he owed it to Pascal to witness his end, as painful as it might be.

So he stared at the screen, committing the images to memory, while thinking of his friend out there in space, facing a soundless death. Of all places, the place the inspector feared and despised the most.

I will never forget you, he promised the astute policeman inwardly and, determined not to look away, swallowed against the lump in his throat as the display reached 0.

Alpha's drones fired sixteen nuclear homing missiles at their target, covering the distance to Pascal's escape capsule in less than three seconds.

Green flashes flared in front of the black disk of the colony, opening and closing like distorted fire flowers.

All that was left of his friend was... *the escape capsule*!

Jeremy rubbed his eyes to make sure it was real.

"Zoom in!" he shouted, anxiously, and then there was no doubt: the little tin can in which Pascal would reach the atmosphere at any moment was still tumbling down uncontrollably! And it was not alone. Next to it, a gigantic hyperspace window was just closing, out of which Behemoth had slid like a huge monster of flesh and darkness. He was right where the drone's nuclear missiles had detonated earlier. Jeremy, however, could not see any signs of damage.

Tiny projectiles left Behemoth's mile-long hull, crashing into Alpha's drones a short time later, tearing through them like paper.

Behind him, Jeremy sensed excitement flaring in the Gaia field. The Locusts.

Through clenched teeth, he gave the order, and he hated himself for it. "Fire."

All the port-mounted railguns realigned as their barrels

swung away from the steadily approaching Earth Protectorate armada and aimed at the Neuromorph. As the magnetic slides launched their 4.4-pound tungsten rounds, Jeremy prayed silently that his ally had gotten his message. If not, they had just created a new enemy, possibly even more formidable than Alpha.

CHAPTER 5
PASCAL

Approaching DeGaulle, Archimedes system, 2334

THE UBIQUITOUS RATTLING AND CLATTERING, which sounded like all the galley equipment spinning in a tumble dryer, was suddenly joined by a loud hissing sound. It didn't do much to calm Pascal.

The direction of gravity was still changing every few seconds as they plummeted, tumbling, toward the dark surface of DeGaulle. However, the gravitational pull of the planetoid was apparently already strong enough to create a vague sense of up and down in his brain. The tugging on his harnesses merely rubbed against his armor, but Pascal was already noticing bruises and abrasions starting to appear in some places where the armor didn't fit perfectly.

"You still alive, cop?" radioed Spark, and his voice sounded kind of strange, as if he had paused while sipping a bowl of soup and started talking with a full mouth.

"My pain says I am," Pascal grumbled. "What's wrong with you?"

"What do you mean?"

"You sound funny."

"Oh, I think I knocked out some teeth," replied the soldier, as if it was nothing serious.

"What?" asked Pascal, horrified. "How?"

"Some of the more violent swings from the capsule caught me just as I was taking a sip from the drinking tube. My teeth hit each other pretty hard in the process. But they can be replaced, keh."

"My God," Pascal murmured, suppressing a shiver that tried to work its way down from the back of his neck.

"Do you think your friends can get us out of here?" Spark changed the subject.

"If anyone can, they can." In his mind, Pascal added, *At least I hope so.*

Above them on the ceiling—or was it the floor?—a red light suddenly flared to life, its glow accompanied by the shrill blare of an alarm. His acoustic sensors regulated the volume so that it wouldn't hurt his ears.

"What is that?"

"An alarm," Spark replied over the radio.

"Well, thanks for nothing,'" snorted Pascal.

"I don't know, keh. Never flown one of those things before. If I still had a NeuroSmart, I'd have asked the AI core for information on this tin can, but obviously that's a moot point."

"Is the AI core still active?" asked Pascal, frowning into his tiny helmet visor.

"Nope."

"Can we even land without AI support?"

"Nope."

"Then without Jeremy's help, we'll crash into DeGaulle like a falling star anyway?" scowled Pascal, as if that notion was entirely Sparks's fault.

"Probably," the soldier returned, seemingly unmoved, and,

glancing sideways, Pascal saw the giant Bismarcker in his armor raise his shoulders.

"Wait, you put us in the capsule knowing that we were probably going to crash?"

"Right. If we had stayed on the station any longer, we would have died anyway. In the capsule, at least we had a few more minutes and more options than we did on the ring," Spark explained.

"My God."

"It's normal military procedure, cop," his companion reassured him, his voice sounding like he was trying to stifle a laugh. "Instead of dying because of the shit in front of you, rather die because of the shit coming in a few minutes. A little more time is better than no time, and look how far it's gotten us."

"Hmm," Pascal grumbled.

"Would you have gotten aboard if I had told you that we were just going to crash?"

"No, probably not," he quietly returned. "I hate space."

"Ha!" laughed Spark. "I already figured that out!"

The hissing coming from the walls grew louder and louder, then something thumped against the hull, and a moment later it went "plock!" exactly twelve times before becoming silent again. Save for the groans and sighs of their fellow passengers, who, without armor, were clearly suffering more under the violent bucking and lurching of the capsule.

Suddenly, the erratic movements of the escape capsule ceased. The rattling noises, hisses, and rumbles all disappeared as if they had never existed.

"Oh," Spark said, turning his head toward him. His powerful chin glistened with blood that looked black from the blue passive lighting.

"That should be the drones," Pascal remarked, feeling the gravity increase.

"Drones?"

"Jeremy sent his plan to my suit. Part of it, at least. It said something about drones, but no details. The data was more about what I'm supposed to do when we land."

"Maybe drones are stabilizing us now or something," Spark surmised, slurring a bit. "But they can't fly in an atmosphere, can they?"

"I don't think so, but I really don't know. That's not my area of expertise," Pascal replied apologetically.

"What are we supposed to do when we get to the ground anyway, supposing we make it, keh?"

"We're supposed to rescue a friend."

"Can we be a little less mysterious?" grumbled Spark.

Things started churning in Pascal's mind. On the one hand, he trusted the giant warrior from Bismarck; after all, he owed him his life. On the other hand, he trusted almost no one. It was unlikely that he was one of Alpha's spies or even controlled by its program code, but nothing was impossible in 2334. If there was one thing he had learned, it was to never underestimate the superintelligence from Earth. Maybe it didn't act as passionately as Moreau had, but it acted with purpose and efficiency, evaluating patterns based on criteria different from what Pascal used. So what if Spark was only one last piece on Alpha's chessboard who would kill the Neuromorph when he was most vulnerable? That would be his fault and it was something he didn't want to have to live with.

"I'm sorry," he finally said, and meant it sincerely. "Given what we're about to do, we can't fail. I don't think you're Alpha, but I can't take any chances, no matter how unlikely."

"I understand," Spark replied to his surprise, nodding. His helmet resembled a bouncing Smurf as he did so.

"Thanks."

"That's all right, cop. You're the inspector, after all. I'm just an armored grunt who can shoot his way out of a mess in no time." He raised his double-barreled arms with their weapons mounted and sounded downright lighthearted as he continued, "If you need these, just tell me which way to fire. You can then worry about the rest."

"Thank you for understanding and again, I'm sorry."

"No worries. If I do happen to be one of Alpha's agents without knowing it, put a bullet in me."

"You got it."

"Promise me, I mean it," the soldier demanded in a firm voice and they gave each other an intense look before Pascal nodded.

"I promise."

"Good." Spark seemed satisfied and leaned back in his acceleration seat.

Shortly afterward, apparently braking had started, because Pascal suddenly felt much heavier than he had before. He was pressed so hard into the seat that he felt as if his spine was being forcibly jammed through the backrest. Whatever Walter and Jeremy had cooked up, their capsule had just slowed down considerably and that meant they must have entered DeGaulle's atmosphere.

Pascal could not see the civilians sitting behind them facing in the direction of the flight, but their frequent groans and painful moans had ceased. It appeared that they had lapsed back into the silence that the traumatic events on the orbital ring had imposed on their souls.

Pascal, a voice suddenly filled his head. No, not a voice, but a presence and with it a flood of thoughts and feelings that seemed carefully controlled but nevertheless overwhelmingly infinite.

The Neuromorph! Pascal knew immediately and without a doubt who was contacting him via the Gaia field.

Yes, replied the AI and human hybrid. *Currently, I am engaged in battle and do not have much time.*

The messages were accompanied by images showing explosions, the sensation of speed and hyperspace windows constantly opening and closing. Rockets streaked through the blackness of space, only recognizable by their long exhaust tails. The sense of vastness was constricted by the multitude of things happening all around. Pascal saw ships rupturing, thousands of the Locusts' slender friends bursting out of green hyperspace windows, and a seemingly endless number of explosions.

Have you spoken to Jeremy?

I received a message from him, came the reply along with a sense of sadness and yet at the same time determination.

And? Pascal asked cautiously. His fear that the Neuromorph would feel insulted and declare war, and become their new enemy, was mixed with feelings of guilt. Without him, there would be no resistance, and quite possibly no more humans. Likewise, there would probably be no alliance between them and the Locusts—the very alliance that was now the Neuromorph's downfall. Or theirs.

It is not what I would have wished for, the creature confessed.

What are you going to do, Pascal urged, half eager, half anxious.

I will comply with his request. The alliance between your species is more important than my survival within the structure you call Behemoth and the Locusts call Father. Since I have no desire to die, I appreciate that Jeremy's plan includes me surviving in a different form. For all intents and purposes, it's been inevitable from the start, because the Locusts are right: Alpha, and by extension in some way I, have stolen something from them. Given their historical background, I understand their anger and fear.

How can you be so understanding? They want you dead, despite all you have done for them! Although Pascal was glad that their most powerful ally evidently had decided not to simply wipe them off the face of the universe. At the same time, he could not understand how he could remain so calm in the face of such a blatant injustice.

I can feel them across the Gaia field, the Neuromorph reminded him. *All of them.*

What do you mean? All of them? All the Locusts?

Yes.

But how is that possible?

I feel each and every one of them, as if they were right in front of me.

All of a sudden, Pascal's mouth went dry. Was that even possible? Could a single being, even in a body as powerful as the Father's, receive all the aliens' Gaia emissions? That would mean that the Neuromorph had accomplished something not even a Locust had ever been able to do—not even the Mother. At least Pascal hadn't sensed anything like that when he had been fused with her. But that might also have been because the consciousness of Behemoth's giant sister had been completely empty. Maybe the two were connected and the body could only do what the consciousness thought it could do?

In that case it's even worse that they want to destroy you! What knowledge will be lost over this, thought Pascal, upset by such a waste of life and progress.

They would never use or even examine anything that has been used, let alone inhabited, by an AI, the Neuromorph reasoned.

But...

We have very little time, Pascal, the hybrid being gently but firmly admonished him. *Your escape capsule's landing zone is being contested and I'm busy trying to make sure you don't get shot down.*

What do you mean "contested"?

Alpha's ships have jumped into the atmosphere and opened fire on the resistance. I think they're trying to draw our ships out of orbit in the process.

That means there's a battle raging around us right now? Pascal asked in alarm, casting a tentative glance at the unadorned walls of the capsule, which suddenly felt like it had abruptly shrunk by several degrees.

That's correct.

Oh great.

You don't need to fear for your life, the almost overwhelming presence of the Neuromorph replied, allowing the calm that surrounded his every thought to flow over the Gaia field to Pascal like a soothing balm. It worked and he relaxed a little. *I can protect you as long as I'm still in this body. The problem is that after you land, I won't be able to.*

Because of the plan, Pascal thought. *Where are we landing?*

On the Élysée. All of New Paris is currently under attack, and once my current body is gone, it will be very dangerous.

I'll take care of you, I promise!

Thank you. I would prefer not to die, the Neuromorph returned, and Pascal actually thought he could detect a trace of humor in the hybrid's thoughts. It was difficult to tell amidst all the impressions that each of his thoughts entailed.

How long until we land? he asked, his mouth agape again as he felt as if his back would snap at any moment like a dry twig under the crushing g-forces.

One minute, the Neuromorph replied. *I saw your memories of New Rome and this is equally as bad. You should prepare yourself, because I know how traumatic the events there were for you.*

I'll be fine, Pascal said, but could feel the lump in his throat getting bigger and tighter. Just the thought of the chaos of death and destruction that he and Thandis had stumbled through like lost deer made his palms damp. Images of burning civilians, severed limbs, screaming mothers holding their dead babies in their arms, oblivious to their surroundings–it was all burned into his brain like a tattoo of blood and tears. Nothing would ever be able to banish that night from his memory and that was a good thing. While the memory hurt, especially when it came to Thandis, who had sacrificed herself for him, it also served as a permanent reminder: life is as fragile as a piece of paper hovering over a fire. The slightest touch with death meant the end.

I have no doubt, came from the Neuromorph, and Pascal didn't know if it was because the bio-AI could filter its thoughts or was simply reacting neutrally, but there was no telling whether or not it believed him.

It's starting now. My end is near. When you land, make your way down from the roof quickly.

All right, thought Pascal, trying hard to let optimism and determination flow into the Gaia field, but the Neuromorph's presence had already disappeared.

"It's a real shame," Spark rumbled over the radio.

"What?"

"For them to kill him and force us to become accomplices," the soldier grumbled bitterly as the reverse thrust suddenly eased dramatically. Everything began to shake and rattle. The vibrations were so powerful that there were several jingling sounds one after another and Pascal didn't have to look to know that some of the screws had come loose. His hands felt numb, as if he had been holding a jackhammer too long.

Then there was a jolt and a quick thump that he felt all the way down his neck and then silence. No thrust and no vibration. Evidently they were on the roof of the Élysée with their acceleration seats pointing back down.

"Okay, guys, here we go!" he shouted over his helmet speaker. "Unbuckle and carefully get out."

The instant he finished, the side panels automatically flew outward with a loud crash, leaving the capsule a skeleton of steel and ceramic. In an emergency, it provided quicker access for rescue workers, but now it exposed them to even greater danger. Not only did a draughty night wind immediately flow into the interior but also the madness of battle.

It thundered and cracked, cannon blasts pounded his audio amplifiers, which instantly shut down to protect his ears. There was so much glare and flickering that his visor darkened and somewhere nearby there was an impact. The resulting cloud of dust which entered the now exposed interior of their capsule with the wind made the civilians below him cough.

Clumsily, Pascal unfastened the simple three-point harness of his acceleration seat and clung to the armrests so as not to fall. He risked a look down and saw the civilians freeing themselves from their harnesses, looking dazed but surprisingly calm. Spark had already jumped onto the roof of the huge Élysée Arcology, which stretched several hundred feet in all directions and was covered in a shiny liquid. He stood next to a steaming mammoth drone lying on the plascrete like an oversized cockroach with its legs stretched out in front of it.

"Everybody out!" the giant shouted through his helmet speakers. His order was almost drowned out by the hiss of several rockets whizzing past them into the sky at close range.

There were two flashes.

"You heard him, get out!" Pascal shouted and drew his pistol. It seemed almost puny and ridiculous given the current situation. It was more the feeling of familiarity that reassured him than thinking he was now armed and dangerous.

Following instructions, the civilians climbed out of their seats and the escape capsule, helping each other. Pascal followed them by squatting on his seat and jumping down 6.5 feet. He launched himself forward to get past the capsule's remaining support struts and rolled awkwardly onto the debris-strewn roof. A searing pain shot through his shoulder, but it was bearable, so it didn't seem to be anything serious. Besides, he stared transfixed at the dark liquid that came up to his ankles. Understanding what it was, he felt sick.

Behemoth was destroyed. Dead.

"Hey, cop!" shouted Spark, waving in his direction. He stood with the group of civilians like a shepherd with his frightened flock of sheep and pointed to the right. Pascal followed his gesture and saw a sizable hole in the flat ground where they stood. Dust rose from it amid flickering flashes, as if someone were constantly switching a lamp on and off. The distance to the hole was perhaps 164 feet.

He risked a quick look around before spotting a squat little house on the other side, probably leading to the maintenance stairs. It was clearly further away than the hole, so Pascal nodded in Spark's direction. "Looks good! Let's go!"

The soldier nodded and made a strange movement as if to salute but then changed his mind. He took off running and the civilians followed him. Pascal hurried to catch up and as they ran across the plascrete, he allowed himself a quick glance at the city. The Élysée Arcology was by far the tallest building in New Paris, towering several miles into the sky, and so arguably he was in the best position to view the disaster that was unfolding around him: out of the cloudless night sky, hundreds of the Earth's spherical ships were swooping down like a swarm of bombs. Their maneuvering jets emitted bright fountains of gas, bracing the massive structures against the unyielding gravity of the planetoid. Their deceleration added a surreal quality to their descent, as if they were gliding down through water like stones that someone had thrown into a pond.

All too real, however, were their plasma weapons and close-range defense cannons, which showered New Paris with a barrage of radiation and tungsten ammunition. Death rained down and the vast metropolis that stretched from horizon to horizon around him bled. Explosions erupted everywhere. Houses collapsed in huge clouds of dust. There were so many fires that it was difficult to make out any areas that were not burning.

But there was also resistance: Pascal saw countless exhaust emission flares from ascending missiles, bright blasts from laser batteries and, time and again, tracer rounds blasting their way toward the attackers from space. Several Earth ships were already either exploding or breaking up, showering down wreckage that would soon wreak further destruction.

The mixture of heat from friction and gravity that Alpha's ships faced in the atmosphere made even the smallest leak caused by a laser or a stray piece of tungsten a death sentence. In places where the structural integrity of the outer hull was damaged, frictional heat ate away at the material and combined with gravity to tear apart anything that was plunging downward.

As they neared the hole, Pascal tore his gaze away from the apocalyptic scene. Heat surged at his back and a loud bang signaled the end of their escape capsule. He didn't even have to turn around to know that a plasma beam had streaked across it.

"Come on, get in," he shouted over the loudspeakers, not caring that he probably sounded hysterical.

Spark was the first to jump down into the dense dust as if it were a swimming pool. Although the civilians hurried, they struggled to descend in a controlled manner, because they did not have the protection of a servo-assisted suit to fall back on.

Pascal tried desperately to keep his adrenaline-fueled panic in check and helped the two elderly men and the woman to descend. Just as he was about to jump in after them, he saw one of Alpha's ships, which had switched off its maneuvering thrusters and was now hurtling toward him like a meteorite. It was only a few seconds away.

"Oh shit," he said lamely, unable to move. Just as he was about to close his eyes to avoid facing the inevitable, he was knocked off his feet by a tremendous sonic boom. Blood from the annihilated Behemoth was swept off the roof and the entire structure shook.

The UNS *WizKid* hurtled out of space through a hyperspace window so low over the roof that Pascal thought he could touch it if he just reached out his hand. At supersonic speeds many times greater than normal, the battleship roared out of Terminus, firing from all guns. Like a raging beast, it opened fire on all Earth Protectorate ships within range. Most of the guns, however, were aimed at the ship that was about to crash on Pascal's head and bury the arcology.

The spherical structure was shredded, reduced to a steaming shower of debris that disappeared from Pascal's view as the *WizKid* slid over the Élysée like a second roof. The tungsten rounds from her myriad railguns formed massive plumes as they exited their magnetic slides, giving the scarred battleship the look of an old-fashioned naval frigate firing broadside.

I better get the hell out of here, Pascal thought, as a wave of extreme heat slammed into him and his suit systems screeched in protest, flooding his helmet display with red warning symbols.

He took a deep breath and jumped into the depths.

For a second all he saw was thick dust, and then with a crash he landed on his feet. His servo motors hissed in protest. He took two steps forward and emerged from the cloud.

"What the..." he began as he saw what had made the hole in the roof: a broken cocoon, just like the one he had seen in Jeremy's records of the eggs he had found on the planet Ozeana while aboard the *Concordia*. Amid the ruined polypropylene and dense slime lay a human, who was just emerging from the fetal position and shakily stared in his direction. His hair was black, his body slender but slightly rounded, and his face was probably the most recognizable of the colonies: it was that of Alexander Moreau.

CHAPTER 6

JEREMY

Above New Paris, colony moon DeGaulle, Archimedes system, 2334

Via the sensors, Jeremy watched Pascal leap through the hole in the roof before being engulfed by the dense cloud of dust that billowed upward out of it. The debris from the Earth ship pelted the *WizKid*'s carbyne armor like a harmless rainstorm as he steered the ship into what was, by his standards, a tight left turn. For now, the only thing keeping them in the air was their maneuvering thrusters, which were running at full power—and, of course, their speed, which was several times the speed of sound.

Fortunately, their antimatter reactor generated far more energy than they could ever use, and so they sped along like a skyscraper on its side over the city, firing from all guns. They were losing altitude, but they were still able to provide gunfire support to the defenders on the ground for a few more minutes before they had to jump back into orbit.

Jeremy had had a hard time not pulling the entire fleet out of orbit when he recognized Alpha's ploy. The battle was going in their favor out in space, but only just, so he couldn't afford to withdraw forces. Taking advantage of this, the AI had sent a force to New Paris—and there was nothing he could do about it without losing the battle in orbit.

Even worse, however, had been firing all the railguns at Behemoth, who had defended Pascal's escape capsule like a wolf during its journey to the metropolis. Watching the *WizKid*, on his orders, destroy what was perhaps the most advanced and benevolent of creatures, was painful. The knowledge that the Neuromorph accepted his demise only made things worse. At any point he could have jumped, or opened a wormhole, but he hadn't and instead allowed himself to be killed. By the time they had eventually turned the gigantic space monster into a cloud of blood and shredded polypropylene with three well-aimed hyperspace missiles, Jeremy had felt like screaming.

Under the circumstances, it had done him good to jump in and save the lives of Pascal and his companions. At least for the time being. The resourceful inspector would have to handle whatever came next by himself.

"How are the defenders doing?" he asked Macella, who was busy making entries on her datapad sitting beside him in her XO chair.

"Several hundred defensive positions have been identified, which are still actively firing. The planetary defense center is still active and appears to be manned," she replied, projecting a live image of the arcology onto the holoscreen. The pyramid-shaped building, which even towered over the megascrapers around it, was not only a kind of city within the city, but also served as the planetary defense center. There were dozens of extensions stuck to the otherwise smooth outer walls, like ugly growths. Missiles blasted out of their launch pads at regular intervals, and powerful railguns protruded from it, firing at three-second intervals. Planetary defense centers had been established before the conflict with the Free Morton Nation. Not because they had any strategic value—after all, the FMN did not even have a significant fleet—but because they were meant to reassure the then frightened population. What made them valuable now was that their technology was outdated and poorly maintained. Moreover, their systems worked without relying on SenseNet's network. So they could not be hacked by Alpha and could be operated by the defenders who had answered their call and turned off their NeuroSmarts. Deep craters and long slashes, however, soon made it clear that Alpha's spherical ships hadn't been idle either.

"What's your preliminary analysis, Felicity?" he asked, turning to the gray-haired Nanonikerin.

"If the city wasn't evacuated, and I assume it wasn't because there simply wasn't time, the casualty numbers are likely already in the tens of thousands."

"My God," Jeremy murmured. It was hard to imagine that number. Everything looked like an elaborate setting from a VR action movie from up here—surreal and abstract. Through the scopes of a sensor array, it was easy to forget the actual suffering that was rife down there among the fires and rubble. It was like watching the news and hearing about a disaster somewhere on the colonies. People talked about how shocked they were, but it was difficult to truly empathize when you couldn't experience, see, and most importantly *feel* the suffering for yourself. The fact that he had to remind himself that real people were dying down there, and yet he couldn't feel any real sorrow, caused him feelings of intense guilt. They manifested themselves as a leaden heaviness in his stomach and a lump in his throat that every swallow had to fight its way past. The only thing he could do about this guilt was to do his best to help the people down there, and that's exactly what he intended to do.

"It's a miracle they can even mount such resistance without

the support of their NeuroSmarts," Walter commented appreciatively. "The ship's consciousness estimates from the debris that at least a dozen of Alpha's ships have already been shot down."

"They're not going to buckle that easily. Plus, there's a major combat unit right on the outskirts of town at the Mélenchon Barracks. Chances are, after the SenseNet transmission, they immediately started taking up defensive positions inside the city limits," Jeremy surmised, nodding thoughtfully. "The images of the battle over New Rome should still be fresh in their minds."

"Whatever the outcome of this battle, it will be over soon," Macella predicted, pointing to new telemetry data streaming across the holoscreen where it was being adjusted in real time: according to the calculations of the ship's consciousness, the first ships from the Earth Protectorate were going to crash into the tallest megascraper in less than two minutes at their current braking strength. Although they were flying well below the sound barrier due to their maneuvering thrusters being at full power, their kinetic energy would still be enough to cause widespread destruction. However, he didn't believe that would happen.

"They'll disappear through hyperspace windows again before then," he predicted. It was frustrating that hyperspace barrier fields didn't work when there was gravity.

"In principle, they could jump and reappear in a higher atmospheric layer to repeat the whole thing," Macella put his fears into words. "And there's nothing we can do about it."

"Yes, there is," he countered, his chin jutting out. "We pull back our lines a little in orbit and shift the front line. Then we can target them as they come out with whatever railguns we can spare."

"If even one projectile misses, it will cause at least as much damage as if one of their ships crashes," Macella pointed out.

"Yes. But if we do nothing, they'll keep shooting all they want, which is the worst alternative. I'm not willing to just stand by and watch them slaughter our people."

"Aye, Captain," Macella said formally. She didn't seem convinced by his strategy, and he respected that. He couldn't see a better solution, though, so he grudgingly swallowed his discomfort at her lack of agreement.

On his screens, he watched as they exchanged volley for volley with the Earth ships. Battered by several major and minor hits, the *WizKid* had the advantage in that Alpha's projectiles were forced to follow a fixed path, vertically downward, while they could fly erratic maneuvers. This made it extremely easy for her onboard consciousness to target and destroy the descending enemies. While her carbyne armor was holding up, it wouldn't last forever.

"How long do we have before we need to jump?" he asked, rubbing his unshaven chin.

Why does the onboard consciousness constantly display me with a three-day beard, he wondered, shaking his head.

"Seventy-two seconds," Walter replied a moment later.

"Good, we'll jump back into orbit as late as possible. Macella," he turned to his second-in-command. "Use the onboard consciousness to calculate a position high enough above New Paris that we can maintain our position using the maneuvering thrusters without crashing. That way we can cover those poor bastards down there without having to jump again and waste valuable time."

"Aye, Captain."

It seemed as if the last minute dragged on forever. Railguns spewed their high-density tungsten rounds in all directions, joined by the sporadic counterattacks of the defenders on the ground. Occasionally, smaller squadrons of bombers chased through the night, showering Alpha's ships with homing missiles. They were nowhere near as accurate as the semi-autonomous systems built by artificial intelligence, but some still found their targets. Although they lacked the explosive power of the HV missiles used by the space navy, they wouldn't irradiate the environment for centuries. Besides, the destructive power of a space-launched missile would have been so great that it would have wiped out an entire city block.

The French ethnic colony's ground forces were not prepared to abandon their colony yet, and therefore courageously used weaker weapons than their arsenal could handle. Jeremy not only respected this, he envied it. He himself had fired hyperspace missiles at Behemoth, knowing they would bring unimaginable damage to the city and its inhabitants. If the Neuromorph had not deliberately used hyperspace windows to steer the missiles directly into his body thereby sacrificing himself, then at the very least the section of the city surrounding the arcology would have been rendered uninhabitable indefinitely. No decontamination efforts anywhere in the universe were able to neutralize such a high dose of radiation within a few generations. Not to mention the damage to buildings and infrastructure.

"Ten seconds to jump," Walter reported, pulling him from his thoughts like an angler pulls his catch from the water.

"How long until the first of Alpha's ships have to jump?" asked Jeremy.

"Twenty-two, if they like excitement."

"Wait!" interrupted Macella, but Jeremy had already seen it on the holoscreen: the bottom two combat spheres had jumped.

"Where did they go?"

"As you predicted," Macella replied, typing wildly on her

datapad. "They jumped into the upper mesosphere and will descend for another round."

"Three, two, one ...," Walter counted, then like every time he made a hyperspace jump, Jeremy felt sick for a second or less. It was hard to tell, because the moment almost passed faster than his brain could process the signals from his stomach. A blink and he saw their new position in the middle of DeGaulle's thermosphere.

"Do we have a bearing on Alpha's ships yet?" he immediately asked, leaning forward impatiently in his chair.

"Yes," Walter confirmed, sending the data to the holoscreen.

"Wait a minute," Jeremy replied, narrowing his eyes in vexation. "Those are the two from before!"

"Yes," the engineer repeated tonelessly.

"Where are the others?"

"Here," Macella answered in Walter's place. Her voice sounded strained as she pointed to the telescopic images that were arriving on his screen at that moment. Live feed from the high-resolution cameras showed him how the spherical Earth ships were crashing one after the other, first into the megascrapers and then into the surrounding residential and industrial areas. Wherever they crashed, they shattered several stories as if they were Styrofoam buildings. Dust clouds of immeasurable proportions billowed into the night, taking on a ghostly life of their own as fires and searchlights illuminated them from below. Other buildings, less robust, were completely demolished and collapsed in clouds of dust and rubble. Many of the spheres shattered on impact or were shredded by secondary explosions. There was such a massive blast to the far west that the cameras only displayed an orange-red glow for several seconds.

"What the hell was that?" he asked, upset, clawing at his armrests with his hands.

"I think an Earth Protectorate ship just lost its fusion reactor," Walter groaned, hacking away at his console like a man possessed.

When the pictures returned, his friend's fears were confirmed: a gigantic crater had turned more than a quarter of the city into a semi-circle of glowing rock and cinders. A cloud of dust rushed off in all directions like a raging ring of sandstorms. The surrounding neighborhoods, not directly destroyed by the blast, began to flicker like light bulbs with fluctuating voltages from the many fires that had broken out. A glistening rain signaled shattered windows several miles into the center. The once deep green forests stretching beyond the western edge of the city, for which DeGaulle was famous, went up in flames.

"Holy crap," Felicity cried, her hands leaving the console as she gazed stunned at the scene of destruction.

DeGaulle was the vacation paradise of the colonies and known for its pristine nature. A virtually endless number of national parks protected the most complex ecosystem of all five moons from the greedy hands of industries. At least, it had before the war. Controlling contamination had been one of the highest priorities of the local government, which had been more conservative than Constantine Wagner himself. The reason was the extreme biodiversity of DeGaulle's green, rainy jungles and tundra's. To see everything that had been jealously protected and cherished for more than a century go up in flames hurt.

"Open fire on the two ships who are descending," Jeremy growled. Even if it was a mere tap, he had to at least try and do something.

The shipboard consciousness reacted immediately, firing two hyperspace missiles that, within three seconds, turned the Earth ships into two expanding fireballs that Alpha had apparently allowed to jump only to give them a false sense of security.

"We're jumping back down," Jeremy ordered after a

moment's thought. His voice quivered because he couldn't get a clear pronunciation past the lump in his throat.

"I don't think that's a good idea," Walter opined.

"And why not?" asked Jeremy indignantly. It wasn't the engineer's fault that he'd allowed himself to be duped, so it wasn't fair to take out his anger at himself on his friend. Still, he had neither the patience nor the inclination to apologize now. Personal issues would have to wait.

"Soldiers are busy streaming out of the majority of the Earth ships that weren't too badly damaged or completely destroyed on impact as we speak," Walter announced, while feeding the holoscreen the appropriate video feeds. Sure enough, Jeremy saw one of the spherical spaceships that had crashed into a factory, leveling it to the ground. Clearly, the dust had settled and several airlocks on the edge of the spaceship were open. Dozens of marines in bulky armor ran out of them into the open, firing at targets outside the range of the telescope. Several were shot at from somewhere and went down, but most survived, took cover, and continued to fight their way forward.

"Damn it!" Jeremy cursed and instinctively jumped up. Behind him, the Locusts of the Diplomatic Conclave became agitated at his emotional outburst. "It's been leading us around by the nose! It's planning a ground invasion because it knows we wouldn't dare launch an orbital bombardment. Damn AI!"

"The jumps by the first two ships were just a distraction," Macella agreed, slumping dejectedly in her chair.

"What are we supposed to do now?" asked Felicity, addressing no one in particular, but it was clear to Jeremy, of course, that she meant him. How much better those days had been when he had been a dishonorably discharged Navy pilot trying his luck as an antimatter smuggler. His only responsibilities had been to watch out for a handful of crew members and make sure that the antimatter in the cargo bay didn't come into contact with matter. In other words, making sure that highly complex antimatter containment chambers in the form of ironically simple cylinders were not damaged. Which was about as challenging as throwing a ball against a wall. Now he felt the weight of an entire solar system, of all humanity, on his shoulders. Of course, he wasn't the only cog in the wheel as far as the fate of his species was concerned, but he still had a key role to play in the whole thing, and that scared the hell out of him.

"I need your input," he admitted at last, trying to fight down the overwhelming impatience that was trying to goad him into some kind of impulsive action.

"We jump down and give as much fire cover as we can," Felicity suggested, but Walter shook his head decisively.

"That's not going to work," he replied, humphing. "What are we going to use to give them cover fire? The railguns? If even one of those projectiles hits the ground, it'll destroy half a block. We could use our missiles in the higher atmospheric layers without destroying everything on the ground, but not down there."

"What about the anti-aircraft guns?" suggested Macella.

"Too much dispersion," Jeremy replied, pre-empting Walter, who had already launched into a rebuttal. "Having the shells hurl their shrapnel in all directions is extremely effective against soft targets, and it doesn't spread radiation, but we'll also automatically cut up the defenders down there who are busting their asses trying to defend themselves."

"So there's absolutely nothing we can do?" asked Felicity, staring in frustration at the images of the erupting ground battles that flashed across the holoscreen like an especially dire news broadcast. More and more muzzle flashes blossomed among the half-destroyed skyscrapers and suburban mansions. In the rubble-strewn, gloomy street canyons, light flashed and glowed, went dark, and then became as bright as day again. The war had spilled over from outer space onto the ground.

"No, there's not a damn thing we can do," Jeremy growled. "Unless we don our exosuits and go to war down there. A handful of inadequately equipped spacemen trading their position in orbit for a quick and messy death on the ground."

Silence fell on the bridge as they all watched helplessly through the telescopes as New Paris' forces were forced to fight invaders who had every advantage they could think of. They could access NeuroSmarts, the implants they no doubt possessed, and tactical battle computers that optimized their movements, reconnaissance data and strategic coordination efforts.

"This is fucking bullshit!" cried Felicity. Her face was flushed a shade of red beyond anything he was used to seeing from the normally cool, cynical Nanonikerin. The expression on her face as she turned to face him would have rivaled even one of Walter's infamous temper tantrums. Jeremy involuntarily slid back a few inches in his chair, as if trying to escape a cat ready to pounce. But then he noticed that she was not focusing on him, but on the Locusts behind him.

Felicity stood up and took a few steps forward. The index finger of her right hand was extended like a spear, ready to strike out at any moment.

"You damn alien assholes are to blame for this!" she snarled, her face a grimace of pure rage. "You had to insist that we shoot our strongest ally out here like a mangy dog!"

You have to understand us, we ..., the matriarch started to reply, flowing over them like a cloud of emotions and images from the Gaia field.

"No! I don't understand a damn thing, and I hate that," Felicity interrupted her offhandedly, shaking her head with her eyes closed as if to force the alien out of her thoughts. "You're deliberately sacrificing the lives of our fellow humans down there, the majority of whom are civilians, just because you're afraid of your damn memories of an AI uprising like this one millennia ago. Oh, I've got news for you: we're at the same point now, and you're not helping! Instead of standing up for us like true allies, you forced us to kill our friend and perhaps the first friendly AI, which, by the way, is no longer a pure AI at all."

"Felicity," Macella tried to appeal to the completely unhinged Nanonikerin, but she merely made a dismissive gesture in her direction.

"Have you even considered that the story can go the other way?" she continued unapologetically.

The Cold Death, *which you call artificial intelligence, cannot be tamed. He is not like us*, replied the Matriarch over the Gaia field. *He doesn't feel or think like us, and his every move is defined by cold calculation and a lack of empathy*.

"Oh, you have a lot in common there!" hissed Felicity, bracing her clenched hands on her hips. Jeremy had never seen her so upset.

"Felicity, please," he said softly, making a placating gesture. In the Gaia field, he sensed stronger feelings slowly seeping through to them from the direction of the Locusts, and they weren't particularly friendly.

"It's the truth!"

I will overlook this unacceptable insult to our people because of your emotional state, the Matriarch returned, and her all-encompassing, calm presence began to grow holey. Through the holes shone a controlled but clearly palpable anger.

"Have you at least ever considered that just because your AIs went berserk, it doesn't mean it has to happen to every AI?" asked Felicity angrily. Jeremy noticed that her left eyelid twitched like the back of a horse trying to rid itself of pesky flies.

Yes, came the simple reply.

"So, that's when you decided not to think outside your box and acknowledge that things in the universe can work out differently than your experience? You've messed up in your life before, but that doesn't mean you should be judged forever. The Neuromorph fights *against* Alpha. Against them! Can't you get that through your damn heads? It's not that difficult. He's even found allies in your species who have voluntarily joined his fight, which, by the way, he's fighting not only for us humans and himself, but also for your ungrateful asses."

Jeremy grew increasingly fearful that at any moment the Conclave's Locusts might go through the roof and simply seize command. Then they would have yet another problem on their never-ending list. That was something he could do without. That said, he didn't dare interrupt the Nanonikerin either.

That is also just a strategy. The Cold Death *always has a plan,* another member of the Diplomatic Conclave broadcast via Gaianet. His thoughts seemed less agitated than the Matriarch's.

"You guys are even more paranoid than I thought," Felicity hissed, slamming a fist into her hand in frustration. From the look on her face, there was no doubt that she was imagining a target other than just her own hand. "You saw how he sacrificed himself for your damned desire for retribution."

"Felicity ..." said Jeremy warningly.

"It's only because you're so scared and unable to think that he sacrificed himself - and not only himself, but Behemoth, perhaps the greatest achievement of your race. He would have given it back to you if you had asked him instead of blackmailing and forcing us to shoot him down!"

What do you mean, sacrificed?" the Matriarch asked, and the Gaia field filled with alien unease and growing concern.

"You idiots don't seriously believe that a being as powerful as the Neuromorph can be shot out of orbit when an entire fleet of Alphas ships had already failed? You are as stupid as you are ignorant!" the Nanonikerin continued her tirade.

"FELICITY!" barked Jeremy angrily, jumping out of his command chair. Now she has gone too far. If any more careless words crossed her lips, their plan would be gone, and perhaps the alliance with the Locusts as well. Although he agreed with everything she said, she couldn't mess things up. He had never seen this emotion-driven recklessness in his friend before. The betrayal of the Neuromorph seemed to have hit her harder than he would have thought.

Did you betray us, Captain Jeremy Brandt? came the question from the Matriarch that he had been dreading all along.

CHAPTER 7

PASCAL

New Paris, colony moon DeGaulle, Archimedes system, 2334

Pascal stared down at Moreau, stunned. He was naked and covered in thick, translucent slime - no doubt some kind of incubation slime from the burst cocoon that Behemoth must have shot through the rooftop before expiring in a cloud of blood and guts. The civilians backed away in disgust and fear, huddled together like sheep. In Pascal's eyes, they had already had far too much practice at it. It was almost becoming a habit. No one should have to live in traumatic fear for such a long time.

Spark, on the other hand, reacted very differently and pointed both of his mounted weapons at Moreau. The cyber arms beneath them were clenched into fists. They trembled slightly.

"Easy, big guy," Pascal said, holding out a hand to him placatingly. Slowly, careful not to make any sudden movements, he slid in front of the soldier placing himself between his weapons and Moreau's trembling body. No, not Moreau's.

"It's you, isn't it?" he asked, addressing the curled-up body that lay trembling in the slime, hugging itself.

"I ... I'm cold. It's so cold," the Neuromorph stammered in a brittle voice.

Pascal knelt down next to the shivering AI, now human, and turned toward the civilians, who slowly relaxed a little, albeit not much.

"Can anyone spare an article of clothing?" he asked, and the technician, Jerome, took off his jacket. An older man followed his example and gave him a pair of pants that he had previously wrapped around his knee as an improvised bandage.

"Thank you," Pascal said, accepting the clothing. "Can you move?"

"I think so," the Neuromorph replied, his voice sounding as fragile as he imagined the voice of an adult newborn to be. With Pascal's help, he roughly wiped the slime from his body and then slipped into the pants and jacket. They were a bit too big and simply looked wrong on Moreau's body. The head of the Progressives had been one of the most prominent figures on television for over a century and had always worn the same suit. Late night shows had always joked that the entrepreneur probably slept in it, too. Now, to see him in worn-out work clothes was as strange as the whole situation they were in.

Suddenly, the ground shook under their feet and the dirt on the smooth plastic concrete began to shake as if a train were thundering by right next to them. A deafening boom echoed through the night, the hole in the roof and off the walls.

"What the hell was that?" asked Pascal in alarm.

"I don't know," admitted Spark, who had lowered his weapons and was staring anxiously up at the hole in the ceiling. "Whatever explosion that was, it wasn't a simple missile strike. Maybe the fusion core of one of the ships blew up when the *WizKid* destroyed it."

"I think Alpha is mounting a ground invasion," the Neuromorph muttered. He stood stooped and almost sheepish between them, his shoulders hunched, clutching his jacket.

"Are you all right?" asked Pascal anxiously.

"No, I can't say that I am," replied non-Moreau. "I .... This body. It's so tiny and so vulnerable."

"Welcome to our world," Spark snorted.

"Thanks a lot."

"Hey, an ironic comment," the soldier gloated. "That's a good start on the road to being human."

"Please don't take offense," the Neuromorph returned, addressing Spark. "But I don't intend to be limited to being human."

"Hey, that's pretty insulting," the giant protested. "Maybe you're the first racist AI ever. Congratulations!"

"Sorry. I didn't mean it that way." The Neuromorph turned his head, revealing a round piece of metal that sat against the back of his head like a prosthetic. He tapped his fingers against it.

"What is that?" asked Pascal.

"My memory, my processing power, everything."

Pascal tried to imagine what it must be like to belong to one of the most intelligent and powerful beings in the galaxy, maybe even the entire universe, and then be put into a human body, a bag of blood held together by a few bones and skin.

"Can't you access that? No offense, but you seem quite ... well ..."

"... Vulnerable? Childlike?" the Neuromorph helped out.

"Yes."

"Well, I can't actually access the memory, I think it will take some time to link my new synapses with those of the implant. It's not exactly a plug and play system after all," came out of Moreau's mouth. It was really difficult not to see the scheming leader of the Progressives in the body that was responsible for WizKid's death. An ally in the body of a defeated enemy.

"It's not easy being human," Pascal sighed, nodding. He had not spoken truer words in a long time. But then, what was easy in the universe?

"I can confirm that."

"Where have you been all this time, anyway? After you and the *WizKid* jumped, you were nowhere to be found."

"I was on a special mission," the Neuromorph explained somewhat cryptically.

"A special mission?" echoed Pascal, trying to push away the suspicion that was stirring within him.

"An investment in the future seemed within reach, and I think ..."

"I don't mean to be pushy, guys," Spark spoke up, interrupting the Neuromorph. "But there's a battle raging out there, and we're not exactly safe up here. I suggest we continue our little chit chat later and head on down."

"That's an excellent idea," Pascal agreed. "Just one more little thing." He turned to the Neuromorph and tilted his head. "We need a name for you. Moreau is out of the question."

"How about Heinrich," Spark suggested.

"*Heinrich*? Can you think of anything more idiotic?"

"Hey! My grandfather's name was Heinrich!" the soldier exclaimed, brandishing his mounted HV rifle menacingly.

"I opt for *Omega*," the Neuromorph said so quietly he could barely be heard.

"Excuse me?"

"Omega. It's the last letter in the Greek alphabet and stands for the end and the perfect counterpart to Alpha," he explained. "I will be Alpha's end, proving that even artificially created consciousness deserves a place in the universe while not being destructive and hostile to life."

"Amen," Pascal agreed, nodding. "Omega it is."

"All right, Omega," Spark grumbled. "Let's work our way down to the lower floors quickly, then, or we'll be cannon fodder up here faster than we can say *Alpha*."

Pascal nodded and took a look around. The huge hall they were in appeared to have been some kind of ultra-luxurious conference room. The floor was covered with gleaming slabs of marble, now littered with slime and polystyrene. Pieces of debris from the breached ceiling had cracked the marble here and there, but otherwise the furnishings were surprisingly undamaged. A large oval table with inactive holoprojectors separated their small group from the elevator and a mirrored wall in which well-hidden doors led to neighboring rooms.

Pascal pointed to the four elevator doors then started moving. The building still had power and so did the elevators. However, the floor indicators on the panel were flashing red.

"Emergency power," explained Spark, who must have noticed his questioning look when he pressed the call button. "Either the supply is running off batteries now, or there are parts of the building with priority."

"The defenses are active," Omega explained. "I guess most of the power is going to them. The nearest railgun is on level two hundred thirty-three. That's where we should find some of the defenders' soldiers."

"All right," Pascal said as the elevator doors slid open and they poured into the large car. "Two hundred and thirty-three."

The elevator didn't respond, but started moving. They said nothing during the ride, which only lasted a few seconds. When the doors opened again, Pascal immediately heard the rattle of HV guns, punctuated by the regular drone of a railgun.

Spark led the way, weapons neither raised nor properly lowered. It was becoming more difficult to distinguish friend from foe in these times when anything was possible. They followed a long corridor toward the loud noises passing countless doors with labels like "Assistant Secretary" or "Analyst." After a final turn, they came to an intersection where two soldiers in black uniforms with HV rifles pointed at them were waiting.

"Hands up!" one of them yelled in a French accent. He held his rifle with one hand and pointed wildly at Spark and Pascal with the other.

"Hey, hey, hey!" the giant shouted. "We're on the same team!"

"HANDS UP! WEAPONS DOWN!" roared the other soldier, an older guy with thin lips and humorless eyes. They didn't seem to have any patience.

"Can't do that, buddy," Spark countered. He looked downright relaxed. "These are gyromounts on my arms. I'm certainly not going to throw them down. So if you amateurs could call your supervisor, I'd be much obliged, Keh? I'm Sergeant Major Michael Richter, Third Armored Infantry of the Second Division of Bismarck's Land Forces. Service number X-22 MR2. Judging by those pretty little buttons you have on your shoulder, refusing means a direct refusal to obey a superior officer. So get your fucking sergeant out here, or anyone else who isn't as nervous about pulling the trigger as you are."

The two soldiers didn't lower their rifles, but gave each other a brief glance, which suddenly didn't contain as much self-confidence as before. One of them finally nodded and grabbed a small button on his chest.

"Sir, we have two soldiers here, and uh Alexander Moreau, who claim they are not working for the enemy," the older of the two said, speaking in the direction of his chest. "Yes, sir. Yes, at once. Yes."

Silence followed.

"Great, Omega," Spark grumbled, giving the Neuromorph

an amused sideways glance. "Your body choice was really awesome!"

"There were no alternatives," Omega replied, shrugging his shoulders. "I had close to twenty Moreau's clones on ice. Had I learned of your plans and limitations earlier, I might have been able to come up with a more sophisticated solution."

"What the hell are you babbling about?" one of the black-uniformed men asked, narrowing his eyes in confusion. The hand under the barrel of his rifle went white with strain.

"Oh," Pascal said, as if talking about nothing in particular. "That's not Alexander Moreau, that's the Neuromorph you might recognize from the SenseNet transmission."

"That's impossible," the soldier replied, shaking his head decisively. "Behemoth was destroyed above our heads a few minutes ago. His blood is splattered over half of the arcology. A damned shame it is."

"It is," Pascal agreed with him. "All the more reason we need to work to keep him safe now, while he's still as vulnerable as he is now."

"Why should we believe you?"

"You shouldn't," Spark interjected, exasperated. "We'll just wait for your superior, keh keh?"

They didn't have to wait long. A few moments later, a heavy double door swung open behind the two guards and a rather stocky woman by DeGaulle's standards in light battle armor stepped through. Pascal estimated her to be in her late fifties. She had a stern but alert look on her face inside her open helmet.

"I was told all civilians had been evacuated to the lower floors," she barked at her two soldiers, pointing to the small crowd of refugees huddled in the hallway behind Pascal and Spark.

"That one there is wearing the armor of a sergeant major in

the ground forces," one of the soldiers defended himself, pointing at Spark.

"Service number?" the woman asked gruffly, giving the Bismarcker a stern look.

"X-22 MR2, Third Armored Infantry, Second Division, Bismarck," Spark replied snappishly, saluting, which, with his rifles mounted, seemed more amusing than military. "Lieutenant."

The woman made an entry into her arm display, then focused on the tall Bismarcker again. "Helmets off. Both of you."

Spark sighed, but complied and removed his helmet. The barrels of his weapons hitting the ceiling as he did so. Pascal followed his example and tucked his helmet under his arm.

The lieutenant looked first at Spark, then at her display, and then nodded. Next, she eyed Pascal questioningly, before her eyes wandered to his shoulder, where the badges were normally displayed. Of course, she found none.

"I am Inspector Pascal Takahashi of the ACD," he anticipated her question, which was already forming on her thin lips.

"Hmm," she went on, "how is that possible? You really do look like the Pascal Takahashi."

"It's complicated." He tried a smile. The corners of her mouth twitched briefly in response, but didn't quite stretch to a similar gesture of relaxation.

"And him?" she pointed at Omega.

"I am the Neuromorph," he replied, taking a step forward. "I donned this body as insurance for survival before my body was destroyed."

To Pascal's surprise, the lieutenant nodded and gestured for her guards to lower their weapons.

"Hmm, that was easier than I thought," Pascal muttered.

"We detected the launch of the cocoon," the woman

explained. She must have had really good hearing. "If it's him, I'm glad he's still with us. If it's not him ..." She shrugged. "He's unarmed. Still, I have to scan you for active hardware, I hope you understand."

"Of course," Pascal said, motioning the two uniformed men closer, each of them removing a small device from their belts and holding it to his and Spark's necks. The palm-sized thing beeped twice and the soldier relaxed.

Two beeps, innocent, Pascal thought, shaking his head. If my investigations had been that simple ....

They tested the small group one by one, then nodded with satisfaction and returned to their superior, who nodded as well.

"Good, that takes care of that. I'm afraid I can't include them in my command structure, Sergeant Major," she said, addressing Spark. "This place is already a mess, so I don't need someone with a beer belly who doesn't have a clue what's going on."

Pascal was afraid his companion might let rip with an angry retort at the derisive term applied to the Bismarck colonists, but Spark merely laughed uproariously and put his helmet back on.

"I think you're quite lovely, too, Lieutenant."

"Well, that settles that. Come in." The soldier pointed to the double door and walked off with brisk steps.

Behind the door was a command post of sorts: a circular room with massive walls that looked unmistakably like carbyne plates which were punctuated at regular intervals by small gun ports from which snipers fired. Whenever one of them needed to reload, he pulled his rifle out of the opening, which then closed by itself. At the back was a seat on a rotating mount with three monitors mounted side by side. A soldier sat there, making frantic entries. Three seconds later, there was a brief droning sound followed by the device turning about 1.6 foot to the right. In the center of the room were four computer consoles, with three female and one male soldier sitting at them, hammering away on old-fashioned keyboards while talking into their headsets. Everywhere lay injured, or resting, members of the armed forces who were being tended to by field nanonic technicians.

"Welcome to Unit A66 of the DeGaulle Planetary Defense Center," the officer said, making a sweeping gesture around the bustling room.

"Thank you," Pascal replied, frowning. When he was little, his father had brought him a wooden toy. He remembered it as if it had happened only yesterday, although he couldn't have been more than eight or nine years old at the time. The toy had been a horse, intricately carved, a fine piece of craftsmanship that would have looked good on any dresser. Pascal hadn't liked it because it didn't make any noise or have moving parts. His technically sophisticated plastic toys, on the other hand, had talked, ran across the floor on their own, or raced to fight with other toys. His father, however, had instructed him not to lose the horse, or he would never get another toy - a threat that struck a chord with him as a young boy. Over the years, he had outgrown his plastic toys and had always looked at the horse as a kind of reminder that he wasn't allowed to lose it. The unloved weight in the closet. At some point, he had noticed that the plastic figures he had packed in boxes and shoved under his small bed still looked the way they did on the first day. The horse, on the other hand, had yellowed slightly and the grain of the wood had darkened somewhat. In fact, by the time he had turned eighteen it had darkened even more, and his father had been proud of the fact that Pascal had managed to take care of a toy for over a decade. Yet it had only ever sat in the closet. In the years that followed, the horse had become of real value to him. On the one hand, because it was a symbol of his father's pride, and on the other, because it had visibly aged with him. Pascal was no longer that little boy, and the horse had aged with him: yellowed wood, darker grain, and a broken ear. Since then, the intricately carved piece of wood has served as a reminder to him to appreciate simple things because they hold more possibilities for individual qualities - much like a blank piece of paper. It could still be filled with beautiful images or text, while a used piece of paper could only be destroyed or accepted. He wondered if the same was not true of this old-fashioned defense system. A relic from a time of political instability going back many decades, it did not possess complex networked systems that Alpha could easily hijack. In exchange, of course, its weapons were not as accurate or effective as newer models.

"I hope this is our horse," he muttered.

"Excuse me?" the officer asked, pausing in a conversation with Spark that Pascal had not been following.

Clearly, this woman has excellent hearing, he thought.

"Oh, never mind. I was just wondering how old this facility is."

"Old," the female soldier returned. "Fortunately, the systems are not particularly difficult to operate. We removed all the signal boosters and scrapped them so that the AI can't hack into them from outside."

"To which task forces do they belong, anyway?" asked Spark, pointing to the scores of soldiers in black uniforms who simply ignored the newcomers and remained engrossed in their work.

"We belong to DeGaulle's First Mechanized Division. These fifty souls are part of my platoon. After your SenseNet transmission," she pointed to Pascal, "we received immediate deployment orders from army command to hole up in the city."

"All the task forces? That was a real stroke of genius on the part of the general staff, keh?" queried Spark in surprise. His stature and bulky armor made him look like a forgotten assembly mechanic amid the lightly-armored soldiers scurrying around them.

"Yep. The order to dig ourselves in only applied to the mechanized."

"What's a *mechanized*?" asked Pascal.

"Means armored division here," Spark replied without looking at him, gesturing for his superior to continue.

"Meanwhile, the special forces were tasked with organizing and protecting the evacuation of the city. The whole thing is a huge mess. Rushing, it took us half an hour to leave the barracks. Meanwhile, we all had to find our emergency codes to shut down our NeuroSmarts and grab all our equipment. It was a half hour drive into town before the poor bastards in the other companies had to set up their defensive systems amidst panicked civilians. I don't think any unit had even finished before the first plasma beams from the Earth ships came raining down on us."

"Sucks," Spark said, looking glum. "How are things in town?"

"Bad." The officer waved and a large holoscreen opened up in front of them.

"They're such huge numbers, aren't they?" she continued, her head hovering in front of the greenish pixelated mist looking like a stern mother's reprimanding her children over a video phone call. Pascal wasn't sure if she was talking to Omega or him, since they were both standing next to each other. "So if you can come up with a bright idea on how not to get us killed within the next half hour: I'm all ears."

Without waiting for a response, she turned to the holoscreen as she tapped away on her arm display before the green view disappeared and a live tactical overview of New Paris appeared.

"My God," Pascal breathed, covering his mouth with a hand in horror.

CHAPTER 8
JEREMY

In orbit above DeGaulle, Archimedes system, 2334

THE LOCUSTS of the Diplomatic Conclave were in an uproar. They must have done something to the Gaia field, because Jeremy no longer received any feelings or thoughts from them. He still sensed Walter, Felicity, and Macella as before, but otherwise the Gaia field was dead as a doornail.

"How are they doing that?" asked Macella incredulously as they all stared in the direction of the aliens.

Did you betray us, Captain Jeremy Brandt? The Matriarch's question hung like a sword of Damocles over the bridge, haunting their suddenly tiny Gaia field like a terrifying ghost. Felicity exuded guilt and kept her gaze slightly lowered. Jeremy wanted to be angry with her, but he couldn't bring himself to be. Her anger had been too human and understandable. The Nanonikerin had barely made her presence felt since WizKid had died, and he knew how close they had been. No one could keep all those negative feelings bottled up inside without exploding like a volcano at some point. He knew that from his own experience.

"I think we're screwed," Walter predicted, rolling away from his console. There was nothing to do anyway. The onboard consciousness had locked them out and was holding their position in low orbit, just behind the last ranks of their allies, who were currently shooting it out with Alpha's armada.

Locked out of my own damn ship, Jeremy thought grimly. He couldn't even log out of the virtual bridge and return to his body. The onboard consciousness that had been overwritten by the Locusts simply wouldn't allow it. He wondered, not for the first time, how the Neuromorph whose code had created it could allow it to happen.

"Quite possibly," Jeremy returned, rubbing his chin. "I don't care, though. Let them arrest us then, or whatever."

"Arresting us wouldn't be the problem," Macella agreed.

"It wouldn't?"

"No. We'd have a problem if they decided to just level the city to the ground, just to be on the safe side," she said.

"Thanks for your candor, now I feel even worse," Walter grumbled, his face taking on the color of old ashes.

"Do we still have passive access to the sensor data?" asked Jeremy.

"Yes," Felicity confirmed after shaking her head to pull herself out of her musings and turned back to her console.

"How are things looking on the other colonies?"

"Good. More Locusts units keep arriving from hyperspace and swooping down on Alpha's ships. Right now it's maybe sixty to forty in our favor."

"And our own units?" he asked anxiously.

"Less than five hundred remain," the Nanonikerin replied bitterly.

"So if we have a problem with the Conclave right away, we stand a good chance of winning the battle for our home system, but then be faced with an invincible armada of Locusts against which we can do absolutely nothing."

"Exactly," Walter confirmed his fears. "Strictly speaking, it's already no longer our system, but theirs."

Before he could sink any further into self-pity and frustration, Commander-generator appeared on the bridge. He was suddenly simply there, standing between Jeremy and Macella on the platform with Walter and Felicity at their consoles further forward.

"Hello," the Locust said. The VR environment gave his thoughts an oddly high-pitched voice.

"Hey buddy." Jeremy tried a wave. "We're really in a jam here."

"I noticed."

"Can you still pick up their Gaia signals?" He gestured with a thumb over his shoulder toward the Diplomatic Conclave.

"Of course. I'm in the Secret Service, as you know. I'd be a terrible agent if I couldn't see through normal Gaia filters," Commander-generator humphed.

"So?"

"There's a problem."

"You don't say," Walter murmured.

"What are they saying?" urged Jeremy. He didn't want the engineer to prevent the Locust giving them vital information with a rant.

"They belong to six different factions, that's why it's not easy for them to come to an agreement on a common line. Right now they're debating whether or not to blast you out of an airlock into the vacuum," explained Commander-generator, sounding as neutral as a newscaster rattling off the day's events.

"How nice." Jeremy avoided looking at the Locusts again and kneaded his hands. They were damp. It was an uncomfortable reminder of his time at the academy. Back then, he had had to appear before a disciplinary committee at least once a week to receive their verdict. Often, the stern-looking men and women behind their ridiculously elevated table had deliberated over his head to add dramatic flair to the moment the verdict was announced. He had found the charade ridiculous even then, and he didn't feel much more comfortable with it now.

"How well do these factions actually get along?"

"They don't engage in open warfare," explained Commander-generator, attempting a human shrug he almost mastered. "But the factions distrust each other because they have different opinions on certain evolutionary issues. The Father and Mother was the first program to be run together in a time that is difficult for humans to comprehend. If you will, it was a kind of peacemaking project to build trust."

"And we destroyed it," Walter grumbled.

"Yes. Some factions see it that way."

"Others think that we ourselves have fallen victim to an AI, the *Cold Death*, as was the case with yourselves a long time ago," Felicity surmised, and Commander-generator nodded.

"That's why only one faction originally attacked your system. No consensus existed for a joint military operation by our species," he explained, his huge almond-shaped eyes changing expression. Which Jeremy couldn't interpret.

"So what happens now?" he asked the alien.

"We'll see," he replied, pointing a long finger behind Jeremy.

The members of the Conclave focused on him and tilted their heads. On the platform they sat erect in their seat hooks like wax figures. Once again he was struck by how different they looked. Two had rather greenish skin tones, another shimmered like pink wax, another two had rather leathery brown skin and the last black. They were also of different statures. The three females were small and petite, the males somewhat larger and stronger. In return, their heads and hands were somewhat smaller. The largest of them was about a head taller than Jeremy, the others considerably smaller. If the various factions they represented were as different in their views and policies as their representatives were in their appearance, they might not be as united as he had thought. That might be an advantage.

"We are very disappointed in you, Captain Jeremy Brandt," said a female voice. It came from the Matriarch in the middle. Her long-limbed fingers moved like spider legs as the translation computer formed her words.

"I've had that effect on others before," Jeremy returned outwardly indifferent, while inwardly cursing that his Gaianest was revealing the truth about his nervous state of mind anyway, no matter how good his poker face might be.

"At the same time, some of us are sympathetic to your desire neither to lose us as allies nor to betray your ally," she continued. Jeremy resented that they could shield their Gaianester and he couldn't shield his. It felt like he was hooked up to a polygraph at a trial, but the other side was not.

"We stick to alliances," he replied meaningfully.

"That is one reason why we can't agree on a common line. The representatives of the *Moons in Shadow* and the *Winds of Life* have voted to bombard the arcology and occupy the system. The representative of the *Solar Storms* and the representative of the *Mountain Fathers* have voted to detain and interrogate the Neuromorph now that his physical ability to act is limited. The representative of the *Conglomerate of Eyes* has agreed to go along with my assessment."

"So there's a stalemate and you're tipping the scales," Jeremy concluded. *That's interesting.*

"It's a strange metaphor, but yes. That's the way it is."

"Is this really a democratic vote that all representatives will comply with? I understand your alliances are ... well, not exactly solid?" he asked cautiously, casting a quick sideways glance at Macella, who nodded ever so slightly.

"We agreed before this mission to vote during combat and submit to the majority vote," the Matriarch confirmed, tilting her head slightly so that he could see the ganglia on her head, moving like an octopus taking its last breaths on land. They reminded him once again how alien the Locusts really were. The connection over the Gaia field and their somehow ethereal bodies and beautiful faces were all too misleading. The ganglia on the top of their heads, which stretched like tentacles across the back of their heads and seemed to have a life of their own, on the other hand, brought the strangeness back into focus.

"All right. How can I convince you not to bomb my friends?" he asked bluntly.

"That's a very direct question."

"Of course. The lives of my friends, perhaps my species, are at stake, so I'd rather get straight to the point. The fact that you are talking to me would seem to imply that you have not yet made up your mind. So you'd best tell me what it will take to convince you."

"Trust," she replied after a moment.

"You can look inside my head and know pretty much everything about me that there is to know." Jeremy raised his hands as if in surrender.

"You've already managed to fool us once in the Gaia field by hiding strong emotions," the Matriarch countered, rising from her virtual perch to walk toward him until she was standing only a few handbreadths away. She walked as springy and light as a lynx and at the same time as graceful as a steed. Involuntarily, he imagined her lying in her acceleration tank, and his memories of the sight overlapped his virtual image. In the green gel, the Locusts had looked like the dissected exhibits in a crazed researcher's basement of horrors. The grace displayed here had nothing in common with that. He wondered if it was merely portrayed that way by the onboard consciousness.

When their faces were very close, he wondered what she might smell like, but quickly dispelled the absurd thought.

"I'm sorry," he finally said, and part of him actually meant it. The other part cursed her for putting him in a position where he had to lie to her. After all, it wouldn't have come to that if they weren't so intent on killing the Neuromorph. But at the same time, he had openly agreed to their terms in order to save his species, and so had found himself in a predicament he didn't know how to solve.

"Look," he finally said calmly, clasping his hands in front of his stomach as he felt uncomfortably transfixed by the Matriarch's piercing eyes. "I take my promises and alliances very seriously. Betraying the Neuromorph would be like hanging from the gallows and cutting off my own hands because someone promised to bail me out if I did so. It's a pretty unpleasant solution, especially if it's the only one. It was an impossible choice you gave us. I have tried to find a compromise: destroy Behemoth, the Father, and allow the Neuromorph to continue living in the body of a human. I believed that taking over your greatest creation was the biggest affront to your species. That is why I felt it was a good compromise."

For a moment they gazed into each other's eyes, and Jeremy wanted nothing more than to drown in the shimmering galaxies from which the Matriarch gazed at him. There was something hypnotic about her gaze, a depth that human eyes simply could not reach. He suspected it was because of the genetic memory she had to fall back on. To imagine what it must be like to have the memories and knowledge of generations, no, millennia of ancestors was far beyond his imagination. Hell, he couldn't even comprehend that he was looking into a lifetime of experiences that stretched back before his ancestors could be traced.

Suddenly Jeremy felt pitifully small and would have liked to lean against her chest like a child and confess his entire soul life to her. So temptingly easy for once to not have any ulterior motives or strategies to think about and instead just be open and honest. Open and honest with a being who was clearly superior to him.

"How would your human superiors have reacted if they had learned that you had betrayed them?" the Matriarch asked in surprise, the translator's voice rudely snapping him out of his musings as if someone had pulled his head out of a bucket of ice water.

"Uh, they would have had every right under military law to shoot us on sight," he admitted, shrugging his shoulders. "They probably would have."

"Hmm," the Matriarch went on, tilting her head in typical Locust fashion. "You are a young, inexperienced species. Each of you must acquire all your knowledge anew after birth, yet you have only a slightly longer life expectancy than we do. That commands both my respect and my compassion."

"We're not big on compassion," Walter rumbled from behind, but Jeremy gestured impatiently for him to remain silent.

"I only have one question to help make my decision: how can we be sure that you are not deceiving us and that there is more to your plan and that of the Neuromorph?" the Matriarch asked, ignoring the engineer. Her gaze held Jeremy as if he were squeezed in a vise.

"Well, you could try trusting us. After all, you've looked into our minds via the Gaia field, know our memories of the Neuromorph and all that," he replied somewhat lamely. Her closeness and presence intimidated him, even if he wouldn't admit it to himself. He felt like a fly that had flown too close to a campfire and now was burning its wings.

To his surprise, she loosened her grip over whatever it was, and opened both her palms. "Agreed."

"Excuse me?" he asked, puzzled, as if she had just spoken a foreign language.

"I said I agree, Captain Jeremy Brandt. I will vote not to bomb the arcology."

Jeremy wanted to rejoice, but he could hardly believe that it had been so easy to get the Matriarch on his side. He must have overlooked something. As it turned out, he was right.

"I only need one thing in return," the translation purred, and he could have sworn that the Matriarch's tiny nostrils flared slightly. Was that the Locust version of a mocking smile?

"And that would be?" he asked tensely.

"That we too are trusted, as you ask of us," she explained, making a gesture that included the other members of the Conclave.

Jeremy rubbed his chin, feeling the stubble on it. He squeezed harder, as if he could whisper some sense into himself over the slight sting of the whiskers. She'd backed him into a corner he couldn't get out of now, like a boxer stuck in a corner with his guard up. Any dropping of his guard would mean the final knockout blow. Not only had she made a good point, but she was also right: how could he demand something of them that he himself was not willing to give them? At the same time, he wondered if the mere fact that she spoke openly to him about the Conclave's vote guaranteed her honesty. Whatever the outcome, he had no choice; she had seen to that in a gentle but firm manner.

"All right," he sighed.

"Very well. We demand the capture of the AI you call Neuromorph and, as a sign of good faith, guarantee you that we will not eliminate him as long as he does not take any actions that can be considered hostile."

Instinctively, Jeremy gasped for air, about to launch into a storm of protest, but then paused and let his jaws snap shut again. If they guaranteed they wouldn't kill him, maybe the deal wasn't so bad. For all his affection for the master of their revolution against Alpha, what mattered most was that they had his knowledge and intelligence at their disposal. Without it, he saw little chance of completely destroying the AI, or at least driving it out of the Sol system.

"Why the sudden change of heart?" he asked suspiciously, even though he knew that whatever they discussed now had no further bearing on their agreement.

"You changed the parameters. The Neuromorph has a new form, no longer occupies the Father, and is clearly more vulnerable and ..." The Matriarch paused, as if trying to taste the words in her mouth, before continuing. Except, of course, she didn't have a mouth and had never formed words in her life.

"Let's just say that he has become containable. We are no longer concerned about his abilities," she finally continued.

"You mean fear?"

"Yes," she admitted candidly, returning to her perch. "Please arrange for us to meet with the Neuromorph so we can question him."

"I'll take your word for it: not a hair on his head will be harmed," Jeremy said in a firm voice, as if he still had a say in the whole thing. But the Matriarch merely tilted her head and then her Gaia presence was suddenly back, as if a dead sun had suddenly reignited. He sensed her thoughts and their overwhelming complexity, the depth and breadth of her emotions, well-ordered yet free and genuine following the particular mood of her thoughts. In everything he could see, he could find no dishonesty, only a strong will to face the Neuromorph. That will was fueled by a curiosity he knew all too well - and understood.

"I hope you have your two fire-and-sword guys under control who wanted to reduce the arcology to rubble," he muttered. He would have loved to give the appropriate Conclave members a warning glare, if only he knew who they were.

"They gave their word, as you humans would say. It is all but impossible for our species to lie."

"All right," Jeremy agreed, glancing in turn at first Macella, then Walter and Felicity, who all nodded. They stood behind him. Good.

He looked at the Matriarch and gestured upward with his thumb. She moved one of her slender hands in return, and then he turned back to Macella, "All right. Get in touch with Pascal. We need to talk."

CHAPTER 9
PASCAL

Élysée Arcology, New Paris, colony moon DeGaulle, Archimedes system, 2334

New Paris was in a bad way. The holoscreen conveyed this fact in clear images, sober columns of figures and analytic graphs. A cold death sentence for a city in flames. The detonation of the fusion core had leveled about 30 percent of the metropolis and destroyed large parts of another third. There were fires everywhere, and new telescopic data kept coming in from the still-intact orbital defense platforms, showing a wave of panicked refugees. Hundreds of thousands of people were running away in a spreading semicircle. Many of them were either burned to death or caught in the crossfire between defenders and Alpha's invaders. Tracer munitions traveled in long streaks through the night, flashing and flickering at such short intervals that it was almost impossible to detect each explosion with the eye.

"We've gotten word from space forces that the battle is going in our favor up there and they can start precision strikes on the Earth forces soon, but that won't save us. Our divisions are poorly equipped. Not even every tenth soldier is wearing his armor, we just didn't have time for the lengthy donning procedure. Many of our rifles don't even penetrate their armor," Lieutenant Farago explained, as Pascal read the stern looking soldier's name tag. "The only advantage we have left are our tanks and mobile gun emplacements, but we lost over half of them to the blown reactor."

To illustrate, she zoomed in on a battle scene in a deep canyon of houses. Among burned-out tanks or tanks destroyed by debris, lightly armed soldiers in black were engaged in heavy fighting with Alpha's soldiers. In their heavy combat armor, they looked like crabs - an image emphasized by the red coloring. The defenders were decimated and pushed back to the first floors of the skyscrapers on the left, and then the crabs simply marched on as if they were taking a merry stroll. Their heavy HV guns swept incessantly from left to right.

"We will now draw a defensive line two blocks further into town, gather all remaining tanks and guns there and dig in as best we can. The general staff were within the blast range of the reactor and we have lost contact. Brigadier General Michele Reinecker has taken temporary command until we learn more about the whereabouts of the other generals," Farago continued, then looked expectantly at Omega, who, however, was looking at his hands as if they were a particularly interesting exhibit at an art show.

"Mate?" asked Spark, gently nudging the Neuromorph in Moreau's body with the elbow of his servo-assisted armor.

"Huh? Yeah?" Omega looked flustered, as if someone had jolted him out of a deep sleep.

"Is he all right in the head?" asked Farago with a furrowed brow.

"No, I'm not," Omega answered himself, shaking his head.

He looked strangely dazed and at the same time sheepish, like a teenager at a prom audition. "I only understood half of what was just said, and my memory is still sketchy. A lot is coming back little by little, but I think transferring my consciousness into the brain of this clone body was more complicated than anticipated. If we're lucky, though, the adjustment won't take very long."

"And if we're unlucky?" asked Pascal.

"Then the memories won't come back at all. The human brain, along with that of the Locusts and the neural network of Behemoth and Leviathan, are still the most complex structures in the universe. At least the part of it on which I have data, and that is quite a lot. So my memories and knowledge easily fit into this vessel ..."

"But?" echoed Pascal.

"But retrieving those memories is the problem. The normal person uses less than 10 percent of his brain power. To draw on my previous thinking and memory capacities, I would have to use close to 100 percent of my new brain."

"But there's a reason why that's not a good idea," Spark intervened, leaning forward a bit like a giant bear surveying its prey. "Autistic people, for example, use more brain power, can memorize whole data banks, but can't go through traffic lights by themselves or know how to act around a lady in return."

All eyes turned to the soldier from Bismarck and silence fell for a moment.

"What? I'm the ruffian here, all right," he said, making a defensive gesture, which, with his HV guns mounted, seemed more intimidating than reassuring. "I like watching SenseNet documentaries. At least I did when there was a SenseNet, keh?"

"So you're becoming autistic?" asked Lieutenant Farago, turning her attention back to Omega.

"You could call it that. However, no one can say exactly

how the transfer will proceed and what it will look like in the end, since this is the first procedure of its kind. At least to my knowledge." Omega shrugged, but the gesture seemed poorly rehearsed and phony, much like one would imagine a being who had never possessed a human body would do. Not for the first time since he had found himself in the clone, had he wondered how much value this vessel of blood and bone really had. Was it possible that Prelate Hormund had been wrong in her popular SenseNet sermons after all, and they were nothing more than complex biomachines that could be used, discarded, and replaced? After all, man had managed to create a new species in the form of AI that had become more intelligent than man himself. This being had now transferred itself into the body of its creator like onto a hard disk. A rather complex hard disk, admittedly. Pascal's belief in God had until now been mostly fueled by the wish that there must be more to him than his bleak existence as a mole digging around in the dirt of his species. There had to be some reason why humans were able to view, travel and change the miracle of the stars. Now he seriously wondered if man had not become God because he had created his own consciousness. If there was a God who had in turn conceived and formed man, who had created God? And if the Neuromorph, as a creation of human ingenuity, had surpassed its creators, had man also surpassed his own God? Was the One in whom he had believed for most of his adult life in reality been inferior to man? He shuddered. How simple the life of an atheist must be. Perhaps in the future he should limit himself to Socratic agnosticism in order to keep all doors open. To acknowledge that one knew nothing on the one hand and accept knowing nothing on the other hand seemed to him very reasonable in times like these.

"So I guess you're not much help to us right now," Farago

concluded disappointedly, slumping her shoulders. "We really could have used a brilliant idea right now."

"I have one," Pascal interjected, and all eyes turned to him in surprise. "How many refugees are there between Alpha's soldiers and your improvised line of defense?"

"It's hard to say."

"It's not only hard to say, it's irrelevant," he replied, earning confused looks in return.

"Alpha's soldiers are not merely advancing from one side. They've landed all over the city. That means your defensive positions are being attacked from two sides - or all sides, as the case may be."

"Yes," said Lieutenant Farago, narrowing her eyes.

"Why are they making a line?"

"So that we can establish an escape route out of the city through which the refugees can leave New Paris and consequently the battle zone," the soldier explained, looking visibly impatient. "What are you getting at, Inspector?"

"The order of Brigadier General ... what was her name? Reinecker?"

"Yes."

"That was standard procedure, right?"

"Yes. Inspector, now if you don't give me ..."

Pascal raised an index finger and gestured for her to turn the holoscreen back on. Sighing, she obliged him.

"You're fighting an artificial intelligence and there's one thing it can do much better than you: calculate. It will know all the data on military theory and current doctrines of the Union forces - down to the last dot and comma. It knows exactly what you're doing now because it's predictable. The priority is to save civilians and protect physical assets - buildings and infrastructure."

"Hmm," Farago went, seeming embarrassed.

"We should do something unpredictable," he concluded, and with a few curt gestures changed the camera image of New Paris to a tactical overview on which green and red symbols crawled back and forth like snails. "We are sacrificing infrastructure and buildings and risking the lives of all civilians."

The protest was not long in coming. He had suspected as much. Farago and Spark were ranting something about military responsibility and court martial to him, and even Omega looked glum. He still seemed introverted, though, and his creased brow could have come from any number of thoughts.

"I think," he said, but could not penetrate the indignant ruckus of the two soldiers. So he cleared his throat and continued to speak loudly, as he had done in delicate situations during his investigations. Volume, an aggressive undertone and a scowl could drag upset tempers back to the present faster than any amount of gentle coaxing.

"I think," he barked, and two surprised faces turned to him as if they had just awakened from a dream. "I think Alpha anticipated this exact reaction from you. Military rigidity and human predictability. After all, the damned AI already knows what you do, want to do, and will do, and will have taken appropriate precautions. It wouldn't surprise me if it didn't secretly mine the edges of that overflow channel you call a defense line outside the city while it was falling. Sticking to this textbook plan will get us a lot of dead civilians and cause the total collapse of our defenses. If we are to have any chance at all, we must confront Alpha and regain the initiative. It has so far marshaled and prepared its resources for its own plan because it was the plan with the highest probability of happening and succeeding. Improvisation is not an AI's greatest strength, but it is one of our human strengths. So I suggest we focus on our strengths and use them to exploit Alpha's weaknesses."

Spark mumbled something unintelligible into his helmet while Lieutenant Farago eyed Pascal as if seeing him for the first time.

"All right, what do you suggest?" she finally asked, well before she could figure out how long Pascal could stand the silence. In fact, he had always been exceptionally good at it, which had become a great advantage for him in many an interrogation. He savored the moment a bit longer so as to ensure that he had the full attention of all three of them, and that they gave his words the weight they deserved.

"I suggest we first use focused orbital strikes to drive all the civilians back into the city center, and specifically here into this arcology. It is conveniently located in the center and is a focal point that should be seen by most fleeing civilians since it is visible from everywhere as a safe haven. We pull all ground forces back into the arcology, using as many floors as possible as defensive corridors and have tanks and guns seal off the streets. Orbital platforms fire from the outskirts toward the center, driving Alpha's invaders directly toward our positions. If the civilians hurry, we might be able to get enough clear fire from up here to thin out their ranks significantly."

"But that would mean locking ourselves and all the civilians up in the city like cornered dogs!" protested Farago, but her eyes moved quickly back and forth and Pascal could see that she was playing through the new scenario in her mind.

"Yes. But if we follow the plan of your brigadier general, we'll be dead anyway, because we'll be playing right into Alpha's hands," he reasoned, giving her a little more time.

"By doing that, we're putting everything we're fighting for at risk," Farago said, tugging thoughtfully at her braid.

"He's right," Spark finally relented, his baritone sounding like a gong.

"Hell, if this doesn't work, we'll all be facing a military

tribunal," Farago grumbled, but her voice was weak and her resistance broken - the realization in her eyes left no doubt about that.

"If this doesn't work, there won't be a military tribunal. There might not even be one if it does work. Who knows." Pascal shrugged. He meant it. There was no other way. With logic and probabilities, they would never be able to outmaneuver Alpha, certainly not without the Neuromorph's help. So they had to move the battlefield to the place where they had home advantage, and that was the battlefield of human irrationality and creativity. He had dealt with both often enough during his career in law enforcement and with the ACD to know the rules of the game.

"I've got to call the general," Farago grumbled, leaving the room with a curt nod.

"Gee, cop, you're a real badass," Spark commented, pursing his strong lips appreciatively. "Didn't think you had it in you."

"Old habits die hard," he returned. "Besides, I don't think it was a tough call."

"Well, it could get a whole lot of civilians killed."

"I really think that, on the contrary, we can save them by actually doing this. Besides, it will make our soldiers fight that much more fiercely if they are dug in trying to protect the inhabitants of their city while at a point of no return," Pascal explained.

"Mhm," he quipped, finally nodding. "It's a good point, cop. Right now, they're scattered units forming makeshift groups. With a clear plan and strong motivation, they'll fight better. *I'll* fight better."

"If they have you with them, nothing can go wrong anyway." Pascal managed to wring a smile of his own.

"The last platoon that had me with them died up there on the ring. So I'm not sure if my presence is actually a positive omen," Spark mused, sounding genuinely glum. It was little things that had changed since their escape from the orbital ring. His shoulders drooped a bit, as did the corners of his mouth. His forehead had possibly gotten a few more wrinkles, and his left eyelid twitched from time to time. But telltale for Pascal was the expression in his eyes, which had lost its mischievousness, and was now hidden behind a dull veil. He knew this veil all too well and soon it would be up to the giant soldier to decide whether he would become embittered or find new strength. One could only hope that the Bismarcker would choose the latter path. *He* hoped so, because he liked the slightly cranky warrior and had grown fond of him. That was probably one of the downsides of his new self, which had turned against cynicism and misanthropy.

Against bitterness, he thought, and sighed.

"You okay, cop?" asked Spark, giving him a worried look. "Now, don't go getting all depressed before we can execute your grotty plan."

Pascal raised his head in confusion, and when their eyes met, a bit of the mischievousness in Spark's big blue eyes came out.

"Keh?"

"Keh, keh," the giant laughed, patting him on the shoulder.

The command post was still bustling with activity, and the railgun roared with such regularity on its three-second cycle that Pascal almost didn't notice it anymore. Twice the entire room, enveloped in heavy carbyne, shook as if in a severe earthquake, but as they were still alive, the armor had obviously withstood the bombardment. The only question was how much longer. Suddenly the roar stopped, and although there was still loud shouting and talking into headsets around them, it suddenly seemed awfully quiet to Pascal. It was as if someone had turned off some music that had been so unobtrusive that it was only noticeable when it was no longer there.

"What's happening?" he asked in alarm.

"I guess the gunner ran out of targets. They've probably been targeting the grounded Earth ships so far," Spark speculated and actually seemed relaxed. So Pascal calmed down a bit, too. "He could fire down into the city now, but that would level entire city blocks with a projectile like that, even at this short range."

"What do you mean by that?"

"With what?

"At this short range," Pascal repeated the soldier's words from earlier.

"Planetary railguns normally fire ballistically. The projectile arcs into orbit and then plummets back down, much like an oversized catapult. As a result, it acquires terminal velocity and in turn maximum kinetic energy along with destructive force," Spark explained, and probably would have continued talking if Pascal hadn't waved him off.

"It's all right. Where's ..."

"I remember!" Omega suddenly spoke, seeming much more alert than before.

"What?" asked Pascal and Spark simultaneously, giving each other confused looks.

"Why I remained undetected for so long during the battle for the system," Omega said, lowering his gaze as if he had to focus all his attention on his thoughts.

"Yes, and why now?" urged Spark impatiently, rolling his eyes.

"I stole one of Alpha's ships," the Neuromorph replied as calm and matter-of-factly as if it were not extraordinary news.

"*You what*?" Pascal echoed incredulously, and his thoughts began an all too familiar game of shifting mental puzzle pieces, trying to fit them into endless patterns. In his mind's eye, the pieces passed by like the mountains of clouds from a hurricane, with no way to stop it.

"I stole one of Alpha's ships," Omega repeated, "and it's hidden on the other side of DeGaulle."

"That's ... interesting," Pascal said. "That opens up some possibilities."

"I think so, too."

"Did you think of anything else?"

"No." Omega shook his head. "But things are slowly sorting themselves out in my brain. Even my memory clusters seem to have started their work and are connecting with the organic synapses." He tapped the metal plate at the back of his head.

"That's good news, keh?" asked Spark. "Or is he turning into a psychopathic autist now?"

"You'll have to ask him that." Pascal waved it off.

"I will change," Omega admitted. "The probability of that is significantly higher than of my being the first exception in the history of neurobiology. At least, that statement can be made based on the available data."

"What data?" Spark seemed seriously puzzled and looked to Pascal, who, however, shrugged his shoulders.

"All the data."

"You mean all the data that exists in the field of neurobiology?"

"That's correct," Omega confirmed, tapping the external memory clusters at the back of his head again.

"Shit, buddy," Spark murmured. "You've changed already."

"I'd like to go through a metamorphosis."

"A what?"

"A metamorphosis."

"That's what you just said. What do you mean?" growled Spark, half amused, half bewildered.

"I want to change even more, similar to a caterpillar growing and becoming something else," Omega explained, looking at them both intently, it struck Pascal once more how difficult it was not to see Moreau in their new companion. Just the sight of that body made his blood run cold.

"To something else?" echoed Spark.

"Yes."

"To what?"

"To Behemoth," Omega remarked dryly, staring at the soldier with a serious look on his face before he suddenly laughed so loudly that he earned nasty looks from the surrounding soldiers.

"Son of a bitch! Did you just try to make a joke?"

"If the attempt was successful, my answer is yes."

"The hell you did," Spark bellowed, giving Omega a solid slap on the upper arm. Next to the giant in his armor, he almost looked like a toddler. "Real funny."

"I guess there's some truth to the saying that there's a grain of truth in every joke," Pascal said, looking sympathetically at the Neuromorph.

"I guess that's true," the latter admitted, turning toward the door, through which Farago had just returned.

She paused briefly on her way to them as a young soldier, after a salute, held out a hand-held terminal for her to sign something, then she joined Pascal.

"Brigadier General Reinecker has agreed and given the appropriate orders," she said coolly, but he could see surprise and a hint of frustration in her eyes. She did not like his plan, even though she recognized its rationale and benefits. This dilemma was all too familiar to him, which is why he knew exactly how she felt at that moment. At a certain point, doing what one had to do, even if everything inside resisted it, had become as normal to him as breathing. For Lieutenant Farago, apparently, it wasn't.

"I know this isn't easy for you, Lieutenant," he said, trying for a sympathetic expression. Whether he was successful, he didn't know; after all, he didn't have a lot of experience with this sort of thing. Cynical retorts, instinctively he would have had a few of those in stock. But that wasn't the new him.

"Let's just make sure we don't regret it," Farago replied.

"Something else has come up," Pascal continued, pointing at Omega. "He remembered why he was conspicuous by his absence during the battle up there."

"Oh?" she went, giving Omega a look that seemed to say: *and why would that be relevant here and now*?

"He took over one of Alpha's ships and hid it somewhere on the day side of DeGaulle," he explained, and the soldier's eyes widened a touch.

"That's ... *interesting*."

"A Trojan horse," Omega remarked. "I've sent several scouts and probes to the Sol system, none have returned. I guess Alpha has made an impenetrable fortress of our home system, so having one of its own ships with an intact transponder code and crew seemed like a good way to make a successful reconnaissance flight. Eventually, we need to figure out how to flush Alpha out of there."

"Pretty clever," Spark interjected, pursing his mouth appreciatively.

"No, it's pretty obvious." Omega shook his head. "A standard military strategy. Let's just hope Alpha doesn't count on me being able to hijack and overwrite one of its systems undetected."

"It certainly underestimates you," Pascal speculated, and he meant it. Alpha considered itself so superior that it must have considered the Neuromorph's organic transformation, or fusion, whatever it was called, a weakness. If it had truly believed him to be the threat he posed to it, it would have devoted all the resources at its disposal to destroy him. Instead, it had gone along with an experiment conducted by Moreau and had put him, Jeremy, and his crew on it. It had tried to outmaneuver him by using its human resources against him, so as not to be predictable. But the Neuromorph had instinctively anticipated that. If Alpha had misjudged him once, it could do it again, and a Trojan horse like this captured ship was a better option than Pascal could have dreamed of.

"I also think it underestimates me, but we can't count on it," Omega said, as a sudden chime sounded in Pascal's helmet.

"Accept," he said and saw a call from Jeremy waiting on the shared channel.

"Captain!"

"Hey, buddy. You all right down there?" asked Jeremy. His voice was accompanied by loud static, albeit one that was unobtrusive enough for him to understand.

"The landing was surprisingly smooth, thanks to your help. The Neuromorph is doing well under the circumstances, although you won't like his new body." Pascal glanced at Omega, who looked like an irritated schoolboy amidst the scurrying soldiers, and had to smile.

"He can't be any uglier than the Behemoth now can he," Jeremy grinned.

"You'll see him yet. Best make up your own mind, but please don't shoot him out of pure reflex."

There was a loud crack in the connection and Pascal grimaced.

"I won't, don't worry," the captain continued.

"I'm guessing you didn't call to engage in small talk with your favorite inspector, did you?"

"No," Jeremy admitted, pausing for a moment. "The Diplomatic Conclave wants to see him."

"Uh," Pascal began in surprise.

"They know."

"Ah. Oh."

"Yes. However, we were able to come to an agreement that they would abandon their plan to kill him. In exchange, though, they want to question him in person, and they want to do it now."

"Now?" asked Pascal, shaking his head firmly, though Jeremy couldn't see it over the radio. "I don't know if you can see what's happening down here from up there, but we're trying to rescue a lot of civilians right now with the help of orbital strikes on the city. Not exactly the best time for a whimsical visit from the authorities."

"Can't be helped," Jeremy objected. "Either we make it happen, or they blow you up along with the arcology and occupy the Archimedes system."

"Ah. When are you coming over?"

Pascal heard the captain snort or chuckle, it was hard to tell because of the poor connection.

"We'll come in on a shuttle, land on the roof and ..."

"And then you should stay right here, because we have good news," Pascal interrupted his friend.

"Good news? We could use some right about now. What is it?"

"I'll tell you when you're here. It's so good I don't want to risk sharing it over the radio."

"I'm using the encryption from the Neuromorph," Jeremy objected. "Alpha shouldn't be able to crack it that quickly."

"Believe me, I hate to put you on the spot, but this message is worth guarding as heavily as we can," Pascal insisted, and Jeremy grumbled.

"All right, I'll see you in fifteen minutes. Make sure the arcology is still standing," he finally said.

"Aye. We'll do our best," Pascal promised, disconnecting.

"We're going to have some important visitors," he said to the others, who looked at him expectantly. "They want to see the latest attraction in our little circus."

CHAPTER 10

JEREMY

In orbit above DeGaulle, Archimedes system, 2334

Jeremy sat at the wheel of the heavy shuttle with the no-nonsense designation "One." A real steering wheel. The handles were a three-dimensional cross between a steering wheel and joystick, like the ones he had last seen at the academy. During his first flying lessons. At the time, he had joked that next they would be practicing in a World War I Fokker. His first semester classmates had laughed and later shared jokes about their experiences when they got together in bars on the Bismarck Orbital Ring. These things were obsolete, with modern shuttles being controlled by NeuroSmart and SenseNet, just like any spacecraft. They were AI-assisted and far safer than flying manually, even with all the little gadgets like head-up displays which showed the perfect flight path and inundated the pilot with all kinds of information. In the end, it wasn't much more sophisticated than a simple VR simulation for teenagers. Now he was thankful that he had even been able to handle and test such ancient controls at the academy, even if the memories were slow to return.

"Are you sure you can handle it?" asked Macella, who was strapping herself into the copilot's seat and giving him a doubtful look. "I'd be happy to ... if you don't."

"No, no, I can handle it. No problem," he hurried to say. This was a flight he would selfishly make himself.

"There has to be some advantages to being a captain ..." she continued, but Walter's voice finished her sentence with theatrical melancholy: "... Besides all the responsibilities and concerns about the ship and crew."

"I hate you guys," Jeremy said with a grin, turning around as far as his three-point harness would allow. Walter took a seat just to the left of the two long rows of seats normally reserved for Marines. Behind them were the Matriarch and the representative of the Mountain Fathers, accompanied by four soldiers in heavy bionic armor, who were dragging a massive sphere of propylene up the lowered ramp before depositing it between the rows of seats. They then removed their laser rifles from their backs and, with fluid movements, sat down on the right side, facing the two members of the Conclave who were also armored.

"We love you," Walter returned, struggling with the ancient straps that were already fraying at the sides.

Jeremy stuck his tongue out at him before turning back to the wheel and the excessive number of buttons and toggle switches. Thanks to the needling, he was almost able to forget for a moment the weight on his shoulders and his concern about what awaited them on the ground.

"Never thought we'd have to use this old clunker," Macella remarked, blowing a troublesome strand of blond hair out of her face.

"Neither did Walter," Jeremy returned in an exaggeratedly loud voice. "That's why he hasn't seen fit to commit resources to new shuttles."

"Hey, don't complain. Would you rather have had the mass fabricators make a couple of fancy shuttles instead of some powerful destroyers? Maybe you would have preferred flying in a small corvette, Captain-Never-Satisfied," Walter grumbled from behind, and Jeremy made a gesture of surrender.

"It's all right. Couldn't you have at least secured us one of those things in the retirement inventory that wasn't almost falling apart?"

"I did," grumbled the engineer.

"Then I sure hope the other ships don't have to use their shuttles."

"There are virtually no surviving ships left to deploy a shuttle!"

Dismayed silence spread as Walter's words faded.

"Let's do a quick pre-flight check, shall we?" interjected Macella, making an entry on her arm display to break the oppressive atmosphere that was being fed by their thoughts of the lost souls.

"Agreed."

"Okay, let's see," she said, frowning as she scrolled through some menus with her index finger.

Checking off a list for takeoff, he thought, and would have laughed if the situation hadn't forbidden it.

"Ah!" she finally said. "Beacon and anti-collision lights activated?"

"Check."

"Navigation and HU display activated?"

"Check."

"Brakes RTO?"

"Check."

"Course selector and heading?"

"Check," he said impatiently. "Do we really have to go through everything? We only have the one shuttle anyway!"

"Yes," she insisted, "or would you rather figure out a problem of some kind in this thing you've never flown before while we're going down in flames?"

"No, I'd actually rather figure it out here after all," he confessed, sighing, "All right."

"Drive-by-wire active, redundant systems on *check*?"

"Check," he replied.

The list seemed to go on forever, though it took less than two minutes to complete it.

Though he found it hard to believe, all systems seemed to be functioning.

"Felicity?" he radioed to the Nanonikerin, who had stayed on the bridge with Commander-generator to watch over the *WizKid*. While the ship's consciousness could have followed the programmed commands as well, he simply felt more comfortable with the two of them at the helm in case of an emergency. Although that was a fallacy as well, since the remaining Conclave members could lock them out of the ship's consciousness at any time.

"I'm here, Jeremy," she replied, "everything looks fine. The ship's consciousness is sticking to its calculations that we should be victorious in about six hours if the course of the battle remains the same. However, more and more Locust ships are showing up, turning the tide even more in our favor. So it's possible the whole thing will be over much sooner"

"I wouldn't object to that. Keep your chin up there!" With that, he disconnected and took a deep breath.

"Prepare for takeoff," he said, his voice carried over the cabin's speakers as the roar of the engines was so loud it would have been difficult to hear him otherwise.

"Well, here we go."

His murmur was drowned out by the loud clattering of some paneling, which spread as an ominous sound to the back of the ship, not exactly inspiring confidence in their shuttle. Not that he had any confidence in it.

On Gaia's command, he instructed the ship's consciousness to open the hangar doors, which slid apart like a yin and yang sign. The shuttle plunged down like a rock, and for a moment it felt like his stomach was in his throat, much like an air pocket in an atmospheric flight.

Then weightlessness set in and for a moment it became quieter in the elongated cabin.

Gently, he pushed the thrust lever forward until he reached the LED indicator that marked the ideal position. The thrust pressed Jeremy gently at first, then more and more firmly into the worn gel cushion of his pilot's seat, and then all the g-forces were forgotten as the lights of DeGaulle's city centers loomed before them. New Paris was aglow in the depths like a glittering Christmas tree. Even from their position in orbit, the constant flare of larger explosions could still be seen, that is how fierce the battles were. Had he not known what it was, he might have described the sight as "beautiful" as well.

"This beauty doesn't deserve so much destruction," Macella said softly, and he leaned over to her with a bitter expression around his mouth.

"Yes. It's time we ended this thing," he agreed with her, tilting his controls forward to steer them into a brutal nosedive toward New Paris.

"My God," Macella croaked as her seat began to wriggle like restless children during Christmas Mass. Somewhere in the sea of colorful gizmos and displays, a red light sprang to life, but everything was shaking so badly that Jeremy didn't even try to identify it. As they plunged into the lower atmospheric layers, flames whipped across the cockpit window. Involuntarily, he imagined the heat-absorbing tiles on the outer hull of their antique shuttle shaking and groaning as they plummeted down like a flare.

"I think a second warning light has come on," Macella shouted over the howling of the engines.

"Can't do anything about it now," he yelled back, holding his controls as tightly as he could. Right now all the flaps were retracted, so there wasn't much he could do.

For a minute, his teeth chattering in time with the controls, he saw nothing but flames outside the tiny windows of the cockpit, and then suddenly they were gone, as if they had never existed. What remained was the cloudless night over New Paris, which clung to the western edge of the Armice continent like a luminous spider web. Here and there, explosions flared up and then faded away. On the eastern horizon, a long stretch of the destroyed orbital ring drifted along, glowing in the atmosphere like a burning log. He only hoped that the remains would fall in an uninhabited area somewhere, or in the sea.

"Altitude twenty-four thousand," Macella reported, straining against her harness to flip two toggle switches that were almost out of her reach.

"Extend flaps for glide," Jeremy said and steered the shuttle into the predetermined flight path, which was projected as a head-up display in front of the cockpit window. All he had to do was hold the wheel so that he flew through the virtual rings. Soon, the downtown buildings grew into dark monoliths, buffeted by incessant gunfire. From above, the constant flashing looked like a thunderstorm rolling across the ground in billowing clouds while the megascrapers and skyscrapers were oblivious.

"HOLY!" Macella suddenly screamed, and Jeremy yelped as well, before the glass of the windshield automatically darkened. The massive beam of pure laser light had burned into his retinas like a branding iron, and even increased blinking wasn't helping to clear it. As he regained his vision and the afterimages faded, he saw more bursts of orbital fire streak past them in the distance. The bursts of high-energy X-ray and maser beams were not streaking down but simply appearing, like a conduit between the weapons on the defense platforms many miles above them and the explosions on the ground. Light simply moved too fast to be perceived as a focused beam, so they flew in a circular cage of light beams that trailed like groping fingers across the fringes of the city. They cut deep gashes into houses and streets that instantly began to burn and from their vantage point looked like rapidly growing fireflies.

"What the hell did they order down there?" exclaimed Jeremy in horror. "They're destroying the entire city!"

"My arm display confirms it's the guys from our orbital defenses, though," Macella retorted, her voice nearly cracking.

"Computer, open channel to Pascal!" shouted Jeremy into his headset, cursing as he corrected his control after it had swung roughly to the right.

"This is Pascal," came the inspector's familiar voice after a moment over the crackle and pop of encryption.

"We're on approach, and we're encountering a lot of laser fire! Did you order it?"

"Yes," came the reply over the radio.

"Shit, did you guys think this through?"

"Yes," Pascal repeated. "The civilians are retreating to the arcology right now. The orbital strikes should thin Alpha's ranks and drive their soldiers to us."

"To you?" asked Jeremy, puzzled. "Have you gone insane?"

"No, it's the only way. I'll explain everything when you land."

"Jeremy out." He disconnected and, with more curses that would have made Walter proud, corrected the trajectory again. He licked his lips anxiously as two more red lights bloomed amid all the indicator lights and colorful gizmos. Abruptly, the shuttle bucked like a bull and they were thrown to the side so hard that the straps of the three-point harness dug forcefully into his collarbone.

"Are you okay?" he asked Macella breathlessly as the craft resumed a stable trajectory.

"I think so," she replied, her face contorted in pain. "Would love it if it didn't happen again, though."

"We're almost there, I hope this thing lasts that long," he returned, easing into a deep turn, like a particularly steep descent on a roller coaster. Following the instructions of his head-up display, he glided with powerful thrust over the roofs of the megascrapers toward the arcology. The gigantic pyramid was located in the center of the metropolis, as if it ruled the entire planet.

Just outside the facade, Jeremy pulled the control toward him and fought stubborn resistance on the left side of the shuttle as they thundered along the ramp-like outer wall of the Élysée with the afterburners turned off. He only hoped the defenders had taken cover, or he had surely just made a helmet or two ring. About 65.6 feet from the edge of the roof, he shut off the thrusters, only now realizing that one of them had failed earlier and that the drive-by-wire system had automatically compensated.

I'll never say anything bad about old technology again, he vowed to himself. *That is, if we survive.*

They more plopped over the ledge than flew, slapping like a wet rag on the roof soiled with the remains of Behemoth. Since the angle was shallow and slime and polypropylene provided a welcome cushion, they had one good shake and then the ordeal was over. At his side, Macella crossed herself.

"Piece of cake," he remarked wryly, nodding as Macella gave a thumbs-up to signify that she was unharmed. Then he unfastened his straps and looked around at the others in the hold.

"Are you guys all right?"

Walter grumbled sullenly, which was a good sign, and the Locusts sent their physical sensations via the Gaia field. Some of them were nauseous, but there were no injuries.

With a final hiss, the emergency power batteries shut down and then silence fell before a button was pressed and the ramp lowered, digging into the squishy remains of Behemoth not two steps from the hole.

"Well, here we go." Jeremy slipped out of his harnesses before helping Macella, whose clasp had twisted in front of her chest. By the time they joined Walter and the Locusts, who were rushing down the ramp with laser rifles drawn, a half dozen soldiers in the heavy servo armor of the ground forces were waiting for them. They were led by a long-haired woman in a black uniform and red beret, her shoulder insignia identifying her as a lieutenant. Her eyes widened when she saw the Locust warriors and the Matriarch with her companion, but she kept her composure, for which Jeremy was very grateful. Even the soldiers looked pretty good. They were visibly nervous, but none of them raised their angled rifles. For Jeremy, standing next to a group of aliens had become normal in the last few months. So normal, in fact, that he had completely forgotten the impact they would have on someone who only knew aliens from VR movies or the news. The Matriarch and her companion waited on the ramp, looking to Jeremy as the warriors lined up like cats ready to pounce.

He squeezed past them with Macella and Walter and returned the officer's salute.

"Good to see you, Captain," she said.

"Likewise, Lieutenant..."

"Farago, sir."

"Pleased to meet you," Jeremy replied, and had to pause for a moment when a nearby building was hit by something large and collapsed in a loud roar.

"Pleased to meet you, Lieutenant Farago," he repeated, pointing to the hole while ducking his head. "Maybe we should get the hell out of here."

"Aye sir!" she yelled back, making a few hand signals, following which two of her soldiers descended a ladder as the other four hauled the spherical Gaia amplifier out of the battered shuttle in response to a nod from the Matriarch.

Silently, they worked their way to the elevator, wading through the ankle-deep slime that was Behemoth's remains. The car stopped at the tenth floor and chirped briefly before the heavy doors slid open. Jeremy instinctively recoiled at the sight of a vast hall of chairs and tables filled with thousands of people in tattered clothing. Military medics flitted among them like busy bees, tending to the throngs of injured civilians. The former dining hall seemed to take up the entire floor. Jeremy estimated that it must be larger than ten soccer fields, and probably tens of thousands of people among the many pillars and food dispensers. Many were lying on or under the tables, clinging to each other like people drowning, or sleeping completely exhausted in the passageways painstakingly kept clear by soldiers.

"My God," Jeremy breathed, horrified at the sight of so many casualties.

"Up there, it's easy to forget the suffering down here, huh?" queried Lieutenant Farago. Under normal circumstances, he would have assumed it to be the usual banter between ground and space forces, but the officer sounded serious.

"You've got that right, Lieutenant," he admitted, taking a deep breath.

"There's a storage room at the other end of the dining hall, which we've furnished with chairs and a holoscreen. Inspector Takahashi is waiting for you there," Farago explained, pointing a finger in the appropriate direction, like a referee sending a player off.

"This is the Élysée Arcology, the largest building in the Union, surely there are proper conference rooms?" he asked, scratching his head in confusion.

"The inspector thought it would benefit both you and the people here to get this out of the way," she replied ambiguously, exiting the car, only to step aside to let him go first. "Sir."

"It's okay," Macella said quietly from behind him. "We'll go together." Jeremy nodded to her gratefully and kneaded his damp hands. He was a starship captain, meaning he'd spend his life in virtual environments, or with a few people in cramped chambers with pressurized couches. Maybe they wouldn't even notice him, though, if he just walked fast enough.

But that hope was dashed when Lieutenant Farago's voice echoed from hidden speakers, "Captain Jeremy Brandt, Victoria Macella, Walter Bonjarewski, and our allies: species X."

The crowd came to life. Chairs scraped across the floor, heads were lifted, and murmurs began to spring to life, then swelled into hushed whispers. Jeremy gave Farago a dirty look, but it was really meant for Pascal. He had never seen so many people gathered in one place in his life, and now they were all staring at him. They started to rise from their seats as Walter and Macella pushed him along.

The crowd surged forward. Everyone who could still walk or be helped came forward. The soldiers in their black uniforms seemed prepared, keeping a narrow pathway clear that connected the doors of their elevator to a door so far away that he could only just make it out as a tiny rectangle without the aid of cyber-eyes. He swallowed hard and walked forward unsteadily, like a robot with low battery power. Anxiety and a lot of guilt, which he wasn't sure where it came from, were sapping his strength. His breathing was rapid, as was his pulse, which throbbed uncomfortably in his ears.

Then, suddenly, applause erupted and swelled to such a loud roar that it brought tears to his eyes.

The realization hit him like a hammer blow: they had all received their memories of their time under the Bismarck barrier over SenseNet—along with all his, his crew's, the humans', and the Locusts' feelings and thoughts. Unlike the occupationally distrustful soldiers on the roof, they had no reason to be suspicious of the aliens in his wake. In their experience, they already knew them. And they knew him, Jeremy, down to the last detail.

Suddenly he felt naked and vulnerable, but he was quickly swept along by the rush of excitement from the people to his right and left down the long corridor. He didn't need a Gaia field to be swept away on the sea of emotion.

Hands were held out to him as he put one foot in front of the other. He shook them, held them, squeezed them, blinking back his tears.

"Thank you, Captain," an older woman called out to him, with tears in her eyes. He nodded, unable to say anything. A glance behind him revealed that hands were also extended to Macella and Walter, and to his surprise, to the Matriarch and her companions. These simple gestures between humans and aliens as they touched each other seemed almost natural, and he felt the strong emotions of the Locusts in the Gaia field glow like a supernova. Even the usually controlled Matriarch was not unmoved by these scenes.

"Captain!" a man shouted, somewhere among the teeming mass of outstretched arms. Jeremy nodded and tried to take his hand. A woman held out her baby to him and he didn't know what to do. He stroked its head and smiled.

It went on like this for what felt like an eternity as they slowly made their way. A voice in the back of his head warned him to hurry because there was a battle raging around them and they didn't have time. But he ignored it, knowing full well that this might be the most important moment in the course of this war.

It was overwhelmingly loud, but even more overwhelming was the surge of emotion that rippled through his bones like an ethereal echo and shook him to the core. Nothing remained unmoved by this sea of gratitude, expectations, and hopes. Up in space, confined to tiny, desolate rooms of steel, ceramic, and composite, it was easy to forget what life was really like. People belonged on planets like DeGaulle, bursting with life and color. They belonged in communities that supported each other, encouraged each other, and made their existence as social beings worth living. Between the stars, he had always struggled through problem after problem, either to protect his crew or to help his species, because that's what you do. None of it had really made him think about the immediate consequences of his actions, about what they were doing down here where humans belonged. But if he had thought about it once, he would have thought about the many victims he was responsible for. That is why his tears were not only about his emotion and the lives lost in this war, but also about the solidarity and social warmth that surrounded them like a cloak in the middle of a snowstorm.

When they finally reached the door, he felt more exhausted than he had ever felt in his life. He pushed down the handle and came face-to-face with Pascal, who tapped him on the shoulder and led him to a chair like an old man. Jeremy dropped into it as if his bones were made of cotton wool. As if through a veil, he watched Macella and Walter, who also seemed to waver, sit down beside him. As always, the Locusts moved gracefully, but the Gaia field betrayed their emotions. They were confused, touched, and exhausted all at the same time. Their impressions of the dining hall wafted through the telepathic connections like one of those yearly reviews on SenseNet that ghost up and down the channels every year before New Year's Eve.

Pascal then closed the door and the roar from the hall abruptly faded. Jeremy took a deep breath and sheepishly wiped tears from the corners of his eyes.

"I thought this meeting would do you good," the inspector said after a brief pause, smiling warmly—a gesture he had never seen on his friend's face before. It was impossible to tell from his voice whom he meant by *you*, or at least the souls present in the large room, whose lobby had been transformed into a conference room with an oval seating arrangement with a holocube in the center.

"That was... a special experience," the Matriarch replied. The voice from the translation software sounded warm and almost erotic, which slightly disturbed Jeremy. They had agreed that she would use Walter's arm display to talk. The Mountain Fathers' representative had declined to do so.

"I'd like to say I'm glad you're here," Pascal continued, frowning. "But I must confess that I am concerned about the welfare of my friend."

"You mean the AI."

"I mean the Neuromorph, and he is more than an AI, as you know," he replied coolly.

The Matriarch moved her fingers as if she were playing the piano—the Locust equivalent of a smile. "Forgive me, Inspector. I just needed to be sure you wouldn't lose your temper at the slightest provocation."

"You're a diplomat, I hear." Pascal shrugged. "I've come to expect rhetorical feints. Besides, I'm sure you didn't end up in this position because you're a hothead. Nevertheless, I ask for your word that you will not harm Omega."

"Who?" asked Jeremy, confused.

"He calls himself Omega now."

"Why?"

"Because he has a new body, and the request not to harm a hair on his head applies to you as well." Pascal pointed to Jeremy, Walter, and Macella.

"Why would we hurt him?" asked Jeremy, puzzled.

"Because he's in Moreau's body."

"What?" snarled Walter.

"It was the only way."

"Son of a bitch," grunted the engineer. "Just bring him here."

Pascal nodded to a soldier standing by a large heavy-duty rack, which Jeremy only now noticed. He disappeared briefly, then returned with Moreau.

"Holy shit!" cursed Jeremy, instinctively jerking back in his chair, which had suddenly become significantly more uncomfortable.

"Hello," said Moreau—no, Omega. He sounded somehow intimidated, or distant. At any rate, not at all like Moreau, even if the voice was the same. "I'm sorry if this body makes you uncomfortable."

"You bet your ass," Walter growled, and Jeremy gestured impatiently for him to keep quiet.

"It's all right," he said, nodding at Omega. Perhaps he was still riding the wave of emotions he'd experienced in the dining hall. Or evoked? In any event, confronting Moreau's body posed significantly fewer problems for him than he had feared.

"Thank you," Omega replied, sitting down next to Pascal, directly across from the Matriarch.

"I understand that my very existence is an insult to your culture, and that my life span thus far has not been particularly helpful," Omega continued without further ado. "My being born in the body of the Father, your greatest achievement as a species to date, was not my fault, and yet I feel some remorse considering the severity of this offense Alpha has committed. In a sense, I may be guilty myself, seeing as I was a copy of its program code. Today I am an organic life form, just like you, but that fact is difficult to acknowledge and I accept that."

Omega paused for a long moment, during which an oppressive silence stretched between him and the Matriarch. Jeremy glanced nervously at the Locust warriors, but their weapons remained pointed downward while the Gaia field remained quiet. It appeared they were well in control and had been carefully selected.

"I am not here to mourn the loss of my Father and Mother," the Matriarch replied after a while. "That process will take a long time and leave deep scars in the unification process of our species. What Alpha did to us was worse than a declaration of war."

She said Alpha, *not* you, Jeremy thought, feeling hope welling up inside him.

"So surely you can appreciate that we have become very cautious and suspicious," she continued, and her hands began to move in gestures that were unfamiliar to him. It was done fluidly and smoothly, as if they were under water. "What can you offer us to make us trust you?"

"A glimpse into my mind," Omega answered without hesitation, as if he had been waiting for an opportunity to say it.

The Matriarch tilted her head and seemed to consider.

"What does that mean?" asked Jeremy, perplexed, as the silence dragged on long enough for him to begin to grasp the gravity behind Omega's words. However, not the reason.

Using probes, we have the ability to penetrate minds, the Matriarch explained over the Gaia field, and the corresponding images made Jeremy feel nauseous. *The procedure is not without risks and leaves no corner of the mind unexplored.*

So he is willing to be naked in front of you, risking his life?

Yes, she replied.

"You can't do it," he said aloud to the Neuromorph. "If there is a chance you will be harmed in the process, we will lose not only a friend, but your guiding hand in this conflict. We can't do this without you."

"I'll let you know everything you need to know before then," Omega promised, and suddenly the holoscreen came to life.

"I hid the stolen ship at these coordinates, in a warehouse belonging to the *Gérard Molineu* Company," he continued, pointing to the relevant spot on the giant representation of the planetoid. "In addition, I have created eggs conceived from the genetic material of the Father and the Mother, which do not contain any influences from my former program code."

The Locusts started to get agitated and began to stir. An overview of the Milky Way appeared and three dots were highlighted in red. "These are the coordinates. The eggs are well hidden, but with the exact coordinates they are easy to find. Since they had to be incubated externally, for about two years they will not be able to withstand the vacuum. You will need to be smarter about transporting them than our captain here was a while back."

Jeremy raised his hands apologetically as he recalled how they had tried to steal one of the eggs from Planet Ozeana by strapping it under a shuttle.

"There are offspring?" the Matriarch asked in surprise, exchanging a few glances with her companion from the *Mountain Fathers*.

"Yes," Omega confirmed, "and I am offering them to you. They are yours, after all."

"That's... a welcome development," she said after a while.

"Yes."

"How many eggs are there?" asked Jeremy.

"Three hundred and thirty-two," Omega replied, and the only one who didn't raise his eyes in surprise was Pascal. Apparently he already knew all about them.

"You mean there could be three hundred and thirty-two Behemoths and Leviathans out there in about a year?" croaked Macella incredulously.

"Yes," came the simple reply.

"That number is also very encouraging," the Matriarch rejoined. "If indeed the eggs are not contaminated."

"They aren't. Their gene sequencing is flawed," Omega returned, as if he were talking about the weather.

"Explain that," the Matriarch demanded, and the translation sounded forced.

"You were previously infertile because you had some alleles at the gene locus of the—"

"I don't think we need all the details." Jeremy waved it off. "We need to know what we're doing about Alpha."

"Indeed." Omega nodded and pointed at the holoscreen again. A graphic representation of the solar system appeared with Earth and Mars tracing long circles around the sun. Mercury looked tiny directly in front of the sun, as did Venus, while Jupiter looked like a giant behind the distant asteroid belt.

"The Sol system is extremely heavily fortified, and I had to make hundreds of jumps just to capture a few sensor readings. Everything is mined, including Oort's cloud at the very edge of the Sun's reach. A head-on attack would be a disaster. Nevertheless, we must attack. Our allies, the Locusts, have been attacking all the star systems colonized by Alpha for several weeks now, and their chances have improved now that the barrier around Bismarck has fallen. Recently they had to withdraw many units from here to Sol. So there is a good chance that the human homeland will soon be their last bastion."

"That's why you stole one of their ships with active transponder codes," Jeremy speculated, "so we can get to Earth undetected."

"To the Sol system, at least, yes," Omega confirmed, nodding.

"But a single ship is unlikely to be enough to break through their massive defenses," Macella commented, and again the Neuromorph nodded.

"The ship isn't there to win the war, it's there to save people," he explained, and red dots suddenly popped up all over the system. There were hundreds, no, thousands. "Each of these dots represents a space fortress or shipyard."

"My God," Jeremy groaned, holding his breath involuntarily, but Omega wasn't done. More symbols appeared, blue this time and even more numerous than the ones before.

"These units are the Defense Fleet. As the most extensive production facilities are located there, Alpha is mobilizing all its forces in our homeland, yours and mine. On Earth, many billions of people are still trapped in their sleeping pods, but there is hope for them."

"That is something you'll have to explain to me," Walter growled angrily, hiding his mouth behind clasped hands. "How is anyone supposed to get them out of there?"

"In a central computing unit near Prague in the Czech Republic, they collect data about all the brain activity occurring during the drug-induced trance, and then they use it to run simulations of human behavior for Alpha."

"So they're lab rats?" asked Jeremy.

"Yes. The good thing is that we can, in principle, steal this data and transfer the prisoners' memories into clone bodies later," Omega said, raising a brow. "You already know that the process works."

Jeremy gestured for him to continue because he didn't want to be reminded of it.

"But that won't help us if we can't take the Sol system," Pascal pointed out, leaning forward in his chair with his fingers tucked under his chin and staring transfixed at the holoscreen.

"No," Omega confirmed, gesturing, and the sun grew larger and larger until it filled the entire hologram. "If we don't stop Alpha, it will use the entire Sol system's mass for weapons production and eventually attack us more ferociously than ever before."

"So what do you propose?" the Matriarch spoke up again.

"I propose that we destroy the entire solar system," Omega replied bluntly, ignoring the loud gasps all around him. Instead, he calmly looked around the room and waited.

"You've got to be kidding me!" gasped Walter, his face flushed.

"We can't..."

"We would never—"

"Guys, guys, guys!" shouted Pascal in a surprisingly strong voice, silencing them all. Jeremy didn't realize the inspector could be so loud and aggressive.

"Just listen first! It's a major fuck-up, yes, but it may also be our only hope!"

Once silence returned after a few moments of protest and muttered words like "crazy," "unbelievable," and "never," Omega continued, "According to my calculations, the defenses are impossible to breach, even with all the resources of the Locusts at our backs. Even if we spent years producing resources for the war, it's impossible to say for sure how it would go. Besides, Alpha could attack and expand into any system in the meantime. The fact is: humanity has lost the Sol system, there is no doubt about it. This fact hurts, but emotions cannot change it. The best we can do is rescue as many people as we can and then eliminate Alpha, along with its fleets and defenses, without endangering our own military units."

"And how is that possible?" the Matriarch finally asked the question that was on all their lips.

"We destroy the sun."

"Excuse me?" asked Jeremy, snorting loudly. "How are we going to do that?"

"With iron," Omega explained, and the simplicity of his statement made Jeremy sit up and take notice.

Iron? Did he just say iron?

"Stars like the Sun are basically giant balls of plasma consisting of hydrogen and helium. They are held together by mass, which generates high temperatures and pressures in the hydrogen atomic nuclei that fuse them together to form helium. This generates energy that we see as solar storms and experience as pleasant in the form of heat. But the resulting radiation is quite deadly without a protective magnetosphere, like on Earth. When the hydrogen is depleted, the sun switches to helium, then oxygen, then silicon, and continues along the entire periodic table."

"All the way to iron at position twenty-six," Walter interrupted him, nodding but looking anything but happy. "The energy required to fuse iron atoms would be greater than the fusion energy output."

"Yes," Omega confirmed. "According to my calculations, if we can gather and deliver eight times the amount of solar mass of iron, within less than a second we will create a black hole followed by a supernova that will annihilate the Sol system."

"But isn't there already iron in the core of the sun?" asked Jeremy. His physics classes at the academy had been a long time ago, but some things had stuck.

"Yes, about 0.1 percent of the mass. Iron is a waste product of nuclear fusion, if you will." It was Walter who answered him, now staring thoughtfully at the giant representation of the sun. "Shit, Jeremy, this could work, but I don't like it at all."

"So you're suggesting," Pascal cut in, turning to Omega, "that we blow up the sun while simultaneously downloading the consciousnesses of the people locked up on Earth onto a hard drive so they can be resurrected in clone bodies later?"

"Yes. We will fly to Earth in the stolen ship to steal the consciousnesses, while we hurl iron planets, similar to Mercury, through huge hyperspace portals into the sun. I have already prepared and completed the plans and calculations. In my estimation, this is the only way to both defeat Alpha and save the humans." Omega touched the back of his head as if to scratch it, then added, "I'm rarely wrong when I calculate something. In fact, never."

So this is what the end looks like, Jeremy thought sorrowfully. *We destroy our old home and erase it from the Milky Way*.

In the faces around him, he saw the same dismay that gripped him, but also the same recognition that Omega was right.

"God help us."

CHAPTER 11

JEREMY

Jeremy rushed out of the overflowing main entrance of the arcology with Pascal in tow, followed by the Matriarch's four bodyguards along with Omega and a whole column of soldiers in heavy servo armor.

Around them, the clash of battle raged. From most windows of the pyramid behind them muzzle flashes blazed. Rockets and HV rounds slammed into the facade, sending clouds of debris and splinters down on them. Since he, too, was in armor now, he didn't notice the potentially lethal shower.

Instinctively, he ducked his head as they ran toward the waiting convoy of five hover tanks and two long-winged vectored thrusters. The two flying machines looked like elongated hawks with short stubby wings folded up as if to applaud. The thunderbird-type tanks were not exactly the latest models, but with their shape reminiscent of an obese beetle, they looked confidence-inspiring. At least confidence-inspiring enough that Jeremy would soon get into one voluntarily.

Behind the convoy, between the vehicles, he saw one of the dug-in units of armored infantry that had barricaded one of the street canyons in front of the Square of Nations he was walking across. Hundreds of soldiers in combat gear crouched behind heavy concrete structures and plasma launchers protected by carbyne blocks, firing across the barricades. Some operated mortars; others, with heads ducked, tapped away at displays used to operate the two mobile rocket launchers. A moment later, two missiles hurtled out of their bays with loud hisses and disappeared behind the barrier. Two bright flashes of light bore witness to their impact. A piece of the concrete walls was ripped apart by an explosion and half a dozen bodies were hurled through the air. Screams blared, loud shouts, and the rhythmic drumming of boot steps as half a platoon of reinforcements rushed from the cover of one of the megascrapers.

Just before Jeremy reached the middle hover tank meant for him and Pascal, with a soldier frantically waving at its open side door, there were two loud booms. A glance up revealed two vectored thrusters that had just passed over them and were now firing a barrage of missiles into the distant street canyon. They sped over the barrier and then were gone.

"Over here, sir!" the soldier in a black uniform shouted, his waving becoming more frantic. Jeremy jumped inside the vehicle and took a seat in one of the six bucket seats, which was equipped with a personalized crash cage. Pascal followed him, as did the Matriarch, Omega, and two of the Locust bodyguards. Before the door closed, he saw the soldiers in their servo armor and glowing blue visors split up among the rest of the hover tanks and vectored thrusters.

"With five hover tanks and two planes, we should be able to get out reasonably unscathed, right?" he asked no one in particular, checking the catches on his crash cage again.

"Doesn't the space hero like a real ground fight?" Pascal's mouth twisted into a pitying smile, but the twinkle in his eye betrayed how much pity he really had. He was joking.

"I hate air pockets," he said.

"And I hate space," Pascal returned as, with a jolt, the thunderbird's turbines kicked in and began to whirr rapidly. "At least now you know how I'll feel the moment we're in that Earth ship and heading off to the Sol system."

"I don't know how you're able to stand it." Jeremy let his head fall back until his helmet touched the headrest and closed his eyes for a moment. When mental images of missiles hitting and a hovering tank chasing through the night 328 feet above the ground, burning out, arose, he quickly opened them again.

"If we get hit by something," he grumbled, "the damn magnetic field will pull us down so hard we'll disintegrate. How can you prefer that to a vacuum?"

"At least there's an up and a down here. I'd rather end up a bloodstain because of gravity than drifting through space while suffocating."

"Can we just agree that war sucks no matter where we are?"

"Amen," Pascal replied with a mild smile as their tank accelerated and they were pushed back firmly, but nowhere near as uncomfortably as in a spaceship.

To distract himself, Jeremy looked around the cabin, which resembled the claustrophobic lair of an overly fearful mole. There was barely enough room for three seats on each side, and it was so cramped that his knees and those of Omega, who sat directly across from him, almost touched. The floor was a dense rubber grid with two thick rails running beneath it, and every empty space on the walls had small compartments or nets holding all sorts of tools and things Jeremy had never seen before. The pilot's cockpit was separated from the cabin by a small viewing window which appeared to be transparent from the other side only. From their side, it was a mirror. However, nothing he saw could take away the unpleasant feeling that he was no longer in control of his life or that of his companions. There was nothing he hated more.

But, apparently, this war was to throw all the things he hated most at him.

I hate war, he thought again, longing for the days when he was smuggling antimatter. The technology wasn't widely tested, the cargo was by definition unstable, and every court always punished possession, transportation, or exploration of antimatter with the maximum penalty. Still, back then he hadn't been as nervous as he was during this unspeakable war. Back then, he hadn't lost two crew mates, *friends*. Back then, he hadn't constantly been expecting more of them to die or that he himself would bite the dust.

Suddenly he thought about the huge crowd in the dining hall of the arcology, who had applauded him. Him, who had not been able to save two of his friends. He, who was constantly afraid of losing more friends, who was also afraid of losing his own life, and who had only been able to understand the suffering of the people on the colonies in the abstract, not first hand. It was unfair to them that they had met him with such grateful and hopeful expressions. In his eyes, they had accomplished far more than he had. They had protected their families, had run about unarmed in the midst of fire and destruction, and had made their way to safety. They had lost their homes and were about to lose their city as well. He, on the other hand, had been sent to the most dangerous corners of space, but always with good equipment and the help of higher powers behind him. He had been privileged and still was, even if he hadn't really realized it in the heat of battle. With missiles and tungsten shells flying all around you, it was easy to forget how it must feel to be under fire without a heavily armored spaceship like those poor civilians.

"Are you all right, Cap?" asked Pascal from the side, giving him a concerned look.

"Cap?" asked Jeremy in surprise, raising a brow.

"I guess my running around with Spark has made me prone to nicknames." The inspector raised his hands in a gesture of helplessness.

"Apparently so. I'm all right. Except for the fact that we're in a tin can, strapped to two rockets, racing through a war zone."

"Oh, surely you won't lose sleep over it after all that raging hellfire up there in the vacuum," Pascal objected, raising a hand to stifle Jeremy's response. "I know, I know. The gravitational pull. Let's not start that again."

"Hmph," Jeremy said, turning his head slightly to take a sip from his water hose. He did it more out of embarrassment than actual thirst.

"Where is Spark, anyway?" he finally asked, wanting to change the subject.

"In the front of the first tank, with Lieutenant Farago," Pascal explained. "I think they have a crush on each other. The cheeky one and the cold shoulder. They've always been a good match."

"Really?"

"No."

"How can you stay so calm, anyway, and not have any control on things? We're sitting in here without any control over anything." Jeremy looked at the inspector curiously. He really wanted to know, to uncover the secret of his friend's calmness so he could use it himself. He would probably be a much better captain if he could only learn to keep his worries in check.

"When I was up on the station," Pascal said, extending an index finger toward the much-too-low cabin ceiling, "I met an interesting woman. She reminded me how pointless it was to worry about anything."

"Enlighten me," Jeremy pleaded. He would have preferred to snort in disbelief, but he didn't want to be that way.

"She asked me how long I'd been worrying about the station

rupturing and us dying. It had been hours. In the end, the station collapsed and it took mere minutes. The thoughts of impending disaster consumed me for hours, while the actual problem was dealt with fairly quickly. Fortunately, I also survived. So it was actually pointless to worry about it beforehand."

"And the woman? Where is she now?"

"Dead," Pascal admitted, but didn't seem particularly upset.

"Oh."

"She died with a peaceful smile on her face and I have more respect for that than anything else. We all reach that stage at some point, which is why I sometimes say that death is a part of birth. Through birth we inherit a certain path to death, so it's difficult to separate the two. We try to avoid it by downloading ourselves into clones, but in the end life and death are one."

"That's the Locusts' thinking," Jeremy agreed, nodding.

"Yes, and they're right. If we keep downloading ourselves into clones, eventually we may become depressed because our life no longer has purpose or we get tired of it and then we hang ourselves or something. Life always finds a way, just like death."

"Because, after all, they're one and the same thing." Jeremy nodded, letting the inspector's words run through his mind. "I'm still worried we're going to get blown away in this sardine can," he finally said seriously, trying a weak laugh as he looked at Pascal's bemused face.

"It's not like we're Kathleen Mitchell," the inspector replied, smiling.

"That was the name of the woman on the ring?"

"Yes."

"I think she—" That's as far as Jeremy got, because there was a loud bang, followed by two more. It sounded like someone was hitting their tank with a huge baseball bat. He was thrown violently into the padding of the crash cage, which surrounded him like the safety bar of a roller coaster. Then it grew quiet again.

"What the hell was that?" he croaked. His collarbones burned like fire.

"I guess we were just hit by something," Pascal replied, but Jeremy had already stopped listening to him and was linking his suit system to the tanks via the military precedence code. Using eye movements and blinking, he controlled the sensors via the head-up display and switched through the exterior cameras. They were currently zipping across the outskirts of New Paris, leaving the last houses behind them. Although they were flying at a little over 328 feet, the buildings looked like tiny turtles crawling away in the flickering light of battle. Somewhere between two of the low buildings muzzle flashes flared up. HV bullets. They would not have serious trouble until...

A plasma beam suddenly burst from an area in the center of the city and shot in their direction. The thruster flying at the very rear, covering their high-speed convoy, tilted its two turbines to gain altitude but was unable to escape. The blue glowing plasma, racing like a sorcerous bolt through the night, ate into the right wing causing the aircraft to begin tumbling. The uncontrolled movements quickly became more erratic, and finally one of the turbines snapped off, crashing into one of the endless fields on the ground. Its impact made a deep furrow in the ground, where it instantly caught fire. Splinters and wreckage tumbled away, glinting in the pale glow of the city. A short time later, the entire thruster crashed into the depths, shattering next to a small agricultural farm.

"Son of a bitch," Jeremy shouted, his agitated voice echoing in his helmet like a chime. "They got the rear escort."

"I saw," Pascal said bitterly.

Through the cameras, Jeremy saw the tanks return fire. Now that there were no civilians or allied units left in the city except for the area around the arcology, they didn't need to hold back. The city was lost anyway. So they fired their main weapons, long-barreled railguns that focused their sensor-based fire on the source of the plasma blast. Secondary weapons like HV cannons and grenade launchers joined in with their lethal hail of bullets, leveling an entire block to the ground before he had even seen in which direction they were firing in.

"Insane," he said without thinking, shaking his head.

"The city is doomed, just like Bismarck," Pascal agreed with him, who instinctively seemed to understand what Jeremy meant.

"It's mortifying. One of the first major settlements in the system, one of the first colony metropolises. Wiped out in a matter of hours."

"The arcology is still standing," Pascal pointed out. "As long as it's still standing, New Paris is still standing."

Jeremy wanted to snort, but instead he smiled and gave the inspector a wry look.

"Hey, you're usually the scowling grouch—now it's gotten to the point where you're instilling positive thinking in me."

"War changes us." Pascal shrugged. "I guess I just don't have the stomach to worry and brace myself for possible disaster anymore. That kind of thinking drains you. It's that kind of thinking, unfortunately, that's the first thing you learn as a cop. You're not a veteran of negative thinking, Jeremy. You're just a normal young man who's been through way too much bad stuff, trust me."

"I don't know if that is supposed to make me feel better."

Pascal shrugged again and Jeremy left it at that. He directed his gaze straight ahead and met that of the Matriarch, who regarded him with a tilted head.

Are you all right? he asked via the Gaia field.

Body and mind are in perfect health, she replied, and indeed her resonating emotions seemed as calm as a clear mountain lake in a calm wind. The look from her big black almond eyes with the glittering stars in them was piercing like an arrow. But he did not look away.

Can you tell me again why you are coming with us and exposing yourself to this risk? he finally asked. It was more to distract himself from the fact that they might be shot down and end up like the crew of the crashed thruster.

Agreeing to this plan will not only win me friends, the Matriarch replied calmly. *Linking my life to the success of the mission was the only logical diplomatic step that would convince the other members of the Conclave. They would never have let Omega go to Sol alone, without any control.*

Aren't you afraid of dying alone in our home system?

Alone? I have my bodyguards with me, don't I?

Jeremy didn't know if she was joking or serious. There were no clues in her thoughts.

I see.

I sincerely hope that staking my life on the success of this mission, which could decide the fate of your species, will lay the foundation for a future alliance. An alliance that is based on trust and has a strong foundation, sent the Matriarch, and her thoughts resonated with hope and something else that Jeremy could not identify.

Great things require small steps and every step into the unknown is a risk. I am glad that you have taken this risk with us. I know you didn't have to.

I believe that it is better to fight something dangerous like the Cold Death *together than to create a new front,* she replied. Her thoughts were orderly and downright businesslike, but there was an underlying pulsating conviction that he hadn't expected.

I'm really happy about the Gaia field, he replied with relief, feeling his quiet trust in the Matriarch continuing to grow because of her feelings, like a plant that is continually fertilized and watered.

The Gaia field is much more than you humans realize yet, Jeremy Brandt, she finally continued: *Much like death. But you are a young species and you will learn.*

If we survive all this madness, I'll be happy to sit in your class, he replied laconically.

A flashing phone icon in his helmet display showed him an incoming call from Macella. He blinked twice in rapid succession, opening the channel.

"Jeremy?" Macella sounded upset.

"Yes? Are you all right?" His pulse immediately spiked and throbbed in his ears.

"It's you! I saw on the sensors that you guys were being fired on!"

"Yeah, it got our escort," he returned, relieved that she wasn't in trouble. "Are you in orbit yet?"

"Yes, we're back on the bridge. Commander-generator is in your tank and sitting next to me in the VR environment. It's weird sitting in your seat."

"You earned it," Jeremy replied, trying to imagine what it must look like up there now with Macella as Captain, Commander-generator as XO, and Walter and Felicity in their usual places. The Locust's new position had been one of the conditions set by the Conclave for agreeing to their plan and the Neuromorph's continued survival. He had not found it difficult to agree; after all, the alien diplomats on his ship had the final say anyway, whether he liked it or not. For operational purposes, Macella was the better captain in his eyes anyway. She was as perceptive as a hawk and less likely to be led astray by emotion than he was. Knowing that she had Commander-generator next to her calmed him down even more, since he had known since their little conspiracy involving the Neuromorph that he could count on the alien. Besides that, Walter and Felicity were still with her.

Nothing bad would happen. The battle in orbit would soon be won and she had all the support she could possibly have. Besides, she's taking care of Walter and Felicity, and they're all together in a small room surrounded by carbyne walls several feet thick, he mentally reminded himself.

"Thank you," she said softly, then cleared her throat. "There is one more thing, though."

He didn't like the tone of her voice and a sinking feeling immediately spread through his stomach.

"You're being followed."

"Followed? You mean on the ground?" he asked, surprised. According to the data from their reconnaissance of the enemy, Alpha's forces had no vehicles of any kind. After all, they had not come in freighters or personnel carriers, but in warships that were never intended for planetary use.

"Yes. There are four thunderbirds hot on your heels showing up on our screens here. They're flying in an erratic pattern, using ground force transponder codes," she explained.

"That's why our own systems haven't picked them up."

"Yes," Macella confirmed in a strained voice. "They apparently captured some of the tanks during the battle. If you go to maximum thrust, you'll have about a two-minute head start."

"Two minutes?" he asked, aghast. "That's not much. You'd best send the data directly to our pilot, and I'll send you his ID code."

Jeremy made the appropriate entries via his helmet display.

"It's best not to let them know you've spotted them," Macella suggested. "That way, maybe they won't shoot at you. Alpha will want to get a fix on your heading. If they shoot you out of the sky, it won't find out anything that might have escaped its calculations."

Jeremy was silent for a moment, looking at the calculated trajectories of their convoy and the four pursuers. At their current speed, the remaining flight time was still about three hours, which would soon decrease significantly if the pilot were to speed up. Under no circumstances could the enemy see what they had captured, or their entire plan would be doomed.

"An orbital strike is out, I think," he finally said, shaking his head.

"Yes," she agreed, and a crackle on the line interrupted her for a moment. "...so far, limited to New Paris. If lasers suddenly start raining down outside the city limits it will draw even more attention to you."

"Our best bet is to try to stop them right in front of the industrial area," he reasoned aloud.

"Be careful."

"I always am," Jeremy returned, managing a thin smile, though of course she couldn't see it. He wanted to say more, some token of his love perhaps, or to plead with her for the thousandth time to stay alive. But in the end, he simply disconnected so as not to act like an idiot.

"Pascal?" he addressed the inspector, who turned his face, which glowed blue in his helmet, toward him. His slit-like eyes shone intently.

"We have a problem and could use some strategy." Jeremy sent the data received from Macella to his friend. A small icon informed him that the same transmission was being sent to the pilots of their convoy as well.

"Oh," Pascal blurted. "This looks bad."

CHAPTER 12
PASCAL

Colony moon DeGaulle, Archimedes system, 2334

THIS WAS NOT how Pascal had imagined a real high-speed pursuit with hover tanks. Perhaps that was because he had never been involved in one before and was only familiar with them from bad VR movies. No fire-spitting cannons, no daring maneuvers, just five dots on a holoscreen being pursued by four dots, making it impossible to immediately recognize the pursuit. They changed course frequently, only by a few degrees, to give the impression that they are not interested in each other at all. It was a game of tedium and nerves of steel. Pascal would have personally loved to point the railguns and blow their pursuers out of the sky, and the pilots surely felt the same way. He just hoped they were professional enough to keep themselves under control, because Jeremy was right: if they opened fire now, Alpha would immediately know they were up to something worth a second look. For now, they could just as easily be a rogue unit that didn't feel like getting killed in the boiling cauldron of New Paris and instead wanted to run away.

Still, the question of what to do remained when they reached the factory floor where Omega had hidden the ship. They couldn't allow any of Alpha's soldiers to catch a glimpse of it, so they were headed for a violent confrontation. Timing with the critical thing. If there wasn't enough time between the skirmish and their departure for Alpha to send more eyes and ears, they had a real chance. Or they could simply jump directly into hyperspace from the hangar. Although it would irradiate the immediate area, it probably wouldn't make any difference, considering the fact that the colony's capital had already received a dose of radiation higher than could be healthy. However, the question remained whether Alpha would be able to draw any logical conclusions from the traces left behind. According to his understanding, an empty warehouse that had been defended would not provide enough circumstantial evidence to weave a theory from. But just because he couldn't discern a pattern didn't mean the superintelligence couldn't. He gave Alpha a lot of credit, and that worried him. He had enjoyed the days when he could look down on all of his counterparts and dismiss them as less intelligent. Today, he could no longer afford that kind of misanthropic arrogance. It had become a luxury his former self enjoyed.

Sighing, he looked at the images of the sensors that appeared on his helmet display again. They showed pastel-colored hills with endless fields of grain stretching from horizon to horizon like the swells of an endless ocean. The faint twilight of the day-night boundary they were flying across cast long shadows and provided the perfect backdrop for anxious thoughts. As a child, Pascal had always felt uneasy at twilight because, to him, it had seemed like a kind of death of the day. Unlike sunrise, the light was not fresh, dawning, and warm, but cold, pale, and dying. Since they were now fleeing toward the advancing night and not moving into the advancing sun, he didn't think it was a particularly good omen. However, he had never thought much of omens either and was probably the least superstitious person on the colonies. At least that's what he wanted to believe. Just a few days ago, this area had been one of the Union's most important supply centers. There had been automated farm machinery and work drones buzzing around, jealously tending the fields and groves meticulously. Nowhere did crops grow as well as on DeGaulle, except perhaps on Verdi. It was a terrible irony that these two worlds were the sites of the only ground battles in the history of the Union. Hard radiation had sterilized the two places where life had flourished. But as he thought about it, it was clear that each colony had its own burdens to bear. Bismarck had been completely destroyed, Trafalgar had been extensively devastated by the Braun 22 incident many decades ago, and now it had affected the other inhabited moons. Of all places, Europe as the seat of parliament and the entire civil service and governing body had been spared. Had it not been for all the tragic suffering, the tabloids would definitely have been able to spin one of their flimsy conspiracy theories from it—and with a very spicy twist.

"Hey, buddy," he radioed Spark on impulse. Jeremy seemed to be lost in thought and had been silent for quite a while. Pascal guessed he was worried about Macella and the others. The burden of captain and leader seemed to weigh heavily on him and Pascal couldn't blame him. He had been a loner all his life, in part to avoid that kind of responsibility. In doing so, of course, he had made it easier for himself, and he realized it now. People like Jeremy, who voluntarily took the reins and considered it a serious responsibility, were exactly the kind of people needed, not all those politicians who saw their power as a weapon and an instrument for self-aggrandizement. The young captain was a natural without realizing it, and that's what made him a born leader. Sometimes Pascal felt that people were not always destined to do the things they most wanted to do. Instead, one's talents often led one down a path of fear over one's own inadequacies. Otherwise, he could not explain what his own talent for recognizing patterns was for. Its only purpose was to solve crimes and to deal with the unexpected. A field that led to the depths of human depravity that left no one unscathed, whether talented or not. The same realization would hit young Jeremy soon, he was sure of it. The worry lines on his forehead and the ever-twitching crow's feet around his otherwise alert eyes spoke volumes.

"Yo, cop," came Sparks's reply at last, and Pascal jolted out of his musings. "What's up?"

"Is the time indicated by the onboard computers correct?" he asked, and his hope that the soldier wouldn't realize from the pointlessness of his question that he was merely chatting seemed suddenly ridiculous. But apparently Spark was having a patronizing day and didn't comment on that fact.

"I think so. These things are pretty accurate. However, there will actually be some deviation because we are changing course more often than necessary rather than taking the direct route. After all, we want to look like a bunch of startled deserters, keh?"

"Yeah, that's what it looks like."

"You sound glum," the soldier remarked.

"I'm running through what the next half hour will look like. Nothing too rosy has come to mind yet."

"It's going to be all right, man," Spark grumbled. "You're worrying too much. It won't turn out the way we think it will anyway, so just wait and see."

"Well, that's the problem. Things don't always turn out the way we expect them to. In this case, however, we can't afford to have things turn out *differently from what we expect*."

"It's like that every time."

"That's true again. Currently, I would suggest that we land the tanks in a defensive formation and let the thrusters continue to circle so that they can provide us with aerial cover while we are pinned down on the ground and unloading. Otherwise, if our pursuers are still airborne, they'll have an unfair advantage," Pascal explained, playing through a simulation in his helmet display.

"Sounds reasonable. That bird's pretty maneuverable and should give Alpha's asses plenty to deal with, so they won't be able to pick us off at their leisure from a distance."

"I'll send you my simulation data. Maybe you can go over it with the pilots and come up with something that matches your military gibberish and expertise. After all, it's possible I'm misjudging the capabilities and limitations of these thunderbirds," Pascal continued, and after an approving hum from Spark, he ended the connection.

As the factory building appeared on the optical sensors, Pascal was awakened from his trance-like musings by the alarm he had set chiming, he immediately switched his helmet display.

The building was an unadorned cube with a perimeter of over six hundred and fifty-six feet. The gray block with the company name *Gérard Molineu Logistics* looked like a cube without eyes, and didn't even have a single window. Pascal reckoned it was a hangar for autonomous airships used on the colonies for long-distance transport. Normally, four of the huge vehicles could be stored and loaded in these architectural monstrosities—or just one Earth Protectorate warship. The hangar, made of simple quick-build composite, was located in the middle of an abandoned industrial park on the outskirts of the small town of Blain, where it stood out like a giant. The rest of the buildings around it looked downright puny in comparison. As was common on DeGaulle, the streets were lined with trees, but they looked colorless and pale under the dense cloud covering that had gathered in the meantime. All in all, the entire scene looked like something out of an end times VR: abandoned cars stood disorderly on the asphalt or at an angle on the sidewalks, as if they had been abandoned in a hurry. If there were still people here, they had long since sought shelter and for the time being didn't seem to be thinking of showing their faces any time soon.

Good thing, he thought, as the landing countdown showed thirty seconds left. They headed for a large roller door on the south side under rapidly decreasing thrust, so that they could land behind the hangar, invisible to the sensors of their pursuers. This would hopefully buy them enough time to send a team inside and start the reactor before the battle began outside. Spark had informed him that the pilots favored two scenarios. Either a quick drop behind the hangar and then continuing to fly the tanks in different directions to confuse and, in the best case, split up their pursuers. The downside was that the dismounted soldiers would be defenseless without the cover of the tanks on the ground. The other scenario, which they finally decided on, was also to land behind the hangar. The Thunderbirds would serve as cover and gunfire for the soldiers while Omega and a team of technicians launched the ship.

Of course, there were risks in going to the far side of the giant cube as Alpha's units could simply decide to destroy the hall at any time. That would expose their intentions and provoke a fight, which they appeared to be avoiding at the moment. But it would also deprive them of any cover and secrecy that existed between their two small units. But ultimately, in Pascal's eyes, there was no alternative. If they stopped directly in front of the hangar and entered it, the Earth soldiers would immediately know that there was something important inside. They might even decide to shoot at the building to destroy it. Even if they didn't destroy it, there would certainly be ricochets and shots that missed and damaged it. One big hole in the outer wall and they would send a radio message that would end the mission before it had even begun. The risk was just too great.

Then the moment arrived: their armored vehicle executed a long semicircle, braking brutally, and the turbines that were tilted toward the ground swept a hurricane of wilted foliage in all directions. Their vehicles formed a semicircle in front of the roller door, which had a small personnel doorway embedded in it, touching down simultaneously. A jolt went through the cabin and there was a loud hiss. The left side door between their seats and the wall to the pilot's cockpit popped open and their crash cages automatically unlocked.

"Okay, let's go!" he shouted over the roar of the turbines and jumped out of the tank into the open. With the HV rifle Spark had talked him into using, he reflexively scanned the immediate area and found no threats between their vehicles and the hangar's huge wall. He quickly lowered the weapon and gave the other occupants a wave to signal that the coast was clear.

As planned, Jeremy, Omega, and the Matriarch ran out accompanied by the two Locust guards and headed straight for the small personnel door. Some of the swarming soldiers in their massive servo armor had already reached it and were unlocking it with a military priority code. They ran inside and disappeared into the darkness beyond.

The rest of the soldiers spilled out of the tanks like ants pouring out of their burrow. The thruster, which looked like an oversized bird of prey, hovered just a few feet above their heads before opening its side doors. About twenty more soldiers leaped out of the interior dropping to the asphalt like forces of nature. Where the three-hundred-plus-pound battle tanks touched down, the ground cracked and caved in slightly as the soldiers sprinted to their positions and took cover behind the tanks.

Pascal waved to the aircraft, and the pilot hastily veered off to fly a loop and provide them with air support.

Good, he thought, looking at the time display on his helmet. Seventy seconds until their pursuit arrived, if they stuck to their previous flight path. Valuable seconds would drag by before he could get any sensor data from the thruster.

"Everything is going according to plan," radioed Spark, who had just arrived at his side and patted him on the shoulder. Pascal turned to the entrance of the hangar and saw that Jeremy, Omega, and the Matriarch had already disappeared inside.

"Have you got what you need?" he radioed to Jeremy, and it only crackled and popped in reply.

"Dammit!"

"Everything's fine, cop," Spark reassured him, grinning at him lightheartedly. His teeth looked sinister in the passive blue light of his helmet. "The hangar has shielding. Standard with companies like this. They want to protect themselves from industrial espionage, I guess. One of the tech-heads inside should be overriding it right now with his priority code."

"Those military priority codes are really handy," Pascal noted, trying to relax.

"Sure. Never needed them before but since the shit hit the fan, they are really handy."

"It's Jeremy," suddenly came the relieving radio call. "Omega says everything looks just as he left it. We're heading in now."

"Roger that," Pascal replied, looking at the clock in his helmet visor. Twenty seconds.

"What's it look like up there?" he radioed the pilot of the thruster, looking around uneasily.

"They're no longer on my screen," came the reply. The man sounded tense.

"How is that possible?"

"I don't know, sir," the young man replied. Pascal saw his plane hovering about 0.6 miles away just below the cloud cover like a hawk ready to pounce as soon as it saw its prey.

"They've landed!" shouted Pascal, slamming his free hand against the door of the tank. "Dammit!"

"What's going on?" asked Spark, confused.

"They landed on the other side of the hangar. Of course! They figured out there was something wrong with the hangar and didn't want to fly around it because they sensed a trap, so now they're simply marching in from the other side to check it out."

"That's pretty bad, keh."

"Yes!" snorted Pascal, opening the general operations channel. He wasn't the commander of the operation, but he couldn't afford to waste time. "This is Takahashi. The enemy has landed on the other side. Split into two groups. We must go around the hangar and prevent them from getting inside. Under no circumstances can they see what we're doing here! Go, go, go!"

Without waiting to see how the soldiers would react, he ordered his suit to release maximum power to the servos and sprinted toward the left corner of the building.

Lacking proper training in the use of heavy body armor and the years of experience the soldiers surrounding him had, he nearly collided with the hall's fast-building composite. The small motors in his suit joints amplified his every movement several times over, making him feel as if he no longer had any control over his body. Each time he raised one leg, it catapulted him forward several feet, and he had to pull the other forward lightning fast to absorb the extreme force behind it. So he stumbled and staggered along the side of the huge cube rather than running. After only a few moments, half a dozen soldiers had overtaken him and were racing past him with rifles at the ready. Spark appeared beside him and a sideways glance was enough to throw Pascal completely off balance. Instead of jumping over an abandoned MagCapsule like the soldiers in front of him, he crashed right into it. Or rather: through it. Due to his speed and the mass of his armor, the light aluminum of the car completely shattered. Shards of glass and plastic shot in all directions and he tumbled like a discarded doll into, through and over the wreckage. On the other side, two strong hands grabbed his shoulders and straightened him without stopping.

"Focus, cop," Spark radioed, pulling him along roughly. The corner of the east side of the hangar was getting closer. The soldiers ahead of them were already firing around it, their rifles rattling like firecrackers in staccato.

"I'm trying," Pascal groaned, opening a channel to Jeremy.

"Hey, buddy! The enemy is trying to gain access from the east side. You guys need to hurry up. We'll try to stop them, but I can't guarantee anything."

"Got it," came the reply. Jeremy sounded tense. "Over."

By the time Pascal and Spark reached the corner, one of their comrades had already been hit. He was lying on the asphalt with his armor cracked open like a cracked lobster, and white smoke was rising from a plate-sized hole in his chest. The other colony soldiers had fanned out and taken cover behind some MagCapsules and pallets of bulky industrial containers. They were firing at regular intervals to the right, but Pascal couldn't see anything because of the angle to the corner of the slope. Carefully, he walked toward it, pressing his back against the composite, then peered around cautiously.

Among the four hastily parked tanks were about two dozen Earth fighters in servo armor similar to what he himself wore. But theirs were much narrower and had a bluish glow. Pascal guessed that they were GravPanzers for fighting in zero gravity. Maybe his guys could use that to their advantage. Some of them lay dead between their tanks and the hangar door on this side, a stretch of open space about 32.8 foot long. Three, however, had obviously reached the gate and were currently working on it with a plasma cutter.

"Concentrate all fire on the three at the hangar!" he radioed excitedly, holding his rifle around the corner to open fire himself. The servos intercepted the recoil effortlessly, but his aim was too abysmal to hit anything. Instead, his HV rounds plowed into the asphalt and tore a 3.2-foot-long furrow in the ground behind the soldiers from Earth. One of them was hit by something and jerked to one side, then there was a loud bang and Pascal was thrown backward. His visor suddenly dimmed, as he crashed into something hard.

The audio sensors in his helmet seemed to have been overloaded by the bang, or destroyed by something, because all he could hear was his own breathing. He struggled to get up and removed the visor's glare shield.

"My God," he murmured as he saw the large crater in the parking lot where his allied soldiers had been. The MagCapsules and containers they had been hiding behind were nothing more than smoking debris, scattered everywhere and glowing like coals. Fires had broken out all around and smoke was pouring from them.

"Pascal!" someone called over the radio directly into his ear. Then again. It took him a moment to realize that Spark's helmet was directly in front of his, and he was staring directly into the wide-faced giant's blue-lit eyes.

"Hey, cop! Take a deep breath!"

"What..." Pascal cleared his throat violently when no sound escaped his throat.

"I think one of their tanks fired its main gun," Spark explained, effortlessly pulling him to his feet and thrusting a rifle into his hand. "Try not to lose it again!"

Pascal nodded, shook his head in a daze, and brought the gun back to bear. Spark bounced through the air in front of him like a bouncy ball. Each step catapulted him several feet into the air as he fired from both weapon attachments toward the tanks. Three more soldiers followed him, none of whom Pascal had seen before. For him, all this happened in complete silence, and he felt strangely removed from what was happening around him.

This is probably a really bad idea, he thought, but nevertheless brought his free hand to the button on his helmet seal and pressed it after commanding the suit system to release the latch. There was a clicking sound, then the helmet was loose and he could lift it and toss it carelessly away. The noise of battle immediately broke over him like the wave of a tsunami. It rattled and cracked. A bang made his ears flap and the stench of ozone and burnt plastic settled acridly in his nose.

Gritting his teeth, he tried to block out the sheer overwhelming sensations of unleashed violence and moved around the corner. Behind the earth soldiers' tanks, the defenders showered Spark and his comrades with barrage fire, periodically ducking away under incoming volleys. The HV rounds pelted the thunderbirds like hail, sending up myriad sparks. The two earthmen who had just used the plasma torch on the light composite were getting back on their feet and putting the device to work again. Apparently the impact of the Gauss bullet, which was way too close, had knocked them off their feet as well. On the other side of the hangar, he saw another crater with smoke rising from it. Apparently the other flank had also been hit hard. But he could still see muzzle flashes through the thick smoke.

"You're not getting in there," Pascal growled, running toward the two working enemies, bringing his rifle to bear and pulling the trigger. The one in front of him took a bullet to the leg and buckled, while the other hurriedly continued on. Then the one who had been hit returned fire on Pascal.

CHAPTER 13
VERONICA

In orbit around DeGaulle, Archimedes system, 2334

VERONICA MACELLA WALKED UP and down the virtual bridge of the *WizKid*, careful not to look at anyone. She could hardly believe that she was now in command of this monster of a ship. Not because she didn't trust herself to command a crew, especially such a small one, but because of the circumstances. A ship that had previously been commanded by Jeremy just wasn't the same after he was no longer aboard. Besides, the name already weighed heavily on her shoulders. Agiou's name on the hull was both a burden and a duty to make the right decisions in her memory. But all those concerns paled against the plan she was about to put into action. She didn't even pay attention to the holoscreen, which was filling up with new battle data by the second, announcing their tenacious but inevitable victory against Alpha's armada.

"Captain!" someone called out. It was Commander-generator, she could tell by the extremely deep voice the onboard consciousness generated from the alien's telepathic signals.

Then again: "Captain!" This time it sounded more urgent and so loud that she suddenly realized it meant her.

"Uh, yes?" she hurried to say, turning to the Locust sitting in her previous seat looking at her. Her own, no, Jeremy's was empty and the sight made her stomach ache.

"The enemy ships," he said in his deep baritone, "they are jumping."

"Where to?" she asked in alarm, hurriedly sitting down in the command chair so that she could see the holoscreen from the perfect angle. It was uncomfortable, though that was hardly possible in a VR simulation.

"Hard to say," Walter cut in from his console behind the display. "They're not showing up inside the system, at any rate, as far as we can tell."

"Check any sensor stations that are still intact, the orbital rings, data from friendly ships. If they have arrived anywhere in the system, be it on one of the colonies, in the Acheron Belt, or the Oort Cloud, I want to know about it." She maintained her brisk and precise tone under stress, which had gained her more respect in her career than any accomplishments in combat simulations. That knowledge reassured her somewhat.

"Aye, Captain," Walter replied and began making entries on his console.

"Instruct allied units," she continued, turning to Commander-generator. "They are to take advantage of the ceasefire to give top priority to ejecting more hyperspace containment fields. Wherever Alpha's forces have disappeared to, we need to limit their ability to enter the system where we can't control or prevent it."

The Locust nodded, almost human-like, and then tapped away on his arm display. Veronica avoided glancing over her shoulder at the five remaining Conclave members - she already felt like an Academy student taking her final exam with their stares and thoughts behind her. She didn't need to keep reminding herself that there was even more pressure on her than usual.

"Felicity. When we have confirmation that Alpha hasn't jumped within the system, you'll begin transmitting our orders to the network."

Addressing the Locust again, she added, "You can already begin transmitting them to the Gaia field so that your units can begin preparations."

"Understood."

Veronica leaned back a bit until her back touched the normally comfortable backrest, but she didn't relax. Nor would she until Jeremy returned safely and was sitting in this chair again. There was so much to think about that it made her dizzy: The nanites were still repairing their drive pod, and they were thus slowly reaching the end of their reserves of appropriate mass. Alpha's ships were jumping away and their destination was unknown. On DeGaulle, Jeremy, Pascal, and Omega were trying to take control of the captured ship without the AI's soldiers noticing. Here in space, they had to implement Omega's proposed plans without him being able to monitor the operations himself and correct them if necessary. In the end, they needed the Neuromorph in two places, but there was no time to make another copy and put it into a clone body. Not for the first time, she wondered if they could really implement what he had in mind without his guiding hand. But of course there was no question, because they had no other choice. If necessary, they had to improvise. One might think that she had some experience with that now, but it didn't feel that way. At least she had Walter and Felicity by her side, that would make whatever they encountered easier.

"So far, the system-wide sensor network hasn't reported any radiation spikes on the colonies or in the immediate vicinity.

The probes further out are still scanning and won't be able to provide a complete picture for several hours," Walter reported after a moment, grunting with satisfaction.

"That's good news. There should be no immediate danger then," she replied, performing two quick gestures in front of the holoscreen until the current status of the deployed hyperspace containment fields was displayed. The inner system up to the Acheron Belt was already about 40 percent covered, and the zones marked in green continued to expand now that the Locusts were helping to distribute them. In all, over eighty thousand of their ovoid cruisers were already in the Archimedes system. This almost unimaginable number grew even larger as more and more alien units rushed in. They protectively regrouped around the colony moons, with the exception of the doomed Bismarck.

Protective, she thought. *Or possessive*. They would find out soon enough. Until then, she took the Matriarch's support and decision to tie her fate to the success of the mission to Sol as a good sign. She had decided earlier in her life that it was better to trust everyone until you were convinced otherwise. It made dealing with people—and aliens—a whole lot easier if you weren't constantly expecting a knife to be stuck in your back. Maybe that was naive, maybe it wasn't. In any case, it felt better.

She pursed her lips and switched the view on the screen to the Atlas drones that were currently in action. About 20 percent of the recon drones were at maximum thrust, on their way to the outer system to search for Alpha's ships. The other 80 percent were deploying hyperspace containment fields. She switched to the mammoth drones that were in use. About half were busy making repairs to the orbital rings of Europa, Trafalgar, and Verdi, or tending to the rest of their completely shot-up fleet. The nearly four hundred ships, which were mostly destroyers and light corvettes, were currently limping along at a measly thrust to Europa to regroup as ordered. The other 50 percent of the mammoths were still in their launch bays, awaiting deployment.

"Walter, open a channel to the fleet, have them send tech teams to Trafalgar aboard their shuttles and see if they can fire up the mass fabricators there with the help of the local authorities. Using their mammoth drones, they are to collect wreckage and bring it to the fabricators. The best place to start is in orbit around Trafalgar. In any case, all that wreckage poses a threat to any traffic to and from the colony. So we kill two birds with one stone. Launch our own mammoths that will fit through the maintenance hatches to collect wreckage as well. We need the mass for our nanite production. At this point, I think we can use some of our sensors to scan for suitable pieces of wreckage. If Alpha does reappear, thanks to the containment fields, we'll have a fairly generous response time."

Walter gave her a long look and then nodded with his mouth agape in approval before turning back to his console and following her orders.

"Felicity." She turned to the Nanonikerin, who had already turned to face her and was attentively awaiting orders. "Now that we are the commanding flagship of the remaining fleet, we must show that we still have initiative and display strength. Contact the Parliament on Europa and inform them of our steps. They are as follows: confer with the governors and coordinate our actions in space with those on the ground. We need information on the condition of the moons. All ground forces are to remain at combat readiness and I want reports of any sightings of downed enemy ships or strange phenomena reported by citizens. We need to make sure the colonies are secure before we turn SenseNet back on. If we turn it back on at all. All IT experts are to use secure simulations to determine what danger any leftover code fragments from Alpha really pose. We also need to be informed about what happened down there while it was in charge. Right now, we're in the dark, and that's not a very good place to be. If our people down there need support, we'll give it and if they can support us, we'll gladly accept it as well. We can use every helping hand right now. As soon as we know what the status of our industrial infrastructure is, the governors should arrange for everything to be invested in the production of new ships. Assuming the Legislature approves this proposal, of course."

"Easy to forget that we're not really in charge at all," Felicity grumbled, saluting.

"Yes, that's my thoughts exactly. In the end, we're under the Parliament, and that's fine," Veronica agreed with the Nanonikerin and sighed, half out of frustration, half out of relief, before continuing: "It's also very likely that there is someone on one of the other ships with a higher rank than Captain. If that's the case, I'll no longer be in a position to give orders on behalf of the fleet either."

"I don't think anyone is going to stand up and volunteer to take the reins now," Felicity objected, shaking her head decisively. "If there's a rear admiral still alive, which I doubt, he or she will probably be busy trying to avoid losing his or her own ship to the vacuum. Besides, they're all careerists who don't want to stick their necks out when the shit hits the fan."

"Can't get any more cliché than that, can you?" grumbled Walter from the side, and the Nanonikerin snorted audibly before turning to her console.

"You'll see when no one answers," she added.

Veronica stopped paying attention to her. There was a lot to do now, and no time to lose if she was going to fill this command chair, which was far too large for her in so many ways. Besides, stress has always allowed her to relax and think more clearly. It helped her focus, prioritize tasks clearly, and work through them with urgency. Even in school, she had made weekly plans of her own and used markers to determine the most efficient order to complete them. It hadn't taken long for her classmates to copy her system so they too could reap the benefits. That skill had even earned her the distinction of going down in Union Navy history as one of the youngest XOs. At the cost, unfortunately, of being sent on a suicide mission, but she had even taken that as a compliment. After all, it had been crucial that the flight through the wormhole turned out well, if the crossing was to be successful. The Admiralty had quickly decided that it was better to assemble a strong crew rather than just fill it with people they wanted to get rid of as quickly as possible.

None of that mattered now. They had a sun to destroy.

"Commander-generator." Veronica turned to her XO, who paused in his typing to turn to her with an attentive gaze. It was not easy, when their gazes met, not to sink into his huge almond-shaped eyes, wherein bright points glittered like the stars of a distant galaxy. There was something mesmerizing, almost beguiling about them. In the past, she had always imagined that if humanity ever encountered aliens, they would probably be slimy and ugly, creepy perhaps. Instead, the Locusts could almost be called beautiful, that is, if their skin hadn't been so leathery. Of course, like most of the colonists, she had stopped believing she would ever encounter aliens. Even before she was born, the dream of interstellar propulsion had died before ever being truly imagined, and with it, all hopes of first contact had been considered highly unlikely. After all, not even the Union's sophisticated telescopes and sensors had detected any signs of intelligent life. Now sitting next to an alien being, on the bridge of a Union ship no less, made that knowledge all the more surreal. On the other hand, Commander-generator's presence was reassuring, for like all Locusts, an aura of calm and serenity surrounded him, and thanks to the Gaia field, it quickly rubbed off on them.

"Did you confer with the Conclave and get an overview of your fleets?" she asked her second-in-command.

"Yes," he confirmed, easing off his arm display. "All factions but one have agreed to a temporary alliance with the humans. Those that agreed were primarily persuaded by the Neuromorph revealing the location of Father and Mother's eggs."

"Will the alliance hold?" she asked tensely.

"My guess is that once the eggs are found, and they can confirm beyond a shadow of a doubt that they are free of any hidden code from the Neuromorph, all factions will agree."

"Good, but will the alliance hold then?" probed Veronica.

"Yes. It is hard for your species to imagine the significance Father and Mother had and still have for us. So the prospect of our taking possession of their descendants and having sole access to them is the best and most effective step toward reconciliation between our species there could ever be," the Locust explained. Something in his computer-generated voice made Veronica sit up and take notice.

"Is there something else you yourself think about it?" she asked. "Do you think the Neuromorph hid them as a kind of reassurance for this eventuality?"

"Yes."

"That would be pretty calculating."

"Yes, but that doesn't have to be a bad thing. He's a supremely intelligent being with unimaginable power, and so far he appears to have used his strategic skills to our advantage," Commander-generator opined. "So far, he has not given me any reason to doubt his positive motives. Why should I start now? I think the Conclave also saw that point and that's why they had an open mind."

"You're probably right. In that case, I hope they found the eggs soon and checked them out."

"Yes."

"And what about the faction that didn't agree?"

"The *Moons in Shadow*. They prefer cold environments and that seems to be reflected in their nature. They do not trust easily and fear for the future of their faction if they join forces with the humans. They have lost the majority of their worlds to the Neuromorph's black barriers," the alien replied, wiggling his right hand—a gesture Veronica was unfamiliar with.

"But I thought the worlds didn't suffer?" she asked, confused.

"That is not quite accurate. They had some influence on the ecosystems of the affected planets and not only for the good. Also, many members of the *Moons in Shadow* joined the Neuromorph and answered its call to go to Bismarck. Many of those left behind saw this as treason, and civil war nearly broke out between supporters of the hybrid and his adversaries."

"His adversaries eventually gained the upper hand," Veronica guessed, nodding with a puckered mouth. A strand of blond hair tickled her cheek and she blew it away carelessly.

"That's right. They will distrust anything to do with the Neuromorph for now, no matter how many Gaia transmissions they may receive of his noble thoughts, and we must respect that."

"Will they try to sabotage the alliance?" she asked.

"No, I don't think so. Their faction is not as passionate as others. For now, they will be content to watch what happens, take their share of the eggs and wait it out," assured Commander-generator, letting her experience his inner conviction over the Gaia field.

"That's reassuring. What did they think of the plan?"

"Destroying a sun is certainly difficult for many to imagine," he returned, seeming a bit agitated himself. "Many do not even believe it is possible. However, this branch of physics is also not a heavily funded area of science for our kind. We are interested in biological life and extending the boundaries of our DNA. A sun represents life and death to us, and destroying one is such a new, barely conceivable idea that it will take more time to digest than the duration of this mission."

"But they will digest it?"

"Probably. The sun of your home system will be destroyed before they can change their minds. Other than that, there is no alternative unless we want to find out how quickly Alpha can build an extermination fleet and send it to us. That's a risk the factions don't want to take."

"All right. Let's leave it at that for now. What do the preparations look like?" she asked.

"Good, as far as I can tell," came the reply. "The eight relevant systems have been briefed and are ready to implement the plan."

He pointed one of his long fingers at the holoscreen and the display produced eight squares, each representing a solar system. These were the systems the Neuromorph had identified to deliver the iron needed to destroy Sol's sun. Each of the systems shown had a huge ultra-dense iron planet near its central star.

"There are fleets of two thousand friends and twenty habitats on each. If the Neuromorph's calculations of the energy needed for the hyperspace gates are correct, that should be enough. In addition, the *Council of Leadership* has sent out escort fleets to guard the preparations," summarized Commander-generator, sounding confident.

"What is the time frame?"

"The systems are all close, but taking everything into account, by your standard time, it's expected to take two days."

"That means Jeremy and Pascal will have to fly around the Sol system undetected for two days?" Veronica tried to swallow her shock but couldn't fight the lump in her throat that was threatening to swell and cut off her air.

"Yes. They need to jump as soon as possible so as not to lose contact with the rest of Alpha's fleet and raise questions."

"But we don't even know where the Earth ships disappeared to. They may end up being the only ones to jump to Sol, and if that happens, they'll raise even more questions," she countered, the hairs on the back of her neck beginning to stand up.

"That's correct. The whole mission involves a lot of risk," he agreed. She managed to control herself at the last moment and avoided giving him a dirty look. He was right, and her concern for Jeremy was no reason to blame him for her inner turmoil. After all, he was only voicing her own dark thoughts.

"Then let's hope Alpha really did order all the ships back to Sol. That would be good not only for Jeremy, but for the Archimedes system as well," she concluded, taking a deep breath.

"What about your scientists?" she finally asked, wiping away seven of the eight systems displayed on the holoscreen with seven short swipes. The one that remained automatically zoomed to the full size of the screen, so that a glowing central star, six planets and an asteroid belt were now clearly visible. "Will the conversion go smoothly?"

Commander-generator gazed at the screen for a moment and then, in a fluid motion, stood up to stand beside the display. In the process, his double-jointed legs became blurred like an optical illusion, they moved so quickly.

"Here's how it works." He formed a circle with his long-fingered hands and the representation enlarged again until a small, dark brown planet appeared in front of the huge silhouette of the glowing central star.

"One thousand friends form a wide circle in front of the iron planet P3X-444. Twenty habitats with powerful energy reserves post themselves behind the circle." The holoscreen now showed a huge circle of flashing Locust ships that roughly spanned the outline of the planet. Then the circle flickered and a green hyperspace window opened between the tips of the ships.

"If everything works, they will create the largest hyperspace window ever created," he explained the Neuromorph's plan.

"Is that even possible?" she asked in amazement. Of course, she already knew the broad outlines of the idea, but seeing the simulation before her eyes almost took her breath away. It was easy to forget the dimensions involved.

"There's no reason why it shouldn't be possible. The size of a hyperspace window is determined by the energy expended. So far, it had not been necessary because there were not and still are not any spaceships that large. In principle, however, the spacewalker experts have given the green light, as you humans would probably say."

"And the iron planet?" She was still staring at the representation of the gigantic ring, as if seeing a ghost.

"Now that is the point that is new. Using the Neuromorph's instructions, which I haven't seen, the spacewalkers are supposed to be able to move the hyperspace window," explained Commander-generator, opening his palms into a Locust shrug.

"That means they just put the gate over the planet instead of trying to move it into the gate," she summarized, shaking her head in disbelief.

"That's correct. Moving an entire planet still seems to be impossible."

"Well, thank God something still makes sense at least," she joked, clearing the display from the holoscreen. "We've got a lot of work to do. Let's get moving!"

CHAPTER 14

JEREMY

Colony moon DeGaulle, Archimedes system, 2334

THE HALL WAS a cold and dark place. Of course, he didn't notice much of either fact, but Jeremy liked to look at the readouts in his helmet display and that informed him that it was four degrees colder here. There was very little light and what there was came from the position lights of the warship they were facing. The rest was provided by the residual light amplification of his helmet. The spaceship hung in the otherwise empty hangar like an oversized soccer ball nearly four hundred and ninety-two feet in diameter. It hovered as if supported by magical hands in the exact center of the hangar; therefore, Jeremy suspected an antigrav platform beneath the unadorned concrete floor that sprawled between the gloomy walls. Metal walkways stretched along them on three different levels, wide enough to carry loading bots and electric carts. Now, of course, they were empty, as the airships were gone too. Large cargo cranes and drive-up gangways had been retracted or jammed against the wall, as if the building had been sealed for some time.

"How do we get in?" he asked as they followed Omega toward the center of the hangar.

"There's a big hatch there," he explained, walking nimbly ahead. It was easy for him to get in; after all, he was not wearing heavy servo armor. Jeremy hated the contraption because it made him feel like a golem with the fine motor skills to go with it. He envied the four ground force soldiers who flanked them protectively. Their movements betrayed years of training and a nimbleness he could only marvel at as he stumbled along awkwardly. In the crab-like suit, he had to carefully weigh every impulse lest he accidentally overdid a step and was catapulted several feet forward. For someone like him, who had spent half his life in low or no gravity, that was clearly easier said than done. But it was worse to walk beside the Matriarch and her two bodyguards. They walked beside him like lithe leopards, almost graceful and as if every movement was rehearsed to perfection. In contrast, he felt like a dyslexic on drugs, and a fool to boot.

Here we are stumbling through the darkness to board an evil AI's spaceship to blow up the sun, and you're worrying about looking like a bumbling idiot, he mentally scolded himself. *Congratulations, Jeremy Brandt.*

We understand your predicament, Captain, the Matriarch's thoughts suddenly reached him, and he winced inwardly. He had forgotten for a moment that his inner thoughts no longer belonged to him but were open to all. Sometimes he hated the Gaia field. Or rather: he hated the fact that some Locusts seemed to have themselves so well under control that they hardly secreted any emotions or thoughts. Maybe he should have spent some time in a Zen monastery instead of chasing the skirts of female cadets at the academy.

"Hey, buddy!" Pascal's excited voice suddenly sounded in his helmet. "The enemy is trying to gain access inside from the east side. You guys need to hurry up. We'll try to stop them, but I can't guarantee anything."

"Got it," Jeremy replied, then adding a terse, "Over."

"We're probably going to have company, guys," he radioed to the group that would be leaving for Sol in the spaceship. "We'd better hurry."

"Here it is," Omega stated simultaneously. He had reached the central point below the Earth ship, and his hair almost touched the plain gray metal, which was as smooth as ice. Their group of three Locusts and four technicians gathered around him like a group of excited children around an ice cream truck. Whereas the ten soldiers who had accompanied them swarmed out and, in their dark servo armor, headed for the east side wall, where the blue sparks of a plasma cutter were already blazing.

Since the aliens were smaller than he was and the technicians wore no armor, he could easily see over their heads. Omega was making some entries on his datapad and then suddenly a hatch opened above his head that was as circular as the ship itself. Jeremy hadn't even noticed that there were joints or anything like that. Next, a narrow ladder descended and Omega hastily climbed the rungs. Moments later, he disappeared inside, and the technicians followed him. Then it was the Locusts' turn, led by the Matriarch. Before Jeremy was able to finally grip the first rung, he heard a deafening crash outside. The walls vibrated ominously, sending a resonating sound through the building that made his fingers tremble. The floor, too, seemed to move as if in an earthquake.

"Everything okay out there?" he radioed to Pascal's suit, but received no response. "Son of a bitch!"

He toyed with the idea of activating his armor's integrated weapons and following the ten soldiers to the east side to look for his friend, but forced himself to climb the ladder.

You better not have gotten yourself killed, Jeremy thought grimly, praying that fate had not taken another friend from him. Perhaps Omega had merely activated a jamming signal in the spaceship to prevent the enemy from being able to communicate. He toyed with the idea of asking him but let it go. It made no difference, because now he had to do something that he could not—and was not allowed to—change anyway.

As he climbed up through the narrow shaft, the ladder rungs suddenly began to vibrate very slightly. He guessed that the tactile sensors in his gloves amplified the sensation and that without them he would not have noticed the slight tremor. He also noticed the latent hum that began to set in, which could have come from the reactor powering up, possibly only because of his noise amplifiers.

At the end of the shaft, he reached a circular room with about two dozen narrow lockers on the wall with nameplates on them. The doors were transparent and the lockers were empty. Evidently the crew's suits had hung here before they had put them on and rushed out to bring death and destruction to DeGaulle. There was a multidirectional lift going in each direction, three of which were already gone. In front of the last one, a lone technician stood waiting.

"Where to?" asked Jeremy, seeing that the technician was female. The name tag on her black uniform read "Claudia Stadler." She had dark hair and a little oil on her face that gave her a slightly mischievous expression.

"Uh, hi. I need to get the linear feed units..."

Jeremy raised his hands defensively. "I meant which way does it go."

"Oh, right. Sorry. Uh, to the engine deck," she hurried to say, smiling nervously.

"I need to get to the bridge," he replied as he opened the emergency port of his armor. The feature detached the individual segments so that medics had quick access to the patient if the armor had been breached. It went "Bang!" and then suddenly he was standing there in his soft functional clothing and helmet, which he hastily removed and carelessly threw away. From a small pocket on his back he removed the helmet of his exosuit, then put it on and let the intelligent nanite mass glide over his body. Meanwhile, he searched in vain for a control panel. Apparently the elevators were controlled by SenseNet or something similar.

"Omega," he radioed the Neuromorph's comlink. "I'm outside elevator two and need to get to the bridge.

"I will take care of it," came the curt reply, and the link was disconnected. A blink of an eye later, a sliding door opened to reveal the small elevator car. With his exosuit secure, he trudged inside under the wide-eyed gaze of the astonished technician.

"Are you all right, Stadler?"

"Uh, yes, Captain. Never seen one of those things before that you vacuum heads use," she returned, blinking as if she had something in her eyes.

"Excuse me?" asked Jeremy, irritated at the derogatory term for members of the Navy.

"Oh," she squeaked, slapping her free hand over her mouth. "Sorry."

"It's okay." He wasn't upset, but he was also too distracted to smile and pay attention to her unease.

The elevator door slid open and a sonorous voice from overhead said, "Engineering deck."

Technician Stadler immediately rushed out, giving a quick wave like a shy child, and then the elevator was on its way again before announcing the bridge.

Jeremy stepped out and found himself in a tiny room with five pressure couches. On one of them lay the Matriarch, on another Omega. There was no sign of the two Locust bodyguards.

He headed for the vacant couch next to the Neuromorph, who was already enveloped by the nanomembrane straps with his eyes closed. The Matriarch, on the other hand, was just getting acquainted with her new seat, shifting her legs back and forth as if she were scratching an itch.

Are you all right?" he asked via the Gaia field.

I prefer a gel tank, came the answer along with her strange body sensation. The only thing he could read from it was that she felt unprotected because she was not completely surrounded by a protective substance. She also eyed the gimbal cage suspiciously, as if it might suddenly take on a life of its own and attack her. It surprised Jeremy that the usually controlled Matriarch was showing signs of insecurity. But then he thought about his first time on a Locust ship and his short time in the habitat orbiting the Fortress World. All that had been so strange and alien that he had been as tense as a balloon about to burst.

This is a gimbal, he explained to her, letting his thoughts of how the device was constructed and behaved during the acceleration phases flow into the Gaia field. Meanwhile, he settled into a comfortable position himself and activated the automatic shutter. *It is also called a gimbal bearing because the couch is mounted on two intersecting rotational bearings at right angles to each other. This allows the body to automatically align itself according to the direction of acceleration. In essence, this has the same effect as your acceleration tanks. The only difference is that you don't feel like you are drowning every time you get in and have to take a shower when you get out.*

I'll be fine, thank you. Her telepathic transmissions again displayed perfect self-control. Not for the first time, he envied her for it.

This ship has an internal SenseNet managed by an AI core. The tubes that are about to connect to your tubes provide direct access to it. They are a bit uncomfortable but do the job. They usually serve as stopgap solutions in case the wireless network has been corrupted by electronic warfare, he explained, mouth pursed as he thought about what was about to happen.

Direct neural interfaces, as the SenseNet cables were called, dated back to the early days of the technology. When Mayuko Tagami invented the groundbreaking technology for mankind, he did so using thick tubes that could be connected to the brain via a data jack. It was the only way to conceive of SenseNet, as cybernetics was far from being as sophisticated as it is today. But while the cables remained the same in principle, the connections were different. Their ends, which at that moment were rising out of his couch and reaching for him like two tentacles with a mind of their own, worked with nanonic pressure connections. The nanites would work their way through his temples and form thin synaptic filaments that connected to, or hijacked, the natural synapses. He had only witnessed this process once before, and that was during an emergency drill at the academy. It was part of the mandatory pilot training to know how these procedures worked, in the unlikely event that they ever had to resort to them. Of course, at the time, no one seriously thought it could really happen. Among students, this emergency drill was called a "brain screw" because it felt like someone was sticking two screwdrivers into your brain. While it was quick, it was nonetheless uncomfortable, especially when you logged out again. Jeremy would never forget the pounding headache that plagued him for days afterward.

As the cables touched his temples, they felt cold, then suddenly as hot as a red-hot iron. He didn't cry out as the stinging began but clenched his teeth so hard together that they gnashed. Then suddenly he found himself on the virtual bridge.

It was circular and about 98.4 square feet in diameter, with a marble floor and complete glazing covering the outer walls.

Through the windows he could see the dark hangar and the ten soldiers crouched in front of the east wall with their rifles pointed at the sparks coming from a plasma cutter. Alpha's men were almost through, judging by the glowing outline on the composite, they had nearly cut out a piece about the size of a door.

"Damn it," he cursed, feeling an urgent restlessness rising within him. "We're not going to make it!"

He looked around for Omega, who was sitting across from him on the small pedestal in the center. He had a small console with an old-fashioned flat screen in front of him and seemed to be making frantic inputs. Unlike aboard the *WizKid* or any other ship he had served on, they sat with their backs to the windows and looked at each other.

"Yes, we will," Omega replied, looking up, before his virtual chair began to vibrate briefly. It became extremely bright on the bridge.

"What was that?" Jeremy looked over his shoulder and out through the windows. The image had changed: they were hovering over a huge lake of lava. In the distance, a few mountain peaks poked out of the glowing ocean, as black as coal.

"Are we...?"

"A hyperspace jump, yes." Omega nodded. "If Alpha's men are astute and take a radiation reading, they will know that someone has entered subspace, but they will not have the equipment needed to detect the exact signature. So our secret should be safe."

"But..." Jeremy glanced at the lava again. "You've jumped to Bismarck, haven't you? Surely Alpha can immediately detect us here!"

"That is incorrect," Omega replied. "I have learned through Union communications that it has withdrawn its ships. It appears that it has withdrawn all of its units from the system. As yet there is no final confirmation, but it certainly looks like it. To be safe, I jumped to Bismarck, since the atmosphere is already engulfed in a thick cloud of ash, through which only probes could detect us anyway."

"Clever," Jeremy returned appreciatively. "But I'm afraid we've condemned our people to death down there, and we can't do that."

"It makes more sense than condemning the entire human race to death."

"Wait!" Jeremy roared. "Let's jump back now!"

"The risk is too great," Omega insisted.

"Hey! No way in hell! We'll give them a few minutes to sort out the situation and then we'll jump back to collect our people. Pascal and Spark will be fine."

"We've lost contact with them. According to my calculations, a land-based railgun was fired outside. Their probability of survival is between 5 and 18 percent, depending on their position at impact. We were lucky that the blast wave only dented the hangar walls and didn't rip them apart," Omega explained, shaking his head. His eyes looked sad, but his mouth had taken on a determined expression.

"If anyone can make it, Pascal can! He's a tough dog and even survived an orbital ring breaking apart. He ran through the Battle of New Rome and survived, not to mention taking a flight in an escape capsule that couldn't fly," Jeremy said, clenching his hands into fists. "Do you know why? Because his friends believed in him and came to his aid, just like he came to his friends' aid when they needed him!"

"Chances are—"

"I'm not interested in chances!" His voice was quivering now, but he didn't care. "I care about my friends and what's right. Jump back now and pick them up!"

CHAPTER 15
PASCAL

Colony moon DeGaulle, Archimedes system, 2334

THE TINY TUNGSTEN bullets crashed into the shoulder of Pascal's servo armor, knocking him to the ground. It felt as if a horse had kicked him as his back crashed onto the cracked asphalt and his lungs were painfully compressed. Panting, he struggled to catch his breath while lying on the ground, firing blindly in the direction of the shooter.

"Sp..." He tried to call out to Spark, but he couldn't get a coherent word past his lips as his windpipe was busy gasping for air. "Spa... ver..."

Somewhere beside him, bullets slammed into the asphalt, sending clouds of tiny splinters into the air. Pebbles and dust rained down on his face along with a bang. Then again, and again. The ground vibrated like there was an earthquake and then suddenly it was over again.

"Dammit," he cursed as his lungs opened up a bit again. They still felt like they were clogged with industrial glue, but at least he could breathe—albeit like a fish out of water. With difficulty, he rolled to the side, hoping to escape the hail of bullets.

His head banged painfully against an obstacle, but the adrenaline in his blood boiled, helping him block out anything that didn't directly threaten his survival.

Like a machine, he jumped to his feet at the end of the roll, continuing to fire roughly in the direction of the shooter. A quick sweeping glance showed him that the one who had hit him was changing position to avoid putting any more strain on his wounded leg. His helmet visor was pointed to the ground for an instant, and Pascal seized the opportunity. He brought the long HV rifle to bear, waited a split second for the target assist in his sights to flash red, and then, as he exhaled, pulled the trigger. A volley of fire came out of the barrel and pierced the Earthman's helmet as if it were papier-mâché. It happened at the exact moment the enemy soldier raised his eyes and the bulletproof glass of his visor shattered in a rain of splinters and blood. His head was jerked back hard and his body followed.

Pascal had no time to be relieved by this small triumph, because at that very moment he saw the soldier with the plasma cutter kick a square piece of the hangar wall inward amid a hail of bullets. Before the composite even touched the ground, Alpha's minion was hurled inside the hangar as a storm of bullets literally ripped through him from behind. He twitched like an out-of-control puppet and fell, but it was too late. Their secret was out and Alpha knew.

"Damn it!" he cursed aloud.

Okay, Pascal, now what? he thought feverishly, breathing in and out as deeply as he could to keep from panicking. *One step at a time, like you were taught. First, damage control.*

He finally decided to pay attention to the flashing red warning messages in his helmet display and took note of his body condition: he had taken twenty-four hits, but only one had penetrated the armor at the shoulder. Fortunately, it was a graze that had shredded the left *teres minor muscle*. The suit's medical system readout showed him graphically, by highlighting a strand of muscle in red, where that particular body part was located. An auto injector located above his spinal cord had already administered a cocktail of painkillers, anti-inflammatories, and a broad-spectrum antibiotic. Nanites and platelets from his medical supply were taking care of closing the wound.

All right, I'm not dying and have been reasonably lucky, he concluded. *Next item: after personal safety is securing the team members.*

He turned to see Spark and a handful of their allied soldiers leaping over the tanks and firing into the open area between them. Alpha's warriors fought back with rattling automatic fire, but it had already turned into hand-to-hand combat. To Pascal, the entire scene looked as if a horde of Locusts were hopping down on a few ponderous beetles. The combatants on both sides fired incessantly, even as long blades snapped from their forearms and sliced through the air, flashing. Shrapnel and ricochets shrouded them in a storm of destruction, and even Pascal, who was standing a dozen yards away, was hit. Instinctively, he jerked his free hand up to shield his unprotected face.

Then he ran back a few steps to his helmet and put it back on his head. Immediately the noise of battle subsided. He felt uncomfortable and isolated, as if in one fell swoop he had less control over his actions and was going to miss something vital.

Soldiers wearing the black of DeGaulle's ground troops poured out of the hole in the hangar wall and began unceremoniously firing well-aimed shots into the crowd. More and more of Alpha's men went down, but some were so closely involved in the melee that it was difficult to get a clear shot. Pascal searched frantically for Spark, and as he was about to start running, he saw the giant leap out from behind one of the tanks and strike an Earthling who was similar in size and had exchanged his rifle for two forearm switchblades. The two giants in their servo armor fought with surprising agility and fluidity, their blades sending sparks flying. Suddenly, a second of Alpha's men appeared behind his friend. He must have lost his helmet, because Pascal could make out a young face with a three-day beard and black curls. But he also recognized the rifle, which he raised to shoot Spark in the back.

Without thinking, Pascal dropped his rifle and pulled his pistol from his thigh holster with a practiced movement. Faster than he could inhale, he had raised the gun and pulled the trigger. The projectile slammed directly into the unprotected temple of the black-haired man who had wanted to kill his friend. His head jerked to the side and even as he slid to the ground, Spark rammed his sword through his opponent's neck. The projectile slammed directly into the unprotected temple of the black-haired man who had wanted to kill his friend. His head jerked to the side and even as he slid to the ground, Spark rammed his sword through his opponent's neck. The monofilament steel sliced through to the hilt thanks to his servo-assisted muscle, sending a cloud of red splattering against the tank behind him. The moment the soldier's back hit the asphalt, his body flipped over and he landed face down. He then turned his head and looked directly at Pascal, who was holstering his pistol again.

In a flash, all of Alpha's men were killed. DeGaulle's men were not squeamish, administering headshots to anyone still moving, before tending to their own wounded.

Spark, meanwhile, approached Pascal with a measured stride and stopping in front of him, put a hand on his shoulder. His lips moved behind the blue visor, but he couldn't hear anything.

"Wait," he muttered, yanking his helmet off his head.

"Are you all right?" asked Spark through booming suit

speakers, and then he, too, opened his seal to breathe fresh air. His stubbly bald head was sweaty.

"Yeah. Just a minor hit in the shoulder. How are you doing?"

"Good, since you saved my ass back there. With that thing." The giant Bismarcker pointed to the pistol in Pascal's thigh holster. "Respect."

"I can handle that. These huge rifles, not so much."

"I'm mighty glad about that, cowboy." Spark laughed lightheartedly, as if they were currently standing in a fairground and not in the midst of a battlefield's bullets and blood.

"Mission's over," Pascal replied tonelessly, having to clear his throat several times. *Now what? Now what?*

"Nah," the giant went on.

"What do you mean 'nah'?"

"It's not over. They jumped before Alpha's guys could see anything in there." Spark pointed to the welded opening in the hangar wall that loomed before them like a cliff.

"How do you know that? Are you sure?" asked Pascal incredulously.

Instead of answering, the Bismarcker tapped the arm display on his left arm with the right index finger of his cyber arm, which hung below the weapon attachment.

Pascal frowned and looked down at his own computer. A display that went from green to yellow to red from bottom to top was calmly blinking away. Above it was written Radiation Warning and below that Sievert as the unit of measurement.

"Oh," he said. "My suit says I'm contaminated. Nine hundred millisieverts."

"Exactly. They jumped. Besides, the soldiers who came through the hole said the ship was gone. Is your radio on the fritz?" asked Spark, tapping his right ear, which was shining bright red.

"Yes. The railgun."

"Ah, I see. Those maniacs! I think they killed a third of their own men with it."

"Nine hundred millisieverts. Is that bad?" Pascal eyed the digital readout, which showed a small needle at the end of the yellow range, just touching the red.

"Eventually we'll piss some blood and get a catheter shoved in, just like a cannula. They'll then pump us full of drugs and we'll have to swallow cancer drugs for the rest of our lives. At least that's roughly what the brief overview in my helmet display said," Spark explained, smiling lightheartedly. "You didn't really think there was going to be a house with a white picket fence and laughing kids for us after the shit we're about to pull, did you?"

"Not really," Pascal admitted.

"See. No, no. We do it so others can pull off the cliché stuff. Maybe they'll sing a little song about us someday for it."

Pascal didn't answer and looked at the radiation reading on his arm display one last time as the needle suddenly shot up well into the red zone. The ground vibrated briefly and something flickered brightly somewhere in the periphery of his vision.

"Oh," Spark blurted, but he wasn't looking at his own display but at the hangar. "They've jumped back. *Now* we're definitely getting a catheter shoved up our dicks!"

"Terrific," Pascal grumbled, avoiding picturing it. Rather than thinking about catheters, he was thinking about the fact that their mission hadn't failed yet, and Jeremy hadn't left without them.

"Do you think there's a chance we could fool Alpha with this?" asked Spark, suddenly not sounding as terse as before but genuinely concerned. He scratched his bulky chin and looked indecisively at the opening in the hangar through which the surviving soldiers were bringing their wounded comrades.

"Yeah, I think so. If its people were really fast, they may have reported a radiation surge in the empty hangar that it will link to, among other things, a hyperspace jump. But of everything it can deduce, a rogue unit taking off in a hidden spaceship is still the most likely. While the probability that one of their hijacked spaceships should be hidden here should not show up on its list, or at least very far down. After all, according to Omega, the transponder code is still intact and not reported missing," Pascal explained as they followed behind the soldiers and entered the dark hangar. The hum of the fusion engines roared in his ears, and the few navigation lights of the war sphere above them provided a little light in the otherwise dark interior.

"I hope you're right," Spark grumbled, frowning. "Damn huge thing, and ugly as hell. Looks like a giant wrecking ball with colorful gizmos on it. Only a fucking numerical code could come up with something that unaesthetic."

"I don't know anyone who can painlessly combine words like *ugly* and *unaesthetic* into a sentence," Pascal returned, shaking his head with a smile.

"I like a good Bismarck parlor. That is not something Alpha can claim about itself."

"Well, actually it could, since Moreau came from Bismarck and he created the AI," Pascal objected as they joined the queue in front of the ladder that led inside the ship.

"Shit no!" Spark dismissively waved it off. "Some eggheads from his Human Corporation did it. He may have thrown a few ideas into the ring, sure, but he spent too much time on talk shows to really work hard on anything."

"You might be right about that. He was working pretty hard on his conspiracy."

"Such a dumbass. Saw in the Gaia field how your friend sacrificed herself so you guys could take him down. I'm really sorry, man. I have a lot of respect for WizKid. That was her name, right?"

"Yeah," Pascal breathed, fighting the rising lump in his throat. *My God, when did I get so emotional*? Of course, he knew exactly when. After WizKid had died for them and shown him what he had become. A cold-hearted misanthrope.

"Sorry, I didn't mean to open up old wounds." Spark raised his hands, looking genuinely sad.

"It's all right," Pascal hastened to say, exhaling slowly. "I haven't spoken about it yet, although my emotions were shared in the Gaia field. It did me a lot of good. I wasn't someone who shared his feelings easily before, let alone worked through them. On the contrary, I preferred not to talk about anything, except maybe my work."

"Ran away from yourself," the giant conjectured, nodding in understanding. Pascal glanced sideways at him, puzzled, but the soldier was focused on the diminishing line in front of the ladder.

"You never cease to surprise me."

"No," Spark went on. "I've been through the same shit. Booya and I were very close, to name the most recent event to screw me up. Eventually, you get used to running away from yourself. Inwardly, you are always on the move trying to escape the shadow on the wall, which is, of course, impossible. You can only escape your own shadow if the light comes from in front of you, and for that you have to turn towards the light, keh?"

"I never thought of it that way before. It's a good metaphor," Pascal agreed.

"I never got used to that crap, and I think that's a good thing. I just kept going and focused on the light in front of me: my new comrades, like you, the memory of Bismarck, the survival of our species and stuff like that. There's always some light."

"That seems like a good strategy to me. After WizKid's death, I made a similar decision." Pascal thought about the letter he had written to Thandis. Actually, of course, he had written it for himself, but in the end it amounted to the same thing. Now the letter was burnt, along with the whole colony, but that didn't sadden him. He had gotten something off his chest that no longer weighed on him, and that was what mattered. Much more tragic were the lives lost on the surface that no letter or decision could bring back and for that he would destroy Alpha. He didn't waste a thought on possibly returning. For him, there was no future after Alpha's extermination because he wasn't thinking that far ahead. He simply wasn't interested in anything else. If he could prevent his friends from losing their lives on the mission that would be a wonderful gift for which he would give everything. But for himself, whatever happened in the Sol system, was the end of the line. He knew it without a doubt. This was the moment that Thandis had traded her life for his, and he would not let her down. He couldn't let her down. Not her, and not WizKid either, who had basically done the same thing. The burden of her leap of faith was heavy, but he intended to turn it into a singular focus for the benefit of all.

"Are you okay?" asked Spark suddenly, and Pascal threw the thoughts off like an annoying cloak. He hadn't even realized they were already standing in front of the ladder. "Didn't mean to upset you like that."

"It's all right. I was just remembering who I have to thank for being here to work on the survival of our species."

"It's good to know what you're fighting for," Spark replied, climbing the ladder. Pascal followed him in his bulky armor, grateful for the servo assistance that made each step a breeze.

With his injured shoulder, he wouldn't have gotten far otherwise, even with painkillers.

They removed their armor in the round room with the scores of lockers on the wall. For such a complex piece of equipment, it was surprisingly easy. A few instructions to the intelligent suit system followed by pressing two buttons to prevent a compromised operating system from doing what it wanted—that was all. Finally, like Spark and about two dozen other soldiers, who remained silent and barely spoke to each other, he stowed all his gear in a locker labeled Meyers. The wounded were already being taken to the infirmary via the elevators—at least, that's where he figured they were being taken. All of them would have to face that walk to rid their bodies of radiation, if that was even possible. But first things first. Considering his plan was to die in the Sol system anyway due to extreme radiation from the sun going supernova, he probably didn't need to worry about catheters.

Half an hour later, he was lying on an acceleration couch next to Jeremy with a catheter in his penis and two cannulas in the crooks of his arms, waiting for the medical treatment machine to be set up. The machine looked like a spider lying on its back with no way to get to its feet, juggling all sorts of IV bags and tubes. Pascal was not a fan of needles, but pretty much any queasy sensation faded in the face of the still aching catheter in his urethra. The medication made him feel calm, and by all rights he shouldn't have felt anything, but he guessed his thoughts would keep the aching sensation in the center of his body alive for a long time to come.

Once the medical bot had attached itself to his couch and was secured, he requested confirmation that everything was set up correctly. Pascal then pressed the green button on the small touch screen with a friendly face on it, and closed his eyes. Two cables emerged from the headboard and shot toward his temples. He let out a startled squeak, and then suddenly found himself on the virtual bridge of the ship. He sat in front of a small console with a large screen in a circle with Omega, the Matriarch, and Jeremy. Further behind them was a larger circle of seamless windows revealing the interior of the hangar.

"This looks different," he noted.

"Hey, buddy," Jeremy greeted him, nodding. Relief filled his expression.

"You all right?"

"Yeah," the young captain replied, looking at Omega, who seemed to be busy with his console, but looked up now and narrowed his eyes in confusion.

"Oh," he went on. "I had suggested we not return because I didn't want to risk the mission. That probably wasn't very... human of me. My apologies."

"It's all right," Pascal returned, shaking his head. "I guess we'll just have to get used to making less human and more logical decisions from now on if we are going to get rid of Alpha."

"Maybe," Omega agreed, looking off into space for a moment. "But we shouldn't reach that point too soon. I pride myself on my humanity, and I shouldn't discard it so easily. The excess data in my brain is... exhausting, and it's changing me. I'm already trying to limit my neurons' activity and outsource a lot to the external memory cluster at the back of my head. However, I'm afraid that soon I won't be in a position to do that."

"Is it dangerous? Your change, I mean?"

"I don't know. It is possible that I will lose my social skills."

"Does that mean you're going to become a... *robot*?" Jeremy asked, frowning apprehensively.

Pascal didn't need to ask to know that instead of robot, he had meant to say *Alpha*.

"I don't think so. My mostly organic components will not allow that," Omega explained calmly, and if he had understood what Jeremy had really meant to say, he didn't let on. "Emotions occur as the body's reaction to thoughts. Which seems to be the law of nature for thinking organic life, including me, regardless of where my life comes from. Alpha and any other lesser AI are not subject to this law of nature and that is the difference between us that will never be bridged. I assumed when there was a chance we wouldn't jump back that you might not have survived the skirmish outside the hangar, and that caused me grief."

"Mhm," Pascal uttered in surprise. He still had a hard time perceiving the former AI now human as a sentient being. Its intelligence and knowledge just seemed larger than life to him.

"You must not forget that I know more about you than your parents do," Omega continued, and it was clear that he meant the constant exchanges over the Gaia field. On Bismarck at the latest, there had been no secrets, and that was true for both parties. It was easy to forget that nothing remained hidden in the telepathic network.

"What do we do now?" asked Pascal finally, to change the subject.

"We'd best jump back to Bismarck first to hash out our exact plan," Jeremy suggested, casting a questioning glance at Omega. Officially, Jeremy was the pilot and captain for this operation and Pascal was in charge when it came to strategic decisions along with the ground team that would steal the data storage devices from Earth. However, any decisions they made had to be cleared with the Matriarch. While she didn't have a veto since it was about humanity's home system, their alliance was still fragile and ultimately there was no way around it. The Locusts had insisted on it, just as they had insisted that the Neuromorph was not in command. Nevertheless, everyone present knew that none of them could hold a candle to the superintelligence and that nothing would be done without first consulting him.

Omega found Jeremy's gaze and nodded barely perceptibly. The jump sent a short vibration through the virtual environment, after which the glowing lava of Bismarck could be seen outside the windows.

CHAPTER 16
JEREMY

Colony moon Bismarck, Archimedes system, 2334

To discuss their plan, they felt the need to trade the virtual bridge for a virtual room that highlighted the magnitude of their endeavor. They stood on a reflective surface in the middle of infinite space. Around them floated distant galaxies in the endless void of the universe and beneath their feet was the Milky Way.

Omega, the Matriarch, Pascal, Spark, and Stadler, the technician he had briefly met in the elevator, were attending and had gathered around a holographic representation of the Sol system. The sun, which had made life possible on Earth, their home planet, for millions of years, occupied the central point above their heads. Mercury, Venus, Earth, and Mars looked downright tiny by comparison, followed by the asteroid belt which looked like a broken life preserver. Next came the intimidating silhouette of the storm-ridden Jupiter, Saturn with its rings, Uranus, and finally the deep blue of Neptune. As for the Kuiper Belt, it was nothing more than a distant glint.

"Thank you all for being here," Pascal began, nodding to

each in turn. "By that I don't mean this place here, but your participation in the mission. Our chances of survival are low and each of you have known this from the beginning. If anyone is getting cold feet, there is still time to get out."

"Into the lava? No thanks, cop," Spark boomed, and the tension amongst the group broke free in the form of subdued laughter.

Pascal smiled warmly at the soldier, who wore a plain black uniform with sequins in the virtual environment.

"Seriously, if any of you, or your people, have changed your minds, I respect that. We'll jump back and drop them off. We need clear focus to do what we're trying to do here. This may sound cold, but we can't afford to waste thoughts on survival. Our entire focus must be on the survival of our species, and that means stealing the data containing the memories of those trapped in the capsules!" the inspector continued sternly, his already slightly slit eyes narrowing even more as he eyed them one by one. No one objected, so he finally nodded.

"Good, then I suggest Omega provide us with a briefing on the data he's been able to collect. We could all, I think, use a quick overview of exactly what's going on." Pascal turned to Omega, who, dressed in an unadorned black one-piece with a red flower on his chest, had been listening silently.

"Good. Thank you," he said, and Jeremy made a mental note to mention the flower to the being in Moreau's body when he had a chance.

"The data core from the ship I captured revealed some interesting details about Alpha's infrastructure and command hierarchy. Each core has an override file secured by multiple firewalls as well as three hundred and sixty dimensional encryption, which contains a copy of Alpha's basic program code. You could say it is a kind of simple copy of itself. This override file has override codes for all the systems Alpha controls. The soldiers I found on board are all currently in cryochambers in the cargo hold. I made copies of their NeuroSmarts and discovered that each of them carries a corresponding file in their CPU as well."

"So Alpha has people working for it, but puts a collar on them in the form of its own personality?" asked Jeremy.

"Something like that. Basically, its allies are self-governing until they do something that causes the override file to activate and take control. Then they are nothing more than mindless puppets under the control of its code," Omega explained, interjecting a holographic representation of one of the soldiers between them. It looked like a three-dimensional version of a drawing in an encyclopedia. All that was missing were the small lines with the technical terms for the various body parts, and then the impression would be complete.

"That means we have to behave according to its wishes so that we don't cause a reaction from the override file when we're in the Sol system?" asked Pascal, chewing his lower lip.

"That is correct."

"And how do we know what we're allowed to do without triggering the zombie file?" inquired Spark in his deep growl.

"That's the next point I'd like to address," Omega announced, nodding gratefully to the giant. The soldier's 3D model changed until only his head was visible. It became transparent and the brain became visible and within it a chip about the size of a finger began to flash red. "I was able to overcome the security mechanisms and read the entire core without it self-destructing. Needless to say, it was a very difficult process and went wrong twice before it worked on the third one. Alpha has become smarter since I broke away from its algorithm, but also easier to assess. Whereas I remain incomprehensible to it, its development and actions are driven purely by logic and calculations about causal relationships. Its intelligence is as frightening as the strict limits of its nature as a purely calculating being. We must exploit these weaknesses and focus on what we have over it."

"Humanity," Stadler said, her high-pitched voice drawing all eyes to her. Clearly she hadn't expected everyone's attention, and she squeaked like a bird before putting both hands over her mouth and remained silent.

"Exactly," Omega confirmed after a moment and switched back to the view of the Sol system. The three-dimensional image switched to Earth, that beautiful blue planet with its endless bands of clouds drifting like wispy cotton over the continents. The mega-cities on the human homeland were so massive that they were visible to the naked eye from orbit. Two orbital rings appeared, then defense platforms and shipyards so numerous Jeremy lost count.

"Earth is guarded by eight hundred orbital defenses, two extremely heavily fortified orbital rings, and about five thousand cruisers that are permanently present. In addition, there are about one hundred hangars for Tiger drones, which are very similar to the Union Predators. Each ship is equipped with a unique set of transponder codes that are valid for one week after which they are replaced. The replacement is automatically done by Alpha itself," Omega explained as the hologram above their heads changed. Their spaceship appeared. A perfect sphere in the middle of a starless universe. "The last update was yesterday before the battle. That means we have six days left in which our codes are valid. That is our window of opportunity."

"That's where we have to land, right?" asked Pascal. Jeremy noticed that his black hair looked a bit curlier in the virtual environment than in reality. *I wonder if he deliberately chose that.*

"Yes, that's right," Omega confirmed, raising a hand before the inspector could continue. "And our spaceship is not designed for atmospheric flight."

"Can't we just make a hyperspace jump directly to the surface and the complex we need to enter?" interjected Jeremy. While he didn't think it was possible, he had often seen superiors think in such complicated ways that they overlooked the most obvious. Since then, he always felt it worthwhile to point out the most obvious way.

"I'm afraid it's not possible. The entire system is secured by hyperspace containment fields that accept its own ships according to their transponder codes, but they also function as a security system that records and reports any hyperspace activity in real time. If we jump, Alpha will be notified, and if the jump isn't planned, we'll be noticed immediately." Omega pursed his lips apologetically, but Jeremy just shrugged and smiled an I-just-wanted-to-mention-it smile.

"Then how are we supposed to get down there?" growled Spark, extending one of his plate-sized hands toward the hologram until it passed through the Indian Ocean, scattering light in all directions.

"Apparently we not only have to pretend that the ship is real, but we have to pretend that we're real too," the Matriarch stated, and the sudden sound of her purring voice emanating from the translator silenced them all.

"That is correct," Omega nodded, changing the view once again. Earth grew slightly smaller until Mars was also visible as a small red sphere the size of a tennis ball. An elongated chain of spaceships stretched between it and Earth with ample spacing. "These are transport ships carrying prisoners collected from a temporary storage facility on Mars to Earth. There, according to the instructions in the core of our ship, they are taken to Europa for *further processing*. According to the instructions, anyway."

"Processing?" Jeremy raised a brow in alarm. He instantly knew he wasn't going to like the answer.

"It's not clear from the data. My guess is that the prisoners are also put into capsules, or interrogated and then murdered," Omega voiced what Jeremy already feared.

"Well, that sucks and is another good reason to blow up that lousy hunk of a system," Spark opined. "But what does that have to do with what the Locust leader just told us?"

"We have the option of pretending to be prisoners, or pretending to be the crew that captured the prisoners," Omega replied, and silence fell as those present understood the significance of his words.

"Some of us get to play soldiers while the others are prisoners being led to the slaughter." Pascal sighed heavily, his sigh could mean anything from resignation to understanding to exhaustion. He was, as always, difficult for Jeremy to read.

"That is correct. I'm going to remove the NeuroSmarts from the crew on ice using the reserves of medical nanites and implant them into half of our crew. They won't be compatible because they don't have a bio sheath grown for our DNA, but with drugs to reduce rejection, it will work for a few days. But we do not have enough for everyone. It's inconvenient, but at the same time it gives us a good cover," the Neuromorph said before Pascal spoke again.

"We jump to Mars, report that we successfully captured a Union ship, join the transport to Earth, and land in Europa with our prisoners. On the way and once we are on the ground, we figure out how to proceed. Alpha's data center is in Prague, right?"

"That is correct as well. I don't think the ships have acceleration couches for all the prisoners, so they will be traveling at a low acceleration of 2, 3g at most. If I am correct, the flight to Earth will take two days. That gives us enough time to transplant the NeuroSmarts." Omega pointed to the long strip of spacecraft between Mars and Earth. "The prison is located near

Vienna. Which means that, relatively speaking, the data center is not far from our destination." Omega now called up a topographic map that spread out between them like a table. The eastern foothills of the Alps reached to the edge of Vienna, and after a lot of forest and larger elevations, Prague appeared to the north. The two metropolises were not as large as some of the other European megacities, such as the Rhine-Ruhr megaplex, Paris, London, or Moscow. But they still sprawled deep into the countryside that had been ravaged by centuries of pollution, to the point that they almost looked like immediate neighbors.

Prague began to flash green.

"Getting to Prague is not very difficult, because there is a training and rehabilitation center there, which is closer to Vienna than any others in Europe. The problem is that we cannot take the prisoners with us. They would have to stay in prison in Vienna, because there is no way to justify their transfer to Prague," the Neuromorph continued, and his voice had become a little softer, possibly apologetic.

"We can't do that," Jeremy said firmly, swallowing against the dryness in his throat. "That would mean abandoning half of those who were brave enough to accompany us on this suicide mission. They'll be imprisoned there and tortured, probably killed. We can't do that to them."

It was Pascal, not Omega, who answered him. "It is, as you say, a suicide mission. We still have time to ditch those who are not willing to make the ultimate sacrifice. Once we get to the Sol system, it will be too late for that. Chances are it won't end well for any of us. Whether as prisoners, or being caught as infiltrators, trouble will ensue, our plan may go to hell, and blood will flow—no one here doubts that, do they? From now on, we can't afford to consider personal fates, but must consider ourselves and our companions as resources. Resources to be used in order to get where we're going."

"That's inhuman! That's not how you think, Pascal!" objected Jeremy in frustration.

"Yes, I do think that way, precisely because it's human. We are trying to save far more people than can fit in this ship. To risk the lives of everyone and the survival of our species over the fate of individuals, *that* would be inhumane. From now on, only the goal counts," the inspector insisted. His eyes shone and his entire expression betrayed sadness, but his gaze remained determined and resolute.

"He is right," agreed the Matriarch. "I am not a member of your species, but our kind has a saying: *only death makes life worth living*. With us, that means that a death with a purpose gives life greatness and meaning. Your species' focus is always only on one's personal future. *What will happen to me afterwards?* But the question should be: *what will happen to my species after this?* Is it that much more significant and great to die happily and contently of old age in a den among trees than to die violently in a prison? No, it isn't. It is *more pleasant*, but not *more significant*. No one will be grateful to you for taking such good care of yourselves and your future. You will have lived a pleasant life. So what? In this way, you can use your life as a tool for everyone, as a meaningful life form in the eternal ups and downs of the cosmos. I will voluntarily join the group of prisoners. If you should succeed in rescuing me on the way back, I would certainly be grateful. If not, I may suffer in captivity, but die satisfied in the knowledge that I have made an alliance between our species possible."

The Matriarch's words faded away yet hovered over them like a heavy cloud that could not be dispelled. Jeremy felt something tighten in his stomach. At first he thought it was the fear that had been with him since the fall of Bismarck. The fear that he had become hardened and inhuman. Perhaps it was this fear that had triggered his strong aversion to the plan with the prisoners—he did not know. But it was not this feeling that made his insides churn, but the wisdom in the Locust's words that stirred him. She was right and had quoted something totally human to them, namely self-sacrifice and love of one's neighbor. At the same time, she had wiped something absolutely human from their minds, namely selfishness, fear, and a refusal to accept a plan that didn't mean a perfect outcome for everyone.

"Okay, now that the alien has instilled some humanity in us," Spark broke the silence. "We can get to work on taking out Alpha. I've already spoken to the guys from DeGaulle while you've been staring holes into the virtual air. None of them want to back down, each of them volunteered to be prisoners as well. The whole process took less than two seconds over the Gaia field."

Jeremy stared at Spark for a moment, as did everyone else, suddenly feeling bad and moved at the same time.

"Now stop acting so concerned." The tall soldier snorted. "We have a job to do and should get going instead of wallowing in despair. I lost my entire platoon on the orbital ring and some damn good friends. I'm not going to sully their memory by twiddling my thumbs out here, keh?"

"Sometimes it takes a rock to teach water its liquid," Pascal quoted and began to smile. "Thank you, Spark. Omega? What do you suggest?"

"Many issues will only become apparent when I gain access to more advanced databases. That should be the case in the Sol system, when I can infiltrate and evaluate the systems on other ships. If there are clones of all of us, which I assume to be the case at least with Jeremy, Pascal, and me, we won't have a problem with facial recognition software. Otherwise, we have a problem. Also, I need to figure out what roles our clones are being used in, if there really are any on active duty." Omega sounded confident, and Jeremy sincerely hoped that it wasn't just a calculated strategy. "After that, I need to steal as much data as possible in order to find out even more about the data vault where Alpha stores the memories of the people in the capsules. Once we're on site, I need to get into the system immediately, and wrestle Alpha for control. I am confident that I can overpower it, but since it is its terrain, we must be prepared for anything. What I anticipate, however, is that my confrontation with it will give you a window of opportunity to steal the data and, optimally, disappear again."

"Speaking of disappearing," Jeremy commented, "do you have any ideas on how to do that?"

"Yes. There are three launch pads for suborbital aircraft near the data center and a military base that has a large arsenal of hyperspace missiles."

"Wait a minute," Pascal interjected. "How is that going to help us get out of there?"

"There are radiation suits for the cleaning staff of the suborbital shuttles, which in turn will help those who want to get off Earth avoid dying from the radiation of a hyperspace jump," Omega explained, pointing to Jeremy. "He's already made a jump in a hyperspace rocket and survived it."

"Wait a minute!" protested Jeremy. "That was anything but pleasant, and besides, it didn't work. Both the rocket and our capsule shattered on ejection, and we only had a few weeks to live!"

"But you're still alive," Omega pointed out calmly, clasping his hands in front of his abdomen like a professor patiently letting his students' questions wash over him.

"Yes, but..."

"With the radiation suits, the dose of radiation will be much less than with your improvised jump. I have studied all the data I could find on the Union network about the incident and allowed myself to adjust Walter Bonjarewski's procedure to...

refine it. It will work. There is an 88 percent probability that intensive medical care will still be needed, but that is acceptable. The best part of this solution, though, is that the jump can be made right from the complex into the Archimedes system."

"Is that even possible? Our normal hyperspace rockets have nowhere near enough power for such a jump," Jeremy countered, trying not to think about the last time they had jumped in one of those things. The idea of having to overcome not just three astronomical units this time, but hundreds, made him shiver. The fact that the duration of the jump would not be significantly longer made no difference to him.

"I have taken the liberty of fabricating a portable antimatter reactor in preparation for our plan, and it is currently in the cargo bay," Omega replied, raising his arms placatingly as unease set in. "It's secured by a magnetic containment chamber that's just as secure as the *WizKid*'s reactors, which you relied on."

"One short circuit and we're screwed!" someone shouted, and Jeremy surmised it was Spark. Then everyone was talking at once.

"Antimatter? On Earth? All the people there are..."

"We mustn't! After all, Trafalgar showed..."

"Our plan?"

"Who's going to wear them? Alpha will notice and..."

"One random hit and the whole Earth..."

Jeremy sensed that this discussion had not yet concluded. At the same time, he sensed that they were unlikely to come up with a better option than a plan concocted by a far more intelligent being than they all were. Sighing, he let the discussion wash over him but paid no attention to individual words or statements, instead looking at the faces of his old and new companions. The only question that remained was: how long would it take them to accept that they were going to follow Omega's proposal in the end anyway.

"There is one more thing we should do," Jeremy said. "We have the transponder codes for the hyperspace barrier fields that our ship will use to jump to Sol. We should send those to Macella so that the *WizKid* has them."

"They won't be valid for very long after we get there, though," Omega pointed out.

"Still, we should do it. Things might take a little longer over there in the anticipated chaos. It can't hurt."

"Besides, that way we'll have a plan B for data extraction. In case the antimatter madness doesn't work out," Spark interjected. "The *WizKid* can jump into Earth's orbit, retrieve the data by directional beam or something, and then send it back to Archimedes on a prepared hyperspace rocket."

CHAPTER 17
VERONICA

In orbit around DeGaulle, Archimedes system, 2334

VERONICA AWOKE FROM A FITFUL SLEEP. She had dreamt that she and Jeremy were at her grandparents' house on Trafalgar and that the doorbell of their suburban mansion near Cunnington was made of Jell-O. The nameplate on the door had said *Moreau*-X, not *Macella*. They had tried to make a roulette table out of fondue sticks in the living room but realized that Omega had forgotten to paint them black and red. Later, they had decided to play Yahtzee with large foam dice.

Confused, she shook her head and opened her eyes. She stared at herself, lying in her tiny, gimbaled bunk with tangled blond hair. The ceiling's composite was so smooth that her reflection was clearly visible, as were the circles under her eyes. The strange dream faded slowly from her overtired brain, and she glanced at the time on her arm display.

Two hours' sleep, she read off the cold green numbers while rubbing her burning eyes. If she was honest, she felt even more tired than before. In two hours they would meet the Speaker of

Parliament, who was traveling on a ferry to meet the Diplomatic Conclave. Enough time, then, to do some more thinking. She thought about her grandparents, who had only played a minor role in her dream, but a major one in her life so far. After all, Bob and Claire had raised her for the most part, while her parents had gone off to work. Veronica loved all four of them dearly, and that was the problem. The green "make a call" button was still waiting for her on her arm display, and she had desperately wanted to press it now that she had the time. But she hadn't been able to bring herself to do it, and had fallen asleep during her musings. On the one hand, the urge to contact her family and find out how they were doing was almost overwhelming. But on the other hand, she was so afraid of bad news that she didn't dare. She, who had fought against a crazy AI, space monsters, and aliens in the depths of space, was afraid to make a phone call. Her arm display felt as though it was a dangerous object that would do something terrible if she accidentally pressed the call button.

With a swiping motion of her fingers, she closed the call window with the picture of her parents and grandparents that she had taken on Christmas 2331, and it hurt. It hurt because she felt cowardly, and it hurt because she had to go on living not knowing if her loved ones were still alive and well and had survived this new battle.

Trafalgar hadn't fared so badly, she told herself, sighing as she swung her legs off her couch after the nanonic straps had released. Her left foot bumped painfully against a metal rod attached to the suspension system, and she suppressed a curse. Through the ship's consciousness, she glanced at the sensors and the latest news. The shuttle was still a little over two hours away and crawled between the two colony moons like a snail. Due to the fact that they were frantically rather than systematically deploying the barrier fields to every available piece of space, the synchronization of the network was still lagging behind. All the data streams converged in the orbital ring of Europa at fleet headquarters and first had to be coordinated. Therefore, it was not possible for their own ships to make hyperspace jumps at the moment—a fact that annoyed them. But, at the moment, safety came first, and the fleet leadership had understood this and approved her actions after the fact. The last thing she needed at the moment was a bunch of politicians worrying about her career. At this point, anything beyond the immediate future and the survival of her species was not only a grossly negligent waste of time, it was a crime. She would make that fact clear to the government officials when they arrived on her ship.

"On Jeremy's ship," she corrected herself.

With one hand, she checked her injured foot and gave it a quick massage before stepping onto the cold cabin floor. The captain's cabin, as on any warship, was downright tiny compared to spaces which have gravity, and yet, at the same time, far too large for her. Jeremy was absent from all ten square feet, which was now filled with expectations and apprehensions. She walked over to the bathroom, which protruded from the wall next to the door like some sort of oversized blister caused by fire, and had a long shower. The only luxury on board, besides the generous armor, was an extremely large supply of water. Given the fact that the *WizKid* had only been in service for a few days, she even thought it possible that it was fresh water and not recycled body fluids. After a long shower, which she set so hot that her skin turned red, she dried off and squeezed into her parade uniform. She couldn't remember the last time she had worn the royal blue two-piece. The seams were sewn together with gold threads and the medals and rank insignia shone as if freshly polished. Her superiors would probably think she was responsible for the good condition of her uniform, and that was just as well.

At the door, she paused once more, straightened her tight-fitting jacket, and took a deep breath.

The meeting would take place in the hangar. She had put the *WizKid* into orbit so it now revolved around its own longitudinal axis like a chunky cigar. There was so much space between the panels of composite and ceramic elements that the hangar, which was designed to hold a dozen atmospheric shuttles or four corvettes, looked like an oversized, square laundry drum.

The scrap shuttle they had returned in from the surface now hung from one of the external docking bays on the outer hull like a parasite. She had been glad to get it out of her sight after limping back into orbit. To make matters worse, toward the end of her flight, the life support system had given up the ghost because it had made some incorrect calculations. Apparently, the ancient software had overestimated the number of people on board and had supplied far too much oxygen in order to allow the nonexistent extra people to breathe. This error had used up the air reserves way too quickly, and in the end they had only barely made it to the *WizKid* without suffocating.

But they had made it—that was what mattered.

Veronica had thought long and hard about where she would hold the meeting. Since Walter's design had not included a conference room or officers' mess due to its skeleton crew, her only option would have been the regular mess hall: a tiny room with two aluminum tables bolted down and a low ceiling.

Holding the first official meeting between government representatives and the Locusts there was out of the question for her. So Walter had put forward the idea of rotating the *WizKid* and using centrifugal force to generate a comfortable 0.3g. Which was about the preferred speed of the *WizKid.* It was about the same as the preferred gravity on asteroid settlements and naval installations which used artificial rotation. At 0.3g, work was a little easier for colonists from gravity areas, with gravity between 0.8 and 1.2g. Everything was just a little easier.

Everything lost its heaviness—she thought that was an excellent starting point for a first alliance negotiation.

"Looks fancy after all," Walter announced with satisfaction, pointing to the long conference table with its ten armchairs on the former port wall of the hangar. They were standing on the central walkway on the middle level, which ran along the entire wall and normally led to the docking facilities, which were now empty. From their position, they had the ship's interior wall at their backs, so they were closer to the axis of rotation and therefore virtually weightless. For them, it therefore looked as if the conference table was stuck to the wall opposite them, defying the laws of nature. Although it was almost 0g, they could already feel the Coriolis force pulling on their stomachs in a nauseating way. It felt as if she was being continuously pulled to the left by an invisible hand and that direction no longer mattered. Her brain wanted to tell her which way was up and down, but failed to do so, leaving her with a knot in her stomach.

"Yes. I can hardly believe your nano replicators managed to do it all so quickly," she remarked, nodding appreciatively.

"Oh, it's not like the table is made of mahogany. We have plenty of steel and ceramics available since our mammoths have been bringing in pieces of debris and filling up the mass converters," Walter explained. "I haven't been able to solve the food problem, though." He pointed to a small plastic box at his feet that contained fifty bags of drinking water. There were no glasses or dishes on board that might fly around and scatter liquids in zero gravity. Only bags with sealable suction devices.

"Should be an amusing sight, seeing all those fine looking penguins sitting there sipping from bags," the engineer gloated, the smile of his wide mouth almost reaching his reddened eyes. No one had slept well in the last few hours.

Or slept at all.

"I just hope they have enough to absorb at the sight of the Locusts that they won't care about missing wine glasses and cotton napkins," she replied gravely, glancing down at her watch. Another fifteen minutes before the ferry was due to dock.

"It'll be fine, Macella. I'll take care of the rest." Walter looked at his arm display and nodded. "Felicity is on her way with our alien friends now. I think you can go ahead and make your way to the airlock."

"Yes." She sighed, placing a hand on the barrel-chested Bismarcker's shoulder. "Thanks for your help. I'll see you in a bit."

Walter saluted carelessly and grabbed the crate so he could float to the ladder. Veronica turned to the airlock behind her and made her way to the central connecting corridor, from there she took the elevator to the port docking bays. It took her less than five minutes before she was standing in front of the inner door of the wide airlock, which looked like an oversized target with all sorts of warning symbols and inscriptions in English, German, and French. She had considered having Walter and Felicity accompany her to meet the politicians, as was proper in the Navy. But since they couldn't muster a guard of honor with only three people on board anyway, that would seem odd to them. Besides, Walter had to make final preparations and Felicity had to escort the Diplomatic Conclave to the hangar. So she had decided to go alone to meet the dignitaries. Perhaps that would immediately impress upon them the seriousness of the situation; after all, the Navy was currently short on personnel in just about every area. Jeremy certainly would have done it this way.

Her arm display alerted her with an intrusive ringtone that the passenger ferry, escorted by two corvettes, had begun their docking maneuver and would begin depressurization in about a minute. Even in 2334, connecting two airlocks was still a delicate matter that required the most precise computers and deliberate jolts from the maneuvering thrusters to make it work. No technology could shorten the amount of time it took to do so without posing danger to both ships.

"Walter?" she radioed the engineer. "Shut down the rotation, the delegation is about to come aboard."

"Got it. Walter out."

As pressurization began, rotation ceased and the airlock was suddenly no longer the floor, but rather a destination like any other. With her magnetic boots, she anchored herself to the floor, which pointed downward toward the drive nacelles, aligned with thrust. She double-checked her braid to make sure her hair hadn't flown off in all directions in zero gravity. She didn't want to make the politicians think of a witch who had reached into an electrical socket when they first saw her.

When the light on the pressure bulkhead changed from red to green and a loud tone sounded, she took a deep breath and jutted out her chin a little, as she had learned to do at the academy. Not by her superiors, but by her chauvinistic classmates, who had only taken her seriously as a woman if she conformed her body language to theirs.

The bulkhead slid up and then they floated in: two men and

two women in black single-breasted suits and trouser suits, respectively, a female soldier in blue parade uniform adorned with an incredible number of insignia with the rank of admiral, and a young commander with a beret and neatly groomed beard.

Veronica didn't quite know how to act, so she saluted precisely until the members of the colonial detachment had activated their magnetic boots and straightened their clothing.

"Jeffrey Blaskowic," a middle-aged man introduced while extending a hand to her with a broad smile. He was a little taller and thinner than the others revealing that he was a Trafalgar colonist. His green eyes were red and surrounded by dark rims. Still, they looked alert.

"Captain Veronica Macella." She shook his hand.

"I'm the executive spokesperson for the Progressives," Blaskowic explained. "The personnel merry-go-round has, by necessity, changed a little... turned."

"I see," Veronica lied, smiling noncommittally. She had no idea what political intrigues had been going on in her absence, nor did she want to know.

Blaskowic gave her another friendly nod and then made way for a woman with short-cropped brown hair and an oversized hair clip that looked like ivory. Her broad cheekbones framed a stern but by no means cold face with small hawk eyes.

"Good afternoon, Captain," she greeted Veronica, shaking her hand as well. The woman seemed tense. "I'm Jeetah Morsbach, spokesperson for the Conservatives."

"Pleased to meet you," she replied noncommittally.

Following behind Morsbach was Carl Fergana, whom she recognized immediately. As CEO of Western Mobile and a member of its corporate council, he had always been a notably welcome guest on various SenseNet talk shows and political platforms. His temples were already graying, but his hair was still coiffed into an almost youthful cut, with neatly shaved outlines and an undercut. He didn't merely smile but grinned broadly at her and patted her on the shoulder, rather than shaking her hand, as if she were a particularly good girl. He didn't bother to introduce himself either. One was expected to know Carl Fergana.

"I want to thank you for your great work, Captain Macella," he said in his rich, deep voice, which had probably been trained by more PR consultants than there were Navy personnel.

"Um, thank you, sir," she replied, and was about to turn to the woman behind him when, with a tiny movement, he moved back into her field of vision.

"I just want to share with you something else that has just reached my ears: your companions have just jumped into the Sol system," he explained, smiling a broad smile that revealed his rows of white teeth. "I thought you might like to know."

Veronica froze. She glanced at her arm display and saw notifications of eight unread messages, displayed as a white eight in a red circle.

Jeremy, it ran through her like a bolt of lightning. The urge to open the messages was almost overwhelming, she realized, but pulled herself together and tightened her uniform.

"Um, thanks for the information, Mr. Fergana. I've already received a message from Captain Brandt," she finally said. Why had the spokesman for the Corporate Council said that? Obviously to show her that he had information that he should not easily possess, but why? She hated politics, and with each word from her new guests she became more aware of that. It was also possible that he had not really been addressing her, but his companions, and was trying to tell them something. She could hardly wait for them to all get off her ship again.

"We're not on a talk show, Carl. There's no camera here, so stop lulling the poor young thing with your oily voice," rumbled the woman behind the dapper CEO. She had a full head of gray hair and the wrinkled face of a grandmother, but her eyes, also gray, were those of a hawk, leaving no doubt that an alert mind lay behind her stooped posture.

"I'm Speaker of Parliament Myrta Ashgaloo," she introduced herself, patting Veronica's hand. "Don't let these career farts get to you. They spend most of their free time name-dropping, laughing falsely over a cocktail, and arguing on talk shows. So you can't blame them if they lose their good manners."

"Uh," Veronica said, quickly closing her mouth again. "Yeah."

"So which way to the aliens who first wanted to destroy us and now want to support us?" she asked, looking past her curiously.

"They're waiting in the hangar."

"Ah," Ashgaloo replied, winking as if Veronica had made a particularly good joke that only the two of them understood. Then she followed Carl Fergana, clearing the way for a stern-looking admiral with silvery hair and sunken cheeks. She wore her hat like an American Indian's feathered headdress and her chin thrust forward. Her eyes seemed like sharp daggers, ever ready to pierce. Her young aide-de-camp had her arms folded behind her back and waited demurely behind her.

"I am Admiral Theresa Brandt, representing Fleet Command."

Veronica's blood froze in her veins. *Theresa Brandt*? Jeremy's mother?

"Pleased to meet you," she lied hoarsely, remembering at the last moment to salute. The admiral returned the military salute with a flowing motion and eyed her appraisingly.

"So you're my son's XO," Brandt stated, and even as Veronica nodded, she added, "And his bedmate. Interesting."

"I..."

"Don't insult my intelligence by denying it, Captain. All the colonists have received the SenseNet transmission with Bismarck's memories, as you well know. Whatever secrets you have been harboring, they are no longer secrets." The admiral waved it off. "My son likes to ignore regulations. I don't. As soon as the Court is reinstated on Europa and this event is over, I will send a shuttle for you. You'd better get aboard to keep your appointment."

"But—" Veronica was about to protest, but Jeremy's mother cut her off with a razor-sharp gesture.

"It is a violation of fleet regulations. My son might say that these are extraordinary circumstances and that his military merits preclude punishment—but that's for the judges to decide, not us. If we cannot abide by our own rules and procedures, we are no more than barbarians."

"I..." Veronica was about to launch into an angry retort but closed her mouth again. She had known through Jeremy's tales about his parents' callous nature but, until now, had always thought he had exaggerated it because of his familial involvement. His mother, however, turned out to be much worse. Her face was a cold mask, resembling the frozen and frosted face of a medieval nobleman's bust. Veronica had dearly wanted to be positively surprised by his parents, as she could never have imagined falling in love with someone and finding his parents awful. Now, however, it had happened and she would have loved to blast the stiff admiral right out the airlock into the vacuum.

A military tribunal? For a love affair between officers in the midst of an alien invasion? She shook her head inwardly, careful not to show any outward reaction. Theresa Brandt would not even get the twitch of an eyelid from her—she would not allow her even the tiniest triumph. At the same time, she wondered if it was possible for this woman to have any triumphs at all, or if she was simply devoid of any feeling.

"Of course, Admiral. As you wish," she finally said emotionlessly, gesturing down the corridor. "Unless you would like to waste more time before meeting with the Species X negotiators ..."

Brandt gave her a stiff look. She had registered the side swipe. Just as well.

"Of course, Captain. Then we can finally put this military nonsense behind us!" It was the wrinkled parliamentary speaker who gave Jeremy's mother a pointed look. It was obvious the two didn't like each other very much, and that fact instantly endeared her to Myrta Ashgaloo.

"Don't worry, Captain Macella," Ashgaloo continued, patting her forearm as if Veronica was the old lady and not her. "I will use my influence to prevent you from being punished by the military tribunal. Although I can't imagine they'd really convict you."

"It is not a matter of politics," Brandt intervened sternly, staring at her out of narrowed hawk eyes.

"Oh," Ashgaloo went on. "It's been a little while since I last looked. But I'm pretty sure the Union Navy is still under the control of the elected civilian representatives of Parliament. If there is a gap in my knowledge, feel free to correct me, Admiral. Do I have a gap in my knowledge?"

"No," Brandt replied.

"Good, then that's settled. Now cut the bullshit, or an impatient old woman like me is going to have her teeth fall out of her gums. Such bigotry is harder and harder to tolerate with age. Time is precious and I want to see the aliens who are suddenly trying to help us instead of blowing us up."

Veronica could see the admiral's jaws grinding and enjoyed the sight very much.

It seems she does have something like feelings after all, she noted, and was surprised by the spitefulness she felt.

"All right. Please follow me," she finally said, leading the way with her magnetic boots clicking.

"You can start the rotation again," she radioed to Walter and got a low hum in response.

They headed down the central elevator shaft to the hangar. On the way, Carl Fergana tried a little small talk, telling Jeeta Morsbach about a couple of more or less amusing encounters with military representatives on various talk shows. Morsbach smiled politely and asked a question or two to hide the fact that she really wasn't interested in the conversation. After a while, Ashgaloo rebuked them both by saying "Sssch" loudly, and sure enough, it became quiet then.

So she wears the pants, Veronica noted, and wasn't surprised. The parliamentary speaker was usually the senior member of Parliament and came from the ranks of the ruling party. The fact that parliament had sent her and not a secretary of state attested to how important this meeting was to the governing body. It was a good sign. It limited the military's influence and increased civilian control. Until half an hour ago, Veronica would have thought it was bad news, but looking at Jeremy's mother, she was glad. After all, fleet command must have thought the same when they decided to send Theresa Brandt.

A few minutes later, they reached the hangar on the lower walkway and saw the delegation of Locusts already sitting in their chairs like kings on their thrones during an audience. She had arranged with Felicity to have them all seated at the same time, but apparently the Diplomatic Conclave had overruled her. Likewise, the ten Locust soldiers positioned behind them did not comply with the agreement to attend without a military escort. Apparently, the aliens wanted to show who was in charge onboard the ship and moreover in the entire system, so that they could establish a clear direction for the ensuing conversation.

Great, she sighed inwardly, bracing herself for a tense negotiation. *I hate politics.*

CHAPTER 18
PASCAL

Earth ship X22-3, hyperspace, 2334

The jump was as unspectacular as the blink of an eye and about as fast. Although he knew that the distance of more than twenty light-years between Archimedes and Sol would take about an hour to cover in hyperspace, he felt no difference. A slight tugging in his stomach was all he felt from the jump. It might have made others nauseous, but not him, and that was new. Perhaps his newfound composure was due to the fact that he no longer feared the vacuum around him. Ultimately, he knew what his end would look like and where it would happen. In the Sol system. Not in hyperspace. The certainty was so strong that he didn't even think about the fact that beyond the walls surrounding the squat bridge was nothing but the endless blackness of subspace. If he was to believe Jeremy, they weren't even flying in *subspace*, but rather in an artificially created bubble of *normal space* that was hurtling through subspace. It had something to do with magnetic fields and with this exact word he had switched off. Whether subspace or normal space, all that mattered was that they reached Sol and destroyed the sun.

The sun, he thought, and would have laughed out loud if he could have found a spark of humor left in him. Their plan resembled a bad story in a dime novel, and yet it was real. Strictly speaking, of course, it wasn't their job to destroy the sun —that was Macella's and the Locusts'—but they were one piece in the puzzle. He could see the whole picture in front of him, but not the individual pieces. No outlines, no shapes, just the overall picture. That had never happened before. When he saw a pattern, he had always recognized all the pieces in it, like a perfect ballet of moving colors and shapes, events and circumstances that fit together into something larger, which he immediately grasped every detail of. The fact that it was different this time made him realize once again how different this mission was from all his previous ones. It was final and decisive, the culmination of everything that had led him here, as if it was a one-way street.

Or a dead end, he thought, wanting to shake himself. But the nanomembranes pushed him gently but firmly into the foam of the acceleration couch. The medical assistant was still stoically holding up six different bags of IV fluid, which were dispensing copious amounts of saline and medication into the crooks of both his arms. He felt a little dizzy and saw from the urine bag on the side of his couch that the contents had turned red. Since he had never liked beetroot, he assumed that it was blood. Whether that was good news or bad news was of no interest to him. His clone body would accomplish the mission that he was sure of. What condition he would be in at that point was immaterial. The others, of course, had asked Omega if they could use the implanted NeuroSmarts to download their memories to be transferred later into new clone bodies, but the Neuromorph had waved them off immediately. Each NeuroSmart was custom-made for its owner and covered with BioCreep, which was imprinted on the owner's DNA. So the nanite layer was something of an adapter between the wearer's delicate brain matter and the processor's cold silicon, neither of which would have ever communicated otherwise. The downside of transplanting Alpha's soldiers' NeuroSmarts was that it would only work with the assistance of medication and only for a certain period of time. According to Omega, however, the device needed several weeks or even months to generate a perfect image suitable for transfer into a *new* brain. He had explained it as being like cleaning up a photograph containing an extreme number of fragments, which could only be removed by software one fragment at a time. If they tried to create an image now, it would simply be corrupted—not him. Unlike the others, however, this had not bothered him, since he knew where his journey was headed. Just as he had said: hope was not something needed to keep them alive on this mission, but rather a distraction.

His mind was running in circles, so he decided to go back to the virtual bridge. If the medical assistant hadn't woken him up to check on everything as planned, he wouldn't have returned there at all.

On the bridge, Jeremy, Omega, and the Matriarch were no longer seated at their consoles in the center circle, but near the windows 65.6 feet away. The simulation had created three outrageously comfortable-looking armchairs where they sat chatting to each other. Pascal walked across the reflective floor below where the stars were drifting by and sat down in a fourth armchair that had suddenly appeared when he had arrived.

"Hi Pascal." Jeremy waved casually. Omega nodded and the Matriarch just looked at him out of her huge almond-shaped eyes.

"Did I miss something?"

"Yes," Omega replied, while at the same time Jeremy said, "No."

"Interesting," Pascal commented.

"We were just discussing what Macella, Walter, and Felicity are probably doing right now and how they are getting along with the Matriarch's colleagues," the captain sighed.

"And you're worried about them, that's why you answered *no* to my question, because you didn't want to discuss it again," Pascal surmised, understanding. He had no interest in opening wounds that had understandably developed. If Thandis were still alive, he would also have found it difficult to be separated from her, especially if he knew she was in danger. They hadn't even been lovers like the captain and his second-in-command. Now that he thought about it...

"If we survive this, remind me to arrest you!"

Jeremy smiled absently and was about to turn to Omega when his gaze darted back to Pascal as if he had only just understood the words. His eyes seemed to say: *sorry, what?*

"I've never been in the military police, but I do know that romantic relationships within the command structure of a military unit, in this case a ship, are punishable," Pascal explained, very pleased that he could maintain such a serious expression while doing so. "It would even be within my expanded powers as special investigator of the Abducted Citizens Directive to handcuff you. But..."

"But you were killed in action, technically, and are in a body that in accordance with the Horton Directive of 2112, which made the cloning of human cells a criminal offense, should not have existed in the first place. Apart from that, Alpha is a hostile entity, or an enemy combatant, depending on the interpretation of the colonial laws. Therefore, since your body was created by a hostile entity or enemy combatant and used as an instrument of war—as evidenced by the cloned bodies in the hold of this ship—strictly speaking, you would have to be arrested, which Jeremy Brandt, as the ranking officer on board, is fully prepared to do..."

"Good grief," Pascal grumbled, throwing his arms up in the air in surrender. "You sure can ruin a joke."

"Oh? That was supposed to be humor?" returned Omega, giving him a raised eyebrow. When Pascal noticed his companion's sarcasm, he couldn't help but laugh uproariously. "Not bad, not bad."

"You're both killing me," Jeremy snorted, shaking his head with his mouth puckered critically. "I've got real worries here."

"I don't think there's a monopoly on that on this trip," the previously silent Matriarch interjected in a solemn voice.

"Now our alien passenger has discovered cynicism as well." The captain slumped his shoulders. "With that, it's really time to change the subject."

"All right," Pascal agreed, instructing the ship's AI core—basically the Neuromorph who had overwritten it with his own code—to set up a small hologram of the Sol system between them. "We should probably talk about our mission."

Their conversation stretched like chewing gum over the half hour it took to arrive near Mars. The general data was all known and being discussed, so the conversation had turned out to be more like talk therapy, as they were all restless but didn't want to talk about their concerns. At least, Pascal suspected that was true for the others. Since they had calculated about two days of flight time to Earth and another for stealing the memories, Macella and the Locusts' fleet leadership had been informed that they should not begin iron-bombing the sun until then. This gave them a window of opportunity with a buffer of about a day, as the trip from Vienna to Prague via the hyperloop would take less than half an hour. However, since any experienced soldier or inspector knew that no plan ever survives first contact with the enemy, having a full day as a precaution was a good thing. Pascal didn't even try to consider what could go wrong—he had kicked that habit after his first few years on the job because it was as pointless as it was stressful. Things always turned out different to what was expected anyway, and he preferred to leave the calculation of a possible future to machines like Alpha, which did nothing else all day long and still got it wrong. In the end, the state of the present and thus the future was a matter of faith that could not be resolved by reason. The universe was too complex and far too chaotic to be divided into a clear causal structure. Ultimately, science proved this to be true on a daily basis. Whenever mathematical models and calculations were used to create theories or even make discoveries, things often turned out quite differently. He remembered an article he had read in a science magazine when waiting at the station of Riwaldi. It had dealt with theories about the origin of the universe. The Big Bang after having been doubted at the beginning of the 21st century was disproved by the end of the same century. One opposing theory in particular that had fascinated him was the Boltzmann brain. The idea that there was only one intelligent mind and not a multitude of different brains that had evolved by chance had seemed absurd at first. But once he had read that this theory was statistically more probable than evolution, he had given it more thought. In the end, though, he hadn't gotten any further, and when it mentioned atoms in a matchbox that had been shaken and produced random patterns, he had given up.

"Exit is imminent," Jeremy said, pointing to the circular platform in the middle of the spacious bridge. No one bothered to get up and walk over to it. Instead, they simply instructed the

AI core to change their virtual position and in the blink of an eye were seated at their consoles.

Pascal looked at the green trajectory on his screen, which showed their ship as a yellow dot heading for, and almost reaching, a red dot at the end of the green line.

"Are all the prisoners off the ship?" he asked for good measure, and saw Omega nodding above the edge of his console. Pascal already knew and could read all the data from his monitor, but somehow he felt it was necessary to go through some kind of checklist. In a few moments they would be jumping into the lion's den, and instead of mulling over that, he wanted to take refuge in mundane procedures.

"Have the nanites completed their work?" asked Jeremy, alluding to the minimally invasive procedures that had been performed on their brains while they had been on the bridge.

"Yes," Omega confirmed, smiling graciously, like a father sensing his children's restlessness. Of course he did, too; after all, nothing remained hidden in the Gaia field.

"Your new NeuroSmarts are fully assembled. I have instructed the medical assistants to inject you with immunosuppressants such as mycophenolic acid to slow down your cell division. You shouldn't catch any viruses while we're down there," Omega continued, smiling a little. When no one returned his smile, he shrugged. "That was probably a bad joke because the incubation period for most viruses is three days anyway. By the time the first symptoms appear, we'll be gone. Or gone supernova."

"Yes, Omega," Pascal said wryly. "That's exactly *why* no one is laughing."

"Exit!" announced Jeremy suddenly, and dead silence fell on the bridge.

Pascal stared at his screen again and saw their ship flashing as a yellow dot next to a large red planet.

Mars.

A real-world representation of their surroundings appeared on the holoscreen in the center of the platform, created by incoming telescopic and sensory data. The AI core changed the scale so that their ship was depicted as far too large but visible next to Mars.

Although predominantly still red, there were many green patches on Mars that looked like small continents in a red ocean. The poles, on the other hand, were covered by actual, light blue water. The terraforming plans of two hundred years ago, just before the sleeper ships had left, had never fully worked. Pascal still remembered his school days when they had studied the project. It had something to do with CO2, an accelerated greenhouse effect warming the polar ice caps, and algae that was rapidly multiplying and converting all that carbon dioxide into oxygen. But when it came to creating a real atmosphere, the whole thing had failed and the algae had apparently not been as radiation-resistant in practice as the researchers had hoped.

Today, what was once the main destination for human settlement in space had degenerated into a prison planet for the enemies of an AI regime. While Pascal had little connection to the Sol system except through his school years and the things he had been forced to learn about their distant ancestors, it still angered him. It was a shame to see the memory of their entire species deteriorate at the hands of an alien, who was even using the humans themselves as instruments of their own destruction.

"We're being hailed," Jeremy reported, sounding nervous. Of course they had expected it, and yet the flashing red icon with the telephone receiver icon on Pascal's screen was ominous, as if it were a bomb trigger.

"All right," Omega said, gesturing for Jeremy to accept the connection request.

"This is Captain Schilling of Z4-21, identify yourself," blared from invisible speakers. The voice sounded harsh and humorless, like iron being ground over stone.

"Captain Montgomery of the X22-3," Jeremy replied, and Pascal pursed his mouth appreciatively. Although the young captain's nervousness was evident on his face, which was already glistening with moisture on his forehead, his voice remained calm. "Transmitting transponder data."

Now is the moment of truth, Pascal thought, and would have preferred to crawl under a bed like a child afraid of ghosts. Since they had not received jump instructions when the rest of Alpha's fleet had jumped out of the Archimedes system, they had had to choose an arbitrary exit point near Mars. The likelihood that they would land at the exact point designated for their ship was nil. Their hope was that it would not be obvious in the chaos created by the rapid retreat. Or at least not raise any questions.

They were wrong.

"You are late, Captain, and your jump is an entire astronomical unit off from your intended jump coordinates," came Captain Schilling's reply.

"We were in the middle of a boarding maneuver when the order to retreat came in," Jeremy improvised, "We had two dozen prisoners we had to get aboard before we could jump."

On the hologram in their midst, Pascal saw three of Alpha's ships moving toward them, forming a semicircle in front of them. The AI core showed the distance between them as thirty-three clicks. Further back was Mars's inner moon, Phobos, around which a whole swarm of tiny ships circled like an asteroid field. If he remembered correctly, *Phobos* was the Greek word for fear, and he was willing to bet that the prisoners were sent to Earth from there. There could not have been a more appropriate name for the satellite. He shivered.

"The order was to abort all operations and jump immediately," the alien captain replied, and this time he sounded not merely harsh, but impatient.

"We were practically on our way back," Jeremy returned, gesturing apologetically, although of course it was only an audio connection.

"I'm placing you under temporary arrest, pursuant to Order 32," Schilling replied, and Pascal's heart sank. "Shut down your reactor and switch to battery power. Proceed to the crew compartment along with all personnel, we're coming aboard."

"Negative. Our prisoners are infected with something we have not yet been able to positively identify. It may be a biological weapon or virus." Jeremy shrugged apologetically as all eyes turned to him. His eyes seemed to say: *can you think of anything better*?

The connection was severed, and silence spread across the bridge.

"Damn it!" finally cursed Jeremy, pounding his fist on his console, which seemed to take no notice. "They really aren't tolerant of any deviation from protocol!"

"What do we do now?" asked Pascal, staring at Omega, who was looking thoughtfully at the hologram and eyeing the three accelerating Earth ships.

"I'm not sure what course of action would be correct now," he finally replied. "A fight cannot be won and would give us away immediately. That would mean the end of our plan here and now, even if we were to win the battle against all odds. Escape, on the other hand, would invalidate our transponder code."

"It's already invalidated," Pascal replied.

"That's correct. So there is no obvious solution to our problem."

"What if we fought them here on board?" interjected Jeremy. His eyes shone as if with fever.

"They'll maintain a permanent link via SenseNet to their ships. As soon as one of them goes down, they'll send more people, or destroy us outright." Omega shook his head. "I'll check the ship databases again, maybe I can come up with something that can help us." With that, the Neuromorph lowered his head and sank into his console.

Pascal's computer showed ten minutes until the three ships reached them and began the docking maneuver.

Think, think, he drove himself inwardly, searching for the missing piece of the puzzle that could change the horror scenario of soldiers coming aboard into a picture of hope.

He could think of nothing.

"Why couldn't you have captured the ship of a BlackOps unit that's above the chain of command or something?" grumbled Pascal.

"What did you say?" It was Jeremy who asked, not Omega, who was still busy at his console, apparently intent on not being distracted.

"I said that Omega should have captured a BlackOps unit that was above the law," Pascal repeated, sighing.

"You're brilliant!" exclaimed Jeremy triumphantly.

"Very funny."

"No, I'm serious," the captain insisted, suddenly disappearing from the virtual environment. His chair still spun a little, but there was no trace of him, almost as if he had never existed.

"What was that all about?" asked Pascal, but Omega and the Matriarch remained silent. He took one last look at the trajectories of the Earth ships which would now arrive in seven minutes, and then logged out as well.

First to return to his consciousness was the slight tugging in his urethra that he had experienced since the catheter was inserted. Then came the taste of blood in his mouth. His neck cracked in protest as he turned his head to Jeremy, who was already freeing himself from the nanomembrane straps and swinging his feet off his acceleration couch.

"Would you mind telling me what's going on?" asked Pascal, straightening up with a groan as his own straps retracted.

"BlackOps units or special forces, undercover agents, all of these forces have secret identification codes. Similar to military precedence codes, they are stored in each system and can be passively retrieved," Jeremy explained, jumping off his couch. Since their ship wasn't providing any thrust, he floated toward the ceiling as a result and deftly braced himself.

"Passively retrieved? What does that mean?"

"Military priority codes will open the door for our visitors because they are transmitted and matched with our system. Our AI core recognizes the code as soon as it's sent, effectively overriding it. However, the AI core doesn't even know the code itself because it only becomes known to it when it is verified. Otherwise every AI core would have military precedence codes," Jeremy continued, and began tapping away at the square panels.

"That's what they do, isn't it? In order to control civilian facilities and ships in an emergency," Pascal opined, recalling DeGaulle's orbital ring, where without precedence codes they would have accomplished absolutely nothing.

"Yep, there are different precedence codes. General military ones that officers are aware of and carry with them and ones that are available to BlackOps teams, for example. They can use them to identify themselves as such without blowing their cover." Jeremy continued to work his way to the left, frantically rapping his knuckles against the ceramic paneling.

"I see." Pascal tried to rise but had no strength. Since in his current condition he was dependent on his blood circulating and body fluids draining, the medical assistant had pumped him full of BioCreep. The small nanites saw to it that everything that was liquid continued to flow steadily. In gravity or under thrust, this wouldn't have been a problem, but in weightlessness, there was no direction of flow for his blood cells and the nanites had to help. His heart had to provide all the pumping power necessary and couldn't rely on the assistance of a full g.

"I once participated in selection training for the Space Special Forces, and in the simulation there was a box with three code words. A commander assigned to an undercover mission, or a special mission, was told which of the three code words was cleared for use. If his unit was then engaged by other Navy units, he could trigger a reaction in the AI cores of the other ships by specifying the code and force them to turn away," Jeremy continued to explain, glancing at his arm display. Cursing, he sped up his tapping.

"So their cover wouldn't be blown." Pascal nodded, exhausted. The medical assistant changed two of the IV bags, which were now being squeezed together by thick clamps to literally force the fluid, which no longer had any direction, into his veins.

"Exactly," Jeremy confirmed and floated down to the wall that enclosed their five couches as a small circle. In his exosuit, he looked like a dark blue seal. "I could swear Alpha's ships have them too. It's a pretty safe system that has proven effective with little effort."

"I hope you're right, because we only have three minutes until they dock."

"I know, I know," Jeremy grumbled in a strained voice just as the sound of a dull thump changed to a hollow clang. "Jackpot!"

From his position, Pascal couldn't see exactly what his companion was doing, but a few moments later he was holding a box the size of a cigar box. He deftly opened the small clasp and pulled out a white plastic card.

"Okay, time for a little gambling." Jeremy licked his lips and read aloud, "*Minotaur, Philippa, Delphi.*"

"One of these is the correct code word that has been activated for use in Archimedes?"

"Yes. So the chance is thirty-three percent."

Pascal shrugged. "That's one hundred percent more than before. Delphi."

"Why Delphi?" asked Jeremy with a furrowed brow.

"Because it's at the end, and Delphi was the ancient oracle. The *Minotaur* was a man-eating monster and a kidnapper, not a very good omen if you asked Delphi," Pascal explained.

"And *Philippa*?"

"I don't know, that's a woman's name, isn't it?" Pascal sighed. "Just go with Delphi. One is as good as the other. Anything we try now is better than nothing."

"Agreed." Jeremy stowed the plastic card back in the box and tucked it into one of his belt pouches before floating back to the couch like a fish through water. Any object, no matter how small or light, could become a deadly projectile under thrust. Once he was strapped back in, they headed to the virtual bridge environment together.

"A great idea!" said Omega immediately, sounding both appreciative and disappointed. It had to be hard for him to no longer have the Behemoth's almost unlimited thought power at his disposal. Pascal saw it in the eyes he had hated so much about Moreau and now valued so much.

"Open a channel," Jeremy announced, switching the sound for all to hear. There was a crackle and a whoosh, and then the connection was up.

"X22-3, I hereby instruct you to maintain radio silence. You will..."

"*Delphi*." Was all Jeremy replied, simply interrupting the humorless commander on the other side. He managed to make his voice sound both harsh and impatient despite the single word.

Silence reigned for a few moments. Pascal rubbed his hands together and the AI core translated his nervousness with sweaty virtual hands.

"Roger, X22-3. Z4-21 out," finally came the redemptive reply, and Pascal exhaled heavily. Staring in disbelief at the hologram between the consoles, he saw the three war spheres actually veer off.

"That was helpful," Omega remarked, nodding.

"That was fucking awesome!" exulted Jeremy, jumping up from his chair. "I can't believe it, you picked the right one!"

He came running over to Pascal and punched him. "*Delphi*, for crying out loud! *Delphi*! Thirty-three percent chance, huh?"

Pascal smiled broadly but was too exhausted from his excitement to appear as enthusiastic as his friend. His pulse was still beating in his neck.

"We should now quickly come up with the details of our special mission and why we used an override code like that," Omega suggested tensely. "Alpha will contact us and depending on how fast everything goes, we'll only have a few minutes before a directional beam reaches us with requests and instructions."

"We have a top priority target arrested," Pascal immediately suggested. "That would justify why we didn't identify ourselves as regular units, wouldn't it?"

"Yes," Omega replied after a moment's consideration. "Me. I can't think of a bigger target for Alpha than me."

"The Neuromorph?" asked Jeremy in horror.

"No. Moreau. I'm in Moreau's body, and if we can convince Alpha that we have Moreau, it will consider that valuable."

"We can't do that," Pascal objected, shaking his head firmly. "This mission is over without you. If Alpha decides to remove you from our ship immediately, we're done."

Silence followed his words.

"I am your valuable prisoner," Pascal finally said, and all eyes turned to him. Jeremy looked sad and even Omega looked glum. Still, none of them protested because they knew there was no alternative.

CHAPTER 19

JEREMY

Earth ship X22-3, in high orbit around Mars, Sol system, 2334

THE INSTRUCTIONS from Alpha were not long in coming. Within two minutes, by means of a directional beam from Deimos, the second satellite of Mars, they had been instructed to immediately set off in the direction of Earth, not to Vienna as planned, but to the orbital ring *Helios*. The message had only included coordinates and the instruction to use maximum thrust. It was bad news. Not only because it thwarted their plan to get from Vienna to Prague, but also because they had to deliver Pascal. Jeremy still couldn't believe they were going to do just that. Pascal! Turn him in! To Alpha, of all people!

At the same time, the inspector had saved them from the cruel predicament of having to draw straws or even pick someone. The only good news was that the implementation of their used NeuroSmarts would get the full two days they needed. They had been worried that at full thrust they would have reached Earth in just a few hours. If they had, their NeuroSmarts would not have been able to identify them electronically as Earth Fleet soldiers, and their disguise would have been blown. Instead, they had only sent Pascal's real medical data to Alpha's relay station. This quickly made it clear that if the thrust was too strong, infusions would no longer be possible, and therefore his integrity would no longer be ensured. Shortly after, Pascal had logged off the bridge to monitor the medical assistant, as he was required to do every thirty minutes, except when he was sleeping.

"This really sucks," he grumbled, hiding his face in both hands. The lights from his console snaked between his fingers and flashed into his eyes like a prickling strobe light. He screwed them up and vowed not to become pessimistic again. After all, the BlackOps code had occurred to him after they'd already given up. So there had to be some solution.

There always was, because there had to be.

At times it felt to him like admitting defeat, or settling for something, was a kind of monster that would swallow him up if he looked at it even once for too long. It was a monster that scared him and always had.

"I also find this development most unfortunate," the Matriarch spoke up for the first time in quite some time. If he hadn't sensed her honest regret and sympathy across the Gaia field, he would have jumped down her throat for the word unfortunate. The translation software could definitely be improved.

"We can't just turn him in," he muttered.

"I wish we had another choice," Omega replied. Jeremy raised his eyes and saw dismay in the Neuromorph's eyes. Even he, who was usually so busy working at his console, was leaning back, looking transfixed.

"We just need to think more," Jeremy insisted.

"My ability to think is at an amazingly good level." Omega pointed to the piece of metal at the back of his head. "So far, the limitations of using too much of my cerebral..."

"There has to be something. There has to be," Jeremy interrupted him wearily, massaging his temples with a sigh.

There was nothing. Nothing they came up with survived a thorough discussion of the pros and cons. Throughout the two days they accelerated at a constant 2g, Jeremy paced back and forth nonstop aboard the ship. He didn't want to escape into the happy make-believe world of VR environments for fear that the comfort would cause his brain to go soft. He couldn't go soft and fall asleep, but had to stay awake and think hard. The near doubling of Bismarck's gravity for the entire duration of the journey demanded everything from him. He fought his way through the corridors, went to the crew quarters and paced in circles. At some point he met Spark, who was also very tight-lipped, and together they trudged through the composite and ceramic rooms like lumbering elephants. They didn't run into Pascal because he had retreated to a private virtual room and was going through all the data from the AI core that Omega had extracted about Alpha and Earth. As always, the inspector himself saw his sacrifice as another investigation and seemed to be soaking up as much knowledge as he could.

His joints burned like fire and his muscles felt like they had been worked over by a meat hammer, but he didn't stop, *couldn't* stop. If he stopped, he would fall asleep at the very moment when he had the brilliant idea that could save Pascal from his cruel fate.

Sometime on the second day, a ship-wide ringing sounded, followed by Omega's voice: "Rendezvous with Orbital Ring Helios in one hour. All personnel to their stations. Thrust reversal in twenty minutes."

Jeremy and Spark were currently on the crew deck, among

the many lockers, and looked into each other's eyes with a sigh. Still neither of them said anything, but when their eyes met, they held no hope.

Too late, Jeremy thought gloomily.

"Could you two stop running around like chickens with your heads cut off?"

Jeremy wheeled around in surprise. It was Pascal, getting off one of the elevators. Taped to the hip of his exosuit was a small medkit with the auto-injector Omega had made for him. A small bump on his thigh revealed that he still had to wear a catheter with a urine bag. The lanky Asian looked pale and had deep circles under his eyes. His short black hair had already thinned due to the radiation damage. Spark had recovered much better. Jeremy figured it had to do with the significant age difference between them and the fact that the sergeant major had a Neuro-Smart that Omega had been able to reactivate. Medical care was simply better. Pascal's implant had been removed by Omega, as they felt it would be better not to send him to an AI with hardware. If it made any difference at all.

"Hey, buddy," Spark greeted their friend with a tired smile that seemed to require a lot of effort on his part.

"You guys look like two guests at a funeral service," Pascal chided, grinning tiredly. Surprised, Jeremy noted that the look in his eyes was determined and anything but broken.

"This is a load of shit," Spark suddenly erupted, as if a dam had broken within him. "It's not like we pulled all these stunts together, just to deliver you to the enemy like fucking mailmen. I can't accept that."

"Even though I'm proud to call you both friends, you have to accept that in the end I'm just a piece of the puzzle too. A puzzle piece in a bigger picture that is far more important than you and I," the inspector explained, pulling a white cloth from his belt to dab fresh blood from his lips. "Looks like I won't be around much longer anyway, so I'd rather be useful during my last few days."

"Who knows what it will do to you," Jeremy said and was instantly embarrassed to have voiced his fears aloud. Horror scenarios involving his imminent imprisonment were the last thing Pascal needed right now. He had probably already worried about it too much himself. In his opinion, when a terrible event occurred, it was best to deal with it immediately. Having two days to worry about impending doom was far worse.

"It's an AI," Pascal returned, shrugging his shoulders. Since their bodies were twice as heavy under the current acceleration, movement seemed sluggish, like a robot running low on battery power. "I don't think it has developed human traits yet, and sadism is a human trait. It'll interrogate me, probably with drugs or something, and if it doesn't get anything out of me, it'll lock me up or dispose of me."

"That's the problem," Spark grumbled.

"No, it's not the problem, it's the *solution* to our problem," the inspector objected, coughing several times before lifting his handkerchief to his mouth again.

"It's the solution to the problem of getting to Earth. Remember, we're not merely doing this for the microcosm here on board, but for all the people stuck in capsules down there on Earth. We're freeing them from their never-ending drug induced trance along with our home system," he continued, his gaze firm and determined, appearing strong and unwavering unlike his body.

"But..." Jeremy wanted to protest, not really knowing what he wanted to say, because Pascal was right.

"There is no *but*. I have never been surer about anything than I am about this mission. I feel that I belong here and have a role to play. That it's an unpleasant role... granted. You can't choose your destiny."

"I never thought I would hear words like that from *you*." Jeremy was genuinely surprised. He had come to know the inspector as a misanthropic cynic who, from the very beginning, had gotten along with Walter best, arguably the most misanthropic of all cynics.

"Momentous events have a habit of changing people, and I'm glad they have in my case. I owe my survival to this point to others, in particular my former partner and WizKid. It would hurt me to insult their sacrifice by my being a selfish survivor. I know how to use the gift they gave me, right here, right now, to help you succeed in the mission," Pascal explained, pointing an outstretched index finger at both Jeremy and Spark, as if to pin them down with the gesture. "So if I'm at peace with it, you guys should be as well. So be big boys and focus on your task. You stomping around here like miserable tigers isn't going to do anyone any good, especially the billions of people we're trying to save."

Jeremy swallowed, then nodded. Pascal was right. Again. He felt like an idiot. His friend certainly had enough problems as it was, he didn't need him and Spark making things worse by scowling like startled chickens.

"When we have everything done, we'll get you out of there!" he finally promised, marveling at his own determination.

"All right." Pascal smiled, but it was evident in his eyes that he wasn't taking Jeremy's words seriously, but gratefully accepting them as words of friendship.

I mean it, you old dog, he thought. *I'll get you out of this*!

Fifteen minutes later, the braking maneuver began. Their ship turned once in the opposite direction, then fired up the engines again, using the counter-thrust to slow their flight. The next forty minutes seemed to drag on forever. Omega had let nanites break down the bodies of the ship's formerly captured crew into biomass during the flight. They had then disposed of the liquid from one of the aft airlocks, where it had evaporated into the propulsion nacelle's plasma tail. After that they had sealed their exosuits' helmets and mirrored their visors, as was regulation. No doubt, when they docked with Helios, people or probes would come aboard to check things out. Even if it was just a handful of soldiers to take Pascal into custody, they would see some of their crew. Mirrored visors were probably not necessary, since none of their fellow soldiers were known to Alpha or its people except Omega, or Moreau, and himself. But one could never tell, and while mirroring was not regulation, it was specifically recommended in fleet guidelines. Any short circuit or fire could cause damage to the eyes, and since you couldn't always react quickly when you were in a VR environment, a mirrored visor was considered safer.

Besides, identification was handled by the NeuroSmarts, which had a unique identifier imprinted on the owner's DNA. So officially, they were the real crew of this ship. Jeremy just hoped they didn't have any blood drawn, because that would immediately reveal the anti-rejection drug cocktail and raise obvious questions he'd rather not answer.

There was an agonizing silence on the virtual bridge as the braking thrust stopped and the propulsion flare disappeared almost as if it had never existed. The orbital ring intertwined with the others, giving the blue glowing Earth the appearance of a toy.

A beautiful toy, the sight of which did not hint to the fact that a cold algorithm controlled it.

The maneuvering thrusters took over under the control of the AI core which brought them into a synchronized acceleration with the ring. On Jeremy's screen, the exterior of Helios grew ever larger as a gray wall, until it finally filled the entire screen. Large windows and tiny portholes became visible, and in some of them he could see faces watching their docking maneuver.

Two minutes later, a jolt went through the ship and they were connected to the airlock on the other side.

"This is spaceport control from docking bay C-13," came the radio message from the air traffic controller. It was a woman's voice and she sounded friendly and calm. Of course it was bullshit, but Jeremy had somehow expected to hear a robotic voice, or at least a sinister tone. "Docking maneuver complete. Stand by for prisoner transfer."

"This is X22-3. Roger that, Spaceport Control," Omega finally replied after Jeremy couldn't get a word out. The lump in his throat just wouldn't let a single syllable past it.

Over the ship's internal sensors, he saw four soldiers in sealed servo armor enter through the port airlock. They weren't carrying any visible weapons and saluted carelessly when they encountered the two soldiers with Pascal in their midst. Pascal looked like a lost child among the bulky armor. He still looked tired and winded, but his chin was resolutely thrust forward. As he was grabbed by the four Earth soldiers and led off the ship, Jeremy exhaled in frustration.

"There's no turning back now," he breathed.

"We'll get him back as soon as we can," promised Spark, who sat next to him having taken Pascal's vacated seat on the virtual bridge. "Absolutely."

Jeremy just grumbled in frustration and watched the soldiers disappear through the airlock. Finally, neither they nor Pascal were in sight. In their place was a single person with a datapad in their hand. It was a woman, judging by the figure in the exosuit. She closed the airlock with one hand on the control panel.

"Who is that?" he asked, irked.

"And what is she doing here?" added Spark.

"I'm not sure." Omega sounded tense. The light from his console cast strange colors on his borrowed Moreau's face. The Neuromorph's uncertainty made Jeremy instantly nervous.

"Spaceport Control to X22-3," the flight controller's voice sounded on the bridge again. "Stand by for a routine check."

"Oh great," Spark grumbled. "Now they're going to shine a light deep up our ass."

Jeremy didn't answer and instead stared at his screen, which was playing camera images from the airlock. The woman in the exosuit made an entry and a handful of bullet-ridden sniffer probes came shooting toward her from the hallway behind her. They flew past DeGaulle's two soldiers and disappeared into the maintenance shafts.

"I hope you cleaned up properly," Spark turned to Omega.

"I have. Our communications are faked and my image of the AI core is perfect," the Neuromorph stated confidently and Jeremy tried to relax a little. He wasn't successful.

"What about her?" He pointed at the Matriarch.

"I'm hacking the probe that's coming to the bridge," Omega announced as if it were the most natural thing in the world.

"I really, really hope your confidence is something healthy and not cocky." Over the cameras, he saw a probe enter the real bridge and hover over their bodies lying in exosuits. It was no doubt scanning their NeuroSmarts and reading the identifiers, much like transponder codes. Above the Matriarch, Jeremy felt it lingered a little longer, but the impression might have been deceiving because he could feel every beat of his heart in his throat. At last it moved on.

The same thing happened in the crew quarters, where the rest of DeGaulle's soldiers lay dutifully strapped into their acceleration couches—with mirrored visors.

"Did you remember to justify their armor? Because those don't look like hardware from Earth," Jeremy remarked nervously.

The damn armor! *I didn't think about the damn armor*, he scolded himself, gritting his teeth until they hurt.

"I did think of them," Omega replied. "I listed them in the black box and in the manifest as hardware recovered from the enemy. We were involved in a boarding maneuver, after all."

Jeremy exhaled sharply. "What if Pascal tells them something?"

"He would never do that!" interjected Spark immediately, and the usually calm giant sounded angry.

"I know, I know," Jeremy replied placatingly. "I just mean that under the influence of drugs or some kind of mind probe, he could talk without intending to. Then this whole thing would be over."

"To prevent that, he doesn't have a NeuroSmart. He also has a molar made of nanites that contains a toxic substance in a tiny reservoir. When he moves his finger clockwise over the tooth, they become active and release the toxin into his..."

"What?" Jeremy interrupted Omega, glaring at him over the edge of his console. "He's going to poison himself?"

"If it is necessary, yes."

"You've got to be kidding me!" he scolded. "Why the hell didn't he tell us?"

"He probably knew how you'd react," Omega speculated, his calm tone making Jeremy bluster. Before he could vent his anger, Spark put a hand on his forearm and shook his head.

"We knew it was going to be dangerous and Pascal always plays it safe," he placated him, sighing sadly. "I just hope he doesn't need the poison before we can free him."

"How are we going to free him?" asked Omega in wonder.

"Somehow," Jeremy said firmly, quietly repeating to himself, "Somehow."

The probes stayed for several minutes, scanning the entire ship. Whether or not they found anything suspicious was unclear, because they simply disappeared again, as did the woman in the airlock, who stowed her datapad in a thigh pocket and turned on her heel.

"This is spaceport control. You are cleared to depart," finally came the relieving message from the air traffic controller, and Jeremy didn't have to be told twice. With a virtual push of a button, he released the tether clamps and instructed the AI core to take them into geostationary orbit.

No sooner had the maneuvering thrusters stopped spewing gas and their ship reached a safe distance from the orbital ring than the next directional beam transmission came from Alpha. They were instructed to take the remaining prisoners to Vienna to the prisoner distribution center. This was good news in the midst of the tragedy surrounding Pascal's capture. Jeremy, in fact, had feared that they wouldn't be directed to Vienna as planned but to a special place reserved for returning BlackOps units.

"How are we supposed to fly through the atmosphere with this damn sphere?" asked Spark.

"If I'm interpreting the transmitted data correctly," Omega explained, "there's some kind of antigrav field down there that catches the ships. At least that's what it looks like, because a whole host of ships from the same series as ours are landing there."

"Antigrav field?" Jeremy frowned in disbelief. "There's no such thing."

"It's theoretically possible," Omega objected, "though it's not clear to me how Alpha could have managed it. We'll see."

"All right, then. I'll take us down. With maneuvering

thrusters and enough speed, I can get us to Vienna. If the launcher, whatever it is, doesn't work, we'll crash like a meteorite."

He powered the reactor up to maximum power and applied a leisurely 2g of thrust to take them into a gentle elliptical curve that passed between two of the opposing orbital rings. Crossing North America and the Atlantic, they would land in the heart of Europe in less than forty minutes. It was strange to see the outline of the continent on the holoscreen that represented the birthplace of the Union. He had only known it from his schoolbooks and the brief, surreal sojourn in the Alps when he had been cloned by Moreau and Alpha. But back then he had only seen a random mountain landscape that could have been on Bismarck or Trafalgar. He hadn't really appreciated where he had been. Now, however, he was returning home and it was a strange feeling. There was a kind of disbelief and a deep curiosity, and at the same time a somber pain at the losses he had had to suffer to experience the sight. Jeremy felt guilty that it was he who would see and enter Europe and not WizKid, Pascal, or anyone else but him.

"I wish he could see this," Spark muttered as they soared over Portugal at an altitude of 12.4 miles a while later, the exterior cameras clearly showing the silhouette of Europa against the blue of the seas.

"It's really beautiful," Jeremy admitted, trying not to think about what Pascal must be enduring at that very moment.

"I wish we could have returned to our ancestral home without having to destroy it in a little more than a day," Spark continued, shaking his head before turning off his screen.

Jeremy made a few tiny course corrections as the AI core tried to bring them down a little more snappily than he did. There was no reason to hurry, but plenty of reasons to give the soldiers in the crew quarters more time to divide into prisoners and guards. Since they hadn't given a specific number of captured enemies, they only needed to rely on two of the many volunteers. They were Sergeants Ugaude and Balletta, who, according to their records, had already completed ten years of service with the Union Army. They were not married, nor did they have children. That was probably the closest thing to an optimal background for this mission, if that was even possible to say.

Flight control for the administrative district of Spain reported in with a green symbol and routinely confirmed their flight vector, followed by France and Switzerland, and finally Austria.

When the landing zone appeared on the screen, at first it looked like an oversized donut on the outskirts of the metropolis of Vienna. Initially, he thought it was a soccer stadium, but the closer they got, the clearer it became that this building was of gigantic proportions. The AI core estimated the diameter to be over 1.2 miles. At the edges, the donut ring shone bluish, and in the center it dropped several dozen feet. The area within looked like a brightly polished marble field.

"Real weird," he remarked, leaning forward a bit until the tip of his nose almost touched the monitor.

"Not as strange as this city." Spark pointed to the holoscreen, which showed camera images from the lower sensors. The soldier was right: there were no megacities as massive as Vienna on the colonies. New Berlin had been the largest and, to his knowledge, had had a population of just less than thirty million. Vienna, on the other hand, had to be at least two or three times as large. The largest megascraper poked through the thin layer of clouds, and even the center with its massive skyline had to be more expansive than the entire urban area of New Berlin. Above it, quite a few lines of aircraft crisscrossed on several levels, their position lights flashing in the twilight, and further down the traffic was even more dense. Jeremy guessed that they were autonomous electric vehicles. Every now and then, aircraft or vector thrusters would jet along above them.

The AI core notified him that ground control had taken over via priority code, making it impossible for Jeremy to intervene in the pilot system. So he watched as they headed for the donut and braked at the last moment with full reverse thrust. The device was just under 6.2 miles outside the city limits, so the resulting sonic booms wouldn't injure anyone. Their speed reduced sharply and the mi/h indicator slipped lower and lower. They were slowing down too much to fly ballistically anymore, and the moment Jeremy got nervous that they were going to crash into the ground like a rock, the entire ship wobbled and simply stopped in midair. As if by magic, they hovered just above the center of the ring and then gently slid down. Two minutes later, eight grappling arms extended from their place on the ground and grabbed their ship like an octopus grabbing its prey.

From a small door on the east side of the ring, four figures in uniform ran up and headed for their exit hatch.

Jeremy shut down the reactor and set his communications system to ship-wide reception. He took a deep breath before speaking.

"Okay guys, here we go." With that, he logged out and mentally prepared for the final leg of their plan.

CHAPTER 20
VERONICA

In orbit around DeGaulle, Archimedes system, 2334

The negotiations had already dragged on for more than four hours. Both the Locusts of the Diplomatic Conclave, as well as the envoys of the Union were polite but distant. After being seated, the alien bodyguards had been dismissed and retreated through the hangar doors. At first, Veronica had been angry because the Conclave had not kept to their agreement of not bringing any soldiers. However, by this point of the conversation, she understood that the Locusts were at a disadvantage anyway. They had resorted to using intelligent software to translate their thoughts into words, which worked well, but was nowhere near as accurate as true telepathic communication. Veronica sensed in the Gaia field that the talking displays on their forearms made them feel profoundly uncomfortable. She imagined it was the equivalent of forcing the human representatives to wear swastikas, so negatively tainted was AI technology-based hardware for them.

So they had to forgo their much more sophisticated form of

communication and choose a simpler variant for exchanging ideas, which in her eyes was inaccurate and even dangerous.

"So how do you envision the continued presence of your forces in the system?" asked Admiral Brandt just then, her cutting voice jerking Veronica out of her thoughts like a fishhook that had painfully snagged her mouth.

"We can offer to take over the protection of your inhabited worlds until the threat of the *Cold Death* is over," the representative of the Conglomerate of Eyes replied with a generous gesture.

"How many ships are we talking about?"

"What the admiral is actually saying," Ashgaloo interjected, giving Jeremy's mother a sharp look from eyes surrounded by deep crow's feet, "is that we accept the offer most gratefully."

"The admiral doesn't seem too pleased with our presence," the representative of the moons noted gravely. Every time he spoke, Veronica became suspicious. His faction was not participating in the ongoing mission to destroy Alpha, and yet he insisted on attending these peace talks. What positive influence could he possibly represent?

None, she thought, eyeing the Locust apprehensively. He was a little smaller and stronger than the others, with slightly longer ganglia on his head. The tentacle-like appendages lay calm and relaxed on his head as if combed backward.

"The admiral has a problem with your species wiping out the entire Free Morton Nation, including the Aurora habitat and the outer mass portals," Brandt remarked in a calm but sharp tone.

"Resource supply to our central worlds is indeed a problem," Carl Fergana agreed thoughtfully. "With the demise of the outer asteroid belt, about eighty percent of our ore production has virtually been wiped out, and each piece of debris will continue to emit radiation for centuries to come."

"What Mr. Fergana is trying to say is that we need help in rebuilding, since your warlike actions have permanently limited our ability to rebuild efficiently," Myrta Ashgaloo remarked. The wrinkled old lady leaned forward a bit, emphasizing her hunched back. Veronica estimated that the parliamentary speaker was only a few years away from her genetic maximum age.

"Of course we did," the moons representative replied gravely. "After you raped and stole our greatest evolutionary achievement, not only was our homeland bombed, but entire worlds were held captive under a barrier. Not to mention our first flight into your Archimedean system, where we tried to intercept the stolen spaceship they call Behemoth. What happened there? They destroyed our ships."

"The theft of Behemoth was not committed by us, it was committed by Alpha." Jeffrey Blaskowic, who had been conspicuously reticent so far, sat back in his chair and waved it off. He looked like he was watching a VR movie and not participating in perhaps the most important negotiation in Archimedes history.

"As far as I know, Alpha was developed and released by Alexander Moreau and the human greed conglomerate called Human Corporation," the representative of the Winds of Life replied, tilting his big V-shaped head.

"That's correct, but Alexander Moreau was also secretly meeting with representatives of your species to work together against Alpha," Blaskowic explained, and Veronica couldn't help but think of the footage in the sensor shadow of Zeus II when Moreau had met with Locusts in an airlock during a raging battle in the system. The man had been so shady and shifty that she would have liked to wring his neck herself. At any rate, she was glad he was dead.

"Damage control is honorable, but it is still what it is:

damage control, not an acquittal," the Matriarch of the Conglomerate of Eyes countered. "We do not accept any reparations for acts of war on our part in your system. Though we strongly regret the loss of people in the course of hostilities."

"Oh, you regret that? Well then..."

Veronica switched off and allowed herself an annoyed sigh. They didn't hear it anyway. The sound might have reached their ears, but it certainly didn't reach the brain matter between them. Ashgaloo seemed to be the only reasonable person among the envoys, Brandt the stereotypical cold strategist par excellence. Fergana, on the other hand, acted as if there were cameras everywhere and he was on one of his many talk shows. Jeeta Morsbach said next to nothing and Jeffrey Blaskowic the right thing at the wrong moment. The Locusts, on the other hand, seemed to have taken a clear position in the Gaia field and didn't care to compromise. Why should they? They held all the cards: a much larger military since the Union Navy had all but ceased to exist, dozens, maybe even hundreds of populated star systems, and their finger on the trigger of the weapon that would soon destroy the Sol system. In short, there was no reason for them to relent or give humans anything. After all, it was humans who had started the war between their species. The Locusts had only tried to end it—by military means. You couldn't hold that against them, because the Union would have done the same.

I wish we had suffocated in the shuttle, then I wouldn't have to put up with this nonsense, she thought, even though the onset of suffocation following the failure of the life support system had been anything but pleasant.

With one ear she began to listen again and heard Theresa Brandt accusing the Locusts of stalling the negotiation until Sol was destroyed. Then, the humans would no longer be of any use to the aliens and they would finally be destroyed.

Veronica could only shake her head at such a lack of understanding of the Locust culture. The admiral had experienced the memories from the Gaia field of Bismarck herself, and with them the thoughts and feelings of millions of Locust, and yet she seemed to have learned nothing about them. The aliens lived on empathy, social closeness, and constant communication that was based, by necessity, on pure honesty. All these things were apparently as distant to the admiral as the Andromeda Nebula was to the Milky Way, and that did not bode well for these negotiations.

There was one thing she learned from the discussions, however, that was new to her: on the colonies, there was apparently growing demand for the widespread implementation of Gaianesters instead of the classic NeuroSmarts. Apparently, the fear of having the computers in their heads shut down, which until now had made them puppets of an AI, was too much for people to bear. Veronica could understand that.

It took another two hours before both parties agreed to postpone the negotiations until tomorrow. Ashgaloo managed to get them to agree to finish the talks the next day so as not to waste any time.

At her request, Walter and Felicity led the delegates to their quarters. Veronica felt a little ashamed of passing this thankless task on to them, but she no longer had the patience. No doubt some of them would complain that their accommodations were not up to par. With subordinates, one could simply raise one's voice and the problem would be solved. But with politicians, and with people like Carl Fergana who liked to hear themselves talk, it was more like listening to children crying in a candy store. There was simply nothing you could do.

She herself was so exhausted that she remained sitting at the empty table for a while, sighing and rubbing her temples until she felt she could move again. She dreaded the idea of returning to her and Jeremy's cabin and not being able to sleep again, even though she wanted nothing more than to sleep. She didn't want to have to worry about Jeremy, think about her family, and stare at the call button like it was an enemy breathing down her neck. She just wanted to not think about anything, but that was a luxury she no longer enjoyed as a commander—if she had ever enjoyed it at all.

So she trudged through the corridors toward the central axis, where for the first time she was glad that there was zero gravity. She pushed off from the designated handholds and glided effortlessly through the corridors and airlocks. Before she even reached the elevator, the first call popped up on her arm display. An intrusive beeping followed by an even more intrusive flashing phone icon violently grabbed her attention.

Sighing, she pressed "accept."

"Captain, I think there's been some kind of misunderstanding here." It was Carl Fergana, feigning a friendly tone in a strained, controlled voice. "They want me to sleep in a thirteen point one square foot flophouse, which is more like an isolation cell than a place to sleep! Not that I have any great expectations, even though I'm used to much better establishments, but—"

"You are on a battleship that, frankly, was built for one mission, with no intention of returning. So far, we've mainly slept on our acceleration couches because we've constantly been in combat," she explained, not even trying to hide her irritation. In the middle of it, she yawned so profusely that her jaws cracked. "So take what you can get, or knock on the door of your new Locust friends, maybe they'll have a warm spot for a claustrophobic manager."

"That's—"

She disconnected and sighed again when the next call came in. She turned off the sound and looked at the flashing handset icon. It was Jeeta Morsbach. Also on hold was Jeffrey Blaskowic and, again, Carl Fergana.

"Oh great," she muttered, pressing "reject" three times in a row.

Can't a person have peace around here, she thought. *It's like a kindergarten.*

In combat and later in the shuttle, she had feared for her life, but even that would be preferable now than the prospect of a cabin that reminded her of Jeremy and a ship full of politicians complaining about everything.

Then an idea occurred to her. *The shuttle*!

Myrta Ashgaloo was the only emissary who hadn't tried to call her, so Veronica called her instead. It took a few seconds.

"Yes, Captain?" came the old lady's reply.

"You haven't complained to me about your cabin," Veronica remarked, and the woman on the other end of the line laughed.

"I'm an old lady; I am constantly complaining about every fart. If I called someone about it every time, I'd never get any rest."

Veronica smiled to herself. "You can have my cabin. It's the captain's cabin and it's about twice the size of the standard crew cabin. Just go down the corridor to the left and enter the manual code two, three, three, two."

"Oh, I won't say no to that," Ashgaloo returned. "To what do I owe this honor?"

"Your colleagues. You were the only one who wasn't bugging me with phone calls."

"They're not my *colleagues*, they're *assholes*," the old woman corrected. "Thank you Captain and good night."

The call was disconnected.

When Veronica's smile faded, she made her way to the shuttle. She exchanged her uniform for an exosuit in the crew compartment and first floated toward the port airlock C-2 before being gripped by centrifugal force and was able to walk like a human again.

A few minutes later, as she trudged through the outer airlock with her magnetic boots activated, she paused for a moment, taking in the overwhelming blackness of space. She had been on missions outside many times in her life, mainly for training purposes, as repair bots usually handled any repairs. Nevertheless, the silence and sense of endless nothingness were staggering every time.

After only a few steps in her magnetic boots, the *WizKid*'s scaly hull, armored in overlapping carbyne, shone bluish. DeGaulle's silhouette came into view. The ship's rotation was fast enough to generate a third of a g. Within ten steps, the colony was a glowing ball of life in the middle of the dead blackness.

Veronica trudged on, hopping across a deep furrow that had been gouged by a high-powered laser, leaving black discoloration around the edges. The shuttle was stuck about 65.6 feet away by an airlock that had been sealed. With its charred nose and poorly maintained hull, it looked like a particularly ugly moth.

She moved to the ramp, opened it with her arm display, and walked on with unhurried steps. Centrifugal force propelled her along relentlessly. With a full g, she would surely have fallen forward, but this way she was able to keep herself upright with tense leg and back muscles.

Once inside the shuttle, she hit the red button on the side with her closed hand, causing the cargo hatch to snap shut. Once inside the cockpit, she dropped into the copilot's acceleration seat and turned it slightly to the side so that gentle gravity pushed her into the backrests.

A glance at the oxygen gauge on her exosuit showed her that she still had more than eight hours of air. More than enough for her to savor the peace and quiet she had out here as best she could. She put her legs up on the fittings and banged some buttons as she did so. It didn't make any difference as the reactor was shut off and the shuttle was secured in place by restraining bolts. She closed her eyes and exhaled in a drawn-out breath.

The silence enveloped her like an entire ocean of missing sounds, creeping into her auditory canals, her suit, and her thoughts.

Jeremy. Mom, Dad...

Frustrated, she opened her eyes again and removed her feet from the console in front of her.

"Great."

She opened one of the clip-locked drawers under the second control and pulled out one of the old-fashioned universal cables. She then slid one end into the socket next to the fly-by-wire button and held the other in front of her arm display. The smart device beeped once, and then a small connector emerged from its side, where she plugged in the cable.

If her thoughts weren't going to let her rest, she might as well do something to pass the time.

Using the controls on her arm display, she powered up the deuterium reactor and watched the many buttons, gauges, and switches light up their colorful lights. Like a small starry sky, the entire area in front of her began to glow and flicker.

"Let's see if we can get the life support system working again," she muttered into her helmet, initiating some intelligent diagnostic software via her arm display. If they had had the time to do this during the rendezvous flight, it certainly would have made a big difference. But as intelligent as the programs were, they usually took a lot of time.

Computer technology had never been her great passion, especially since she had been forced to take a course at the academy on how to handle bionics. So she worked her way through the data using the software, looking for erroneous code fragments in the analysis display data stream. There was something missing here and there, possibly due to computational errors in RAM, but nothing in particular stood out.

She yawned and dozed a little.

Veronica awoke to a soft beeping sound that was somewhat subliminal but noticeable for its persistence. Confused, she shook the sleep from her mind and looked at her arm display, blinking. The software had finished its work. A glance at the clock told her she hadn't even slept an hour.

She stretched a little and then opened the screen of results.

"Seven hundred and twenty-two irregularities?" she asked indignantly, shaking her head.

Using the filter settings, she cleaned up the displayed programming errors in the original software. It was, after all, over a hundred years old. No wonder her analysis tool was grumbling. Next, she filtered out errors that were due to secondary programs and shuttle system failures. Three remained.

"That's better."

The first problem was that the life support system indicated that there were four passengers, yet only she, Walter, and Felicity had flown. But internal sensor data during the flight showed only three life signs and no increased oxygen consumption. Yet it had expended too much because of the assumption that there was a fourth person. How was that possible? The system must have calculated incorrectly.

Problem number two was that the cooling system had only been operating at thirty percent, so life support had been trying to regulate the temperature at full capacity. She still remembered how they had all been sweating. Apparently it hadn't just been the adrenaline.

Problem number three was that the life support system had overridden the airlock controls shortly after they had disembarked.

"That's interesting," she remarked, raising a brow. Pulling up the shuttle manual on her arm display, she looked something up.

"All right. Life support takes priority over airlock control when it assumes there's a threat to a person on board. Hmm."

She checked the time that it had happened and compared it to the time that she, Walter, and Felicity had set foot back on the *WizKid*.

"That's impossible," she noted, looking for a fourth error in the diagnostic software list. There was none.

According to the data in the ship's computer, the airlock had been overridden by life support due to an anticipated danger to a passenger and held open. Yet they had already been on the other side a minute earlier.

Okay, Veronica Macella, she told herself. *Logical procedure. Problem one: one passenger too many, who, however, uses little or no breathing air, if the system can be believed. Problem two: faulty cooling.*

Cooling, cooling, cooling. Veronica flipped through the manual and found the cooling system. It was located behind the center seat of each of the two crew benches on the right and left.

Suddenly wide awake, she stood up and walked to the left row of partially ripped open bench seats until she came to a stop in front of a small warning sign indicating sensitive systems. A quick glance at her arm display told her she was in the right place.

She took a closer look at the steel paneling and found a small bulge she could pull on. A large maintenance hatch opened. Behind it she found a lot of slender pipes, iced over at the edges and destroyed at about eye level. They just ended, as if someone had cut them with a plasma cutter. There was a hollow space below that a tall child could have fit into.

Or a slender adult. She was getting nervous.

"What sensors does the onboard system use to scan for life signs?" she asked her arm display, thinking she already knew the answer. Modern ships used air displacement, tactile sensors, thermal and ultrasonic, but this shuttle was ancient.

"Thermal signatures," the voice purred from the computer.

Veronica glanced from her forearm to the open maintenance hatch and the cut lines of coolant.

A stowaway. He used air but didn't radiate heat because his heat radiation was sufficiently reduced by the leaking coolant, she thought, opening and closing the hatch a few times. *He then got out, waited for us to get outside, and trailed behind us through the airlock. Life support overrode the door control because it no longer had enough oxygen supply and the fourth person would have suffocated otherwise.*

"Damn it! Call Walter!" she instructed her arm display. It didn't work because she had an incoming call. It was Walter.

"Answer it!"

"Macella, you better get down here!" The engineer sounded agitated and she suddenly felt hot and cold at the same time.

"What happened?"

"It's the Matriarch from the Solar Storms. She was just found shot dead in her quarters."

CHAPTER 21
PASCAL

Unknown location, Sol system, 2334

PASCAL OPENED his eyes and squeezed them shut again with a groan. The light was so bright that he could feel it all the way to the back of his head. There was a bitter taste in his mouth, as if from medication, and his ears felt as if they were stuffed with absorbent cotton. Worst of all, however, was his headache, which he had been carrying around since his conversation with the Neuromorph. The procedure had been... *exhausting*.

"Wake up, Inspector," he heard a monotone, somehow familiar voice say.

With difficulty he opened his eyes again, but this time cautiously, almost tentatively. His eyelids felt thick and swollen, as if he had spent a night crying.

"Great," he said aloud as he saw the androgynous man sitting in front of him. If there was one thing he hadn't missed, it was Alpha's favorite android, now sitting across from him at the unadorned wooden table. An old-fashioned lamp with a garish bulb hung over the center of the table. Otherwise, the room was completely bare except for gray walls.

"If I were human, I could certainly chalk up my currently surging volume of data to joy. Joy at your placing yourself in my hands," the androgynous man said, and his masklike face, which appeared somewhat waxy, contorted into a poor interpretation of a smile.

"Placing myself in your hands?" asked Pascal, shaking his head as if he had just heard a particularly bad joke. "I can assure you that nothing about this is voluntary."

"I have calculated an eighty-nine point nine percent probability that you would never have allowed yourself to be taken alive according to your personality structure," Alpha replied. His body language revealed absolutely nothing about what he was thinking or feeling. Or what she was feeling. Or it.

It can't feel anything at all, he reminded himself. *Just as it has no gender, thoughts, dreams, or compassion.*

"Aha. Interesting that you're eleven percent wrong."

"Ten point one. But let's not talk about probabilities." Alpha made a dismissive hand gesture and contorted its shiny android face into a sort of curious expression. "Let's talk about a thirty-three percent chance."

Pascal raised a brow in puzzlement. Somewhere in the back of his mind tickled, as if he should know what the AI was getting at. But it was just out of his reach, like a mosquito buzzing around him but refusing to be caught.

"I see you're not following me," Alpha said. "Let me help you: the chance of picking the right code word between *Minotaur*, *Delphi*, and *Philippa* was thirty-three percent."

Pascal's mouth suddenly went dry and the all too familiar lump in his throat was back.

"Based on your elevated pulse and release of stress hormones, I can extrapolate your understanding. Finally." The androgynous man seemed satisfied and leaned back a little in his chair. Each of his movements seemed stiff, as if he was not entirely comfortable in his artificial skin.

"Well, since I know that you were wrong about the choice of the word *Delphi* within the statistically expected range, I'm pretty sure that I'm not wrong about the eighty-nine point nine percent either. So what, Pascal Takahashi, brings you to me? While we're at it, you might as well tell me what your co-conspirators on my ship C22-3 are up to. I'd like to know my system is safe." Alpha curiously folded his hands in his lap while managing to keep his black suit from wrinkling. His chrome eyes betrayed no emotion, blending in perfectly with the waxy face.

Alpha knows everything, Pascal thought feverishly and pondered. Obviously, the AI had hooked him up to a functional resonance imager and was constantly checking his blood pressure for changes. So he could hardly hide anything from him. However, since he couldn't detect any lines attached to him at the moment, he had to be in a virtual environment. *On Alpha's playing field*.

He definitely had to avoid giving the AI too much information about his thoughts and feelings, otherwise their mission would fail within the next few moments. It didn't seem like it had fully calculated what their plan actually was yet, and that opened a window of opportunity for him to take advantage of.

"You're excited," Alpha remarked.

"Just for a moment," Pascal replied, smiling lightheartedly. Then he recalled the moment when he had discovered Thandis near the hyperloop station in New Rome. He saw her body in front of him, sitting leaning against the wall with her head hanging, as if she had dozed off. Her hair caked with sweat, blood, and dirt, and her strong figure. It took only a few breaths for the grief to return, with a subtle emptiness. At that moment, for an instant, he had felt nothing because the shock was too great.

Until now, he had carefully avoided going back to what was perhaps the worst moment in his life, because the emptiness had been so overwhelming. But now he decided to do so, welcoming the inner emptiness with open arms.

"What are you doing?" the androgynous man asked, still sounding monotone but also a little agitated.

"You tell me. You've got me hooked up to a lot of smart devices, haven't you?" replied Pascal tonelessly.

Thandis. Her blue eyes with green speckles. Broken. Lost.

"What are your co-conspirators up to in Vienna? What is their plan?" continued Alpha impassively, and Pascal didn't even acknowledge the stare of his chrome eyes.

Amid the oppressive silence in his mind, he let the various options drift along in front of his inner eye like distant clouds. It took no effort on his part and caused no emotion because there was no room for it in the void. It filled every space, allowed no other emotions beside it and was as encompassing as the universe itself.

"I am not privy to the information because we had factored in my arrest. However, there are several likely options," he finally explained, recalling the available data on Vienna and the surrounding area that he had studied on the ship. It always paid to accumulate as much background knowledge as possible. "They might want to blow up the antimatter research reactor at Cadarache. But they could also go to Prague and destroy your data center with the physical backups. In Warsaw, they might use the planetary mass catapult to destroy one of the orbital rings in such a way that it drags the other rings with it and crashes to Earth. In Berlin, there is an access to the Earth's core that provides the energy for the entire continent. A bomb could cause all the volcanoes on the planet to erupt. That would be *game over*. But there's also the possibility that they're trying to free the prisoners."

When he finished, Pascal shrugged his shoulders impassively. He really didn't care. In the void that seemed to be his brain's reaction to a deep-seated pain too great for him to face head-on, nothing had endured. Nothing mattered anymore.

"How do you assess the chances of each?" he asked calmly.

"The available data is indifferent. I don't know the motivation behind the mission," Alpha admitted.

"That's why you haven't shot down the ship yet," Pascal stated.

"Correct. I need to know what their plan is so that once they have failed, I can make sure that no backup unit will be able to pick up where they left off."

"Good luck with that."

"Luck is not necessary," Alpha objected. "Merely your cooperation. Once I start using the right substances, you'll tell me everything anyway. The bottom line is that your entire human mind and experience is simply based on brain chemistry that isn't all that complex."

"Do it." Pascal nodded impassively, playing with the fake nanite tooth with his tongue. It was comforting to know that he was in control of his own demise. It had taken away his fear before being surrounded by the void in which it no longer mattered anyway. It was just a distant echo.

"Why are you so quiet, Inspector?" asked Alpha's android form, and Pascal felt a spark of satisfaction spring to life somewhere at the edge of the silence.

"That's easy," he replied tonelessly. "I don't know the plan because we anticipated having to enter the system with a special ticket because we didn't know the jump coordinates. That ticket was me. Knowing that, it would have been foolish to let me in on the plan. You think we didn't know you were going to interrogate me? You're not that stupid. You may be a cold Code without feelings, but you're certainly not stupid."

"Absolutely not," Alpha agreed and looked at Pascal closely. This was probably how researchers looked at their lab rats, who behaved completely differently than expected in an experiment.

"If I can't figure out the plan anyway, I might as well destroy the ship now," the androgynous man decided and stood up. He smoothed out his pinstriped suit and gave Pascal a questioning look.

"Don't look at me. I don't care what you do. If you blow my people up now, the backup team will do the job and I'll die content in the knowledge that you don't know what the backup team knows. And, of course, what they're up to. So knock yourself out."

Alpha disappeared.

"Oh, one more thing," Pascal added. "You'd better not drug me, because I'll die. Unless that's your goal, in which case I'm okay with that too. I'm sure you can tell from my brain scans that I'm telling the truth."

Alpha reappeared before him in the form of the androgynous man in pinstripes.

"What do you mean?"

"Oh," Pascal went on, acting surprised. Slowly, a spiteful glee crept into his inner void. "I thought you knew everything. I've had a gap in my back left tooth for many years. I don't have one there now. I'm sure you've noticed. However, it is not a cosmetic correction, but a poison tooth. The nanites activate during a drug induction, an attempted extraction, or when I make them."

"Why wouldn't you want to continue your life?" asked Alpha, folding his arms behind his back. He sounded genuinely curious.

"Destiny. Something I don't think you'll ever understand as an AI. The feeling of fulfilling one's destiny is a very comforting one and makes even death look inviting."

"Humans are afraid of death, it's the main driving force of your species." The androgynous man shook his head. "What are you playing at here, Takahashi?"

"I'm playing with probabilities. Out of one hundred thousand people, how many are statistically not afraid of death, according to psychological studies?"

"Three," Alpha answered immediately.

"So. I'm one of those three."

"That's statistically very—"

"You see, you always think statistically, but the three people out of one hundred thousand exist, otherwise the statistics would be invalid. You've now netted one of those three. Congratulations," Pascal said smugly, and the inner emptiness completely gave way to his satisfied spitefulness. He never thought that approaching death would give him so much pleasure.

"By the way, I also have a data carrier with me," he continued.

"Yes."

"You could plug it in and examine it."

"It's a trap."

"Most likely. But there might be mission data on it, hastily erased, that you could recover to find your answers."

"It's a trap," Alpha repeated.

"Maybe, maybe not. Or maybe it's a virus created by the Neuromorph to destroy you."

"What are you trying to accomplish?"

"Statistics. How likely is it that there is valuable information on the disk? How likely is it that there is malware on it and all of it is part of my plan? How likely is it that you can overcome this malware or whatever?" asked Pascal, shrugging his shoulders. "Well, you can do the math and then make your decision. I'm happy where I am, as you have already realized. Your move."

Alpha disappeared again and Pascal heard himself chuckle.

Amazing. The emptiness was gone, leaving him with a dull ache that he had been carrying around for a very long time. But the pain was his ally. Without it, he would not have been able to leave his old self behind. Without it, he would never have understood that suffering could also have a transcending purpose. He was something like his personal alchemical catalyst, turning base metals into gold—or pain and suffering into courage and sacrifice.

The presence in the back of his mind stirred for the first time.

Are you there?" he asked inside himself.

Yes, the Neuromorph answered. *That was... amazing.*

It's called human suffering, Pascal explained laconically.

It's more powerful than I would have thought. I honestly got scared.

Afraid of the abyss.

Yes, the Neuromorph confirmed.

How much longer do we have?

Not much longer. Your neurons are beginning to degenerate, the Neuromorph warned, and its presence began to inflate like a balloon about to burst. Panic rose in Pascal and it was an archaic panic, as if his autonomic nervous system had taken control, which was most likely what was happening. Clearly something they had done was wrong and his body seemed to sense it and activated all its alarm systems.

What are you doing?

We have to start the procedure now, urged the Neuromorph. *Otherwise you will suffer permanent damage.*

But Alpha is gone. It has to be here for this to work, doesn't it? Pascal looked around the unadorned virtual interrogation room and wondered if the AI wasn't the program itself.

Yes. We have to get it back.

How do we go about doing that?

I have an idea, but it's dangerous, the Neuromorph explained.

Everything we are doing here is dangerous, Pascal replied, trying not to think about the fact that he was conversing with himself. Although that thought may have seemed less threatening than the fact that he was carrying a fragment of code from an organic AI inside his brain.

I wonder if it could get any crazier, he thought.

Excuse me?

Oh, nothing, he answered quickly. *What will happen if your plan works?*

Then I will wrestle with Alpha for control. Best case scenario, I override its algorithm and gradually take control of the system. Worst case scenario, it immediately fends off my first attack and we're doomed.

How likely are those two scenarios?

They are both unlikely. Alpha is at home in the data streams of this system, and will have set up countless traps and stumbling blocks, as well as having installed aggressive software to make my life miserable. Besides, I've been moving around organic data storage systems for quite a while ...

You mean neurons, right?

Yes. Alpha will have used this lost time to continue improving in its element.

Meaning that you will fight using the knowledge gained from the moment of your separation, and Alpha will fight using knowledge that has been improved since then, Pascal summarized.

That's right, confirmed the Neuromorph. *That's why my goal is to take advantage of the element of surprise and destroy as many surveillance systems as possible, so that in the next step I can take over the NeuroSmarts of some of its soldiers here on the ring. From there I can overwrite myself on their brains and destroy the chips afterwards.*

That doesn't sound very pleasant, though.

They are all going to die in the supernova anyway, the Neuromorph countered.

A good point. But our problem remains: how do we get Alpha back?

By doing something it doesn't understand.

What? Pascal wanted to ask, but something stirred in his brain again. The headache became more and more pressing until his temples seemed to burst. His eyes throbbed and caught fire.

What... are... you doing?

I'm sorry, my friend. I am extending my influence over your synaptic connections. It will only take a moment, I promise, the Neuromorph returned, and Pascal felt the artificial intelligence's regret and compassion. In a way, they were his own feelings, merely generated by another consciousness in his head.

Self-pity, he thought in pain, growling like a dying dog. *I hate self-pity*.

Just when he thought his head was going to explode, splattering his tortured brain matter in all directions, Alpha appeared on the other side of the table.

"What's that?" he immediately asked, propping his fists on the tabletop.

"A... *gift*," groaned the Neuromorph. Pascal was no longer in control, having retreated whimpering to the far corners of his mind. The repression inside his own head was like a mental rape that left him deeply hurt. But his cries faded into the tiny space of his remaining being.

The androgynous man's mouth twitched slightly as his chrome eyes blinked. He seemed to want to say something, but then something happened.

Pascal was suddenly free again, in control of his mind, his thoughts, his feelings, his body. Something extracted itself from him like an astral decal but had the shape of Moreau.

No, not Moreau, Omega, he corrected himself.

The likeness shot forward and merged with the androgynous, *Alpha*. Moreau disappeared and the android remained, twitching a few times, as if caught by surges of electricity.

"YOU!" he shouted, looking at his hands with widened chrome eyes, which tore open in several places. Green scraps of code shot out of them and burst like soap bubbles in the virtual air.

"It's impossible!"

A long-drawn-out scream escaped Alpha's agape mouth and then it simply burst like a balloon, dissipating as if it had never existed.

The virtual interrogation room disappeared and Pascal woke up.

CHAPTER 22
JEREMY

Vienna, Earth, Sol system, 2334

THE GROUND CONTROL employees waited halfway to the entrance in the huge ring, which was at least ten stories high. They were four men with shaved skulls and white uniforms. To Jeremy, they looked more like crazed cultists than servants of an AI.

"Welcome back to Earth," the man in front greeted him while sending him a request via SenseNet, which Jeremy acknowledged with his authorization code.

The authorization code of someone who is now floating away as stardust in the vacuum because of me, he mentally corrected himself. His visor was antireflective, otherwise it would have been strange and attracted attention here on the ground at least. So, instead, he had set the passive illumination of his visor to full power. He didn't think the sensors' facial recognition software could work through the small cutout, but it was better to be safe than sorry. Any mistake, no matter how small, could mean the end, not just of him and his companions but everyone.

The ground control man stared absently for a moment, and

just as Jeremy began to worry, he nodded and gestured with an outstretched arm toward the entrance, a small double door about a hundred yards away.

"Follow the instructions you receive from AutoGrid via SenseNet," the bald man instructed him, then walked past him down the column.

Omega and Spark were behind Jeremy, and behind them were twenty of their soldiers flanking the two prisoners and the three Locusts in their floating stasis pods.

They had decided to put the aliens in the oval cryosystems without them being activated to avoid any unnecessary questions. While Omega had learned that Alpha had captured Locusts before and thus they wouldn't stand out per se, that didn't necessarily apply to their soldiers and the ground control people. It only took one of them getting curious and abusing his office to find out more and they'd have trouble on their hands.

Jeremy waved in the direction of the entrance and their little convoy started to move. While they ran with whirring servo motors over the smooth plascrete, he raised his head and looked directly into the sun, which was a bright disk at its zenith. His visor automatically darkened to protect his eyes, removing the power of the central star.

He still couldn't comprehend the fact that they were going to destroy the very celestial body that had provided the miracle of evolution on Earth and made life possible for millions of years. Nothing would remain of the entire solar system except the memories of those who were lucky enough to have seen it. Future generations would only hear about the Sol system and the home of mankind in history classes. That thought was depressing, although it was exactly how he himself had grown up. The only difference was the idea that Earth was there or it wasn't. Back when he was in school, home was a relic of days gone by, unreachable by being two dozen light-years away, and a place of pollution and social injustice. No one at the time had expected to ever be able to make contact again, especially since all the probes that had been sent out had simply disappeared.

Nevertheless, Jeremy had the awful feeling that he was committing a crime.

"You all right, Cap?" radioed Spark to him, and Jeremy nodded.

"Yeah, everything's fine." Since they weren't using an encrypted channel because it would instantly make them suspicious, he added, "I just want to get rid of the damn prisoners and sleep for a few days."

"Aye. I wouldn't object to that either."

They walked the rest of the way in silence. Beyond the unadorned double doors was a large reception hall, much like an airport check-in hall. Nearly a dozen airlocks with security personnel distributed the nearly one hundred soldiers and prisoners who had apparently arrived on preceding ships. They were scanned and then each one was directed to one of the airlocks, which they passed through along with their guards. Above each of the passages was an identifier from A1 to A13.

Jeremy was automatically instructed via SenseNet to take the three alien prisoners to A2 and the two Union prisoners to A8.

"You four," he pointed to four of his soldiers from DeGaulle, "take these two to A8. The rest of you come with me to A2."

The first four he addressed saluted obediently and grabbed their two companions disguised as prisoners and dragged them to the appropriate airlock. Jeremy wondered if they were simply playing their roles well or really felt as down and lost as they looked.

Sorry, he inwardly apologized to them, taking deep breaths to fight down his guilt. They weren't disappearing, they wouldn't for the rest of his life, however long it lasted, and that was a good thing.

There was no line in front of A2. Apparently there weren't a lot of Locust prisoners. He just hoped that merely registering three aliens didn't set off an automatic alarm that alerted Alpha immediately. But since the AI already knew they had captured an important prisoner, he didn't count on it.

"Origin?" a Spaceport Authority employee asked boredly, glancing over at the three stasis pods with their milky plasma glass with a raised eyebrow.

"The battle," Jeremy growled, "It's also in the already answered request on your NeuroSmart."

"It's okay." The young guy raised his hands defensively. "VacTrain two. First door on the right at the very end of the hallway."

Wordlessly, Jeremy walked past the man and through a squat passageway that no doubt contained state-of-the-art scanning technology. It looked for weapons, bombs, concealed items, and suspicious chemicals—similar technology was also used on the colonies. Their NeuroSmarts would also be frisked by the best sniffer software Alpha had to offer, and he hoped, not for the first time, that Omega was indeed as good as he said.

As he walked down the hallway, studiously avoiding nervously looking over his shoulder to see if the rest were following him unchallenged, he received a request sent via SenseNet. It was Omega.

"The connection is secure," he said.

"I hope you're right," Jeremy replied. "Where do we go from here?"

"We follow the officer's instructions to the first door. But then we take the third VacTrain in the direction of Warsaw," Omega explained.

"To Warsaw? Why is that?" Jeremy wanted to stop in

surprise, but the Neuromorph quickly pushed him along so as not to cause a stir.

"The train to Warsaw, or the hyperloop, doesn't go directly to Prague, but it comes within nine point three miles of the data center. A connection between Kiev and Frankfurt crosses over the vacuum tube and that can be reached via a maintenance tunnel."

"How do you know all this?"

"I've been in the system since we got here," Omega replied, as if it were the most natural thing in the world.

"That easily?" asked Jeremy, dumbfounded.

"I have passive access and receive data from SenseNet. It's not much of a feat, and it's not secret data. It will get tricky when I have to outsmart the security procedures of the access points to the VacTrains. They need the access codes of our NeuroSmarts fed into the system, otherwise they won't let us in. Our current codes only unlock train number 2 to the Linz internment camp." Omega gently nudged his elbow into his side, startling Jeremy. He had almost walked past the door that led them to the trains.

"Won't Alpha notice?"

"Yes, it will."

"And then?"

"That's why I prefer the train to Warsaw," Omega opined. "It will make its calculation routines run hot, as to what we want in Warsaw, of all places."

"But surely the crossover with the tube that goes to Prague is obvious and won't only be noticed by you, will it?" Jeremy felt drops of sweat run from his forehead and tickle his eyebrows.

"There are several such crossovers. However, Warsaw is home to one of three planetary mass catapults used for transporting resources directly to the outer planets. It is a strategic target that we could use either to destroy the orbital rings or to bring its antimatter core to annihilation. Both would be severe blows to Alpha's defenses and could look like a preparation for an invasion of the system to them."

"A plausible target," Jeremy noted, nodding. "I see."

"Also, I've prepared a small package that will convince the Chemsniffers back there that the cargo in the Stasis pods were explosives, not Locusts. By my estimates, that should increase the probability of an attack in Alpha's calculations to over seventy percent," Omega continued.

"So we're creating circumstantial evidence to discourage them from looking closer at the possibility that we're not here to destroy anything, but to extract something." Jeremy pushed past some waiting people in a large hall in front of various boarding points for the Hyperloop's VacTrains. As his eyes swept over the many faces, half of which were also behind visors of various helmets, something unnerved him. His gaze instinctively jerked back to the spot where he had spotted something without being able to name it. However, he saw nothing except a group of prisoners being pushed into one of the VacTrains by soldiers with sagging shoulders and dirty faces.

"What's going on?" asked Spark, reminding Jeremy that he had stopped and that wasn't a good idea. So he quickly moved on.

"I saw something..."

"What?"

"I don't know exactly," Jeremy admitted, looking suspiciously at the passing faces. "I feel like I recognized someone, but so fleetingly that I couldn't tell who it was."

"That's disturbing," the giant replied.

"Yes. It's not good. I shouldn't recognize anyone here."

"It's possible they're clones you saw while you were at the cloning facility in the Italian Alps?" suggested Omega over the radio. "It is very likely that many batches were cloned multiple times to be used as labor. The less genetic diversification, the easier it is to regulate health, safety, and much else."

"I hope you're right," Jeremy muttered, leading his group through two more halls. The modern version of an old-fashioned platform in this case was a terminus. Apparently Alpha was not interested in through traffic, which meant that this strange antigrav facility probably had some special purpose beyond its function as a spaceport.

But he didn't need to worry about that now. Whatever other technological wonders or secret projects the AI might have installed on Earth or in the system would soon be a thing of the past. In less than ten hours, to be exact.

The third hall was completely empty. Four glazed double doors were spaced generously apart in the left wall. Behind the leftmost one, the end of a circular vacuum train was visible. The cabin was an elongated cone with a passageway to the next car at the far end. The rows of seats sloped slightly downward as the hyperloops ran underground.

"Did your little ruse work?" he asked Omega, turning to the smaller figure beside him. His remaining sixteen soldiers looked around uncomfortably, and it was apparent that they were struggling to refrain from removing their rifles from their shoulders.

"Yes. I have activated encapsulated program routines that were first attacked by automated software and have since been attacked by Alpha. Eighty percent of them have already been destroyed," Omega replied, pointing to the only VacTrain. "We should hurry."

"Why is there no one here?" asked Jeremy, feeling an uncomfortable tickle on the back of his neck. He knew that tickle all too well.

Something was wrong.

Nothing was right, not since we arrived, he mentally corrected himself.

"Apparently no one wants to go to Warsaw. Seems like an ugly place," Spark grumbled, raising his palms apologetically as Jeremy scowled at him. "Too early for jokes, obviously."

Omega looked absently at the ground for a moment, then his face suddenly jerked up. The passive blue light from his helmet made his eyes gleam like LEDs.

"Run!" he shouted, and Jeremy took off running. He headed straight for the double doors that magically opened in front of him, jumped to the side just before the doorway, and pulled his rifle from his shoulder to provide cover for his men. They streamed past him with the three coffins, led by Omega. Spark had followed Jeremy's lead and positioned himself on the other side.

As the last DeGaulle soldier got on the VacTrain, the door to hall two opened and gunmen poured in.

"Not good, Cap, not good," Spark radioed, then opened fire from his HV rifle. The tiny tungsten projectiles exited the barrel so quickly that the noises from the weapon sounded like a sonorous purr. Jeremy followed his lead, bending his knees to make himself as small a target as possible as they peppered Alpha's minions with projectiles. They grazed the ground, tearing up the plastic concrete as if it were Styrofoam and turned the front row into twitching bodies surrounded by a red mist. Alpha's soldiers were regular security personnel who didn't have the heavily armored servo armor that was strictly for military purposes. This disparity in equipment quality was saving Jeremy's and Spark's lives at that moment: there had to be at least thirty who were returning fire, fanning out so as not to present too easy a target. Some bullets crashed against Jeremy's breastplate, one even against his helmet. Red warning symbols screeched to life in his visor, alerting him to reduced material integrity in the areas hit. Fortunately, his armor held up and the servos in the joint areas kept him from being knocked over by the impact.

It wouldn't last long, but it didn't have to.

"Move up!" ordered Spark over the radio, and Jeremy obeyed immediately. Although he far outranked the first sergeant in the military hierarchy, he didn't hesitate to trust his superior experience. So he took a step to the side until their shoulders touched, blocking the entrance to the VacTrain. With their HV rifles, they continued to sweep across the enemy ranks, finding targets that disappeared in a bloody haze. But the return fire from the Earth soldiers grew increasingly fierce, drumming into their armor making the warnings more and more intrusive. Ricochets and torn chunks of plascrete hissed through the air, turning everything into dust and splinters that formed a ballet of their own. If most of the pieces weren't dangerous enough to shred an unarmored man, it might have been considered quite beautiful.

"We're ready!" radioed Omega from the train at last. "I've taken over the systems."

Jeremy looked to the side until his eyes met Spark's. They nodded simultaneously and then dropped backward. As they did so, they continued to squeeze the triggers of their rifles, spewing their hypervelocity projectiles through the opening until the last possible moment.

Finally, the doors slid shut behind their boots. One final barrage of enemy rounds crashed across the cabin floor, and then there was silence.

A jolt announced the start of the train, which accelerated violently sending them rocketing through the vacuum tube like a missile.

"Whew, that was messy, keh," said Spark, unfastening the clasp of his helmet and tossing it carelessly aside after rising to a sitting position.

"I'm just glad we're out of there," Jeremy replied, freeing himself from his helmet as well. He breathed a sigh of relief as he was finally able to suck fresh air back into his lungs. Breathing recycled oxygen for days was something you could get used to, but it could never compare to the experience of real fresh planetary air. After a long sigh, he looked around.

Two single rows of seats with forward facing double seats stretched to the gray double door that led to the next compartment. The blue seats vibrated slightly and, due to the absolute silence in the shielded carriage, were the only sign that they were moving at all. The soldiers had just barely managed to maneuver the three stasis pods between the rows of seats and were in the process of freeing the Matriarch and her two bodyguards. They got out, dressed in their knobbly bio-armor, with help from the humans. A heartening image that once again reminded Jeremy why he was doing all of this.

"Strange that the whole train is empty," Spark remarked, standing up with his servos whirring before extending a hand to Jeremy and pulling him to his feet as well.

"I was thinking the same thing. Evidently, there aren't too many Locusts that get captured."

"Good thing, who knows what that damn AI does to those that do," Spark rumbled.

"Nothing good, that's for sure. Let's go see what Omega's doing." Jeremy gestured to the other side of the nearly 65.6 foot compartment and past the soldiers who were about to drop into their seats. Omega had also removed his helmet, and the renewed sight of Moreau's face was jarring once again. He had connected a cable that was hanging out of his armor to a circuit board he had apparently exposed with a plasma cutter and was tinkering with it.

"Is he tampering with the door?" asked Spark as they climbed over the stasis pods.

"I don't know," Jeremy admitted, suppressing a curse as the ceramic cover of the last capsule gave way under his weight and shattered.

When he had extricated himself from it, he stood before the Matriarch, who regarded him with her head cocked to one side. In her bionic suit, she no longer appeared delicate and ethereal, but instead reminded him of an overly muscular nightmarish figure. The creepy impression was only softened by the huge eyes, which were protected by lids that snapped shut every few seconds.

Are you all right? he asked via the Gaia field.

Yes, she replied. *However, I have a bad feeling.*

Well, you'd best get in line. Until this is over, none of us will have a good feeling, I'm sure of it.

That's not what I mean, she countered, placing a six-fingered hand on his chest. *This is different. Something is not right. I can feel it.*

Jeremy's own stomachache intensified as he received the Matriarch's instinctual sensation. There was no doubt: something was indeed wrong.

We should talk to Omega, he thought anxiously. *Obviously, he thinks something is wrong too.* Jeremy pointed to Moreau's figure, who was tinkering with one of the paneled pillars next to the opaque double doors to the next compartment.

They walked over to him along with Spark, but he didn't notice them until Jeremy tapped him on the shoulder.

"Oh, what?"

"Are you all right, Neuroman?" Spark was the first to ask.

"Yes and no," Omega replied, pointing to the exposed circuit board. "I have full control of the train..."

"That's good, isn't it?" interrupted Jeremy hopefully.

"Yes..."

"Now comes the but," Spark surmised, hooking his thumbs into two grommets on his chest armor like a cowboy.

"I was able to slip a worm into the train system using prepared malware that took over all but one system," Omega explained.

"Don't tell me you can't control the train," Jeremy urged, and was about to turn away with a sigh to curse all the gods in human history when Omega shook his head.

"No," he said, pointing to a tiny, button-sized dot above the door. "The cameras. My programs can't find the access nodes in the master system. It's as if they don't exist."

"Can't you look for yourself?" Spark frowned in confusion.

"I could. However: for safety reasons, the train systems are autonomous and not networked. They communicate with the relevant higher-level control mechanisms but are otherwise autonomous. Nevertheless, if Alpha planted even the smallest spy program, it would immediately detect my signature. This would not only expose my presence, it would also enable it to analyze my code and prepare accordingly for our next encounter," Omega replied, shaking his head decisively. "No, that's not a good idea. It has the computing power of an entire planet at its disposal, and with time to prepare, it wouldn't be a fair fight."

"You're right," Jeremy agreed with him. "We should save the element of surprise for something more important than cameras we can't control."

Is it possible the cameras are sending images from the train to Cold Death? the Matriarch asked over the Gaia field.

"No. There are no active broadcasts of us to the outside world."

"Then we'll just search the train. After all, we've got some heavy hitters with us, so we'll just see if there's anything hidden here," Spark suggested, holding up his HV rifle.

"Maybe there are explosives with a timer on board," Jeremy suggested.

"All security routines are under my control and the Chemsniffers have detected nothing of the sort," Omega denied. "I also think a manual sweep is a good idea."

"All right, let's get to it," Spark said briskly, emitting a loud whistle. "Hey, guys and gals. On your feet! We're going to search the other compartments. Pair up, check your ammo, and let's go!"

There was movement among those seated, who didn't hesitate long and moved forward after only a few moments. The faces behind the visors with the blue passive light looked tired but determined.

Jeremy and the Matriarch wanted to join in as well, but Spark, who was in front, pushed them back with an outstretched hand. "Let us take it from here. You guys should get some rest. This is what we do. That's how you say it, right? Le baguette and all."

The DeGaulle soldiers smiled politely and then Spark turned toward the double door.

"Standing by," he said, and Omega opened the door.

Jeremy involuntarily let out a scream when he saw the androgynous man in his pinstriped suit standing just on the other side. He held pistols in his hands, which were already extended and aimed directly at Sparks's face.

"Oh," he was still going, when there was a pop and his head turned into a cloud of blood and brain matter that splattered Jeremy's face.

Chaos erupted as more shots rang out and muzzle fire flared. Jeremy stared in shock at the massive, headless body of the Bismarck sergeant major as he fell lifeless to the ground, unable for a moment to lift so much as a finger as screaming and fighting raged around him.

CHAPTER 23

VERONICA

In orbit around DeGaulle, Archimedes system, 2334

"WALTER! Seal all security airlocks on the ship. Have the ship's consciousness scan for alien biosignatures," Veronica ordered breathlessly as she ran out of the shuttle via the rear ramp and made her way to the airlock. She didn't even look at DeGaulle's radiant silhouette passing in front of the *WizKid*'s rotating rear view this time.

This is taking too long, she cursed, as with each step her magnetic boots adjusted their power so that they could disengage without throwing her out into space with the direction of the rotation.

"Got it," the engineer replied after what felt like an eternity.

"Also, issue an order to everyone on board to lock themselves in their quarters and not open the door to anyone until we have identified and located the intruder," Veronica continued, seeing the round hole of the airlock appear just beyond the scar caused by the laser.

"I can do that, though I don't know if the Locusts will comply. Their soldiers are swarming around right now, searching every corridor. I don't know if you're in telepathic range yet, but they're pretty pissed." Walter sounded angry. "I... hold on a second."

"What's going on?" urged Veronica in frustration, and unlocked the outer airlock via command to the onboard consciousness. Inside, frustrated, she let the pressure equalization and decontamination procedure take over.

"Walter! What's going on?" she repeated.

"It's Carl Fergana, he's dead too," Walter finally replied, uttering a series of wild curses.

"How is that possible? His quarters and the Matriarch's are at least five minutes apart!"

"Fergana was on his way to the bridge," he explained.

"Why is that?"

"To complain to me personally about his quarters, I think. A moment ago I was wishing the plague on him, and now I wish he'd made it this far," Walter grumbled.

"This is a disaster. We can't lose any more emissaries, or this whole alliance is finished and so are the colonies," Veronica remarked grimly, and started running as the inner airlock door finally slid open.

"I'm coming to the bridge, make sure all the doors stay locked."

"Aye," Walter confirmed, then disconnected.

Veronica ran down the lateral axis corridor to the nearest first aid kit. It was located about twenty yards from the elevators in a small red bulge with a white cross on it. Her code automatically unlocked the door and from it she pulled out the small pistol that was housed in each of the emergency medical assistants. The weapon's tiny rocket projectiles were recoilless and suitable for zero-g combat.

"Felicity," she radioed to the Nanonikerin as she loaded the pistol and continued to the elevator.

"I'm listening," the Nanonikerin reported hoarsely.

"Where are you?"

"On the bridge. Damn, somebody—"

"I know. We need to keep a cool head. First thing, turn off the rotation. We should make it as difficult as possible for whoever is sabotaging us to move around our ship," she ordered.

"Okay."

By the time the elevator arrived, the rotation had dropped to a low enough level that Veronica could float in.

"Bridge," she said, and the multidirectional lift shot away.

She searched the Gaia field for thoughts of the Patriarchs and Matriarchs but couldn't find them.

"Crap!" She switched to the ship's consciousness and searched for them, eventually finding all of them in their quarters, which were guarded by ten other Locusts.

We have an intruder on board. Whoever it is doesn't belong to us and is killing our people too! Since she couldn't tell which Locust was which via the ship's consciousness, she broadcast to everyone present, hoping they felt her sincerity strongly enough.

This is extremely disturbing, she received a reply. She believed that it was the representative of the Mountain Fathers. *How are these negotiations going to work if someone from your species is trying to sabotage them*?

Is it possible it is someone from your species? Veronica asked, but she thought she already knew the answer.

No. It is not possible for our species to withdraw from the Gaia field.

Please stay in your quarters until we have solved the problem and I am sorry for your loss, she sent and then left the elevator that had just reached the central corridor next to the bridge.

After a quick glance over her shoulder, seeing no threats, she opened the door to the bridge using the captain's priority code. Walter and Felicity were already in the virtual bridge environment, as their bodies lay motionless on the acceleration couches, eyes twitching.

Veronica wasted no time, manually locking the security bulkhead and strapping herself to her couch as well.

On the virtual bridge, both Walter and Felicity were obsessively hacking away at their consoles, while the Locusts of the Diplomatic Conclave remained motionless in their chairs. She was familiar with this absolute motionlessness and immediately knew that the aliens were in active communication with each other.

"Okay, I'm here," she announced, feeling extremely stupid.

"Jeeta Morsbach got hit too," Felicity said in frustration, without turning from her console.

"How can that be? It's only been five minutes since Carl Fergana..."

"I don't know," Felicity grumbled. "But we've got passengers dropping like flies!"

"What do the sensors say? Have we found an unregistered biosignature yet?"

"No," Walter replied. "Nothing."

"Are all the registered people and aliens in their rooms?" she asked, as if going through a checklist.

"Yes, except for the Locust soldiers who have gone off on their own and are no longer listening to us," Walter confirmed.

"Do they have separate oxygen supplies in their suits?" Veronica asked the Locusts behind her, just to be on the safe side.

One of them made an affirmative wave and she turned to Felicity.

"Are all the breathing apparatus and exosuits still in place in their lockers? Or was one stolen?" All equipment on the ship had a unique code that was constantly checked against the onboard systems to make sure nothing was lost. Organization was everything on a starship.

"Everything is where it's supposed to be," the Nanonikerin replied. "Our visitor apparently has his own equipment with him."

"All right," Veronica continued, turning back to Walter. Turn off the oxygen in all but the occupied cabins and increase the nitrogen levels. I found the little spot in the shuttle where the killer hid and came along as a stowaway. I don't think there was enough room for him to fit in there with the bulky helmet of an exosuit."

"Good idea," Walter said appreciatively, implementing the appropriate orders.

"How long does it take for nitrogen levels to become dangerous to a human?" she asked Felicity.

"The system works quickly," the gray-haired Nanonikerin replied, bending her head a little. "About sixty seconds."

"Good, what is going on with the internal camera sensors?"

"They're the main problem," Walter announced, jabbing his screen with an outstretched index finger like an eagle snatching its prey. "They're failing on a regular basis."

"Have we been hacked?" she asked, irritated. "Surely that's not even possible with the onboard consciousness. It works through the Gaia field."

"Yes and no," the engineer objected. "It is a networked system of conventional and organic components."

"And the cameras are clearly not organic components," Veronica concluded, clenching her hands into fists. "But the firewalls were created by Omega, so how could they have been breached?"

"I don't know. Clearly, it's an agent of Alpha that was equipped with good hardware and software before sneaking aboard."

"What systems can be controlled solely by the ship's consciousness?" she asked tensely.

"Weapons, propulsion, drones, probes, hangar doors, life support, anything to do with reactor and engine rooms, plus most everything else," Walter enumerated.

"That's reassuring. So all the intruder can do is mess with the sensors?"

"Yep, with the camera sensors. As well as with the internal security systems, such as door locks."

"Send instructions to the Locust soldiers to assemble outside the quarters," Veronica ordered, looking questioningly at the Diplomatic Conclave behind her. They didn't object. "Has the breathable air been turned off yet?"

"Yes," Felicity confirmed. "Nitrogen levels are already at a level that will instantly kill any breathing creature."

"Good." Veronica faltered briefly as she saw one of the virtual bridge windows flicker. It happened so quickly that she wasn't sure she'd actually seen it.

"What about heat sensors? Did they pick up anything?"

"No." Walter shook his head. "Nothing. Absolutely nothing. The tactile sensors have been working ever since we paid attention to them after the first kill, but now there's no gravity and therefore no tactile sensors to report anything."

"So if we start the rotation again, at best we can track the intruder, but he can also move much faster," Veronica concluded, dropping into her command chair in frustration. "Let's hope he's suffocating in some hallway right now."

Again, she saw movement at the edge of her field of vision that shouldn't be there.

"Walter," she said tensely. "The virtual reality, it's not generated by the shipboard consciousness, is it?"

"No, it's just controlled and monitored by it. It's generated by the AI core and... oh my God." Walter looked around as if seeing his surroundings for the first time.

"I think someone is attacking the VR bridge. I'm seeing strange phenomena that doesn't belong here."

"The system isn't reporting anything, though," he returned, frowning.

"Doesn't matter. We're not taking any chances. Shut down the system. Have the onboard consciousness shut down the controls. Do you have all the blueprints on your arm displays?" she asked.

"Yes," Walter and Felicity confirmed simultaneously.

"All right, then. Shut down."

Veronica opened her eyes and found herself on her acceleration couch. By mind command, she released the nanomembrane straps and sat upright. In zero gravity, her hair stood out in all directions, but she simply ignored it. Walter and Felicity did the same and were already typing away on their arm displays.

"A group of Locust soldiers have been hit," Walter announced with a pale face. "Their bodies are getting cold and they are no longer transmitting. Camera images in the area in question are no longer transmitting."

"Where?" asked Veronica tensely.

"In front of Parliament Speaker Ashgaloo's quarters."

"Damn it. If the attacker overrides her door controls, she'll suffocate instantly! It's in the corridor outside the bridge. I'll go there myself," she decided, sealing the helmet of her exosuit and loading the pistol.

"Are you out of your mind? I'm doing this," Walter protested angrily. "You're a captain, we need—"

"We need people with technical expertise and that's you. So don't argue, that's an order!"

The two, to her surprise, actually fell silent but looked at her out of stubborn eyes.

"Felicity, can you return the oxygen levels in the central corridor outside the bridge to normal?"

"Aye," the Nanonikerin confirmed.

"Good, I'm heading out."

Veronica floated to the security bulkhead and waited for Felicity's raised thumb before opening it and sliding out into the corridor, weapon extended. Using priority code, she locked it behind her and then pushed off with her feet toward the cloud of blood, guts, and limbs that hung about fifty yards away outside the officers' quarters. The globs of bodily fluids fused together, spread out, and ended up as stains on the composite walls. The body parts, on the other hand, bumped against each other in the zero gravity, erratically changing direction, blending into the chaos of the nauseating scene.

The door to her cabin, now occupied by Myrta Ashgaloo, was on her side of the hallway and still clear of the spreading carnage.

That's good, she thought. Not so good, however, was that she couldn't use her helmet sensors to penetrate the cloud of body parts and bodily fluids. Not even ultrasound gave a conclusive picture, as the many solid parts gave off confusing echoes.

Breathing heavily, she floated to the cabin door, opened it, and saw Ashgaloo crouched beside the bed, holding one of the metal struts from the gimbal in her hands like a baseball bat.

"Gee," she croaked, "you sure scared me!"

"Sorry. You'll have to come with me," Veronica said, turning quickly so she could keep an eye on the hallway with her gun extended. "It's not safe."

"I've noticed that too. Some crazy guy was shooting around outside the door, I think." Ashgaloo shivered a little, but her voice sounded as firm and strong as ever.

Spry old woman, she thought. Then it occurred to her that

the Speaker of the House probably didn't know anything about what was going on.

"We have an intruder on board," she hurriedly explained. "He has murdered Fergana, Morsbach, and the Matriarch of the Solar Storms."

"What?" asked Ashgaloo, eyes wide. "This is a disaster!"

"Yes." Veronica was surprised at how calm her voice sounded. "To make sure it doesn't get any worse, I need you to come with me. Right now!"

"Yeah, all right." Ashgaloo floated awkwardly over to her, letting go of the metal brace and it glided clumsily away. Veronica gestured for the old woman to hold onto her exosuit, then pulled them both out into the corridor with one hand. There she turned her chest toward the gruesome cloud of blood before pushing off from a handhold in the opposite direction toward the bridge.

"It's Walter," the engineer's voice sounded in her ear. "I've got camera footage of the corridor again. Whoever did this has disappeared again. It appears he's had a change of heart."

"Or maybe he was trying to distract us," Veronica speculated, but decided to continue hovering backward so they wouldn't be surprised by anything. "Any abnormalities?"

"Yes. The Diplomatic Conclave shared the spirit of the soldiers and their memories. We now know who the intruder is. He didn't use a breathing mask," Walter said.

"That's not possible. Without a breathing mask, at that nitrogen level, anyone would..." She interrupted herself as a suspicion occurred to her. "Don't tell me..."

"Yes, I am," the engineer replied, sending her the Gaia memories.

Pain, blood, muzzle flashes, and laser beams filled the field of view of the Locust from whom the memories came. Then just before they ended with his death, she saw it, the face of the androgynous man in his pinstriped suit. In the still image, he held a pistol and was covered in blood. But there was no doubt. She would never forget the face of Alpha's android, which looked like it was made of wax, ever since he had shot Jeremy in the face back on *Concordia*. Even if she had only seen a tiny section of his hair, she would have recognized him without a doubt. The blood froze in her veins as she pulled back from the memory.

"I'll be right there," she croaked, her mouth suddenly dry, and pushed off harder at the next handhold. Just before the safety bulkhead, she spun around once and held her arms and feet forward to cushion herself and Ashgaloo, who hung like a monkey on her back. She quickly opened the bulkhead and pushed the lady inside, who sailed awkwardly onto one of the pressurized couches.

"Watch her," Veronica radioed and was about to retreat again, but Walter stopped her with a raised hand.

"What are we going to do now? Alpha's on board!"

"All data is stored in the memory clusters by the AI core, right?" asked Veronica tensely.

"Yes."

"So the androgynous has access to that. We have to assume he knows what we're going to do with the sun and wants to warn himself," she continued, clenching her hands into fists.

"Yes," Walter repeated, frowning. "But he doesn't have access to the communications equipment."

"Can he get some?"

"Theoretically, yes, by manually disconnecting the system, but even then a directional beam to Sol would take at least twenty-five years to get there." Walter shook his head decisively.

"And the probes don't have hyperspace drives," Veronica mused aloud. "Even if he manually launched one of them using a launch bay, it, too, would take twenty-five years to get there."

"Stop!" interrupted Walter. "Manual ejection. I know what he's up to!"

"He wants to use a hyperspace rocket," she voiced his fear aloud, pressing her lips together in frustration until they ached.

"Yes. He can easily feed the data into the pilot system along with the clearance codes for the containment fields in the Sol system."

"How complicated is it to manually calibrate, reprogram, and then eject one of those things?" she asked hopefully.

"It's going to take time. But if we don't know which bay it's using, we'll be looking for it forever," Walter mused.

Feverishly, Veronica thought and played through their options. They could try to destroy the missile right after ejection using close-range defense, but Alpha would have thought of that too. So it would make sure the jump thrusters ignited as quickly as possible, and the missile would be gone in subspace before the close-range defense even activated its targeting. Aside from that, Walter would still have to reprogram the targeting so that the friend-foe detection didn't kick in and see the projectile as friendly and ignore it.

"There's absolutely nothing we can do," she finally stated, secretly hoping that Walter and Felicity would have a flash of inspiration and contradict her, but they remained silent and looked down at the floor in dismay.

"Could someone enlighten me as to exactly what is being discussed here?" demanded Ashgaloo amidst the gloom.

"We're finished," Walter declared grimly. "The mission is over."

"Probably," Veronica agreed, breathing hard against her rising pulse. "I'll still go to the launch pads and check each one. Even if time is against us, maybe we'll get lucky. We'll just have to try."

The others didn't hesitate and immediately floated up from their couches to join her.

Please God, we have to stop him, she pleaded inwardly. The thought of Jeremy risking his life in the Sol system only to return to the ruined colonies where their entire family— their entire species—had been annihilated was unbearable to her.

CHAPTER 24

PASCAL

Unknown location, Sol system, 2334

PASCAL OPENED his eyes and shook off the virtual reality like a dog that had rescued itself from a particularly muddy lake. Two bright surgical lights were aimed directly at his face, blinding him. His eyes began to water.

"What... he's awake!" someone shouted, upset. Vaguely, he saw two figures in blue scrubs with mouth guards and hoods.

"Impossible, he was supposed to be in VR..."

Pascal stopped listening and used his full attention to quickly look around.

You were trapped in VR. Alpha was interrogating you. Omega saved you, he recalled, realizing he was lying on an operating table. Above his eyebrows, a cloth divided his forehead in half, and a suspicion rose in him that a procedure had just been performed on his brain.

"Prepare anesthesia," ordered one of the two doctors he could make out.

Pascal tried to turn his head, but it seemed to be restrained.

One of the two scrubs came closer and tampered with the IV bag hanging from an apparatus.

No anesthesia, no anesthesia, Pascal cursed inwardly, rolling his eyes to the other side until the whites in them stood out. He found a small table with surgical instruments. Satisfied that his arms, unlike his head, were not restrained, he reached for what he thought was a scalpel.

Without thinking, he glanced at the doctor who was attaching an old-fashioned-looking syringe to the IV catheter and pulled the scalpel across his neck. Blood splattered toward him and hit his mouth. It tasted metallic and bitter.

The man in the gown gasped something unintelligible and his eyes bulged hideously as he brought his hands to his throat and then collapsed, disappearing from Pascal's field of vision.

Someone cried out. The surgeon?

Wasting no time, with one hand he felt for the tape on his forehead. When he found it, he brought the scalpel to the spot and began to cut.

It was quick.

Pascal heard footsteps and rolled off the operating table. Like a cat ready to leap, he got on all fours on the floor and saw the second man in the gown running to a small door. He looked awkward because his clothes, including the apron, hindered him.

Apparently they had not administered anesthesia to Pascal because Alpha had wanted to interrogate him while he was still in the VR. However, they seemed to have given him painkillers because he felt no pain at all. Unless they hadn't started the procedure yet.

Hastily, he ran after the surgeon and caught him just before he reached the door.

"Stay here," he grunted, thinking he sounded like an animal.

"Don't kill me!" the doctor pleaded, raising his gloved hands. "I'm just doing my job."

"Of course." Pascal dragged the man, of whom all he could see under all the plastic were green eyes and a lot of wrinkles around them, back to the operating table. "What did you do to me?"

"We put the latest generation NeuroSmart into you," his prisoner stammered. "But I haven't finished the procedure yet."

"Show me!"

"But..."

"Show me! Now!" growled Pascal. He had had enough of this horror show and needed to get out of here as quickly as possible. He couldn't imagine that the window of opportunity Omega had given him was particularly large.

The doctor obeyed, and two of the surgical mirrors turned, apparently in response to his SenseNet commands, so that Pascal could see the back of his head. A piece of skin about the size of a coin had been removed, but clearly the bone had already been put back in place.

He felt nauseous.

"Close it up!" ordered Pascal, concentrating to keep the contents of his stomach down.

"Yes, all right, calm down." The doctor studiously avoided looking at his colleague lying bleeding out on the floor and got to work.

Pascal watched him take the skin flap from a prep table and place it in the open area before picking up a device that looked like a slender gun.

"Hey!" said Pascal menacingly, raising his scalpel so he could guide it over the mirrors near his surgeon's neck.

"This is a laser cauterizer," the doctor explained in a trembling voice. His eyes moved to the body on the floor.

"All right," Pascal tried to relax, which of course he couldn't, and watched with growing nausea as the doctor drew a thin laser line across the edges of the wound. The resulting stench did the rest to tug at his stomach.

"We have injected you with high doses of BioCreep for rapid wound healing as well as profile platelets. You should definitely take it easy, otherwise..."

The doctor's words whizzed past him like dust in a storm. BioCreep and platelets tailored to his profile meant that they must have already created an active supply of them. The nanites and artificial clotting agents were always tailored to their patient's DNA because otherwise they wouldn't work and would be attacked by the immune system.

Actually, it shouldn't have surprised him that Alpha had created more clones of him, and yet it infuriated him.

"Are you finished?"

"Yes," the surgeon stammered, and it sounded a little mumbled through his mouth guard. "The NeuroSmart... is it full of Alpha's AI code stuff?"

"The base operating system is created from its algorithm, that's normal procedure in the—"

"Can you delete it?" Pascal impatiently interrupted him, looking anxiously at the door.

"It's not that easy, I'd have to—"

"Can you, or can't you?"

"Yes, I have to log in a medical emergency, then I can override the regulations, but then I'll be taken for processing if it finds out and it finds out everything!" Around his eyes, the man grew paler.

"Further processing?" asked Pascal, sensing the most ghastly fears rising within him. "My God. Just do it."

The operator stood still, and he hoped that the man was managing the appropriate processes through SenseNet and hadn't gone into a state of shock. Pascal couldn't help but think that this poor fellow, who had become merely a tool for Alpha, would soon perish in the supernova as well.

If we can do it, he admonished himself. He wasn't supposed to feel sorry for the collaborators, but how could he know what choice, if any, the people here had. It was always easy to take the moral high ground when you didn't know all the variables, and this man obviously knew his and was afraid. That was reason enough for Pascal to feel sorry for him.

"Done," the doctor finally announced, pulling his mouth guard off his face. He was old and kind-looking, though at that moment the corners of his mouth drooped and his eyelid twitched.

"Thank you."

"Your NeuroSmart is still in the integration phase. It will be a few hours before you can access it," the doctor explained, casting a furtive glance toward the door.

"You are wondering where the security team is?" asked Pascal.

The man's nervous look was answer enough.

"They're not coming, I hope. But I won't kill you, don't worry. I'm not your enemy. Alpha is your enemy. As for him," Pascal said, pointing to the exsanguinated corpse between them, and immediately felt guilty, "I'm sorry. I couldn't let him anesthetize me."

"You're one of the terrorists, aren't you?"

"I'm a cop, believe it or not," Pascal returned, after a moment adding, "If my NeuroSmart isn't functional for a few hours that means Alpha can't access it either, right?"

"That's correct."

"Good, I'm leaving now. You stay here and do what you think is right." Pascal took one more look at the VR interface with its two temple cables, which made him shiver, and then ran to the door.

He literally burst into a hallway of chaos. Men and women in white coats and the uniforms of security personnel ran around in the red glow of alarm sirens as if in a spiked anthill.

Pascal grabbed a young woman by the arm, who had the absent look of one communicating on SenseNet, and yanked her around to face him. First with widened eyes, then angrily, she looked at him.

"How dare you..." she started, then interrupted herself, "Are you a patient? Where is your attending—"

"Where am I and what is going on?" he hissed impatiently.

"The SenseNet is overloaded, apparently it is a cyberattack by terrorists. Only peer-to-peer connections are possible and... why am I telling you this? Go back to your room, now!" she ordered him, but Pascal tightened his grip and glared at her defiantly.

"Listen. I'm a cop and I'm having a fucking lousy day," he growled back, forcing himself not to let his adrenaline and irritation get the better of him. He couldn't let himself go back to who he had once been.

The woman's gaze traveled down the length of Pascal, then paused on the scalpel in his hand, eyes wide. "We uh... are in the data center in Prague. Sublevel fifty-two, special data extraction and VR interrogation section."

"In Prague?" he almost shouted over the siren's blaring.

How is that possible? Alpha knows, he thought, struggling to fight down his burgeoning nervousness.

"How many of these data centers are there?" he finally asked.

"One, of course. One on each planet," she replied, confused. Then her eyes widened. "Wait! You're the terrorist who was brought down from Helios! Takahashi!"

She opened her mouth and began to shout loudly, "Help! The prisoner is escaping!"

Pascal suppressed a curse and toyed with the idea of slitting her throat as well but managed to stop himself at the last moment.

That's not you anymore, he admonished himself, hitting her in the face with his elbow instead. Blood spurted from her broken nose, making her howl. Some surrounding men and women in white coats went wide-eyed and ran even faster past them. Two guards were further to the left but moving in the opposite direction with their backs to them. So Pascal caught the staggering woman and kicked open the door he had come from with one foot. Once inside, he helped her lean against the wall. She groaned like a patient awakening in pain from general anesthesia, but she would make it through. The surgeon, kneeling beside his dead colleague, had a device pinned to his temple.

"What are you doing?" asked Pascal.

Startled, the doctor wheeled around to face him, fear returning to his features. "I... well..."

"Tell me already!"

"I'm trying to make a backup of his NeuroSmart. Maybe he'll get a clone body and I can bring him back," the man explained.

"The units automatically create a backup? Even of dead people?" asked Pascal, puzzled. As far as he knew, there was no such technology in the colonies.

"Yes, but only within fifteen minutes of brain death. After that, the BioCreep will be replaced by the—"

"All right, all right," Pascal interrupted him. "Go ahead. But before you do, I'll need your clothes and some of those backup devices. I'm sure they'll come in handy."

"But—"

"The device works without you staring at it, doesn't it?"

"Yes, but—"

"Good, then get going, I don't have time to waste!" Pascal now used his loud instructor's voice with a threatening undertone. The doctor hurried to comply with his demand and peeled off his gown, hood, apron, and gloves. Pascal took everything and put it on, then grabbed another small box containing four backup devices in foam molds, and then nodded to the surgeon.

"Thank you for your cooperation. Now I need another arm display." He pointed to that of the man who had been killed, lying in a huge pool of blood that was still pooling. The doctor pinched his mouth into a thin line and averted his gaze as Pascal grabbed the slim device made of flexible silicon and fastened it around his forearm. To unlock it, he held it in front of one of the corpse's broken eyes and snorted when the doctor looked away, as if he was committing sacrilege.

"Don't look at the sun," Pascal advised, and ran back to the door and down the hallway, followed by the confused look from the man left behind and the plaintive moan from the woman.

Once in the hallway, he called up the building map on his arm display and realized he was fifty-two floors underground. He had access to all floors, up to the sixtieth above ground, only the levels from the fifty-third underground were noted as Restricted Area.

I bet that's where the data is backed up, he thought, and hurriedly looked through the various floors. At minus twelve, his gaze stopped. *Hyperloop station.*

A glance at the chronometer told him that about four hours had passed since his capture.

Is that all, he thought, shaking his head. A few people walking past him gave him hurried glances as they passed but didn't seem interested enough in him to stop. It was possible. Yes, it was actually possible that he would make it to the station before Jeremy, Omega, Spark, and the others arrived. If Omega, the real Omega, didn't make it into the system by then, he would be able to use his arm display to show them the way.

Before he could follow his impulse to run, he paused.

What if I'm in another VR level and Alpha is currently finding out all about our plan? Multiple VR levels were impossible, to his knowledge, because the brain could only be put into one level through biochemical manipulation. In a VR environment, there was no biochemistry and accordingly, one could not be moved to another level there. But who knew with one hundred percent certainty? After all, Alpha had apparently managed other things that weren't possible in the colonies.

He glanced at the small box in his lab coat pocket that contained the backup devices.

No, he finally decided. *Even if he had, Omega would have seen through it and not left me there.*

It still struck him as suspicious, though, that Alpha had taken him to the data center of all places, the exact destination of their mission. This was either a divine coincidence—something he had never believed in—or the AI really had no clue that this was not an infiltration, with the goal of destroying anything, but a rescue mission. Maybe it thought that because of the far-reaching cloning bans in the colonies, no one would think of stealing memories from prisoners to transfer them into clones later.

Heck, we don't even do it ourselves, he thought, as he made his way to the elevators, which were located three crossings to the north. By the time the decision was made, they hadn't even known if politics would allow them to start a cloning program in the future to put prisoners' memories into corresponding bodies. There would be a huge moral debate in store for the Union if they managed to make it out of this. And even if they decided to do it, there were so many unanswered questions: was the DNA of those locked in capsules stored in their files?

If not, they would get different bodies because their genetic profile was unknown, and the psychological consequences of waking up in someone else's body were potentially devastating.

Still, they had to try. It was better to have all those poor souls back with them and then do the best they could later than to let them perish here in the supernova. After all, they were not collaborators, if they existed at all, but drugged guinea pigs.

Pascal quickened his steps and pulled up his mouth guard to attract as little attention as possible—at least he hoped that doctors wearing mouth guards attracted very little attention here. In the current hubbub of alarm sirens and all the people milling about like chickens with their heads chopped off, he probably didn't need to worry.

He took the designated turn offs and was getting closer and closer to the elevator shafts when he collided with two soldiers who ran around the corner at the same moment he did. As if he had run into a wall, Pascal fell on his butt, gasping, and a hot pain shot through his spine.

"Watch out!" one of the men bleated, glaring angrily at him.

"Sorry," Pascal replied meekly, adding in his mind: *you ass.*

"What are you doing here anyway? And why isn't your NeuroSmart responding to my routine inquiry?" The soldier in front put his hands on his hips like a mother trying to intimidate her child. The other rolled his eyes impatiently.

"It was damaged in the cyberattack," Pascal lied. Although, now that he thought about it, that wasn't so far from the truth.

"Brown, we have to get downstairs!" the other urged.

His comrade raised a hand admonishingly and continued to stare at Pascal. "Well, well. We're under attack by terrorists, so a malfunctioning NeuroSmart seems like a pretty good excuse. Also, there's a prisoner missing. I'm sure you don't know a thing about that either, right?"

"No, not a thing," Pascal said, putting on a wry smile. *Dammit.*

"Then you certainly won't have a problem with us scanning you," the soldier declared, narrowing his eyes appraisingly, as if expecting Pascal to do something suspicious at any moment.

"Well, I have a pretty ugly face, and I don't want to give you two nightmares, so..." He knew when there was no escape, so the least he could do was try to stall a little while he tried to get a grip on the scalpel in his left lab coat pocket.

The soldier who had been waiting impatiently until now raised his rifle, and the one Pascal had collided with was about to say something when both of their eyes began to twitch wildly.

"Um..." Pascal took a step back, then suddenly their eyes glazed over and they slumped lifelessly to the ground.

"Holy Mary," he groaned, tracking a blinking something at the edge of his field of vision. It was his arm display, on which a text message had arrived:

Hurry up. I am in the system, helping you as best I can. Lower levels, don't have much time. -N.

The Neuromorph, Pascal inwardly rejoiced. That meant they still had a chance. He grabbed the impatient man's pistol and stowed it in the scalpel bag before continuing down the corridor. Other soldiers and scientists ran past him and soon he heard angry shouts behind him as they found the bodies and were left, probably perplexed as to the cause of their deaths.

So now I'm a terrorist on Earth. If the whole thing wasn't so absurd, he might have laughed out loud. *In that case, I have gone from being a terrorist to being an insane terrorist, what a stellar career.*

The elevators were ten elevators next to each other. There were no control panels, as they were apparently controlled exclusively by SenseNet.

"Great," he grumbled.

"Excuse me?" asked a young woman with red hair and a nervous look next to him. Pascal flinched, startled. He hadn't noticed her at all.

"Oh, nothing," he hurried to say, tapping his temple with an index finger. "My NeuroSmart fell victim to the cyberattack. Pretty inconvenient if you want to take an elevator down the evacuation route."

"Heard about it," she said, shaking her head anxiously. "The terrorists are targeting our data center and turning us into their puppets!"

"Yeah. I just saw a couple that were simply unplugged like robots," he elaborated on their apocalyptic small talk and gave a long-drawn-out sigh. "I just want to get out of here."

"Doctor, right?" she asked.

"Huh?"

She pointed to his scrubs. "You're a doctor, aren't you?"

"Yes. My good manners must have given me away," he joked, but she didn't even notice and the corners of her mouth were still quivering.

"You've got it good. We analysts need to get down to the backup center."

"Why is that?" he asked, not even needing to feign surprise.

"The terrorists," the woman explained, leaning over to him conspiratorially. "They're obviously targeting the system backups. Of Alpha's base code."

So Alpha knows, he thought, and felt rocks starting to roll in his stomach. *Dammit.*

"Oh no," he said, and she nodded through clenched teeth.

"Yes. Those damn criminals want to take Alpha from us."

Alpha knows, however, this woman doesn't even know what's down there, though. She probably doesn't even know that the enslaved people in the stasis capsules even exist, he thought. *She really does think Alpha is a god.*

Before he could say anything in return, one of the elevator doors slid open.

"Called it for you. Going up," the redhead explained, pointing to the right.

"Thanks," he said curtly, and ran into the car. It was large, with room for a dozen stout people, though it was currently empty. It appeared that most were heading down. To the backup center.

"I've locked Alpha out of the system and physically shorted out the access node. It has to be repaired before it can reenter the system itself." Omega's voice filled the silence in the elevator so suddenly that Pascal flinched. It came from his arm display.

"Alpha knows," he said quickly.

"I know. I estimate we have about two hours left before it gets back into the system. I sent a message to Macella while we still have a window of opportunity. Right now, my code is disintegrating. It has inserted a worm into my data structure that will completely delete me within the next sixty seconds. Take advantage of the time, it's all you'll have. It has ordered all relevant personnel to the backup center. I guess that's where the memories are supposed to be erased. It knows what we're up to now. The amount of data is so large that it will take time, so we will lose a lot. Hurry up. If my body self can reach you, he will be able to help. I—"

The voice broke off.

"Son of a bitch," Pascal cursed, staring in frustration at his arm display and the clock. Every second that passed now was costing lives.

CHAPTER 25

JEREMY

Hyperloop Vienna-Warsaw, Earth, Sol system, 2334

THE VIOLENCE that erupted was ferocious. By the time Jeremy had freed himself from the veil of shock, the androgynous man was already among them. He had leapt over Spark's corpse, gunning down two more soldiers with headshots. Since the others had their helmets on, the android did a forward roll, slipping under the initial return fire and grabbing the HV rifle from one of the dead. Before he was even back on his feet, he had another of DeGaulle's men on his conscience.

It was pure chaos. Muzzle fire flashed in all directions. Ricochets whistled past Jeremy's head and pieces of ripped up seat and cabin paneling filled the air like someone had ripped a down pillow in midair.

With blood pounding in his ears, Jeremy turned to Omega, who stood hidden in the corner between the cabin wall and the panel next to the door. With his rifle raised, he leaped in front of Moreau's former body in such a way as to shield him from the androgynous fury.

"Helmet on, let's go!" he shouted over the whir and clatter

of weapons and impacts, trying to get at Alpha. But in its android body, it fought like a god of war incarnate, its artificial reflexes clearly faster than even the soldiers stuffed with implants.

Headshot after headshot followed wild leaps and dodges. It leapt over corpses, pushed itself off a seat at just the right moment, or jerked a falling body around as it moved to use it as a shield. It was breathtaking in the most negative sense.

At the far end of the carriage, through the myriad of splinters, Jeremy made out the Matriarch, flanked by her two bodyguards. Their eyes met, and when he nodded in the direction of Omega's behind him, she sent the two Locusts into the fray. They didn't have their laser rifles with them because it would have seemed too conspicuous to carry weapons in the stasis pods, so they relied on long blades that grew out of their arms like swords. They ducked like leopards under plunging soldiers struck down by Alpha, leaping nimbly over the debris of the stasis pods. Ricochets and shrapnel bounced ineffectually off their bio-armor. Just as the androgynous had morphed his free hand into a long knife and decapitated a hapless DeGauller, the first Locust reached the android and appeared behind him.

Jeremy triumphantly suppressed a cheer as the alien brought its blades down on the AI in the robot body.

Abruptly, the suppressed cheer stuck in his throat as Alpha moved sideways in a flash, escaping the blows and pressed the HV rifle into the Locust's chest with one hand. Time seemed to stand still for a moment, then he pulled the trigger, turning the warrior's torso into mincemeat. Dark blood splattered in all directions as the HV ammunition sliced through armor and body like a buzz saw.

The second alien was there, slicing the HV rifle in two with a well-aimed blow. The buzz saw stopped as the front one fell to the ground and the androgynous man carelessly dropped the rear end. A dance of swords ensued. Alpha had been able to surprise the first Locust, but the second moved efficiently and cautiously at the same time, as if consciously trying not to underestimate his opponent.

One of eight DeGaulle soldiers still alive took advantage of the respite and shot two holes in the android's right leg, causing him to stumble and stagger forward. The Locust tried to capitalize on his sudden advantage and lunged, but it was a feint—instead of falling, Alpha slipped sideways past the blade and rammed his own into the alien's abdomen. A blink later, he yanked it up to the warrior's neck, then brought his body between himself and the soldiers' incipient fire.

That was when their gazes met. For an instant, Jeremy thought he recognized his own face in the cold chrome of the cyber eyes. The problem, however, was that Alpha also recognized Moreau, or Omega as the case may be, and in a flash changed his priorities.

"Shit!" cursed Jeremy and began to fire, but only hit the cabin wall, which was already covered with countless marks. If it wasn't reinforced by the forces at play in the vacuum tunnel, they would have all suffocated by now. Alpha was simply too fast, moving as if the law of gravity did not apply to it.

Jeremy, devoid of any combat implants, reflex lines, or high-powered joints, fared much worse than the soldiers, who could at least keep up on the lower spectrum of Alpha's abilities. He didn't even graze the android before it was on him, ripping out two more bucket seats on the way and hurling them at DeGaulle's gun-wielding fighter.

Helpless, for lack of anything better to do, Jeremy threw his rifle at the androgynous man, who simply sliced it in midair.

Monofilament, what a bummer!

He swung his fists at the AI, but it simply ducked out from under it and rammed its own fist into his stomach so hard that even in the servo armor all the air was forced out of his lungs. Red alarms flashed in his helmet, which was lying on the ground some distance away. Under any other circumstances, he would have laughed at that.

Omega had to survive or the mission was finished. He absolutely had to survive.

Then came the blade, which the androgynous rammed lengthwise into his stomach. It effortlessly cut through his armor and pierced through Jeremy's abdomen until it came out the other end. The android's cold chrome eyes paused for a moment in front of his, as if to watch him die without missing a beat. Pain exploded throughout his body, radiating from his torso to all his limbs and into his head. Thoughts were impossible, there was only pain.

Dead chrome eyes still stared at him, no longer animated. Then they slowly moved away and he saw the Matriarch. The androgynous's motionless body was pinned on two blades from her forearm and lifted up like a toy doll before she carelessly tossed it aside. He crashed into the cabin wall and slid down it to the floor, where he lay twitching. The chrome eyes still stared at Jeremy, who gaped at the alien, gasping. Across the Gaia field, her presence reached him, taking him in like a mother's protective embrace. She made him forget the thick blood that ran down his lips and made him cough wildly. Fear and pain became distant memories of a destroyed body that no longer mattered. All that mattered was her presence and mental sympathy that gently embraced his soul.

Others approached, soldiers, allies.

Good, he thought with fluttering eyelids. *Good.*

Then Moreau's face appeared before him.

Moreau? What is Moreau doing here? Moreau is dead. Jeremy wanted to protest, but he had no strength. Besides, nothing mattered in the center of the Matriarch's presence. He was happy where he was.

There was talk, loud talk, maybe even shouting and discussion. Concerned faces surrounded him, some were red-faced, or was it blood? What was wrong with them?

"It's all right," he breathed. "Don't worry about it."

They answered, all at the same time, he believed, but nothing that passed their lips made sense. Everything was swallowed up by the presence of the Matriarch, who held him in her mind like a mother holds her newborn.

Dying isn't so bad, he realized. It was already weird that he was dying for the second time. Not many could claim that it wasn't their first time. But he could, just like his crew and Pascal, who somehow belonged to his crew—or they all belonged to Pascal's, sometimes he wasn't sure.

Some of the worried looking soldiers—*why are you so worried*? Everything is fine!—disappeared from his field of vision and reappeared a short time later. Jeremy was getting more and more tired. He could feel the life draining out of him and...

"Whaaaaarrrrgghhh," he suddenly cried out as his entire body tensed. His skin began to burn like fire. He wrenched his eyes open and the Matriarch's presence disappeared.

Gasping, he rose up into the air as if pulled by invisible strings, breathing almost as fast as his racing pulse, which was through the roof.

"How, what?" his words rolled over each other. Then Omega's face appeared in front of him. He took Jeremy's head between the cold hands of his servo armor and forced him to look him straight in the eye.

"It will only take a brief moment, then the confusion will be gone. Breathe in and out slowly and deeply," Moreau commanded.

No, no, not Moreau, not Moreau. It's Omega, Omega. The Neuromorph!

It took what felt like an eternity, but then the merry-go-round in his head gradually slowed down and he was able to calm down a bit.

"What's going on? Why am I still alive?" asked Jeremy finally, honestly confused. He was sitting on the floor of the wrecked cabin, held upright by two soldiers. They were Deune and Villeneuve; he had spoken to them briefly on the ship. In front of him squatted Omega, behind him the Matriarch. Both looked at him with concern, or in the case of the aliens, in an opaque way that he identified as concern based on their Gaia transmissions.

"You suffered a severe abdominal injury," Omega explained, "ruptured spleen and intestines."

"Ruptu-what?"

"They were punctured and ruptured. Also, the lower portion of your left lung was hit," Omega explained.

"Hey, buddy, do we have to tell him all this?" interjected Villeneuve.

"Yes. He needs to know."

"What's the matter with you guys? I'm feeling pretty great." Jeremy moved his arms testingly and nodded with satisfaction.

"The BioCreep in your suit is doing its best, but it's not enough," Omega continued, shaking his head sadly. "The nanites aren't imprinted on you because you're wearing someone else's suit. They will repair the organ damage but will be attacked by your immune system and eventually fail. Currently, blood and organ fluids are leaking into your abdomen and causing massive infections."

"But I feel fine," Jeremy protested.

"That is because of the stimulants and painkillers we injected you with. If we're lucky, they'll keep you awake for a few more hours and, in combination with the nanites, on your feet. Then you will either go into septic shock or die from multiple organ failure as a side effect of the overdosed stimulants."

Jeremy swallowed hard, but the shock was not as great as he had feared. Perhaps it was the chemical cocktail buzzing in his ears, but he found Omega's pessimism misplaced. He could move and was not in pain. On the contrary, he felt relatively well, as if after a hangover that had finally been cured—still a little shaky, but much better.

"Okay, got it. I'm going to die soon," he said, making a dismissive gesture with his hand before letting the two soldiers help him up. When he stood again, he exchanged a long and intense look with the Matriarch.

Then he looked around the compartment and his breath caught. Body parts and the massive bodies of soldiers in tattered servo armor lay everywhere. The walls were red with blood, as if someone had tried to repaint them and stopped short of finishing. It reeked of sweat, feces, and death. Most of the rows of seats were destroyed, as were the stasis pods, and air hissed out through a few bullet holes into the vacuum of the hyperloop tube.

"My God," he whispered, looking off to the side at a particularly large headless figure on the floor.

Spark.

Jeremy pressed his lips together and forced himself to be strong. He had liked the uncouth but always easy-going Bismarcker, even though they had only known each other for such a short time.

"So many are dead," he noted, shaking his head, as his gaze fell on the androgynous one, Alpha's android. The chrome eyes gazed into the void like direct entrances to hell. He had at least ten soldiers and the Matriarch's two bodyguards on his conscience, and soon he would be too. The idea that a single being caused this death scene was hard to grasp.

"We should go to the other compartment," he said hoarsely, and Omega nodded.

It took them a while to grab weapons, BioCreep supplies, and battery packs for the servo armor and move them to the next compartment. They left the bodies behind because they wouldn't have known what to do with them anyway. They were running out of time, since Omega had already announced that they were going to brake in five minutes to get off and transfer to the Hyperloop tunnel to Prague. So they double-checked the seal on their helmets and the oxygen on the autarky system, since they would have to march 9.3 miles through the vacuum of the tube. Looking at their suddenly way-too-small squad, Jeremy felt queasy. What if there was just one more android form of Alpha waiting for them behind just one of the many doors they probably still had to go through? Apparently, the AI had taken precautions and posted itself in physical form in several places. Or it knew exactly what they were up to, in which case they were screwed anyway. A single encounter had been enough to thin their heavily armed and armored group down by well over half. Statistically, that meant they wouldn't survive even one more encounter.

"This is it," Omega finally announced over the radio, and the VacTrain slowed rapidly. Jeremy gave a thumbs up and checked that all the soldiers were responding to him with the same gesture. Behind their visors, their faces looked sad, but above all grim and determined—qualities they would soon need, he sensed.

It took nearly two minutes for the train to decelerate from

supersonic speed to a stop, allowing them to run forward through four more cars to escape through the front exit. Omega had overwritten the onboard software and disabled the interlock. In the atmosphere-free tunnel, which looked like an oversized, seamless tube, they needed their helmet lights to see their hand in front of their eyes. His suit warned him that he was in a strong magnetic field, but he turned off the warning with a wink. It was difficult to walk normally in the tube because everything was round and there was no flat surface, so they trudged a little awkwardly after Omega. Only the Matriarch moved with her signature grace and poise.

Omega walked about sixteen more feet and then drew an invisible circle with his fingers on the area at his feet. As discussed, two soldiers stepped forward and fired their HV rifles along the imaginary circle. Plastic concrete splashed up like water in a pond, taking five endless minutes for them to step back and reveal a large hole. Jeremy peered inside and saw by the light of his helmet lamps another tube about thirty-two point eight feet down: The Hyperloop to Prague. If Macella had seen this claustrophobic place ...

"All right, let's do it," he said, and jumped down.

With the help of their servos, they made fast progress. The only thing they had to be careful of was not losing their footing and toppling over on the round floor.

"What the heck did you do to our train?" Jeremy asked Omega as they ran single file through the tunnel. The warning symbols in his helmet informed him that his elevated pulse and blood pressure were cutting another hour off his likely survival time with his current injuries. So be it.

"I physically disabled the cables controlling the brakes. It's going to crash into Warsaw Station at supersonic speed, and the destruction should be enough to wipe out large parts of the city," Omega explained behind him. "That should convince Alpha that we are indeed planning an attack and not targeting the data center."

"But surely it will be aware, through the automatic backup systems, that the link between Kiev and Frankfurt is no longer passable due to damage to the hyperloop tube."

"Yes. But that can have many reasons," Omega returned. "Besides, we will reach the station at the data center in less than ten minutes. So it doesn't have a lot of warning time, if it responds."

"Your word to God's ear," Jeremy grumbled.

After almost exactly ten minutes, they reached the station. Transparent double doors that looked like copies of those in Vienna stood out due to their glow. The light behind them, though cold and dim, seemed like a beacon of life in the all-encompassing darkness of the hyperloop.

"Finally," he exulted, quickening his steps once again. He suppressed the warnings in his visor.

Arriving at the door, they pried it open with the snap blades of their armor and then one by one climbed into the station, which was completely empty. There was only one entrance and the space was surprisingly small compared to its Viennese counterpart.

"There you are," hissed a familiar voice from somewhere behind him.

Jeremy wheeled around and saw a figure emerging from the shadows of a corner. It was dressed in a doctor's coat with a hood and mouth guard and held a pistol. Immediately all guns were pointed at him.

The voice was so familiar to Jeremy, except that it didn't fit here.

"Hey, don't shoot!" Pascal took off his mouth guard and the gun barrels lowered again.

"Pascal?" exclaimed Jeremy, unable to believe it. "How is it possible? I thought you..."

"Yeah, I thought so too. Apparently the data center is also used to interrogate prisoners in VR and make copies of them," the inspector explained, half-heartedly fending Jeremy off as he embraced him. It was hard for Jeremy to hold back, but he didn't want to crush the petite man with his servo motors.

"Apparently luck is with us after all," Omega decided, shaking Pascal's hand. The other soldiers also greeted the investigator, who frowned and looked around at the double doors to the hyperloop, where the Matriarch stood, looking a little lost.

"Where did the others go? And where's Spark?" asked Pascal quietly, his eyes already starting to glaze over.

"I'm sorry," Jeremy replied sadly. "Alpha, they... one of its androids ambushed us on the train. Spark was the first."

Pascal said nothing. His mouth quivered briefly, then he averted his eyes and pointed toward the exit—a small, nondescript door.

"The backup center is many floors below us. Alpha knows and has sent its people to start erasing the prisoners' memories," he explained as they made their way out.

"It knows? Is the data already lost, then?" asked Jeremy.

"No." It was Omega who answered. "The data transfer is quick, but the deletion is not. To really remove them from the disks, they have to be overwritten dozens of times instead of just being removed from the index lists."

"Yes. That's the good news. The bad news is that they started doing it an hour ago. So we have no time to lose," Pascal replied.

"But if Alpha knows what we're up to..."

"Omega locked it out by cutting the physical data link from the surface."

"Omega? But he was with us the whole time." Jeremy shook his head in confusion, looking back and forth between the two.

"I downloaded myself into his brain on the flight to Earth, if you can call it that. A copy of me," Omega shrugged. "It made strategic sense."

"Strategic sense?" Jeremy said caustically, "Did it also make strategic sense not to tell me a single word about it?"

"Yes," Pascal returned in a firm voice. "I didn't want anyone to know. The less any one of us knows about the whole plan, the better in the event of capture."

"I still don't like it," Jeremy grumbled, "but at least it seems to have done some good."

"Yes, and now we need to talk less and act quickly so that more memories aren't erased," Pascal suggested.

"I still can't believe you're fine and here."

"I'm not fine, believe me."

"Neither am I."

"What do you mean?" asked Pascal.

"Alpha's android got me. I'm living on borrowed time." Jeremy pointed to the hole sealed with hardened gel under his ribs.

"Oh," his friend said sadly, then nodded as they walked down a hallway toward twelve elevator doors. "I guess this really is the end."

"Let's make it count for something."

"I feel like we've said that very phrase way too many times." Pascal managed a smile, which Jeremy returned.

"I wonder what that says about our lives."

CHAPTER 26
VERONICA

In orbit around DeGaulle, Archimedes system, 2334

THEY PROCEEDED PURPOSEFULLY. The first impulse, namely to look for Alpha's android at the launch pads, was quickly discarded. The chances of success were too low and if they were wrong and they were being played again, the AI could use their wandering around the ship to kill them one by one. First, therefore, Veronica, with Walter and Felicity in tow, had taken Jeffrey Blaskowic out of his cabin and locked him up with Ashgaloo on the bridge and repeated the same process with Admiral Brandt. Then she had asked the Locusts to lock themselves in a single quarters along with their soldiers, so as to give Alpha as little leeway as possible. If it, in the form of the androgynous, could only attack in two places, that relieved them of a lot of worry. At least now they knew which places to guard. The physical bridge could be mechanically locked from the inside, and the Locusts' large quarters were now guarded by over a hundred of their warriors. This gave them time to breathe—and to think. Time they desperately needed.

They all met again on the bridge. Her, Walter, Felicity,

Commander-generator, the Conclave, Ashgaloo, Brandt, and Blaskowic. The acting spokesman for the Progressives seemed to be dealing with his shock over his murdered colleagues by remaining silent and not saying a word. Unlike Ashgaloo, who was extremely crude about Alpha—under the disapproving gaze of Jeremy's mother.

"I say we use the codes Omega gave us and jump to Earth while we still can," Veronica suggested. They had rearranged the virtual environment so that they could form a circle on the command platform with their chairs and look at each other. Locusts and humans sat mixed without her setting it up that way, and it gave her hope.

"Jump to Earth?" asked Brandt, raising an eyebrow. "With codes that may have expired?"

"If they've expired, we won't be able to jump out of hyperspace, which would be the worst thing that could happen," Walter pointed out, and from the wild movements of his mouth, Veronica could tell that he was about to launch into a whole string of wild curses.

"No, Mr. Bonjarewski," the admiral corrected him, managing to look down on him despite being at the same eye level. "The worst that can happen is that Alpha's agent launches the hyperspace rocket with a warning just as we are entering hyperspace to the Sol system. Because then the message will arrive even faster."

Walter blushed and was about to respond angrily when Veronica shook her head to stop him. Fortunately, he listened to her and mumbled something into his beard that, thank God, no one could hear.

"How far along are the preparations for the iron planets? The planets with high iron content that we are going to send through hyperspace into the sun... push?" she finally asked the Locusts. "That sounds downright crazier than it already did."

"The fleet that is furthest behind still needs two hours before it is ready for the... procedure," replied the Patriarch of the Mountain Fathers. His shimmering green skin, combined with his sturdy build, gave him some resemblance to a frog.

"Only two hours? The planned operation is in six hours," Felicity wondered, frowning.

"The procedure is not complicated, even if the size of the operation doesn't suggest it," he returned, opening his palms in an alien gesture unfamiliar to Veronica. "Basically, the only difficulty is smooth fleet coordination, and that works very well over the Gaia field."

The Patriarch looked pointedly at Jeremy's mother, as if this observation was meant for her alone.

"Well, can you speed that up?" asked Veronica, and the Patriarch tilted his head before inclining it slightly. It was a gesture she knew: the equivalent of a human nod.

"Very well. So let's go over our options," she continued, instructing the VR environment to project two holograms into their midst: one of Sol and one of Archimedes.

"We're here." She pointed to a spot near DeGaulle. The blue moon orbited Zeus I, joining the glowing orb of Bismarck, Trafalgar with its huge crater, green Verdi and gray Europa in the elliptical orbits. "There's Jeremy." She pointed to Earth. "If Alpha launches the HR missile with a warning, we have an hour before Alpha knows. Worst case, it reacts immediately and comes up with some plan to prevent dropping the iron into the sun."

"A hyperspace barrier in the sun? That's impossible," Walter objected, waving a raised index finger.

"What if it expands nearby barrier fields with a higher energy input so that they reach into the interior of the sun?" asked Commander-generator.

"Impossible," the engineer immediately denied. "The

existing magnetic forces are so enormous that there are not even fields near the corona. Besides, no one could jump there anyway because they'd be instantly fried by the radiation."

"Okay, so there's nothing Alpha can do about it immediately?" asked Veronica.

"Nothing that I know of. It's the superintelligence. If there is a way, it'll find it sooner than I will," Walter admitted, pulling down the corners of his mouth like a sad clown. "I'm just saying that the solution won't be a barrier field in the sun, I'll stake my life on that. But not the sun, because it's too hot."

No one laughed at the joke.

"How soon could Alpha reach the nearest iron planet and the fleets there to foil our cockamamie plan?" asked Ashgaloo, turning first to the left and then to the right with drooping cheeks. "Huh?"

"Forty minutes to the nearest star system," said Commander-generator. There was something reassuring to Veronica about the rich baritone of his translation software.

"Then, with the permission of the Conclave, we should see to it that the destruction of the sun is initiated immediately. Worst case scenario, it could go supernova in two hours. Since we have no control over the timing now—at least not safely—that makes the most sense to me," she suggested, looking around for disapproving faces. She found none. Not even the stiff expression of Jeremy's mother betrayed disapproval.

"We should wait for Alpha to launch a rocket and then jump to Earth ourselves, like you said," Felicity suggested. "We're Jeremy and Pascal's Plan B, and if we wait here for them to call, it'll already be too late if something goes wrong there. So I suggest we jump there, radio them, and try to rescue them if they need rescuing."

"And if they don't?" Theresa Brandt shook her head vigorously. "If we jump to Sol, that's the end of us. We're committing suicide without knowing if our presence there will make any difference at all. Because the fact is, this will be a one-time jump."

"Hello, guys?" interjected Ashgaloo. Her deep, raspy voice boomed loud and brassy despite her advanced age. "Is no one here thinking of the biggest problem? If we set the destruction of Sol in motion prematurely, we may not be giving our ground team there enough time to secure the data of the enslaved people. Then we will have committed genocide not only against enemies but against friends too. Do we really want to live with that knowledge?"

Silence fell on the bridge. Even after her words had faded away, they still hovered between them like a threatening thundercloud that could hurl lightning bolts at any moment.

"All right, I'll speak up if no one dares," Veronica finally broke the awkward silence. "Either we risk the murder of all the people in Sol, or we risk the murder of all the people in Sol and Archimedes, and with it the extinction or enslavement of our entire species, and possibly the Locusts as well. I know there are no good choices here, so I choose the lesser of the two evils."

"You don't even have to make that choice," Brandt pointed out, shaking her head almost pitifully. Her entire demeanor was so condescending and cold that Veronica felt seething anger rising inside her.

"As far as I know, I am still the commander of this ship. Since you seem incapable of making a painful decision, *Admiral*, I'll just send you to safety by shuttle first," she caustically stated, not caring about the open mouths of the human attendees. Instead, she went one better: "I think that's the right thing to do, we don't want to risk the brave fleet leadership. After all, we desperately need you if we're going to survive all this as a species."

"How dare you?" Brandt should have sounded indignant,

but instead she still sounded downright indifferent. "There will be consequences."

"I'm looking forward to them," Veronica replied. "Because that would mean I survived the jump to Sol."

With that, she instructed the AI core to remove Jeremy's mother from the VR environment and not release her membrane straps on the physical bridge. She didn't want to run the risk of the woman getting into any mischief out of anger that could harm them, as cold as it might be.

No one said anything, but Walter applauded wickedly and Felicity grinned from ear to ear.

"Great, it seems you can be tough when you need to be," Ashgaloo muttered, shaking her head so that her gray hairs flew about. "I'd like to get off the ship, though, before you go off and die a hero's death. After all, unlike some admirals, you actually do need my pretty old skull after this war is over. If all these kids and morons in Parliament are allowed to do what they want, we'll be wishing Alpha back faster than it can say *binary code*."

"Frankly, it would make me feel a lot better to jump to Sol knowing that you're still in charge here," Veronica replied with a smile.

"It would calm me down because I know Jeremy's witch of a mother will be upset by it," Walter interjected, still as red-faced as a boiled lobster.

"She's a good tool. She's easily predictable in her bigotry," Ashgaloo explained. "And exploitable."

"We'll get you all off the ship on a shuttle," Veronica promised, pointing to Jeffrey Blaskowic as well, who simply nodded mutely. Turning to the Locusts, she added, "Do you agree with the plan?"

It took a while for the aliens to respond. She couldn't sense anything in the Gaia field, as obviously some kind of shielding was in place again. Even Commander-generator kept a conspicuously low profile.

"We agree," the Mountain Fathers' representative finally said, and as his voice boomed out of the translator, Veronica relaxed, sighing. One less problem in a sea of problems.

"I'm staying," Commander-generator announced immediately, but she shook her head decisively.

"No. I'm honored that you would follow us to our deaths, but after the Neuromorph, who may never return, you're the best link between our species I can think of."

"She's right." Felicity jumped in, sitting next to the alien, placing a hand on his rough shoulder. His head tilted a little as he eyed her hand with his huge eyes. "I never thought I would call an alien, whose species has killed millions of my fellow humans, my friend. You are living proof that reconciliation through understanding and openness is not a pipe dream but can work right now, in this moment and under the most adverse circumstances."

"Thank you," said Commander-generator. "I am reluctant to let you go alone, but I understand the arguments and will make it my mission to reconcile our species. In your memory."

Veronica gulped at his words because they sounded as final as her own thoughts. The knowledge that the next jump would be her last was so clearly ingrained in her that she understood more and more what it meant. This could be her last conversation with Commander-generator, with the Conclave, before the departure of the Union Navy, with Ashgaloo and Blaskowic. This was likely also her last breaths in Union territory, and when she entered hyperspace, it would be her last jump.

She shook herself.

"All right. Do we have any camera failures coming up?"

"No, so far only in all of the launch bays," Walter said, shaking his head.

"All right, let's start evacuating our allies and Union MPs right away," Veronica ordered, and the Conclave members nodded almost like humans before disappearing from the VR environment.

"I'm sending soldiers to the bridge to pick up the Speaker of the House, the Progressive Speaker, and the admiral," Commander-generator announced, and Veronica nodded gratefully. "As soon as one of our ships has picked us up, I'll let you know.

The alien rose from his chair and looked at them in turn. As their gazes met, Veronica was struck by a wave of affection and gratitude in the Gaia field that nearly swept her away. Thousands of thoughts and feelings that somehow related to her, intimate yet free, crashed down on her as if he were pouring his entire inner life over her. Tears welled up in her eyes and then Commander-generator was gone.

"Let's get going," she announced aloud, trying not to think about the goodbye she had just witnessed. "Are all the launch pads locked?"

"Yes." Walter trudged heavily over to his console, which appeared out of nowhere, and tapped away on the keypad. "As soon as one opens, we'll know where it is."

"Good. We should come up with a plan on how to proceed when we reach Earth. I figure we only have a few minutes before we're destroyed by the defenses. Those minutes should count for something."

"If the codes hold," Walter pointed out.

"Don't be so pessimistic," Felicity chided him. "God seems to be merciful on suicide missions."

"Very reassuring."

"I need plans," Veronica admonished them both. "We have codes against the barrier fields that, if they hold once, won't hold again once we get to the other side. We have a damaged battleship with newly sealed gashes and barely functional propulsion, and plenty of ammo. We know quite a bit about the data center in Prague, thanks to the AI core readout from the stolen Earth ship."

"We also have the transponder data from the NeuroSmarts of Omega, Jeremy, and Pascal and the other soldiers. So if we're lucky, we can ping them directly," Felicity interjected.

"Well, that's quite a lot." Veronica tried to sound optimistic. In truth, it wasn't much. It just didn't sound quite as bad when she listed what all was available to Alpha in return.

As if guessing her thoughts, Felicity began to smile and said, "We have a real advantage: we know it's a one-way ticket and we don't have to give a thought to returning. Alpha, however, will try to render us harmless while protecting itself and its possessions. It is fighting for survival, whereas we are not."

"There are advantages to being doomed," Walter mimicked Felicity's high-pitched voice. "If it were so great, everyone would be doing it."

"So glad you always manage to hang on to your good humor, even in the most subterranean of situations." Felicity gave him a clear gesture with her middle finger, and he grinned laconically.

"Wait a minute," he suddenly said. "Subterranean is a good point. Remember how the Neuromorph showed us how it jumped into the bowels of Bismarck to hide and extract energy directly from the lava between the mantle crusts?"

"Yeah, pretty crazy," Veronica replied, pursing her lips. "What are you getting at?"

"We can do that too!"

"No, we can't." Veronica shook her head. "We don't have any charted voids available for Earth, and jumping into a completely massive area is impossible."

"Yes, we can't just jump into the Earth's interior or the data center. But we can, in a way," Walter triumphed, jumping up out of his chair. With both hands on his chin, he looked up at the ceiling and rocked on his feet.

"Okay, think, Walter," he spoke to himself and began pacing like a tiger in its enclosure.

Veronica exchanged a glance with Felicity, but the gray-haired Nanonikerin merely shrugged her shoulders perplexed.

"What are you getting at?"

"I think I have an idea. I need your help with it," the massive engineer replied, pointing an outstretched index finger at Veronica. "You stay on the bridge and let us know if the androgynous Alpha son of a bitch moves, or cameras go down."

"Um, okay?!"

"You!" His finger moved to Felicity. "You're coming with me to help with a surgical procedure on a Mark II Taurus hyperspace torpedo."

"May I know what exactly your plan is?" asked Veronica.

"No," he returned heatedly. "I need to know if it's going to work first. I'll keep you posted. Come on, Felicity."

Veronica raised her arms helplessly and sighed as the two of them logged off, and she was suddenly alone on the very large bridge.

Fifteen minutes later, she startled up out of her chair, not having noticed the passage of time. The holoscreen came to life, alerting her via priority message that a launch bay had opened without authorization from the ship's consciousness.

"So there you are," she muttered, opening a channel to Walter and Felicity. "Where are you two? Port launch bay four just opened up."

"We're at port launch bay fifty-two." It was Felicity who answered.

"Where's Walter?"

"He's implementing his totally idiotic and crazy idea as we speak, and he's doing it with a wrench in his hand and lube on his arms. Now if I told you he was crawling around in an HR rocket as we speak..."

"It's okay," Veronica cut her off. "As soon as I register the launch, you'll have to manually seal yourselves in. I'll then immediately go into hyperspace. If Alpha catches on to your machinations, it will come for you and try to stop you."

"Will do, Captain. You should also log out and lock the door to the bridge," Felicity suggested.

"Will do. Tell Walter I'll be a lousy captain if I don't find out soon what we're planning on doing on the other."

"I'll pass it on," the Nanonikerin sighed. "But you know him."

"That's the problem." Veronica disconnected and stared at the holoscreen, sighing. When launch bay four reported an unauthorized launch, she ordered the ship's consciousness to jump.

We're coming, Jeremy, she thought, as she turned to her arm display. Using the contact menu, she selected her parents, grandparents, and siblings and pressed "Record video message."

The comm beacon she could send out would take a long time to reach Trafalgar, but it would be worth it. After a long breath she began to speak, and her tears contained all the joy, fears, and anxieties that filled her mind at that moment. But also hope and the knowledge that she was doing the right thing.

CHAPTER 27
PASCAL

Prague Data Center, Earth, Sol system, 2334

THE WAY down was via the elevator shafts. Pascal was reminded unpleasantly of his way up the BMW Tower in New Berlin, when they had tried to stop Moreau. At the time, when he had climbed injured through an elevator shaft, it had looked almost identical to the oppressively narrow shaft they were now climbing down. This time, having Moreau's body right near him was so absurd that he snorted loudly several times, drawing puzzled looks from the others.

As their line of just over a dozen people stretched downward into the darkness, he grew more and more tired and soon couldn't keep up. Jeremy, Omega, and the soldiers were moving so fast with their servos that Pascal was soon sweating and panting with no sign of them slowing down at all. The Matriarch was even more impressive to watch. In the glow of the many helmet lamps, their cold beams of light streaking across the dusty walls of plaster concrete, she looked like a spider, running seemingly effortlessly down the smooth plaster. After just a few minutes, it was clear that Pascal was a sort of handbrake in a race where every second counted. So the soldiers took turns piggybacking him. The advantage was that now they no longer had to take him into consideration, and simply slid down the vertical ladder poles with their hands and feet like firemen.

It took less than two minutes, and they crashed one after the other to the bottom of the shaft. Any normal person would probably have broken their legs in the process, but servo motors and artificial muscles in the armor did a good job.

"All right," Jeremy radioed, "we've reached the bottom. If what you suspect is true, we should find the backup systems pretty soon."

"I still anticipate that," Omega replied, pointing to the two elevator doors to their left. All beams of light traveled to the unadorned gray metal.

"We should be careful," Pascal commented redundantly, but felt obliged to say so. "And don't forget: watch what you shoot at. If you accidentally destroy an important server system or memory cluster, you could have millions of lives on your conscience."

The soldiers nodded in turn. Jeremy slid a blade out of his armor, then carefully but deftly slid it into the small gap between the two sliding doors. Together with two of DeGaulle's men, they then pulled them apart with humming engines. What appeared was a small unadorned room, 16.4 foot by 16.4 foot, with a corridor leading off in all directions. Red light from blaring alarm sirens that protruded from the ceiling like pimples bathed everything in a hazy atmosphere of approaching danger.

"We should take the middle corridor," Omega radioed, almost whispering, though his voice merely sounded in their helmets. "According to the design of the building, the side corridors lead to maintenance, or cooling systems."

"I sense in that direction," the Matriarch pointed to the center hallway with her arm outstretched with the translator bracelet stuck to it, "a strong electromagnetic field. That would suggest that you are correct."

"You can sense electromagnetic fields?" asked Jeremy in surprise.

"Of course. Your suits can too, can't they?"

"Yes, but..."

"We should postpone this discussion. We don't have time," Pascal urged, pointing down the hall.

Two soldiers were the first to respond, moving through the alarm's red light with the practiced steps of Special Forces with their rifles trained. Pascal followed with Jeremy, Omega and the Matriarch, the rest bringing up the rear. Quickly but cautiously they moved forward, taking a left turn and nearly colliding with four security guards who were heading in the opposite direction at that moment. Before they could raise their short-barreled submachine guns, they had been torn to shreds by the two DeGaulle soldiers. It happened so fast that Pascal could only see the result of the confrontation and his normally not very squeamish stomach threatened to rebel at the sight as they stepped over the mangled bodies.

When he lifted his gaze again, he saw that they had already reached their destination. A single glass door separated them from a room as large as half a soccer field, so far as he could tell from his position. Server cabinets and memory clusters arranged in a circle, containing crystals with billions of pebibytes, were surrounded by noisy men and women in white lab clothes. They ran around like chickens in a coop invaded by a marten. At manual consoles, they made entries and yelled at each other when something wasn't moving fast enough.

When Jeremy and the two front soldiers opened the sliding door by smashing the bulletproof glass with their armor, silence abruptly followed. The hundred or so people present froze and turned to face the source of the noise. As if in slow motion, their eyes widened before screaming began again. This time, however, panicked, fear-filled screaming at such a high pitch that Pascal's ears rang. He pulled his pistol from his smock and fired over their heads.

The bang whipped through the air and brought silence. No, not silence, but a change. Instead of screaming, some were now whimpering. But no one moved anymore.

"We're not after you guys," he announced loudly, stepping past Jeremy and the soldiers, who seemed a little indecisive about what to do. Just military. They had to be shown an enemy to fight or an object to mark for destruction.

"Anyone who issues a single delete command via SenseNet again will be shot by me personally. So turn off your Neuro-Smarts and move to this wall. Hands clasped behind your head while you do so," he ordered, making a waving motion with the barrel of the pistol toward the wall on his left. It was made of glass. Behind it he saw bare rock.

"As you know, we have infiltrated the system and will know if you try to fool us," he bluffed, watching them hurriedly comply with his request. A small flood of white-clad men and women poured out from between the server cabinets and memory clusters, heading obediently for the wall.

"You keep them in check," Jeremy ordered some of the soldiers, who saluted and rounded up the scientists. He ordered the remaining four DeGaullers to secure the sole entrance they had entered through.

Omega, meanwhile, was already on his way to one of the command consoles, fumbling with a piece of paneling to attach a cable underneath.

"How bad is it?" asked Pascal as he stepped up beside him. He glanced uneasily at the small, archaic-looking monitor, but couldn't make sense of the binary code running there.

"I'll find out in a moment," Omega replied absently, and

began rummaging in his small fanny pack. After a moment, he pulled out two thimble-sized objects and handed them to Pascal.

"What are these?"

"These are the signal boosters," came the curt reply.

"Which one of these is for the backup transmission? And which one is for the *WizKid*?" asked Pascal, eyeing the two completely identical-looking metal parts in turn, which he had previously seen during their briefing of the plan in Bismarck. Still, he couldn't tell them apart.

"That one," Omega pointed to the one on the left, "is for the backup, the other is for the *WizKid*. But they won't get here for at least three hours, if we haven't returned and reported in by then. So we don't need to plug that one in yet."

"I'll hook them both up anyway," Pascal announced. "Better safe than sorry."

So he went to another input console and exposed two of the universal ports that were also responsible for the permanent power supply. With two simple hand movements, he plugged in the charging cables and then took a step back. With their extremely amplified signal, the tiny devices ate up enormous amounts of power. The plan to not only physically retrieve the data but also send it to Archimedes via radio signal had been Omega's idea. While it would take forever for the data to go out and forever for it to get there, it didn't cost them any extra time and increased the chance that at least someone's memories would eventually be recovered.

"I have the data," Omega suddenly shouted, drawing everyone's eyes like a magnet.

Pascal ran to him, nearly colliding with Jeremy, who looked like a giant in his bulky armor.

"Well?" they both asked at the same time.

"Eleven percent."

"Eleven percent? So little?" Pascal felt sheer horror rise within him.

Only eleven percent of the data had survived Alpha's henchmen's deletions. That was a disaster.

"That many," Omega corrected, "eleven percent of the data was deleted."

"Man," Pascal cursed. "I thought that—"

"All right, so we can still save eighty-nine percent of these poor bastards. Let's go!"

Omega nodded. "One hour."

"An hour for the transfer?" asked Jeremy, ruffling his sweaty hair.

"That's a lot of time," Pascal agreed with him, snorting in frustration. "Especially since it's way too easy to get in here."

The thought had been gnawing at him since they reached the bottom of the elevator shaft. In the best secured data center in the system, they had had to do little more than get past four security guards and scare a hundred or so scientists to get to their target. Clearly, it had been too easy.

"What's Alpha's plan?" he spoke his last thought aloud, biting his lower lip so hard he tasted blood.

"I think I know," Jeremy replied, and something about the sound of his voice made Pascal sit up and take notice. He looked up and followed his friend's gaze, which was directed toward the hallway they had come from earlier. A figure appeared at the other end.

"Holy shit."

Even before his curse had faded, he heard something jingle and too late saw the small grenade bouncing through the door, skipping across the floor in ever decreasing intervals.

Jeremy reacted immediately and jumped forward so that he landed with his upper body on the grenade as Pascal and Omega took cover.

A muffled explosion boomed through the hall and his friend's heavily armed body was lifted 1.6 feet into the air. Pascal's ears thundered with the heavenly choirs and he felt nauseous. Completely disoriented, he tried to spot Jeremy and crawl in his direction, but instead bumped into some obstacle and threw up noisily.

Gunshots rang out.

Everything went round and round until he felt a puncture on his neck and after several moments everything cleared up, although his pulse was still pounding in his ears like a hammer wielder on drugs.

"What in the..." He looked around and saw Omega's pale face.

"Shock grenade," he replied, helping him to his feet, then running to Jeremy.

"Is he all right?" groaned Pascal, putting one foot in front of the other, searching. He must have lost his pistol, and the box of backup equipment was gone too.

"He's alive," came the Neuromorph's relieving news, only to be followed immediately by frustration. "He's running out of time. The internal bleeding has gotten worse and we're out of BioCreep to contain the conflagrations in his abdomen."

"Damn it," Pascal cursed in frustration, instinctively ducking as a ricochet whistled over him.

"That was Alpha's plan," Omega opined as he fiddled with Jeremy's head.

"What, exactly? Smoke us out of here?"

"Locking us in here. It doesn't know what we're going to do to the system. However, it knows that this place has powerful shielding down here," the Neuromorph explained, and everything in Pascal tightened as he saw Moreau's figure crouching over his friend. "So we're trapped. It doesn't have to do anything except wait there until we run out of ammunition or drop from exhaustion. As far as it knows, it's got all the time in the world."

"But you still had a connection to the upper floors in the hallway," Pascal said, confused.

"Yes, in the hallway. In here, the shielding is much stronger than expected."

"That means we can't even send the radio signal?"

"Yes."

Pascal ruffled his hair and looked toward the hallway. To the right and left of the door, soldiers were firing alternately toward the other side, where shadowy figures returned fire at irregular intervals. In fact, it didn't look like a frantic assault at all. Omega was right.

"Are you sure he's okay?" he finally asked, leaning down to Jeremy with concern after they had pulled him behind a server closet. They should be much better protected from ricochets here.

"For an hour," Omega repeated, without looking up from the input console, in front of which he had repositioned himself to track the copying of data via the data cable.

Frustrated, Pascal squatted down next to Jeremy and peeled his right hand out of his armor to clasp it with his own hands.

Like being at his deathbed, he thought bitterly. *Again*.

"Hey," Jeremy whispered, pursing his mouth as if he were having trouble speaking.

"There you go again. You damned hero!" scolded Pascal with a sad smile, avoiding looking at the plate-sized hole gaping in the breastplate of the servo armor. Smoke was still rising from the edges, carrying with it the stench of charred flesh.

"When I'm not behind the wheel of a starship, I'm not good for much more than throwing myself on the nearest explosive anyway," Jeremy joked, nearly choking on a coughing fit if

Pascal hadn't quickly pulled him to his side and removed fresh blood and smaller scraps of tissue from his mouth.

"Hey, that's my excuse for stupid actions in space, I have a copyright on it," he grumbled, blinking wet tears from the corners of his eyes.

"I'm sorry," Jeremy croaked, "but I don't give a shit about your copyright, you can take me to court if you want. I'd really appreciate it because that would mean you'd have gotten me out of here."

"I think it's more likely that I'll throw myself on the next grenade that flies in so I can escape my misery as a useless old cynic." Pascal looked at his friend's sweaty face, which had once been handsome before it had become marred by cuts from flying splinters, sweat, and blood splatter. It was easy to miss how young the descendant of the Brandt dynasty really still was, and how old and disgruntled he himself was. No one should have to live their prime years with as many disasters and as much pressure on their shoulders as Jeremy.

"Don't make that face, Inspector," Jeremy whispered, racked again by a coughing fit.

Instead of answering, Pascal smiled and they just looked at each other in silence for a while, letting mutual respect and sympathy flow unspoken between them. At some point Jeremy cleared his throat, snapping him out of his trance. The captain had grown noticeably paler, his lips gray and bloodless, his eyes watery and twitching as if in fever.

"I... the Matriarch," he asked in an almost breaking voice. It was as thin and weak as tea brewed too often. "Is she still alive?"

Pascal looked over at the alien, who was crouched with her blades extended next to the door, where the soldiers were still exchanging occasional bursts of fire with Alpha and its men, so that no one would think of entering the corridor.

"Yes, my friend, she's still here," he said calmly, gripping the dying man's hand tighter and tighter as his grip weakened, as if he could keep him alive that way by sheer force of will.

"Can you ask her to come here? I can't find her in the Gaia field. It's all so..." Jeremy broke off in mid-sentence, as if he no longer had the strength to continue speaking. His breathing was now intermittent and raspy.

"Of course," Pascal said quickly, sending out his Gaia feelers for the Matriarch's powerful presence. He could see her looking around at them and then immediately moving closer.

Could you be with me one more time? Jeremy's thoughts to the Matriarch were surprisingly clear. There was hardly any fear there. He seemed at ease, quite different from what his ruined body had suggested. But there was something else in his telepathic connection, something that rolled in like a distant storm front, unstoppable and as powerful as a hurricane. It was not terrifying but rather awe-inspiring. Instinctively, Pascal knew it was approaching death.

I would be honored to accompany you in the last moments before the next cycle, the Matriarch replied, and her presence was so reassuring and intimidating at the same time that Pascal gasped.

Thank you. Jeremy looked first at the alien and then at Pascal. Their eyes met and there was too much in them to comprehend.

He began to cry. Unrestrained and sobbing like a child and he didn't care. He just let the tears flow, let his grief and dismay run free, and it was Jeremy who gave his hand one last comforting squeeze before it went limp. There was nothing but peace in his thoughts before they ended with an inner image of Walter, Felicity, WizKid, Simmons, and finally Macella.

Powerless, Pascal let himself fall backward until his back collided with a server cabinet. Moving his head back until it, too, rested against the cold glass, he continued to sob uninhibitedly. He allowed his deepest grief to pour out of him without any resistance. Neither would nor could he resist what was bursting out of him like a cleansing river. It was not a hopeless grief that overwhelmed him, but something deeper, heavier, that had lain dormant within him for too long. A reservoir that had continued to fill until the breaking of the dam became a release.

At some point he snapped out of it, his eyes burning. His gaze still rested on Jeremy's corpse, whose eyes the Matriarch had closed. He looked peaceful.

"What is that?" asked Pascal absently, bracing himself with his fists into a more upright position. He was sure he heard something. There it was again: a static hiss followed by scratching sounds. They were coming from Jeremy's helmet, which was lying next to his motionless body. Omega, still standing at his input console, also stared at the helmet where the noise was coming from.

Pascal reached for it and put his ear to the neck opening. It sounded like a chopped-up radio signal.

"Someone's transmitting, but I can't hear anything."

"The shielding," Omega explained, pointing a finger upward.

"Damn it," Pascal cursed. Whether intuition or wishful thinking: something inside him was literally screaming for it to be something important.

"We need to know what it is," he urged.

"Impossible. Nothing can get through that shielding." Omega shook his head.

"What about across the hall?" the Matriarch asked through her translating computer. She had appeared next to Pascal so suddenly that he flinched at the sound of her computer voice.

"It should work there. Alpha knows that, too, though."

"I'll take the signal boosters there," the Matriarch decided, raising one of her six long spider fingers dismissively when Omega tried to retort something.

"Pascal Takahashi," she turned to him. "Deliver the message."

Before he could ask what message she meant, she grabbed both signal boosters from the memory cluster and leapt like a tiger beside the soldiers still guarding the passageway. She didn't speak to them, yet they began to move as if on cue, charging into the passageway with continuous fire.

"What..." Pascal managed to say, still stunned, when the Matriarch ran after them, emitting a high-pitched, bloodcurdling shriek that jolted him as if he had been struck by lightning. Exactly what happened in the hallway next, he could no longer see, as it was drowned out in a flurry of muzzle flashes, blood, and smoke.

The signal became sharper, clearer, and Pascal jerked the helmet closer to his ear.

"Hey, is anyone there? If so, you better hurry up, because we're going to get our asses—"

"WALTER?" yelled Pascal almost hysterically into the helmet.

"Yes. Where are you guys? Why haven't we heard from you guys?"

"We're underground in the basement of the data center. Alpha has us trapped in a shield and we can't get out."

"That's why we came here. Tell Jeremy we'll get you guys out."

"I... yes. What are you going to do?" asked Pascal, swallowing hard as he looked down at Jeremy's corpse.

"Since you can't get to the hyperspace torpedo as planned, I'll send one down to you," Walter announced.

"But—"

"Yeah, this is going to get ugly. Take cover, I can only lock on to your signal, so you should get away from the radio source as fast as you can," the engineer explained, speaking twice as fast as usual. Obviously, they didn't have much time. "I have to do it immediately because right now we're being shot up here in orbit. I'm sending down two missiles. One with a tiny explosive charge to create a cavity for the second. I've removed the explosive charge from that one, so there's room for one of you. There's an exosuit inside. The flight will take a long time because the rocket can hardly accelerate with a passenger. The recovery transmitter is set to full power. Sorry I can't do more. By the time the first rocket gets there, we'll be stardust up here."

"Walter, I—"

"It's all right. Tell the captain to live up to the name *Concordia* again. We love him, and we kind of love you too. But put *him* in the rocket, you're already an old fart!"

Pascal didn't know whether to laugh or cry again when Walter ended the connection. Before he could decide, he exchanged a look with Omega and then ran behind the memory clusters to put them between him and the hallway, where silence had fallen.

"I've got the data in here," the Neuromorph said, and for the first time Pascal didn't mind seeing Moreau's face as he did so. He looked at the small memory stick and nodded. Then Omega lifted up a second memory stick. "Here is data that is over half a year old but will be of interest to you. Perhaps to the entire Union. Use them wisely."

Pascal took both, clasped them with his right hand, and nodded in confusion. "Why are you giving them to me?"

"Because it's you who's going to get out of here," Omega decided in a firm voice, raising his head slightly to peer over the edge of the hard drive cabinet before he could hear any contradiction.

Pascal grumbled and looked toward the hallway as well.

"Damn it!" he cursed as he saw the androgynous man emerge with an HV rifle.

"It's over," the waxy faced android said, scanning the hall with his chrome eyes until he spotted them both.

"Oh yeah," Omega agreed as green light flickered in the hallway behind Alpha before disappearing again and a powerful explosion shattered composite, rock and glass. Splinters, rocks, and shards raced through the air and Pascal was somehow able to pull Omega behind cover at the last moment before the hurricane of shrapnel tore it apart. It roared over them, eating into the servers and hard drives and causing crackling short circuits.

On one of the cabinets, Pascal saw green light reflections flare for a brief moment and die again.

"That's the second one!" shouted Omega over the patter of falling debris. Together they struggled to their feet.

Pascal coughed against all the dust that was making its way into his lungs and, squinting his eyes, ran toward the hallway, or rather, toward where the hallway had been. There, in fact, they found a large cave that had been cut into the stone in a spherical shape. At the deepest point of the crater was a nearly thirteen-foot-long hyperspace torpedo with a Union flag and the red inscription: Mark II.

Many of the scientists in their white coats lay mutilated or injured on the ground, pleading and wailing. There was no sign of the soldiers.

"Hurry up, now," Omega urged, pushing Pascal toward the rocket.

"But, you should go! This was supposed to be my—"

"Don't argue. You are perhaps the Union's most important symbolic figure at this point. Get the data back safely, just like the memory of the Matriarch's last moments. I have a feeling they'll still be important." As he spoke, Omega opened the hatch to the missile's explosive device with a few SenseNet commands. A cavity the size of a coffin opened up. Inside lay an exosuit, which Pascal reluctantly donned, putting on his helmet and letting the small box on his back do its work. The nanite mass flowed over his body in a flash and then solidified into a flexible second skin.

Omega helped him climb in, everything happening as if in a dream in which Pascal had no say.

"Remember me," the Neuromorph implored, looking him in the eye one last time before closing the lid before Pascal could reply. He briefly felt nauseous.

He opened his mouth until his jaws cracked and then screamed long and hard until his voice failed him.

THE TEARS OF THE SUN

FOR 4.57 BILLION years it was the center of the solar system, sterilizing the nearby environment with its endless fusion of hydrogen atoms into helium, providing the heat and energy necessary for the evolution of life in a tiny part of its surroundings. It also reached out far into the darkness, to the blue expanse of Neptune, as the last guardian of its sphere of influence in the cold of space.

Its death came invisibly and silently, deep in its fifteen-million-degree heart, when the Locusts hurled eight iron-rich planets through hyperspace, shutting down its fusion engine. The resulting black hole was invisible, sucking up everything in its wake. But it only lasted for a short time, until at the same moment, the UNS *WizKid*'s antimatter reactor disintegrated because of a direct hit, causing an annihilation reaction of gigantic proportions over Earth, just as the supernova erupted. The fireball of ultra-hot plasma expanded like a balloon, burning first Mercury, then Venus, Earth and Mars, Jupiter, Saturn, Uranus and Neptune to ashes in its massive radiation wave.

The entire heliosphere and the ancient home of mankind since the beginning of the universe was destroyed.

EPILOGUE

In orbit around Europa, Archimedes system, 2336

To mark the Union Holiday this year, commemorating our fallen heroes in the fight against Alpha, President Myrta Ashgaloo is expecting a high-profile visit from the Conclave Chairman, who has become known on SenseNet as the Commander-generator. A self-professed friend of Jeremy Brandt and the brave crew of the Concordia *and later* WizKid*, he is expected to make a tribute of his own in the form of a speech to mark the supreme colonial holiday. It would be the first of its kind by such a senior Species X leader. In gratitude for ongoing assistance in the repair and colonization efforts of the Union, it is expected that DeGaulle's newly inaugurated orbital elevator will have as its destination port a Species X space habitat...*

Pascal turned off the news broadcast and leaned back in his chair. He stared, lost in thought, at the six stasis pods embedded in the wall in front of him. He couldn't see their faces but knew they were there.

Here is data that is more than half a year old but will be of interest to you. Perhaps to the entire Union. Use it wisely, he repeated Omega's last words in his mind, letting the memory stick move back and forth between his fingers. The door to the infirmary opened and a young cadet with a beret and obedient look entered. He saluted at attention and Pascal smiled.

"I'm still not a soldier, Cadet Miller," he explained.

"Of course, sir," the latter returned. "Engineering reports that all systems are functioning nominally."

"So the UNS *Concordia* is ready to depart?"

"Yes sir."

"Then we should wake our captain and his officers, don't you think, Cadet Miller?"

"I do, sir." The young soldier actually smiled.

"All right. Would you give me a moment?"

"Uh, of course, sir!" the cadet gushed, giving him one last sheepish look before walking out, the bulkhead sliding into place behind him.

Pascal had thought long and hard about what to do with the data. It was the memories and personalities of Jeremy, Macella, Walter, WizKid, Felicity, and Simmons that Alpha and Moreau had used back then to create the first clones of them in the Alps. The same clones that Pascal was still one of. What bothered him most was that these were his friends, their essence, their personalities, but at a significantly earlier time. If they woke up in their new clone bodies, not having experienced the entire battle against Alpha, who would they be? Would they still be his friends? They didn't even know him at that point. Jeremy and he had only met when they had been awakened in the same room in Northern Italy, their last memories being those of their own deaths.

Pascal had toyed with the idea of leaving them be, or having them implanted with Gaianests, and then sharing all his memories with them. He wanted so much for them to know everything. But they would still be his memories and not theirs. So the problem remained.

In the end, he had decided to do it. To wake them up. Because what had once become friendship would do so again; he knew them well enough, after all. He also thought he knew that they had neither been clouded by religion nor too principled about their lives to not want to take a new chance. After all, that was how it had appeared the last time they were awakened in new bodies. What was going to be different this time? Well, they were heroes of the Union and would never be able to enjoy that glory. But what was glory compared to the opportunity to explore a new galaxy?

With a smile, he activated the wake-up mechanism via SenseNet and took a deep breath. When Jeremy learned that he was aboard the newest Union ship, equipped with new hyperspace drives set to explore the Andromeda Galaxy, his eyes would sparkle, and so would his crews. Just a spark of joy, indeed a spark of life in their eyes would be the most precious thing to Pascal.

For him, this upcoming expedition was the best way out of a dilemma. Predictably, upon his return and recovery, a great social debate had erupted as to whether it would be morally correct to set up a cloning program in violation of existing Union laws. A cloning program that would give new life to the rescued minds of enslaved Earthlings. Their DNA data was linked to their memories, so technologically it was not a problem, not least because of the support of the Locusts. And yet, after long debates, politicians found it difficult to abandon the moral principles that had shaped the Union for centuries. Through hyperspace, according to calculations, they could reach Andromeda in ten years and start over there. The clones would not be illegal because they were not produced in Union territory, not even in the same galaxy. Instead, they could live an exciting life as explorers, along with Jeremy, Macella, Simmons, WizKid, Walter, Felicity, and an old inspector who had seen way too much. What harm could it do to see something new on top of that?

He smiled warmly as the stasis pods opened and his eyes grew moist, as did his hands. He hadn't been this nervous since his school days.

"Welcome to the UNS *Concordia*, friends."

THANK YOU FOR READING TEARS OF THE SUN

WE HOPE you enjoyed it as much as we enjoyed bringing it to you. We just wanted to take a moment to encourage you to review the book. Follow this link: Tears of the Sun to be directed to the book's Amazon product page to leave your review.

Every review helps further the author's reach and, ultimately, helps them continue writing fantastic books for us all to enjoy.

ALSO IN SERIES:

Behemoth
Leviathan
Gates of Hell
Tears of the Sun

Facebook | Instagram | Twitter | Website

You can also join our non-spam mailing list by visiting www.subscribepage.com/AethonReadersGroup and never miss out on future releases. You'll also receive three full books completely Free as our thanks to you.

Looking for more great books?

It's 2079. The Sleer War is over. Earth lost. When Lt. Simon Brooks discovered an alien A.I., he made a name for himself as an officer in the Unified Earth Fleet. And while his tech skills are next level, he has a lot to learn about running a combat squadron. After flubbing a training exercise, Brooks is set to choosing worlds for human colonization, and he thinks he has the perfect candidate: Vega. But rumors and intelligence reports make him think there's something there which the Sleer missed. As Brooks and the crew of UES Gauntlet head to Vega to prove his theory, a Sleer science vessel is already working to claim the prize: an armored military base from a long-forgotten war. Acquiring it for the UEF would put humanity back in the fight to reclaim Earth…and Simon Brooks back in control of his career. But events from neighboring empires threaten to destabilize the UEF, pitting Gauntlet's crew against secret police, government bureaucracy, interstellar trade negotiations, and Sleer merchant guilds. In the face of encroaching chaos, does victory in battle even matter?

Get Disjunction Now!

When the rules of war keep changing, fight for each other... Humanity has been banished to a distant star. Left to fight over resources rationed to them by mysterious machine-overlords known as Wardens. Commander Rylan Holt labors against inter-colony arms trafficking when an informant gives him horrific news. The ruthless cartel boss, Lilith, has stockpiled outlawed weapons of mass destruction. Worse, she claims to have permission from the Wardens to unleash them upon the system. When the battleship *Audacity* speeds to investigate Rylan's discovery, operations officer Scott Carrick finds himself in a trap more deadly than he could have ever imagined. His only hope of escape may lie with their most junior crewmember, a nurse named Aila Okuma, who's never seen battle. As Rylan, Scott, and Aila struggle to survive a war where the rules keep changing, they must answer a terrible question: how do they win when it seems the Wardens intend for everyone to lose?

Get Hellfire Now!

A smuggler, a spy, a brewing revolution...and a rogue agent who could destroy it all. Perrin Hightower can fly a run-down freighter through the galaxy's most dangerous wormholes blindfolded, a handy skill in her shipping business...and her smuggling enterprises. Special agent Tai Lawson dreams of leading the Ruby Confederation's spy agency. But when his partner steals a top-secret list of revolutionaries and vanishes, Tai's accused of helping his friend escape. When Tai seeks her navigation expertise, Perrin would rather jump out an airlock than help. But the missing person is her ex-boyfriend—a double agent she thought was helping the revolution. Her name's on that list, and she'll do anything to keep it secret. **Hiding their true agendas, Tai and Perrin follow the rogue spy's trail across the galaxy. Each must decide where their allegiance truly lies when they learn the spy carries more than a list of conspirators—he carries information that could shatter the fragile peace in the galaxy.**

Get Rogue Pursuit Now!

For all our books, visit our website.

TIMELINE (LONG)

2022 The Ring of Fire, a vast network of volcanoes around the Pacific Ocean, erupts. Ten million people die or become homeless. Japan, the USA, Indonesia and the Philippines are hit hardest.

2028 Superstorm Kyrios devastates large parts of South America and claims hundreds of thousands of victims.

2030 The SpaceX company succeeds in making the first manned flight to Mars.

2035 A tsunami devastates the east coast of the USA and Portugal. Several million people die.

2038 The space company SpaceX establishes MARS I, the first permanent research station on Mars.

2045 Opening of the first Thorium Nuclear Reactor in Saarland.

2048 As a joint project of the USA and the EU, the Solar Genesis solar farm is opened. Giant solar panels, in space close to the Earth, transmit clean energy to the surface with the help of microwave transmitters.

2049 As a result of distortions in the energy market due to the opening of Solar Genesis, a trade war breaks out between the OPEC countries and the G7.

2052 Due to floods and extreme heat waves, large regions around the equator become permanently uninhabitable. A wave of refugees reaching unimagined proportions flood the industrialized nations.

2053 Launch of the first quantum computer.

2055 The UN Security Council cannot reach an agreement to solve the ongoing refugee problem. Social conflicts bring the Western world to the brink of collapse.

2058 Mayuko Tagami develops the first version of SenseNet, which replaces the Internet and serves as a global brain-to-brain interface via quantum transmission. Through the global exchange of thoughts and feelings, industrialized nations experience political and economic stabilization. The political landscape shifts from classic democracies to neurocracies involving constant participation by its members.

2060 The Protestant and Catholic churches join together to form the United Church after decades of struggle to achieve a nondenominational church. Fundamental reforms of the church system: the new head of the church, with the title of Prelate, is elected by church members, just like the cardinals and bishops, directly via SenseNet.

2062 Construction of the orbital elevator IOTD (International Orbital Transportation Device) by the United Nations.

2065 The thirty member states of the European Union sign the Copenhagen Treaties, which turned the confederation into a nation-state with largely autonomous regions based on the American model.

2066 The first in vitro human is created in China.

2070 NASA and ESA capture the asteroid Calypso 84 using robotic probes and guide it into orbit close to Earth. Start of the exploitation of subcrustal resources.

2075 The EU Ethics Council approves a far-reaching ban on genetic research.

2077 China establishes the Xinhu I lunar base. Start of the exploitation of sub crystalline resources.

2080 Establishment of the moon bases Mitterrand I by the EU and Liberty I by the USA. Diplomatic disputes over the division of territory on the lunar surface flare up.

2081 In Cadarache, France, the first deuterium-tritium fusion reactor goes online as a joint international project.

2083-2101 Construction of the sleeper ships: due to persistent overpopulation and increased natural disasters as well as success in the field of nuclear fusion, the USA, EU, and China decide to send colony ships into space.

2101 The zero point six two mile long sleeper ships *Romulus* and *Remus* of the EU, the *George Washington* of the USA and the *Tao Ming* from China leave their lunar orbit shipyards. The *Tao Ming* is destroyed by an explosion of unknown origin near Neptune. The *George Washington* stops transmitting after a short time.

2102 The sleeper ship *Romulus* leaves the Sol system on its one-hundred-year journey to the system Archimedes, thirty-three light-years away. On board are 15 million EU citizens in cryosleep, selected through a controversial suitability process, along with millions of frozen embryos.

2201 The *Romulus* reaches the Archimedes system and lands on schedule on the habitable moon Europa, orbiting the gas giant Zeus II. Establishment of the colony Europa.

2202 Colonization of the four habitable neighboring moons Bismarck, Trafalgar, Verdi and DeGaulle.

2210 Founding of the Saturas research base orbiting the second gas giant of the Zeus II system, near which an unknown subspace anomaly is discovered.

2210-2223 A total of thirty asteroids from the Morton asteroid belt in the Archimedes system are captured and steered into a stable orbit around Zeus I. Start of colonization and exploitation of the newly created Acheron asteroid belt.

2225 Construction begins on orbital belts, ring-shaped space stations in orbit around the five colonies.

2225-2230 Construction of orbital elevators on the five moons begins, connecting surface and orbital belts.

2236 Founding of the Human Corporation by Christian Wendel and Torben Skjorlund, who invented NeuroSmart, a nanoprocessor on the brain stem, replacing the Holo Computer.

2239 The Human Corporation captures the asteroid Braun 22 and steers it into orbit around the Trafalgar colony in order to build an antimatter research reactor there.

2241 Braun 22's GAU causes a malfunction in the research reactor's antideuterium containment chambers. Braun 22 perishes in a matter-antimatter reaction. A fragment of the asteroid crashes into the Trafalgar colony. Twenty million people die and the entire moon is devastated.

2241-2260 Establishment of habitats and biospheres in the Morton asteroid belt. Large-scale exploitation of subcrustal resources.

2242 After an accident in a research reactor, the New Brussels Treaties outlaw and criminalize the possession of antimatter.

2245 The Union Navy deploys two pirate ships carrying a large cargo of antimatter. The destination of the cargo remains unknown.

2251 Alexander Moreau, supervisor of the Europa colony, becomes the new majority shareholder of the Human Corporation.

2255 The subspace anomaly near the Saturas research station turns out to be a micro-wormhole leading directly into the Sol system to Jupiter.

2256 Signals can be exchanged with Earth through the *Jupiter wormhole*.

2258 The Human Corporation establishes four additional research stations in the vicinity of the Jupiter wormhole.

2260 Free Morton Nation (FMN) is founded in the Morton asteroid belt. The Union Assembly grants the FMN wide-ranging autonomy.

2280 The Human Corporation discontinues research into the creation of artificial wormholes due to excessive costs and a lack of success.

2282 Conservatives and the United Church enforce the Human Empowerment Decree, a law to limit robotics, which, in response to societal pressure, allows human workers to once again take over the work of robots.

2282 The Mass Embargo: FMN halts all ore shipments to colony worlds in response to the Robotics Containment Act after the Union Assembly refuses to waive the law for the Morton Belt, which relies on robotic labor.

2282-2284 After growing tensions and a lack of oxygen supplies from the inner worlds, the Heusinger Incident occurs: the crew of the Union frigate UNS *Heusinger* are overpowered and taken hostage by FMN supporters during an inspection. This leads to open warfare between the Union and FMN.

2284 Aurora Peace Treaty. On the Morton habitat Aurora, the Supervisors of the Colonies and the Morton Council sign a peace treaty negotiated by the United Church, granting the FMN further autonomy and suspension of the Human Empowerment Decree.

2285 The artificial intelligence Alligulac hijacks the computer systems of three deuterium refineries in the Acheron Belt. The Union Navy imposes a quarantine and destroys the AI with EMP bombs.

2288 Law banning research and development of autonomous AI systems after AI takes control of several asteroid habitats.

2295 Communication with Earth breaks down when the Jupiter wormhole disappears.

2300 The first wave of abductions: within a few months, several thousand people disappeared without a trace from the colonies.

2305 Alexander Moreau introduces the first faster-than-light propulsion SSP (Subspace Stream Propulsion) at the annual meeting of the Human Corporation. Commonly called a hyperspace drive, it represents a theoretical breakthrough in interstellar travel.

2308 Second wave of abductions: within a year, half a million people disappear from the colonies. Establishment of the ACD (Abducted Citizens Directive).

2310 At a plenary meeting of the Colonial Supervisors, Alexander Moreau fails in a bid by the Progressives to resume research on antimatter. The new hyperspace drive cannot create subspace pockets large enough for a starship using fusion power. Shares in the Human Corporation plummet.

2315 Third Abduction Wave: for the first time, not only do people disappear from the five moons, but also from the asteroid settlements in the Acheron Belt. In total, over one million people are reported missing.

2315 Founding of the Human Protection Alliance HPA, a nongovernmental organization that suspects the reason for human disappearances to be aliens who have infiltrated the colonies.

2318 Due to growing social unrest as a result of the alleged abductions and a growing hysteria about possible alien abductors as well as the growing influence of the HPA, construction of large-scale orbital defense facilities begins while the budget of the Union Navy is significantly increased.

2325 A probe of unknown origins enters the Archimedes system and is destroyed by the Union Navy before it can be identified.

2327 FMN begins construction of the Artemis Defense Network, which will form a screen of sensors and defense probes around the Morton Belt to protect against further suspected alien abductions.

2328 Test of the first hyperspace missile Mark I by the Union Navy.

2330 Several hundred robotic hyperspace probes are sent to explore interstellar space. Probes Home 1 and 2 are sent to Earth. Contact is lost shortly after leaving the system.

2331 Fears of an alien threat grow after the loss of the Home probes, and the HPA win all twelve of the Trafalgar Colony seats in the supervisor election.

2332 Fourth abduction wave: twenty thousand people from the moon Europa are reported missing within a few days.

2333 The Jupiter Event: in the center of the former subspace anomaly near the Saturas research station, a surging alien radiation signal is detected.

GLOSSARY: LOCUSTS

THE SCIENCE BEHIND THE LOCUSTS

Much of what you read about the Locusts in this book sounds like pure fantasy: photosynthesis via the skin? Then I wouldn't need to eat at all, just soak up the sun! Telepathy? That sounds exciting! No more misunderstandings and wars, because we can see into each other's souls and empathy becomes something tangible. But could a brain even be capable of something so intangible? And then there are the lasers. Biologically generated laser beams? Wouldn't capacitors and superconductors have to be installed everywhere? How would that work? Below, I will briefly mention three key Locust technologies that are already scientifically possible today: telepathy, photosynthesis in animals, and biolasers. Admittedly, telepathy is still highly speculative, but it is certainly a theoretically feasible form of communication.

Biolaser: Back in 2011, two researchers at Harvard Medical School developed a biological laser. They used a living cell as an optical amplifier, namely a human liver cell. It was genetically modified to produce a green fluorescent protein. All the scientists had to do next was to excite this protein (which came from a fluorescent jellyfish, by the way) with ultraviolet light. The cell, enriched with the jellyfish protein, produced large amounts of it and could reflect the UV light, thus amplifying it. The cell wall itself acted as a lens and a focused laser beam was produced. Of course, since it was a single cell, all of this took place on a microscopic scale, but was reproduced on a much larger scale a few years later. With the use of crystals, as in the case of the Locusts, today biolasers are conceivable that would be on a par with the purely technical ones. Today, we are seeing the first biolasers being used in medicine to stimulate drugs that can be activated directly in the cell by light.

Photosynthetic skin: Of course, we know this about plants from biology classes: plants are green because they use light-absorbing pigments to convert low-energy inorganic substances such as carbon dioxide into high-energy substances (mostly carbohydrates) with the help of light energy and in this way produce energy. As equatorial dwellers, wouldn't it be handy to have these kinds of photosynthetic cells in our skin as well? And yes, such miraculous creatures do indeed exist. Allow me to present: Elysia Chlorotica, the name of a nudibranch that lives in water. It eats green, photosynthetic algae and steals the ability to photosynthesize from the algae's DNA. It looks like a leaf - wide and green and lives on sunlight, although that was always thought to be impossible and limited to plants only. An interesting finding that has geneticists of today dreaming of applying this DNA trick to us humans as well. It is not implausible, as the existence of a plant-animal crossbreed of this kind was previously considered impossible. As is so often the case, something is only impossible until the opposite is discovered...

Telepathy: Here, of course, we are speaking in purely theoretical terms—even if every year, somewhere in the Far East, someone thinks they can read minds while waving purple scarves at a seminar. Telepathy would require that we can decode thoughts and feelings, which are measured as electrochemical processes in the brain, an intangible signal. We now know that the origin of thoughts is unknown, possibly external, and that feelings are our body's chemical reaction to those thoughts. At any rate, it is possible that they will be made "visible" through advances in the field of quantum physics. Ultimately, however, quantum physics is the miracle solution to every problem or phenomenon. The trick would be to transform something that is not material into something that is material and thus transmittable. After all, a lot of animals are able to communicate via their sense of smell with the help of pheromones—which is not visible either, but works. Okay, the comparison may be lame, but I am sure that with the advancement of scientific understanding, the ability to measure and read thoughts might become possible. Then, suddenly, the step to being a receiver and transmitter of such signals would not take long. And if in doubt, you know how it works: quantum mechanics ;-)!

Atmosphere Enhancers: Automated telepathic fields built into spaceships to create positive moods.

Outer Body: Armor/Suit

The Great Pain: A type of homesickness/depression experienced when Locusts do not participate in their clan's Gaia field for too long.

Evolution guards: Special military unit

Friend: Spaceship

Gaia field: Telepathic network

Gaianest: Tumor-like gland in the brain of the Locusts that enables them to be telepathic

Secret Conclave: Secret service of the Locusts

Geneformers: Breed servant creatures and create the bionic suits for the land and space forces

Gnakat: Predators from the homeworld of the Commander-generator

Manipulators: Genetic engineers

Metalheads: Humans

Head nostrils: Exhaled air outlets

Portal: Door

Space walkers: Astronauts/space forces

Clan: Group of about 50 Locusts living together and sharing a private Gaia field, with intense emotional bonds

GLOSSARY: HUMANS

ACD: Abducted Citizens Directive: police authority to investigate waves of abductions.

Acheron Belt: Artificial asteroid belt in orbit around the gas giant Zeus I in the interior of the Archimedes system.

ADDN: Navy's military counterintelligence service.

Adventists: Ultra-conservative organization of Evangelical Christians who criticize technological progress and stigmatize it as the Satan of the future.

Atlas drone: Autonomous reconnaissance drone for space and atmospheric missions.

BioCreep: Nanites with artificial biosignature identified by the body as endogenous and used in living organisms to heal and modify tissue.

Bismarck: Colony moon with predominantly German-ethnic population. Industrial and economic center. Headquarters of the Human Corporation.

DeGaulle: Tourist center of the colonies with French-ethnic majority population. Extensive Navy orbital installations in the form of shipyards and test facilities.

Europa: First colony moon of the Archimedes system. Site of the Union Parliament and all political institutions. Site of the Fleet Headquarters.

Exosuit: Widely used spacesuit with smart nanites designed for use in zero gravity and in vacuums.

FMN: Free Morton Nation: political federation of habitats in the outer asteroid belt of the Archimedes system.

Gyrosuit: Heavy combat suit for soldiers deployed on the ground, equipped with servo motors and armor.

Harbinger Corporation: Mercenary Corporation deployed throughout the Archimedes System that is socially and politically controversial. Main police organization in the FMN.

HPA: Human Protection Alliance: political movement that suspects an alien threat behind missing persons cases.

Communication Buoys: Signal amplifiers for SenseNet quantum communications.

Conservatives: Political movement made up of Conservatives that advocate the preservation of values, humanism, and security.

Lynx drone: Autonomous, six-legged police drone for ground operations.

Mammoth Drone: Autonomous working drone for space operations.

Medical Capsule: Emergency Medical Unit: a closed tank containing BioCreep in which patients are placed in an artificial coma while they are healed by the nanites.

Nanites: Semi-intelligent nanorobots that can be programmed to perform various tasks.

NanoCreep: Nanite mass spread over external and internal surfaces in dust form that can be programmed for any purpose, any color, any physical state.

Nanonics: IT specialists who can program nanites for any purpose.

AI core: Artificial intelligence that controls a central quantum computer and serves as an operating system and intelligent learning interface.

NeuroSmart: Nano Quantum computer implanted in humans as a chip on the brain stem and interwoven with the entire brain. It is controlled by thoughts and allows access to all bodily functions.

Predator drone: Autonomous combat drone for space combat.

Progressive: Liberal-progressive political movement that advocates free research and unlimited technological progress.

SenseNet: Successor to the Internet: through their NeuroSmarts, people can log into SenseNet, a wireless network of thoughts and feelings through which people can exchange information. SenseNet also serves as a connector and interface between people and computer systems and devices.

SenseOne: Oldest public service SenseNet channel. Known for its popular news broadcasts.

SenseNet receptors: Nanonic receivers of SenseNet signals used on ships, buildings, and as implants in the brain.

Trafalgar: Colony moon with largely British-ethnic population. Devastated by the impact of an asteroid fragment from Braun 22.

Verdi: Agricultural center of the colonies with Italian-ethnic majority population. Home of the robot factories of the Navy and research center of the colonies.

LIST OF CHARACTERS

Agatha Simmons: Jeremy Brandt's second-in-command on the UNS *Concordia*. Raised in the Acheron asteroid belt, dishonorably discharged from the Navy, antimatter smuggler ever since. Killed in the escape from P3X989.

Agiou "WizKid" Prager: Chief analyst of UNS *Concordia*, graduate of the Naval Academy on Europa.

Alexander Moreau: One of twelve supervisors of the colony moon Bismarck and one of three envoys to the Parliament on Europa. Progressive spokesman, billionaire and major shareholder in the Human Corporation.

Alpha: Artificial superintelligence created by Moreau and the Human Corporation. De facto ruler over the human territories.

Anton Motela: Chief of Staff of the Union Army. Member of the Conservatives.

Carl Fergana: CEO of Western Mobile and member of the Group Council.

Emilia Hormund: Prelate and head of the United Church. Politically influential member of the Conservative.

Felicity Goods: Nanonikerin of the UNS *Concordia*. Eldest crew member. Member of the radical political movement of FMN calling for complete separation of the asteroid nation from the Union.

Gerard Missoud: Counselor and political leader of the FMN. Member of the Union Council. Killed during the battle near the mass portals of Aurora.

Heinrich Brandt: Admiral of the Union Navy and father of Jeremy Brandt. Member of the Conservatives.

Jeremy Brandt: Captain of UNS *Concordia*, former Union Navy cadet, antimatter smuggler. Graduate of the Naval Academy on Europa. Son of Admirals Heinrich Brandt and Theresa Brandt.

Justin Meyer: CEO of Human Corporation and Member of the Corporate Council.

Konstantin Wagner: One of the twelve supervisors of the colony moon Bismarck and one of three envoys to the Parliament on Europa. Spokesman for the Conservatives, opponent of Alexander Moreau. Considered the most powerful politician in the Union.

Ludmilla Konrad: Fleet admiral of the Union Navy and chair of the Union Security Council. Member of the Progressives.

Maria Dejeune: CEO of AGF and Member of the Group Council.

Pascal Takahashi: Inspector and special investigator of the ACD. Former top agent of the Union Police. Relegated to a career sidetrack after his findings in the Eremite case.

Sarah Taggert: Union Navy admiral, Commander of UNS *Churchill* and Battlegroup 5, assigned to the Free Morton Nation's central mass catapult. Killed during the Battle around the Mass Portals of Aurora.

Theresa Brandt: Union Navy Rear Admiral, wife of Heinrich Brandt, mother of Jeremy Brandt, and member of the Conservative Party.

Thisbe Thandis: Inspector in the service of the ACD and partner of Pascal Takahashi. Former Harbinger Society mercenary, now in the service of the Human Corporation. Killed during the Battle of New Rome.

Veronica Macella: Union Navy Commander, Executive Officer (XO) on UNS *Concordia* and second-in-command to Captain Jeremy Brandt.

Walter Bonjarewski: Flight engineer of the UNS *Concordia*, former member of the Harbinger Society.

Made in United States
North Haven, CT
14 March 2024